About the Author

Cathy Williams can remember reading Mills & Boon books as a teenager, and now that she is writing them she remains an avid fan. For her, there is nothing like creating romantic stories and engaging plots, and each and every book is a new adventure. Cathy lives in London, and her three daughters—Charlotte, Olivia and Emma—have always been, and continue to be, the greatest inspirations in her life.

Mills & Boon Stars

COLLECTIONS

January 2019

February 2019

March 2019

April 2019

May 2019

June 2019

Mills & Boon
Stars Collection:
Sinful Proposals

CATHY WILLIAMS

MILLS & BOON

First Published in Great Britain 2019
By Mills & Boon, an imprint of HarperCollins*Publishers*
1 London Bridge Street, London, SE1 9GF

MILLS & BOON STARS COLLECTION: SINFUL PROPOSALS
© 2019 Harlequin Books S.A.

Seduced into Her Boss's Service © 2016 Cathy Williams
Wearing the De Angelis Ring © 2016 Cathy Williams
The Surprise De Angelis Baby © 2016 Cathy Williams

ISBN: 978-0-263-27544-5

0319

MIX
Paper from
responsible sources
FSC® C007454

This book is produced from independently certified FSC™ paper to ensure responsible forest management.

For more information visit: www.harpercollins.co.uk/green

Printed and bound in Spain
by CPI, Barcelona

SEDUCED INTO HER
BOSS'S SERVICE

CHAPTER ONE

'HE'S HERE!'

Sunny looked up from where she was buried in a mound of paperwork and reference books. The paperwork was to be filed, the reference books to be consulted for precedents on a complex tax issue which her boss was working on.

With a workload that barely gave her time to escape to the bathroom, she had still not been able to ignore the fever-pitch excitement that had gripped Marshall, Jones and Jones ever since they had learned that Stefano Gunn was going to be throwing some business their way.

Literally, Sunny had thought, *throwing business*, in much the same way as someone might throw a bone for a dog. Marshall, Jones and Jones was a recent addition to the legal scene in London. Yes, some really bright lights had been poached from a couple of the bigger firms but essentially it was still just a fledgling medium-sized firm without the decades of experience a man like Stefano Gunn would be looking for.

But he had *thrown some business* in their direction and speculation was rife.

Even lodged in the smallest honeycomb of rooms at the furthest end of the building, with her head firmly in her work and her body language projecting all sorts of *not interested in rumours* signs, rumours had still trickled down to her.

He had chosen their firm to handle some patent work

for him because of Katherine, one of the partners. He fancied her and so he had chosen to sweeten her up by flinging a bit of work at them.

Sunny thought that that was a stupid piece of pointless speculation. Why on earth would the man do that? When he could make a simple call and ask for a simple date? Like any other normal person? Not, she knew, that Stefano Gunn was like any other normal person. Most normal people weren't capable of holding the city of London in the palm of their hand at the tender age of thirty-something.

Not that she was giving any of the fuss much thought. At the end of the day, all work was good work for a new company and the work he would be giving them might be peanuts for him but, for them, it would result in a hefty pay packet for the company.

Now, she propped her chin in her hand and looked at Alice, who shared the office with her.

Alice was small, plump, talkative and found it almost impossible to sit still for any period of time. Hence, out of all of the juniors who worked at this end of the building, she had been the one who had made it her duty to find out as much as she could about the billionaire.

For the past two weeks, she had carried every file and report from their offices to those of the bigwigs who occupied the other two floors of the building. Every time she had returned, she had brought with her more titbits of information Sunny had largely ignored.

'And did you manage to get a glimpse of The Big Man?' Sunny asked, eyebrows raised.

'Well…'

'Just a simple *yes* or *no*…'

'Don't be such a spoilsport, Sunny.' Undeterred, Alice dragged a chair over and positioned it directly in front of Sunny's desk. 'You can't be *that* uninterested!'

'I bet you I can be,' but she grinned back. Alice was

everything Sunny had always imagined would get her back up. She spoke in just the sort of cut-glass accent Sunny had always found irritating and offensive, bounced around with the irrepressible self-confidence of someone for whom life had always been kind and, to top it off, had only got the job at the law firm because, as she freely admitted on day one, her father had connections.

But, mysteriously, Sunny had taken to her and so now, although she just wanted to get on with her work, she was willing to take a bit of time out to indulge her colleague.

'No,' Alice sighed and pouted. 'And I couldn't even quiz Ellie for details about him because everyone out there is on good behaviour. Anyone would think that she'd suddenly had a personality transplant. She's *always* happy to chit-chat...'

'Perhaps she just had a heavy workload,' Sunny said gently, 'and didn't think that ten-fifteen in the morning was the right time to settle down for a good gossip about a new client.'

'Not just *any old client*...'

'I know. We've all heard about the wondrous Stefano Gunn...'

'And you're really not impressed, are you?' Alice said curiously. 'How come?'

'I'm hard to impress.' Sunny was smiling but she had tensed up inside. She wondered when she would be cured of that, when she would be able to deal with personal questions without freezing up. Would she ever really be able to relax or was that something that would always be denied her? Alice hadn't been prying, hadn't actually asked her anything that could be called *personal* and yet Sunny had not been able to prevent that instinct to withdraw.

She knew she was buttoned up. She knew the group she worked with, who were all her age, found her pleasant enough but distant and unapproachable. She guessed they probably gossiped and speculated about her behind her back. She was the way she was and she knew why she was the way she was but she still couldn't change it and sometimes, like now, she wished she could.

She wished she could lean into Alice, who was gazing at her like a good-natured, eager little brown-eyed puppy, waiting for her to say something.

'Someone like that just isn't the type of guy…er…that I could ever find…well… I'm not impressed by someone because they're rich or good-looking…' she finished lamely, before gesturing to the pile of paperwork on her desk. 'It's good that he's going to be letting the company handle some of his business. I'm sure all the partners will be thrilled…but anyway…'

'Who gives a hoot about all the partners? If he's after Katherine, I think she'll be thrilled by more than just the business he's bringing to the company.' Alice grinned. 'I'll bet he'll be thrilling her over more than just a desk and a cappuccino…with Sammy sitting in the corner taking notes… I'll bet he'll be thrilling her in all sorts of different ways tonight when they celebrate the business he's given us without a bunch of prying office eyes on them… Although…' she ran a canny eye over Sunny and grinned '…if it's looks he's after, you're a hottie—if only you'd dress the part. And whoa! I'm going before you shoot me down in flames for saying that!'

She stood up briskly, still grinning as she brushed her short, short skirt and asked whether there was some paperwork she could take to the third floor. No? Well…she'd better be off and do a couple of minutes' work…

Sunny watched her saunter back to her desk but her mind was off her work now. As if a man like Stefano Gunn would ever find her in the least bit attractive. Ridiculous.

Everyone had heard of Stefano Gunn. The whole world had heard of Stefano Gunn. Or at least anybody who was anybody and didn't live with their head buried in the sand. The man was ridiculously rich and stupidly good-looking. Not a day passed without his name popping up in the financial pages of a newspaper, reporting some deal or other he had secured which would boost his already inflated bank balance.

Sunny never read the tabloids but she was pretty sure that if she had she would have found him popping up there as well because ridiculously rich and stupidly good-looking men never led monk-like lives of self-restraint and solitude.

They led playboy lives with Barbie-doll women tripping along behind them and hanging on to their arms like limpets.

None of this was any of her concern, but Alice had opened up a train of thought which was normally kept safely locked away and, like opening a Pandora's box, Sunny could feel all those toxic thoughts uncurling from their dark corners and slithering through her head.

She stared at the computer winking at her and at the dense report she had been instructed to read. What she saw was her own life staring back at her—the pathos of her childhood, the foster home and all that horror, the boarding school to which she had been given a scholarship and all those girls who had made it their duty to sideline her because she wasn't one of them.

Self-pity threatened to engulf her and she had to breathe deeply to clear her head, to focus on all the positives in her life now, all the chances she had grasped and the opportunities she had taken that had led her to this up-and-coming law firm where she could gain experience whilst completing her LPC.

Deep, deep, *deep* inside, she might carry those scars that could still cause her pain but she was twenty-four now and grown-up enough to know how to deal with that pain when it threatened to surface.

Like now.

The report swam back into focus and she lost herself in her work, only surfacing when her phone buzzed on the desk. Internal line. When she looked at her watch, she was startled to find that it was already twelve-thirty.

'Sunny!'

'Hi, Katherine.' In her head, Sunny pictured Katherine, one of the youngest full partners in any law firm in the city. She was tall, slim, with a sharp brown bob and open, intelligent brown eyes. Her impeccable background had primed her for a life of solid achievement and she had fulfilled all her potential. Every so often, she joined some of the other girls lower down the pecking order for drinks after work because, as she had once said, it didn't do to wedge yourself into an ivory tower and pretend that anyone who didn't live there with you didn't exist. So she would come out for a drink and, on one of those rare occasions when Sunny had actually been coerced into joining her colleagues, had confided that the only thing missing in her life was the husband and the kids, which she never tired telling her parents would never come. They just didn't believe her.

Katherine was a one hundred per cent career woman and Sunny's role model because, as far as Sunny was concerned, the only reliable thing in life was your career and, if you worked hard enough, it would never let you down. The letting down always came from people.

'I realise it's your lunch hour and I really do hate to impose but I'm going to have to ask you to do me a small favour… Perhaps you could meet me in the conference room?'

'Is it to do with the files Phil Dixon asked me to go through? Because I'm afraid I'm not finished with them just yet...' And she'd been working flat-out but, unlike most of her other colleagues, she had debts to pay and the after-work job she held down left her precious little time to devote to work once she finally made it back to the flat she shared with Amy.

She heard anxiety creep into her voice. The files weren't due back for another week but she still tensed up in preparation for disappointment or a reprimand.

'Oh, no, nothing like that. Meet me in the conference room and of course bring whatever you're working on with you. And don't worry about lunch. I'll have whatever you want sent up to you.'

Inside, the building was cold, thanks to air conditioning. Outside, the sun was shining, the skies were blue and, as she walked up the two flights of stairs to the conference room, she noted that a lot of the offices were half empty.

St James's Park was only minutes away from the building and, on a fine summer day, who would want to stay indoors and eat at their desk? Or even bring a sandwich back to their desk? Not many people.

She hit the third floor and immediately went into the plush cloakroom to neaten up.

The image that stared back at her was as tidy as it always was. Her long silvery-blonde hair, flyaway fine and, when loose, a riot of tumbling curls, was tightly pinned back into a chignon at the nape of her neck. Her white blouse was pristine, as was the grey knee-length skirt. There was no need to inspect her pumps because they would be shiny and unscuffed.

She was a businesswoman and she always left the flat every single morning having made sure that she looked the part.

The striking looks, which had never done her any good at all, were always ruthlessly played down. Occasionally she wished she had poor eyesight so that she could play them down even more with a pair of thick-rimmed glasses.

Alice had called her a *hottie* and she had flinched from the description because it was the last thing in the world she wanted to be seen as and she made strenuous efforts to make sure she wasn't.

Katherine was waiting for her in the conference room, a large space impeccably decorated in muted colours. Long walnut table which could seat twenty people around it, a matching sideboard to house coffee- and tea-making facilities, pale tan carpet and vertical blinds at the floor-to-ceiling windows. No bright colours, no demanding paintings, no eye-catching plants.

And next to Katherine was...

A small child mutinously sitting with her arms folded and a variety of gadgets next to her—iPad, iPhone, sleek, slim computer.

'Sunny, this is Flora...'

Flora didn't bother looking up but Sunny's mouth dropped open.

'I know you're probably surprised but I need to ask you to sit with Flora until my business with her father is over.' She mouthed something over the child's head that Sunny didn't understand and then eventually said, moving to stand next to Sunny and out of earshot, 'Her grandmother was supposed to be looking after her but she's been called away and dropped her off half an hour ago.'

'I'm babysitting?' Sunny was appalled. She had never been one of those girls with a driving maternal instinct. She'd had no experience to speak of with kids and the little she did have had not left her with glorious rosy memories. The kids she had met at the school she had attended off and on until the age of ten had been horrible. Even then she had been a victim of bullying by most in her peer group because of the way she looked—blonde-haired, green-eyed with, she had overheard one parent telling another with just a hint of malice, the face of an angel. At an age where the most important thing was to blend in, she had stuck out like an elephant in a china shop and had paid the price.

Life lessons had taught her that the safest route to follow was the most invisible one and being highly visible had not drawn a vast circle of friends around her.

She'd never babysat for anyone. She had grown up fast. There had been no room in her life for playing games and especially not playing games with young children.

What on earth was she supposed to do with this one?

'She's hardly a baby, Sunny,' Katherine corrected with a smile. 'And you really won't have to do anything, which is why I told you to bring whatever you're working on with you. It's comfortable here and I've booked you in for the afternoon. I should be wrapped up with Mr Gunn by around five-thirty.'

'This is *his* child?' Sunny's jaw hit the ground with a thud and Katherine grinned.

'Unless he's having us on and, trust me, he's not the sort to have anyone on. We're not exactly rolling in the aisles from his sense of humour in there.'

'So…!' She stepped briskly back towards the child, who eventually looked up when there was no choice because Katherine had made introductions and was heading at speed towards the door.

Sunny got the feeling that the other woman was probably as awkward around young kids as she was.

The door shut and Sunny walked towards Flora and looked at her for a few seconds without saying anything.

She was a beautiful child. Long dark hair flowed down her back; her eyelashes were so long they brushed her cheeks, the eyes staring right back at her were huge, almond-shaped and as dark as night.

'I don't want to be here either.' Flora scowled and folded her arms. 'It's not my fault Nana had to drop me off.'

A surly, rebellious child was more what Sunny felt she could deal with and she breathed a quiet sigh of relief. 'You've brought all your toys to play with?' She eyed the collection of high-end gadgets and wondered how many other children of eight or nine walked around with thousands of pounds' worth of electronics to amuse them.

Faced with this unexpected job, she had had no time to ponder over the weird fact that the billionaire Stefano Gunn had a child. He might feature in the *Financial Times* with the regularity of a subscription holder but she had to concede that he was very private when it came to his personal life because, as far as she knew, no one was aware of the fact that he had a daughter.

For that she owed him more credit than she had otherwise thought.

'I'm bored with them.' Flora yawned extravagantly without putting her hands over her mouth.

'How old are you?'

'Why do you want to know?'

'You may think you're tough but you can never outdo me when it comes to being tough,' Sunny said honestly, which provoked a fleeting spark of interest. 'How old are you?'

'Nearly nine.'

'Good.' She beamed and walked towards the files she had lugged into the room with her. 'In that case, if you're bored with your toys you can help me with my work…'

Long legs stretched out at an angle, Stefano did his utmost to stifle a yawn.

This entire situation could have been handled by one of his employees. In fact, had it not been for his mother, this entire situation would not have been happening in the first place.

He had a perfectly competent team of in-house lawyers and had they not been up to the job of dealing with this particular slice of intricate patent law then he would have immediately gone to the biggest and the best.

Instead, here he was, at his mother's instigation, sitting in the offices of a company that was so new that it had barely left the embryo stage.

'Jane's daughter works there. You remember my friend Jane, don't you?'

No, he didn't. With those opening words three weeks ago, Stefano had been able to second-guess where his mother was going and Jane's daughter, whoever she was, was going to feature in the scenario.

It wasn't the first time Angela Gunn had tried to set him up. Ever since his ex-wife had died, driving too fast, having had too much to drink in a car that was way too sporty for winding New Zealand back roads, his mother had been keen to find him a suitable woman who could provide, as she was fond of telling him, a stable, nurturing maternal influence in his daughter's life.

'A girl needs her mother,' she had repeatedly said in a wistful voice. 'Flora barely knows you and she misses Alicia…that's why she's finding it so hard to adjust…'

Stefano had had to agree with his mother on at least one count and that was that he barely knew his daughter, although he always made sure to refrain from telling his mother just why that was the case.

His marriage to Alicia had been brief and disastrous. Having met young, what should have been no more than a passing fling had turned into a marriage of necessity when she had fallen pregnant. On purpose? That was a question he had never directly asked, but was there really any need? Alicia had come from New Zealand to study and had decided to stay on to work in one of the larger London hospitals as a nurse. He had met her there when he had suffered three broken ribs while playing rugby and the rest, he had always thought, was history. He had lusted after her, she had played coy and hard to get and then, when he had eventually got her into bed, safe in the knowledge that she was taking the Pill and, as a nurse, would be only too aware of the importance of making sure she stuck to the rigid regime, she had *had an accident*.

'I remember having a tummy upset,' she had told him, winding her arms around his neck and snuggling against him while he felt the bottom of his world drop away, 'and I don't know if you know but sometimes, if you have a stomach bug, the Pill doesn't work…'

He had married her. He had walked up the aisle with all the enthusiasm of a man walking to meet his executioner. They hadn't been married for five minutes before he realised the enormity of his mistake. Alicia had changed overnight. With free rein to more money than she could ever know in a lifetime, she had taken to spending with an exuberance that bordered frenetic. She had begun demanding that he spend more time with her. She had complained incessantly about the hours he worked and thrown hissy fits if he was late back by more than two minutes.

He had gritted his teeth and told himself that pregnancy hormones were to blame, even though he knew that they weren't.

When Flora was born, her demands had become more insistent. She needed constant, round the clock attention. Their London mansion became a battleground and the less he wanted to return to it, the more spiteful she became in her verbal attacks.

And then she began, as she took great pleasure in telling him, to *find stuff to do because she was bored and he was never around.*

He found out what that *stuff* was when he returned to the house early one afternoon and caught her in bed with another man. The fact that he had not felt a shred of jealousy had been the clearest indication that he needed a divorce.

What should have been a straightforward separation of ways, for he had been more than willing to give in to her strident, excessive demands for the sake of his daughter, had turned into a six-year nightmare. She had grabbed the money on the table and fled back to New Zealand, from where she had imperiously controlled his visiting rights, which, from the other side of the world, had been difficult, to say the least.

He had done his utmost to fight her for more reasonable custody but it had been impossible. She had thwarted him in every way conceivable and only her premature death had granted him the child he had fought so hard to know, but in reality had only seen a handful of times.

Now he had Flora but the years had returned him a daughter he didn't know, a daughter who resented him, who was sullen and uncooperative.

A daughter who, having now lived with him for nearly a year, *needed*, as his mother kept insisting, *a mother figure.*

He looked at Katherine Kerr, who was frowning at the various company accounts he had brought with him.

'You mustn't worry about your daughter.' She caught his eye and smiled warmly. 'I've left her in the capable hands of one of our brightest stars.'

Katherine Kerr was intelligent, attractive and empathetic. His mother would be hoping that they would click, that his next step would be to ask her out to dinner. It wasn't going to happen.

'I'm not worried about Flora,' he drawled. 'I'm worried that if we don't put this one to bed soon I'm going to miss my five-thirty meeting at the Savoy Grill.'

'It all looks fairly straightforward.' Katherine closed the file and sat back. 'If you're happy to leave it with us, then I can assure you we'll do an excellent job for you, Mr Gunn.'

Stefano looked at his watch and stood up. If the woman was looking for things to go further, then she was going to be disappointed. 'If you tell me where I can find my daughter, Miss Kerr, then I won't keep you any longer. I take it you now have all the relevant information you need to proceed with this patent case?'

Yes, she did. Yes, it was a pleasure doing business with him. She hoped that should he need any further legal work, he would consider their firm.

Leaving the office, Stefano decided that he would have to gently tell his mother that she would have to curb her desire to find him a wife. It wasn't going to happen. She would have to accept that when it came to women, he liked things just the way they were. Pretty, undemanding and admittedly not over-bright little things who came and went and allowed him windows of fun and sex for as long as he required them. It worked.

He made his way to the conference room, already bracing himself for the expected confrontation with his daughter and feeling mightily sorry for whoever had had the dubious pleasure of looking after her. Flora had a special talent for making her antagonism known and she was invariably antagonistic towards anyone babysitting her.

The offices smelt of recently applied paint and newly acquired carpet and had been decorated in just the sort of style he liked, which was understated and unpretentious.

This wouldn't have been a natural choice for him when it came to law firms but he'd liked what he'd seen and he was toying with the idea of throwing some more work their way as he knocked perfunctorily on the door before pushing it open and striding into the room.

Sunny looked up.

For a few seconds she felt winded, as though the breath had been knocked out of her.

She knew what Stefano Gunn looked like. Or at least she'd *thought* she'd known. She'd seen blurry pictures of him in the financial pages of the broadsheets, shaking hands, looking satisfied at some incredible deal he'd just pulled off. A tall, good-looking man whose roots lay in Scotland but whose looks were far from Scottish.

Seeing him in the flesh was a completely different matter. He wasn't just *good-looking*. He was staggeringly, sinfully *sexy*.

He was very tall, his body lithe and muscular under the hand-tailored suit. His black hair was slightly long, curling at the nape of his neck, and the arrangement of his features…was dramatic. Everything about him oozed exotic sex appeal and she found that she was holding her breath.

Horrified to be caught staring, she pulled herself together at speed and stood up, hand automatically outstretched.

'Mr Gunn. I'm Sunny Porter…'

His cool fingers as they briefly touched her sent an electric impulse racing through her body and when she withdrew her hand she had to fight not to wipe it on her skirt.

'Flora…' she turned to the child, who hadn't glanced up and was ferociously highlighting the photocopied piece of printed paper which Sunny had given her '…your father's here.'

'Flora!' Stefano's tone was sharp but he modulated it to add, 'It's time to go.'

'I'd rather stay here,' Flora said coolly, throwing Stefano a challenging stare.

For a few terse seconds complete silence greeted this mutinous remark. Embarrassed, Sunny cleared her throat and began shuffling her papers together. She could feel his presence and it was suffocating.

'You seem to have captured my daughter's interest with…what exactly is she doing?'

Sunny reluctantly looked up. She was tall, at five eight, but she still had to crane her neck to meet his eyes.

She's beautiful was the thought that sprang into Stefano's head as he stared down at her. Not just pretty or attractive, but a stunner, even though she couldn't have done more to try and conceal that fact.

Her clothes were cheap and drab, the colours draining, but they still couldn't subdue the radiant, startling beauty of her heart-shaped face and those huge green eyes. His gaze roamed the contours of her face, taking in the small straight nose and the full, perfectly formed mouth.

Sunny was used to men staring but Stefano's brooding dark eyes didn't send her irritation levels soaring. Instead, she felt her nipples pinch with sudden, forceful awareness and an unfamiliar, horrifying and unwelcome dampness spread uncomfortably between her legs.

Her response confused and panicked her.

Having lived the unstable, disjointed and bewildering life of a child with a mother whose primary concerns were men, drugs and drink, a mother who had been prone to disappearing for days on end, leaving her with a neighbour, any neighbour, Sunny prided herself on being tough, on being able to handle any situation.

Especially men.

She'd been attracting their attention since the minute she had become a teenager and started to develop. When her mother had died from an overdose, leaving behind her eleven-year-old daughter, she had been fostered by a couple and had lived on her nerves, uncomfortable with her foster father's leering eyes, terrified into locking her bedroom door every night although he'd stared but never touched.

At thirteen she had won a scholarship to an exclusive boarding school and, even there, she had been ostracised because of her remarkable looks. She was the cuckoo in the nest, out of her depth with girls who came from serious money, isolated because whenever boys happened to be around, they drooled over her.

She had hated every second of it all but the shell she had developed had protected her, had allowed her to ignore what couldn't be changed.

Men were driven to look at her. She had learned to blank them out.

She had told herself that the guy for her would be one who would want her for her brain, for what she had to say, for her personality.

Except when, at university, that guy had come along, dear, sweet John, who had been kind and chivalrous and thoughtful; she just hadn't been able to respond physically to him. That had been two years ago but it still hurt to think about it.

Had she, under the tough shell, been secretly searching for love? Had she longed for someone to ignite the sort of gentle romance she'd fantasised about in the deepest, darkest corners of her mind? Was that what had driven her to John, who had ticked all the right boxes as candidate for the Big Romance? If that had been the case, then she'd been way off mark and what she'd got hadn't been a Big Romance, but yet another tough learning curve which had closed the doors, for good, on any stupid belief that she was destined for a happy-ever-after life with the perfect soulmate. John should have been the perfect soulmate and she should have wanted to touch him all the time. It hadn't been that way at all. She'd concluded what she should have concluded a long time ago, which was that her background had irretrievably damaged her. She had moved on and accepted her lot.

So why was she all hot and bothered now? In the presence of a man like Stefano Gunn? Since when had she ever felt hot and bothered when some guy stared at her? Hadn't she stopped being an idiot two years ago when she and John had ended their doomed relationship?

'Flora didn't want to play with…any of her expensive toys—' she fought to remember that this was a very important client and swallowed down her natural instinct to be contemptuous '—so I gave her some work to do and she's been doing it for the past three hours.'

'Work?' He drew her aside while Flora continued doing what she was doing with the highlighters and making a pointed show of disinterest in his arrival.

'Not actual work,' Sunny explained, shifting a few inches away from him in an attempt to ward off the disconcerting impact of his presence. 'I photocopied some pages of one of my law books, Petersen versus Shaw, and asked her to read it and highlight the bits she thought were relevant to Petersen winning the case.'

'You did…*what*?'

'My apologies, Mr Gunn.' She stiffened, automatically defensive. What else was she supposed to do? Magic up some Lego and play building games with her? Was that even what eight-year-old girls were interested in doing? 'She said she was bored with whatever…games are on her iPad…or laptop…and I had a stack of work to get through…'

'I'm not criticising you,' Stefano said drily. 'I'm expressing open-mouthed amazement that Flora was drawn into doing something like that.'

Sunny relaxed and stole a glance at his handsome face. His voice was deep and lazy, as velvety as the smoothest of chocolate and his bronzed colouring spoke of an exotically foreign gene pool. And she could *breathe* him in, a woody, clean, utterly masculine scent that made her senses swirl.

'She's more than welcome to take the little file back with her.' She could feel the hot burn of an uncustomary blush. 'It's a historic case. I would never have given her anything that could have remotely been seen as sensitive information.'

'What are you doing later?'

'I beg your pardon?' Her eyes flew to his face in consternation.

'Later. What are you doing?' The Savoy Grill would have to be put on hold. 'I'd like to thank you for your impromptu babysitting by taking you out to dinner.'

'There's no need!' Sunny was aghast at the thought of having dinner with him. She was aghast at the thought of doing anything with the man, aside from saying goodbye and never clapping eyes on him again. He did something to her that she didn't like—something that made mincemeat of her nervous system—and for someone who valued her control that was tantamount to disastrous.

Stefano eyed her narrowly, taken aback by her horrified refusal.

'I... I couldn't.' She backtracked from being outright rude. 'I...happen to have a job that starts at six so I couldn't possibly...and there's really no need to thank me... All in a day's work...'

'A job?' He frowned. 'What job?'

'I... I work four nights in a restaurant... Qualifying to be a lawyer costs money, Mr Gunn,' she said bluntly. 'I also have rent to pay and food to buy. What I earn here doesn't quite stretch to cover it all.'

'In which case,' Stefano said smoothly, 'have dinner with me. I have a proposition for you and I think you'll find it…irresistible…'

CHAPTER TWO

SUNNY BARELY HAD time to make it home, change quickly and head out to the restaurant, which was just five minutes from where she lived and attracted an eclectic crowd of tourists and students because it was cheap, which appealed to the students, and trendy, which appealed to the tourists.

She had been lucky to get the job. The tips might not have been great because students were notoriously stingy when it came to that sort of thing, but the pay was better than average and the young couple who owned the place were generous, which meant that at the end of the week, if the takings had been particularly high, the staff were all given a small bonus over and above what they were paid.

Every penny went into Sunny's savings.

She was out of breath by the time she flew into the kitchen to change at speed out of her jeans and T-shirt and into the uniform, which was a jazzy red number, trousers and a T-shirt with the restaurant logo printed in bold white across the front, and a cap. Sunny had no idea what the significance of the outfit was and neither did Tom and Claire. They had decided on it because, Claire had confided, giggling, it had been a cheap bulk buy and the punters had seemed to like it so they had stuck with it.

'It's going to be a busy one tonight…' Claire was rushed off her feet. Tom was supervising in the kitchens, barking orders at the staff, and the other two waitresses were already zooming in and out, pinning orders to the cork board in the kitchen.

'I'm sorry I'm late,' Sunny apologised, stuffing her hair into the cap. 'I got held up at work.'

'No matter, darling. Go, go…go! Tom's having a melt-down because the tuna delivery hasn't arrived yet. You don't want to get anywhere near him!'

The trickle of customers was fast becoming a flood and Sunny went into autodrive. She had been working at TWC Eaterie for eight months and she knew the ropes. Take orders, smile a lot, race between kitchen and tables, deliver the orders and as soon as one set of diners had finished eating, get the bill to them as fast as she could so that the table could be cleared, making way for another lot to sit down. Sometimes, if the customers seemed to be dawdling a little too much over their coffees, Claire would turn up the volume on the music, just a notch, and that always seemed to remind them that it was time to go.

Sunny had her patch and she could work the tables blindfold. She chatted without really noticing who she was chatting to and she always added a smiley face to the bill when she brought it because she had read somewhere that it encouraged diners to leave bigger tips than they normally would.

This evening, she was particularly oblivious to the crowd. She'd thought of nothing but Stefano on the Tube ride back and he was still in her head as she dashed around the restaurant, distracting her, which got on her nerves.

The man had got under her skin.

Was it because he was just so good-looking? And why should that have made a difference anyway? Sunny had never been susceptible to good-looking men. She'd been chased by enough of them and heard enough of their corny lines to know that they were usually full of themselves and arrogantly all too aware of the effect they had on the opposite sex.

So why had Stefano Gunn proved the exception? Especially when she had given up on men? If she hadn't been able to feel any sort of physical attraction to a guy who had been perfect, then there was no hope for her. She had reconciled herself to that fact. She had assumed that she was frigid, a consequence of her turbulent background and a mother who had set a poor example when it came to self-restraint and decorum.

She touched the locket she wore around her neck. In it was one of only a handful of pictures she had of her damaged parent. Annie Porter might have been a terrible mother but there was still a big place in Sunny's heart for her. She felt that that must be what unconditional love was all about. Her mother would be the only recipient of that sort of love as far as Sunny was concerned. If she ever loved anyone again, and she wasn't even sure that she had loved John nearly as much as he had loved her, then there would be so many conditions that the weight of them would probably kill off any relationship before it could get going. Suited her.

But she hadn't had a relationship with anyone since John and she wondered whether the effect Stefano had had on her had been a timely reminder that she was still young.

It made no difference anyway. She wasn't going to see him again. She had politely turned down his offer for dinner and had shown no interest in whatever proposition he had for her that she might find irresistible.

Dinner and a proposition could only add up to one thing as far as Sunny was concerned.

Bed.

Perhaps he saw her as a possible easy conquest. He was staggeringly rich and staggeringly good-looking and maybe he thought that if he made a pass at her, she wouldn't be able to resist. Maybe he thought that, as a relative junior in the company, she would be awestruck and open-mouthed and breathless with girlish excitement if he so much as glanced in her direction.

Maybe…no, *almost certainly*, that was where the *irresistible* aspect of his so-called offer came in.

She was so wrapped up in thoughts that she wanted to box away that she was convinced her mind was playing tricks on her when, with the crowd finally and thankfully beginning to thin out, she heard the sound of his dark, velvety voice behind her.

She spun round, only just managing to hang on to the tray she was balancing and stared.

It was a little after ten and he looked as bright-eyed and bushy-tailed as when she had last seen him at five-thirty, although he was no longer wearing his suit.

The suit had been replaced by a pair of black jeans and a fitted black jumper that did remarkable things for his lean, muscular build.

She couldn't find a thing to say. She actually blinked several times to make sure that she wasn't seeing things, that her mind hadn't conjured up his image because she had been thinking so much about him.

'So this is where you work…'

Sunny was galvanised into movement. 'What are you doing here, Mr Gunn?' She wasn't in the office now and she didn't see why she should try and modulate her voice to accommodate him. She stared at his face but she was aware of every part of him with every pore in her body. 'Look, I can't stop to chat to you.' She turned round abruptly and began heading towards the kitchen, heart beating like a sledgehammer inside her.

Fi, one of the girls who worked the tables with her, the only full-time waitress among them and a bubbly brunette who specialised in having boyfriend problems, was taking a little time out to catch her breath because her stint was almost over. Sunny was very tempted to ask her whether Stefano was still outside and, if he was, whether she could take his order but then she knew that that would lead to endless curiosity and, as always, the part of her that clammed up at the thought of confiding slammed into gear.

Maybe he would get the message and leave. Maybe he'd already left. Her hands were clammy and she wiped them on her trousers as she headed back out to the restaurant, which was now practically empty.

There was no avoiding or ignoring him. His presence was so powerful that it would have been impossible to overlook him even though he was sitting right at the back. He had pushed his chair at an angle so that he could stretch out his long legs and he looked utterly composed and relaxed.

Stifling a sigh of frustration, Sunny walked towards him, taking her time.

'I'm afraid we've already taken last orders,' she said ungraciously, 'so if you've come here expecting a meal, then you're going to be disappointed.'

'Oh, dear. And the menu looked so interesting. Perhaps another day. However, that being the case, I'm assuming you'll be leaving shortly?'

'How did you even find out where I worked?' She looked at him with great reluctance and was assailed by the same unwelcome heady discomfiture she had felt before. His eyes were as dark as night and as captivating as an open flame to a moth. There was nothing safe or comforting about him but he had the sort of face she felt driven to stare at and the sort of compelling personality that wanted to suck her in and she had no intention of being sucked in.

Her memories of her mother were scattered but she remembered enough. She remembered how pretty her mother had been and how helpless she had been at the hands of men who had taken advantage of her. The roller-coaster ride that had been her childhood had built in her a capacity for self-control she never relinquished and a determination never to find herself in any situation with anyone that made her feel helpless. John had never made her feel helpless.

But something about Stefano Gunn made her feel helpless.

'Sit.'

Sunny folded her arms and stared at him. 'We're not in an office now, Mr Gunn...'

'Stefano, please.'

She chose to ignore that interruption. 'So I feel it's okay for me to be direct with you.'

'I've always encouraged directness in other people,' Stefano murmured. She was even more eye-catching than he remembered, even though the hair, he noted, was still tucked away and she wore no make-up.

She'd turned down his offer for dinner and rejected what he had to say without bothering to give him a hearing. She'd been pointedly polite about it but she hadn't been able to get away from him fast enough.

He was accustomed to women bending over backwards to attract his attention. He'd never been in the position of being with a woman who so clearly couldn't wait to escape his presence and he hadn't known whether to be irritated or amused by that.

'I don't know how you managed to find out where I work...'

'Not that difficult. I got your address from Katherine, went to your house, spoke to the girl who shares your flat with you, who told me where you worked and here I am.'

'You *spoke to Katherine*?' Sunny was outraged. She glanced round to see Claire looking at her curiously. 'I have to finish clearing the tables,' she muttered.

'I'll wait until you're finished and walk you home.'

'I don't need an escort, Mr Gunn.'

'I told you, the name is Stefano.' An edge of impatience had crept into his voice. Her simmering hostility and mutinous stubbornness, rather than putting him off, was goading him into digging his heels in. He'd come here to talk to her and talk to her he would. Maybe if it hadn't been for Flora, he would have shrugged off her cool refusal to listen to him although a little voice in his head was telling him that she posed a challenge and a challenge was something he had not experienced in a very long time.

Sunny didn't bother to answer. She knew she was attracting interested looks from her friends in the restaurant and that in itself made her bristle with annoyance at him.

How dared he track her down like this?

How dared he think that he could stampede over her very clear refusal to listen to his *proposition*?

How dared he think he could try and sweet-talk her into bed because he was filthy rich and she was just an ordinary junior in a law firm and therefore open to persuasion?

And how *dared* he compromise her position in the company by talking to her boss about her?

Rage bubbled up inside her as she raced through the remainder of her chores, wiping the tables and then, finally, changing back into her jeans and T-shirt and the denim jacket she had brought along because it was now quite cool outside.

'He's still there, you know,' Claire said, lounging by the kitchen door with a tea towel slung over her shoulder. She and Tom would stay on for at least another hour and in the morning they would count the takings. It had been a very good night. 'I know you've made a point of pretending not to notice, but he hasn't gone.'

Sunny flushed and scowled.

'My darling, none of us can miss the way the guys

who come in here stare at you. I don't mean to intrude…
I know you're a very private person, but haven't you ever
been tempted to…to…?'

'Never,' Sunny said fiercely. 'I don't go for guys who
are drawn to me because of the way I look.' She remembered her foster father's lecherous eyes following her
through the house, while his invalid wife remained cheerfully oblivious, and shuddered.

'Who's your latest admirer?'

Sunny sighed and looked at Claire. 'He's not an admirer,' she admitted. Although why else would he be here?
If not to try and get her into bed? She wasn't vain but she
was realistic and being realistic protected her against having her head turned by meaningless, pretty words. 'Don't
worry. I'll get rid of him and I'll make sure he doesn't
come here again.'

Claire laughed. 'He looks rich. He can come whenever
he wants, just as long as he puts his hand in his pocket
and actually shows up in time to order food and drink!'

'I'll pass that on.' Sunny smiled weakly. She had no
intention of doing any such thing. What she intended to
do was find out just what he had said to Katherine and
whether he had compromised her position in the company.

And she would have to do that without letting her temper explode. She would have to be cool, calm and collected
whilst leaving him in no doubt that she wasn't interested
in whatever he had to say to her.

She emerged and Stefano was almost surprised because
he had half expected her to have disappeared through a
back door. But there she was, in jeans and a T-shirt and,
without the cap, her hair was long. Very long. Every shade
of blonde feathering in curls down her back, although that
didn't last very long because, even as she walked towards
him, she was stuffing it into a ponytail.

She had the long, slender body of a ballet dancer and

CATHY WILLIAMS   35

her movements were graceful. She was scowling, but not even the scowl could hide that startling, unusual prettiness. When she had been created, some small added ingredient had been thrown into the mix, elevating her from good-looking to unbelievably striking. Her green eyes were narrowed suspiciously on him as she finally came to a stop directly in front of him.

'I want to know what you said to Katherine.'

'You're not, are you?' Stefano stood up, towering over her, and she automatically fell back a step or two.

'Not what?'

'Sunny.' He shoved his hands in his pockets as they headed to the door. 'Your mother must rue the day she named you that. Unless, of course...' he pushed open the restaurant door, allowing her to brush past him '...you're sunny with everyone else but reserve all your bulldog belligerence for me...is that it? And, if so, why?'

'My mother died when I was a child,' Sunny said coldly. 'What did you tell Katherine?' She didn't want him walking next to her...didn't want him escorting her the short distance to her flat, but she felt as if she had no choice.

'I told her that I wanted to discuss something with you of a personal nature and she was kind enough to provide me with your address.'

'How dare you?' She rounded on him, hands on her hips, so furious that she felt she might explode. 'Do you have any idea how important that job is to me?' A series of scenarios ran through her head, each worse than the one before. He had put poor Katherine in a position...he was so important that she had had no choice but to do as he had asked...but in the morning, she, Sunny, would be called in for a little chat...she would be told that fraternising with clients was frowned upon...she would be warned... she might even be sacked... She hadn't been there very long and the last thing the company would want would be a lawyer who couldn't be trusted around clients...she would lose her job, her career and everything that made sense of her life...

And it would all be this man's fault.

'I don't want anything to do with you and how dare you tell my boss that you want my address? So that you can try and *come on to me*? How *dare* you?' Tears of anger and frustration were pricking the back of her eyes.

With just the street lights for illumination, his face was all angles and shadows. He towered over her and she couldn't read the expression on his face.

Just in case he hadn't got the drift, though, she thought that she should make herself perfectly clear.

'I'm not going to sleep with you, Mr Gunn, and I don't want you *pestering* me. I don't care how rich or powerful you are or how much business you're going to bring to the firm... *I* don't come as part of what's on offer to you!'

Stefano was genuinely outraged that she had pigeon-holed him as desperate and downright stupid enough to think about making a pass at her.

'Aren't you getting a little ahead of yourself?' he asked coolly.

That threw her and for a few seconds she stared at him in sudden confusion.

'Anyway, I hope I've made myself clear,' she muttered, dragging her eyes away from him and walking briskly towards the flat. He kept pace with her.

The flat she shared with Amy was cheap and thus located in a fairly dodgy part of town. A hop and a skip away, smart restaurants and trendy cafés lined the high street but here all of that gave way to rundown houses that were mostly let to people who couldn't afford anything better, and a couple of off licences and corner shops that stayed open beyond the call of duty.

'So—' she stopped in front of the door that led up to

the flat she shared at the top of the converted Victorian house '—I'd appreciate it if you just left me alone, and please don't discuss me with my boss. It could jeopardise my position in the company.'

'Like I said…you're getting ahead of yourself here. I think you're confusing me with the sort of sad loser who's into pursuing reluctant women and can't take no for an answer.'

Sunny stared at him in silence, slowly realising that she had misunderstood the situation.

Mortification swept over her in a hot, burning tide. 'You said you had a proposition for me…' she stammered, so taken aback that she was barely aware of him removing the key from her hand, opening the door and urging her inside.

He shouldn't be coming in. He definitely *should not* be coming in. Amy wasn't going to be there. She was on nights and wouldn't be back until the following morning and Sunny couldn't imagine him being in the flat with her, just the two of them.

Although he wasn't *interested in her*, was he? When you thought about it, why the heck would he be? He could have any woman he wanted. He would just have to snap his fingers! She was so embarrassed at jumping to erroneous conclusions that she would happily have stepped into the hole if the ground had opened up beneath her feet.

While this jumble of thoughts was chaotically running through her head, they took the stairs and he let them into the flat with the key, which she had failed to take from him.

It was a very small two-bedroom flat with barely room to swing a cat. The décor was shabby and the furniture looked as though it had mostly been reclaimed from a skip somewhere. Not even the cheerful prints Blu-tacked to the walls could lift the place into something more cheerful.

But it worked for both of them. They got along very well and, because Amy worked nights most of the month, they tended to see one another only in passing.

Looking around him, Stefano realised that he had never been anywhere like this before in his life. He knew that by anyone's standards his life had been one of unsurpassed privilege. The only child of a wealthy Scottish landowner and an Italian mother who, herself, had inherited a tidy sum of money when her parents had passed away, he had never had any occasion to find himself slumming it. Alicia, of course, had not had money but he had rarely ventured into the quarters she shared with her friends.

Here, amidst this drab, unappealing *ordinariness*, Sunny was the equivalent of an orchid in a patch of weeds. He could almost understand why she had misinterpreted his intentions, although that did nothing to detract from the umbrage he felt.

Although, a little voice whispered in his head, hadn't he looked at her with sexual interest? It wasn't going to happen.

Stefano swept that unwanted thought aside as fast as it had come.

'My daughter liked you,' he said without preamble.

'Did she? I have no idea why. I gave her work to do and I don't suppose many eight-year-olds would have appreciated that.' But she felt a rare bloom of pleasure at his words.

Released from the discomfort of thinking that he was just someone else attracted to her because of the way she looked, Sunny knew that she should be able to relax, but she was still as tense as a piece of elastic stretched to breaking point. He had sprawled out on one of the chairs in the tiny sitting room and he was just so wildly exotic that she could scarcely look at him without her breath catching in her throat and a weird tension invading her body.

'I had to bring Flora in with me because she managed to successfully see off the last nanny and my mother had to go unexpectedly to Scotland…'

'Oh.' Where was this going? Sunny was bewildered. 'When you say *see off the last nanny*…' This for no other reason than to fill the silence.

'Flora enjoys making life as difficult for her nannies as she humanly can.' Stefano sighed and raked his fingers through his hair.

'I don't see what this has to do with me.' His wife wasn't around. He was an eligible bachelor. The office gossip mill had made that perfectly clear from day one, when speculation had been rife that he was only handing them business because of Katherine. She perched on the edge of a chair and looked at him steadily.

'My mother will be up in Scotland for the next month. I have a nanny to cover for Flora during the day, as she's on holidays, but not even the most long-suffering of nannies, and Edith is about as long-suffering as they come, is willing to do day and night cover. I'm wrapped up in some pretty important deals over the next fortnight and my proposal was for you to work for me between five and ten every evening, Monday to Friday.'

'I'm sorry but that's out of the question.'

'Why?'

'I don't have to give long explanations,' Sunny told him stiffly. Something about the prospect of being inside his house sent shivers through her. No matter that she now knew that he had no interest in her aside from babysitter for his daughter. 'But, in case it's missed you, I actually already have a job after work and it's a job I enjoy and wouldn't want to lose. Also…'

Stefano tilted his head to one side. Flora had been animated on the drive back to the house. In fact, she had been the most animated he'd seen her since she had arrived in

London. She had actually spoken to him, as opposed to sitting in surly silence and answering his questions in monosyllables.

'Also…?' he prompted softly.

Sunny shrugged and reddened. 'Nothing. I… I just can't do it. I'm sorry.'

'But you don't know what the terms and conditions are,' he murmured. He wondered what else she had been about to say. She was guarded and that was something he never saw in the women he met. And the way she had rushed into the assumption that he'd been after her for sex. Was she accustomed to having to fend off men? Had she suffered from office pests? They were out there, no question of it, and she had the looks to provoke over-enthusiasm in most red-blooded men, he would have thought.

Or maybe one pest in particular had made her suspicious of all men…

He was a little unnerved at the amount of time he was wasting in pointless speculation.

'Unless, of course, you have a boyfriend…someone who might not want you to spend time away from the flat when you're not at work…'

Sunny laughed shortly. 'I wouldn't let any guy tell me what I could or couldn't do.' The words were out before she could take them back. 'By which,' she continued lamely, 'I mean that I'm…my own person…not that it's any business of yours whether I have a boyfriend or not anyway… I just… I'm sorry…'

'I'm sure the restaurant could spare you for a couple of weeks. In fact, I don't see that as a problem at all. I'll personally arrange for a replacement and cover the costs myself. And with regard to what you earn there…' He paused, allowing speculation to take root in her head and spout tendrils. 'I'll quadruple it.' He sat back and watched her narrowly. 'I'd like you to work for me and I'm prepared to pay you far, far more than you would earn in the restaurant, including tips…'

'I don't understand,' Sunny stammered, thoroughly taken aback. 'Why can't you just go and employ someone from an agency?'

'Flora averages a nanny a fortnight and, during that fortnight, I'm bombarded with complaints from whatever nanny happens to be working for me. I don't need that. She's taken a liking to you and I'm prepared to take a gamble.'

'I have no experience of looking after children, Mr Gunn.'

'For God's sake, there's no need to keep calling me Mr Gunn.' He paused and watched her, trying to read behind the cautious exterior.

Agitated, Sunny looked away. 'Don't you have a… um…a partner?'

'Partner?'

'A girlfriend? Someone who could step in and help out?' She had no idea from whence the rumour had sprung that he was interested in Katherine. Maybe the rumours had been wrong. Maybe there was someone else in the background, although it beggared belief that he would bring work to a new, small company and not use one of the top guns to handle his business.

'Now, now, Sunny—or shall I call you Miss Porter as you seem determined to stick to the formalities?— would you say that you're entitled to ask that question considering you've surrounded yourself with No Trespassing signs?' He watched her squirm for a few seconds. 'There's no handy woman ready to jump in and help out.' He thought of Katherine and his mother's fine intentions to set him up. Nice enough woman but he certainly couldn't picture her in the role of surrogate mother.

Indeed, she had seemed distinctly uncomfortable when presented with Flora.

'What about Flora's mother?' It seemed an obvious enough question and she was surprised when the shutters snapped down, coldly locking her out. As No Trespassing signs went, she'd just stumbled into an almighty giant-sized one.

'Flora's mother died several months ago,' Stefano said abruptly. 'Now, are you willing to take the job or not? I've given you my offer and, from the looks of it, you could do with the money. You can bring your work to the house if you want to do overtime and that's an added bonus, considering working in a restaurant doesn't afford that luxury. And I may be misreading the situation, but if you're intent on a career then the lack of overtime must be a decided drawback to someone young and ambitious.'

'I'm not sure whether it would be entirely ethical for me to work with a client.'

'In which case, I'll take my considerably well-paid work away from your law firm. How does that sound?'

'You wouldn't.' Sunny was aghast at that threat because, if he did that, then the worst-case scenarios would be a great deal worse than the ones she had conjured up in her head when he'd told her that he'd spoken to Katherine.

'Yes. I would. You would be surprised at the lengths I would go to in order to get what I want.' He thought of that small but perceptible change in his daughter on the drive back to his house. For that reason alone it was worth the hassle of being here. He could hardly believe that she was kicking up a fuss at being paid handsomely to do a babysitting job of limited duration. 'And, just for your information, I have already cleared the way with Katherine. I explained the situation and she's more than happy for you to help out.'

'Is she? Didn't she…ah…volunteer to do it herself?'

'Why would she do that?'

'No reason.' Annoyed with herself for being drawn into that faux pas, she stared down at her trainers. 'What if it doesn't work out?'

'I prefer positive thinking. Like I said, Flora doesn't warm to people easily but she warmed to you. It's good enough for me. Now, the job. Yes or no? You'll start first thing on Monday. I'll have my driver collect you from work and return you to your flat. Meals will be provided and you're free to do as you wish with Flora, although she's accustomed to being in bed by eight. I'll open an account for you if you want to take her anywhere. Feel free to use it.'

It was a fantastic opportunity to add to her savings. She knew that. She might even treat herself to some new work clothes. So why was she still hesitating? It was crazy.

'Okay,' she agreed. 'I'll do it. I'll take the job.'

CHAPTER THREE

STEFANO'S HOUSE, on the outskirts of London, was a dream house.

For one man and a young child, it was ridiculously big. There were six bedrooms, five bathrooms, too many undefined reception rooms to count and a kitchen that was spacious enough for a table at one end that could seat ten. It opened out to a spread of perfectly manicured lawns, in the middle of which was a magnificent swimming pool.

Paradise for an eight-year-old child and Sunny wondered whether the pool was used during the day. The weather had certainly been hot enough for swimming.

Life here couldn't have been more different for Flora than her own life had been for her. She wondered what it would have been like had she, as a kid, been exposed to this level of opulence. She would have been terrified.

Now, as an adult, she could see the many material advantages but she was also beginning to see the many drawbacks. After four days of babysitting, she was slowly realising certain things and there was no need for Flora to verbalise them.

Surrounded by all this luxury, Flora was confused and unhappy. Her mother had died and she had been yanked across the ocean to a life she had never known and a father she seemed to resent.

'I hate it here,' she had confided the evening before, as Sunny had been about to switch off the bedroom light and leave the room. 'I want to go back to New Zealand.'

'I get that.' Sunny had sat on the bed. There were no signposts as to how she should connect with a kid and it wasn't in her to be patronising. She had had to grow up fast and that had implanted in her the belief that kids could deal with honesty far better than most adults thought.

They didn't like being patronised and Sunny didn't see why she should patronise Flora.

'Sometimes circumstances change and, when that happens, you just have to go with it because you can never change things back to the way they were. That's just the truth.'

Flora, she had discovered, was as mature as she herself had been at that age, although not for similar reasons. She was just a grown-up child with shaped opinions and the sort of suspicious, cautious nature that Sunny could understand because she, too, shared those traits. She had no time for her father and Sunny could have told her another harsh truth, which was that she was here and having him around was also something she couldn't change so she might as well accept it.

It wasn't in her brief to broker a relationship between father and daughter, however. In fact, it wasn't in her brief to be curious about the dynamics of the household at all. She was there to babysit, no more, no less, but she liked the kid and she knew that Flora liked her, even though she still didn't understand why because they never did anything Sunny imagined an eight-year-old would find fun. When she'd been eight, there had been no exciting trips to Adventure Parks or shiny new toys. She had taken refuge in books and so pointing Flora in the direction of more serious pursuits came as the natural choice.

They watched telly, always the National Geographic channel which they both enjoyed. They'd played a game of Scrabble and Sunny had laughed and told Flora that she could allow her to win or they could both play to the best

of their ability and see what happened. The evening before, after they had eaten an early dinner at six, they had
both attempted to bake and it had been a miserable failure.

'I didn't do much baking as a child,' Sunny had said
truthfully, 'and I don't think I ever got the hang of it.
We'll have to bin the bread. Or else hang onto it in case
we need a lethal weapon.' Which had made Flora laugh
until she cried.

Between eight and ten Sunny worked and then Stefano
would return with his driver.

His presence filled the house. He would stride in and
Sunny would know that she'd been bracing herself for the
brief encounter. They would exchange a couple of sentences and then the driver would whisk her away back to
her flat and once there she would think about him. She
tried to fight those thoughts and when she couldn't she
uneasily told herself that it was only natural that he was
in her head because she was now working for him. If she
hadn't been, she would have forgotten all about him, however startling the impact he had made on her had been.

Now, with Flora in bed, Sunny settled down for her
two hours' work, which was absolute bliss because it was
a luxury she could never had afforded when she'd been
working at the restaurant. She was given the most basic
of tasks but they tended to be time-consuming and it was
good to be able to work her way through them in the peace
and quiet of the sprawling mansion.

Having explored all of the rooms on the ground floor,
she had settled on the smallest and the cosiest as her work
room. It overlooked the back gardens and she enjoyed
glancing up and letting her eyes wander over a vista of
mown grass, sweeping trees and, in the distance, the open
fields onto which the house backed. Compared to the view
from the flat she shared, which gave onto the grimy pave-
ments outside and a lone tree which looked as though it

was pining to be anywhere but on a road in London, the view here was breathtaking and it made her feel as though she was on holiday.

Legs tucked under her, her long hair untidily pulled over one shoulder, she was hardly aware of Stefano's appearance in the doorway until he spoke and then she yelped in shock, eyes adjusting to the impressive sight of him.

When she could predict his arrival back, she had time to brace herself for the physical impact he still seemed to have on her. With no time to prepare herself, she could only stare while her heart sped up and her mouth went dry.

He was tugging his tie off, dragging it down so that he could undo the top two buttons of his white shirt, and she tried her best not to gape at the sliver of brown skin exposed.

'What are you doing here?' she stammered, gathering the bits of paper spread around her and smartly shutting her computer.

'I live here.'

'Yes, but…'

'No need to rush, Sunny. I'm back early so we can have a catch-up.'

'A catch-up? On what?'

Stefano banked down a flare of irritation. Her desperation not to be in his company had not abated. They crossed paths when he returned from work and she was always packed up, jacket on, exchanging a few sentences on the move as she headed out the front door. Whatever she did with Flora, she was doing it right because his daughter, when prompted, actually now deigned to show some interest in his questions rather than sullenly sitting at the breakfast table in front of her cellphone playing games. The top-of-the-range cellphone, in retrospect, had not been the cleverest purchase on the planet.

'I haven't eaten,' he said evenly, keen eyes noting the blonde length of her hair which, for once, wasn't tied back, probably an omission because she hadn't expected him home at eight-thirty. 'Why don't you join me in the kitchen?'

'Of course,' Sunny dutifully replied. She sneaked a covert look as he rolled up his shirtsleeves, exposing muscled forearms sprinkled with dark hair. Everything about him was intensely masculine and her body behaved in disconcerting ways when she was confronted with it.

He was already moving off towards the kitchen and she followed, taking all her work with her and her bag so that she could leg it at speed as soon as their catch-up was finished.

'Drink?' He moved to the wine cooler, which was built into the range of pale cupboards, and extracted a bottle of white wine.

'No, thank you.'

'Relax, Sunny. One drink isn't going to hurt you.' Without giving her time for a second polite refusal, he poured them both a glass, handed one to her and rummaged for ingredients for a sandwich. 'How are you finding the job?'

'Fine,' she said awkwardly and he turned round and looked at her with a frown.

'Is that going to be the full extent of your contribution to this conversation?' he asked coolly. 'Monosyllabic answers? Flora talks about you.'

'Does she?' She fiddled with her hair and reminded herself that this was a perfectly normal business conversation, that of course he would be interested in knowing what she did with his daughter. But she still felt horribly nervous and she knew it was because she was too *aware* of him for her own good. If this strange reaction was her body reminding her that she was still *alive*, then she resented the reminder.

'Tell me what you two do together.' He dragged out a chair, sat down and began tucking into his sandwich.

'Oh, the usual.' Their eyes met and she reddened. Did she really want him asking why she was so jumpy around him? No. But he would if she continued to stutter and stammer and, as he had pointed out, answer his questions with unhelpful monosyllables. 'Nothing very child-oriented, I'm afraid, although we did do a spot of baking yesterday after dinner.'

'A failure, I've been told.'

'I'm not very good when it comes to stuff like that,' she said vaguely.

'No mother-daughter bonding sessions in front of a stove?'

'No.' Sunny heard the tightness creep into her voice and she lowered her eyes. 'Nothing like that.'

A girl with secrets. Was he really interested in finding out what those secrets were? Did he care one way or another? She was here to do a job and she was doing a damn fine job. Then she'd be gone…

He found his curiosity unsettling because it was something he never felt with any of the women he dated. He had been through one disastrous relationship and now he made sure to keep everything light and superficial when it came to the opposite sex. Curiosity was definitely neither light nor superficial.

But it was something she roused in him for no reason he could begin to understand.

'I think Flora's unhappy and lonely.' She rushed into saying more than she had intended because she didn't want him quizzing her about her past. Being here had brought home to her the differences in their worlds and she didn't want him judging her because of her background. She was an aspiring lawyer, coerced into doing an impromptu job for him. She didn't want him feeling sorry for her or pitying her.

'I mean…she's been displaced from everything she knew and I just get the feeling that she hasn't settled here just yet. She hasn't mentioned her school once and that's saying something.'

Stefano shoved his plate to one side and sat back, arms folded behind his head. 'Is that right?' he drawled and Sunny bristled.

'She's just a child and she's had to endure some pretty major life changes.' The way he was staring at her with those dark, dark speculative eyes made her feel all hot and bothered and she was suddenly as angry with him as she was with herself for feeling so *exposed*.

'And I hope you don't mind me being honest,' she said tersely, 'but I don't suppose it helps that you work such long hours.' *Oh, he's never here*, Flora had shrugged apropos of nothing in particular a couple of evenings ago, and Sunny had heard the hurt in her voice and been moved by it.

Stefano stiffened at the implied criticism in her voice, yet she was only stating the obvious, wasn't she? He wondered when positive criticism had become something he could do without. He certainly never encountered it in his day-to-day life.

'It's impossible for me to conduct a nine-to-five existence.'

Sunny shrugged. 'It's none of my business anyway.'

Perversely, the fact that she was happy to back away from the contentious conversation rather than pursue it made him want to prolong it. 'Don't start conversations you don't want to finish,' he inserted. 'I'm a big boy. I can take whatever you have to say to me. Did Flora tell you that?'

'A passing remark. Look—' Sunny raised her eyes to

his and felt heat creep into her face '—I'm not here to have opinions on…on…how you handle Flora. I'm just here in a babysitting capacity. I need the money. I don't suppose any of your nannies tell you what they really think because they'd just be here to do a babysitting job, like me.'

'They don't tell me what they think because they're intimidated by me,' Stefano said drily. 'You don't like being around me but you're not intimidated by me. At least, that's the impression I've got. Am I wrong?'

Sunny had no idea how they had got where they had but this felt like a very personal conversation. Or maybe it was the intimacy of being in the kitchen with him, just the two of them, that made it feel more personal than it really was.

'Well?' he prompted. 'True or false?'

'I try not to be intimidated by anyone,' she was spurred into responding.

'And that works for you?'

'Yes. Yes, it does.' Colour flared in her cheeks but she held his gaze defiantly. 'I like to think, *What's the worst that can happen?* I mean, you can sack me from this job but, if you do, then that's fine. I'd be more than happy to return to my restaurant work.'

'Long hours,' he mused, startling her by the sudden change of topic.

'What do you mean?'

'When do you get time to relax? Do you have a busy social life on the weekends?'

'I'm too busy building a career to have a busy social life on the weekends,' she snapped.

'How old are you?'

'I'm twenty-four, although I don't see what my age has to do with anything.'

'Katherine told me that you're one of the most dedicated employees in the company. You're in by eight every morning, sometimes earlier, and if you leave promptly for your job in the restaurant it never seems to affect the quality of your work, which is always of the highest standard. Which means, I'm guessing, that you work on weekends…'

Sunny was torn between pleasure that her hard work had been noted and dismay that she had been a topic of discussion. 'You have to work hard in order to get on,' she muttered, flushing.

'To the extent that it consumes your every waking hour?'

'It seems that work consumes all *your* waking hours,' Sunny said defensively. 'I'm sorry. I shouldn't have said that, Mr Gunn.'

'If you call me Mr Gunn again, I'll sack you.'

She didn't know whether he was joking or not and she bit back the temptation to keep arguing with him.

'And, believe it or not, work doesn't consume *all* my waking hours,' he told her softly, 'I know how to play as well…'

Sunny stared. The tenor of his voice was so…*sexy*… and when she looked at him it felt as though his eyes were boring straight past her defences, seeing into parts of her that were soft and yielding and vulnerable, parts of her that hadn't been forced into toughening up over the years.

'I… I…' Her voice was cracked and she cleared her throat. 'I plan on getting through my LPC exams and then…then I'll have plenty of time to go out and have fun…more than enough time…' Because, right now, clubbing and going to pubs and bars just wasn't on the agenda.

When did she ever have fun?

That was something that she never really thought about. A history of insecurity and rootlessness had instilled in her a need to ground herself, to have the security she had missed out on and that security, she had always known, would come in the form of her career. She had learned to distrust the attention she got from men and she had learned that at an early age, so fun, for her, wasn't about guys and dates and flirting. Her one stab at *fun* had run aground and she wasn't going to repeat the experience. She just didn't have it in her to enjoy life the way other girls her age did. As she'd told her young charge, what you couldn't change you simply had to accept, like it or not.

So fun for her wasn't about all those things girls her age were interested in.

Suddenly the life she was looking at, the life she had strived with every ounce of her being to secure, looked empty and lacking.

Stefano watched the play of expression on her face. There was a luminosity to her face and a guilelessness that was at odds with the tough exterior.

His eyes drifted lower, to the jut of her breasts underneath the T-shirt. Small breasts, a neat handful. He drew his breath in sharply at the unexpected image of her in his king-sized bed, with all that blonde hair across his pillow...lying naked and hot for him.

His erection was as swift as it was hard and painful, bulging against the zip, and now that his imagination had taken flight, it was flying without restraint.

What would it feel like to have her delicate tongue flicking against his shaft? How would she taste? He imagined her writhing under his exploring mouth and hands, twisting and moaning and begging, desperate for him to take her.

She was too young to be so utterly controlled and he wanted to smash through that control and see what was underneath...

Hell, where were his thoughts going? Aside from anything else, there was no way he was going to jeopardise the tenuous, fragile shoots of a relationship tentatively trying to establish themselves with Flora by hitting on her babysitter.

He shifted uncomfortably, trying to ease the pain of his erection, annoyed with himself for his utter lack of self-control. 'There's another reason I wanted to talk to you.' He dragged his brain back into gear but for a few seconds he had to look outside rather than at her face. 'I have to be at a breakfast meeting on Saturday and I want to ask you whether you would step in and cover here. Naturally, you will be paid handsomely for putting yourself out...'

'Saturday...'

'Day after tomorrow.'

Her fingers were slender and she was raking them through her tangle of fine hair now, frowning slightly as though he had posed a particularly tricky maths problem which she had been called upon to solve rather than being asked a simple question that required a simple yes or no answer.

'You can bring your work,' he reminded her, 'although you might want to do something...a little more fun...unless you have plans for the weekend? Have you?'

More than anything Sunny would have loved to have told him that she had. In fact, she had planned on getting ahead with some studying and then having a lazy night in because Amy was going to be out on another date with yet another hopeless boyfriend.

'What about the woman who stays with Flora during the daytime?' she asked and Stefano shook his head.

He laughed shortly. 'She's been with Flora for a fortnight and so far she hasn't run screaming for the hills. I don't want to test her patience by asking her for anything beyond the call of duty.'

Sunny felt her lips twitch in a smile. It was bad enough that he was so distractingly attractive. Add a wry sense of humour into the mix and that attraction became combustible.

'Why have you run through so many nannies?' She

was genuinely perplexed because Flora seemed a far from difficult child.

'She hasn't wanted to have a nanny so she's made sure to get rid of them,' Stefano said shortly. He stood up and poured them both another glass of wine. 'I mistakenly assumed that someone young and enthusiastic would be the first choice but they've all found her stubborn refusal to communicate unbearably frustrating...'

'I don't try and force her into having fun,' Sunny mused thoughtfully.

'Edith, the woman who comes in during the day to help out, is sixty-three years old, although she's already mentioned that she doesn't like the way Flora talks to her.'

'Which is how?'

'Patronisingly.'

Sunny wondered whether Flora's patronising wasn't a response to the older woman also being patronising and then was surprised that she was finding excuses for her young charge and taking her side over a woman she hadn't even met.

'I... Okay, that's fine.' She stood up and felt the two glasses of wine rush to her head. 'What time would you like me to come on Saturday?'

'My driver will collect you at ten and I'll need you for the whole day, I'm afraid. I won't be home until at least nine in the evening.'

Stefano thought that she looked like someone who had suddenly remembered that she should be fleeing the scene of the crime instead of hanging around making small talk with the officer in charge.

'And don't forget that you have full use of the account. You have the card. Take advantage of it.'

They were at the front door. When Sunny looked up, she felt her heart skip a beat because he was so close to her, almost but not quite invading her space.

For a second, a brief destabilising second, instead of wanting to step back, she wanted to move closer, wanted to place the palm of her hand on his chest and feel the hardness of muscle under her fingers.

'Perhaps I will,' she said shortly, swerving away and opening the door. 'And there's no need for Eric to drive me home.' She felt breathless, as though she'd been running a marathon and now had to steady herself or else fall over from the exertion. 'I can make my way to the station. It's only a half hour walk and the exercise will do me good.'

'I wouldn't hear of it,' Stefano murmured, not taking his eyes from her face even though he was already on his cellphone calling his driver to the front.

Sunny felt herself break out in a fine film of perspiration and she stuck her hands behind her back, clasping her computer case between them and clutching it for dear life.

This was what it felt like to be *turned on* and it was the first time it had ever happened to her. John had never *turned her on.* She had liked him, perhaps even loved him in the way you loved a dear, dear friend, but this overwhelming physical helplessness had been absent.

She didn't know why it had chosen to make an appearance now but she knew that it was utterly inappropriate and complete madness and was to be stamped out at all costs.

Sunny had no idea what she was going to do with Flora on Saturday but the day dawned with the promise of heat.

She had grown up in London and now lived in London and so escaping London, going to Stefano's sprawling mansion in Berkshire always felt like a sneaky escape and even more so now because it was the weekend.

On the spur of the moment, she packed a little bag and thought that if it was hot enough she might dip her feet in the pool.

She'd asked Flora whether she swam in it at all and was told that of course she did.

'I learned to swim when I was two,' she had told Sunny proudly. 'We had a swimming pool in our house in New Zealand and Annie used to take me twice a week to the public pool so that I could get practice swimming with other girls. In competitions. I always won.'

'I bet your mother was proud of you,' Sunny had said, because *she* would have been proud, but her mother, she was informed, had rarely gone to stuff like that because it was boring.

'She liked going out,' Flora had said, shrugging her shoulders, 'parties and stuff. She liked dressing up.'

Lonely on both sides of the world, Sunny had thought. You could be lonely even if you had loads of money because loneliness was very fair and even-handed when it decided to pay a visit. No distinctions were ever made.

Eric came to collect her promptly at ten, always on time, and she allowed herself a sigh of pure anticipation at spending the day out, doing something other than working or household chores. Plus Amy was overjoyed to have the flat to herself for the day.

'I'm going to show him that I can be a domestic goddess,' she had confided.

'Brilliant idea.'

'Something Thai,' Amy had said vaguely. 'A salad or something. Don't worry. I'll be gone by the time you get home…'

Sunny had wondered whether some sort of Thai salad was going to work with her friend's latest big love interest but who was she to say anything? She had images in her head of a guy who was inappropriate on so many levels that it made her feel dizzy when she thought about it.

But today she would just relax and enjoy herself because she had one more week and then she'd be gone.

She'd miss Flora.

In her own way, Flora was as fragile as she had been at that age and Sunny felt a pang when she thought about saying goodbye and walking away, leaving her in the capable hands of another nanny.

It was already baking hot by the time the driver pulled into the long drive that led up to the house. She expected to find Stefano there, had braced herself for some polite conversation but she was greeted at the door by the housekeeper, who came, it would seem, to clean on the weekends.

'We could do something exciting and fun,' she suggested to Flora, racking her brain to think of what might fit the bill. 'Perhaps a zoo…or a park…maybe the movies…or something…'

'I disapprove of zoos,' Flora ruled out that option immediately and Sunny grinned.

'Or we could just…have lunch somewhere nice and then come back here…'

'And swim!'

'I'll have to stay in the shallow end…'

'Why?'

'Because I… I never actually learned how to swim…'

'I'll teach you!'

With a project in hand, Flora was happy to rush through the various *fun* things Sunny felt she should be doing. The zoo, which would have meant trekking back into London, was fortunately ruled out and instead they went to a nearby beauty spot for a picnic. There was a huge lake, acres of woodland and many, many people also out enjoying the area with their kids and their dogs.

Flora talked about New Zealand, about what she had done there and about the open spaces and natural beauty. Her mother rarely featured in these accounts, except in passing, and her father not at all. Had he been over to see her at all? Sunny wondered. Or had he washed his hands of his own child the second he had obtained a divorce? Strangely, although he was a workaholic and although, as far as Sunny was concerned, he needed to take way more interest in his daughter, she didn't see him as the sort of guy who would ever walk away from responsibility.

Walking around the lake, she realised that speculating about Stefano Gunn was becoming a full-time occupation. When she wasn't thinking about work she was thinking about him and having told herself that there was no way she would allow herself to be curious about him or his circumstances, she still was.

Eric, fortunately, was there to save them the huge walk back in blistering sunshine and it was a little after two by the time Sunny had stripped down to the modest black bikini she had brought with her.

She had always wanted to know how to swim. Indeed, she had started a few swimming lessons less than a year ago but time had been in short supply and she had stopped them. The fact was that her life had just been too disordered, too unpredictable for something as constant as swimming lessons and when she had earned her scholarship to the boarding school she had made sure to steer clear of the enormous swimming pool. With few close friends, no one had questioned her reluctance to go swimming and, as it was a voluntary after-school activity, there had been no awkward or embarrassing confessions about her lack of know-how.

But this glittering turquoise pool in the calm peace of the countryside was irresistible.

She stayed at the shallow end and watched a different Flora prance around, diving and flipping and swimming underwater like a little darting fish.

Instructions were given, with Flora stepping into the role of stern swimming teacher.

Little by little, Sunny relaxed and began enjoying the weightless feeling of being in the water. It was a very big pool and she tentatively edged away from the shallow end, growing in confidence as she remembered some of the instructions from her brief foray into swimming lessons months before.

Don't panic and swallow lungfuls of water while trying to scrabble and touch ground...

Brilliant, sensible advice.

Except...

How was she to know that Stefano wouldn't do as he had promised? Wouldn't stay out of the house until at least nine in the evening? In other words, how could she have guessed that, daringly halfway across the pool, trying her luck with paddling from one side to the other, she would look up and see him? Standing right there? Looking right back down at her?

All the brilliant, sensible advice flew straight out of her head. She panicked. She gulped down water and panicked more, scrabbling to touch ground but, in her confusion, sinking and flailing.

Flora was the first to dive in, slicing through the water and grasping her under her arms.

Convinced that she was on the verge of drowning, Sunny still wanted to yell to her that she was way too young to be trying a rescue mission on an adult.

But she didn't have to because Stefano wasn't far behind his daughter and then bigger, stronger arms were around her, firmly gripping her ribcage and pulling her with consummate ease to the side of the pool, where he heaved her out with no trouble at all.

'Good job, Flora,' she heard him say, to which Flora muttered something in reply, but when Sunny opened her eyes and looked at her she was blushing as she turned away for a towel, which she brought to her.

Humiliation washed over her in waves. She could barely look at him and, when she did, he was leaning over her with a concerned expression.

He was soaking wet. He'd kicked his shoes off before diving into the pool but he was dripping.

Sunny squeezed her eyes tightly shut and prayed that she had somehow imagined the whole horrible episode but when she opened them he was even closer to her, kneeling with his big hand propping up her head.

The spluttering was thankfully done but shock was setting in.

'We need to get you upstairs.' He'd taken the towel from Flora and sat her up so that he could wrap the towel around her as best he could.

'No,' Sunny pleaded. 'I'm fine.' She was trembling violently even though she was doing her best not to.

'Flora—' he turned to his daughter '—do you want to start running a bath for Sunny? And make sure there's a dry towel there. And Flora...you would make a fine life-guard, once you've grown a little...' He smiled crookedly and felt a burst of something he had never felt before— sheer pleasure and warmth when she half smiled back at him. 'Change into some dry clothes before you run the bath,' he instructed. 'And then wait for us in the sitting room. We need to do something a little special after this...'

'Okay. 'Cos she'll probably be all shaken up.'

'Exactly.' He turned back to Sunny as Flora disappeared inside the house. 'And you,' he murmured, 'I don't want to hear a peep out of you...you've had a shock. Just relax and let your breathing return to normal.'

Relax?

When her practically naked body was pressed against him? When his arms were so close to her breasts that one inadvertent shift in position could have him touching her?

When her head was against his chest and she could almost hear the beating of his heart under his wet suit?

After this, there was no way she could stay on here...

CHAPTER FOUR

SUNNY HAD NOT explored this section of the house. She knew where Flora's room was because she settled her to bed but all the other rooms were always closed off and somehow it would have felt nosy to open doors and peer inside.

So she had no idea where she was being taken and she was far too busy trying to deal with her mortification to give that much thought.

She heard the sound of a bath being run and when she opened her eyes she could instantly see that she was in Stefano's room. It was massive, with a super-king-sized bed in solid dark wood dominating one side of the wall. Everything in the room was overwhelmingly *male*, from the dark wood of the bed and the chest of drawers, to the sleek lines of the built-in wardrobes and the lush fall of deep burgundy velvet curtains that had been pulled back to offer spectacular views of the rolling lawns at the back.

Including, she suspected, the treacherous swimming pool, which had glittered so temptingly before subjecting her to this horrendous attack of pure humiliation.

He kicked the door to the en-suite bathroom fully open and deposited her gently on the chair by the window.

Immediately, he began undoing the buttons of his shirt and Sunny nearly leaped out of the chair in horrified consternation.

'What are you doing?' she yelped and he shot her a dry look.

'I'm getting out of my wet clothes to forestall an attack of pneumonia. Where are your dry clothes?'

'I changed in the bathroom downstairs. They're… they're in my backpack. Please, there's no need for all of this.'

He didn't answer. Instead, he continued getting out of his clothes as he vanished out of the bathroom and she distantly heard him shouting to Flora to hunt down the backpack and bring it up. When he reappeared, he had changed and the bath was now completely run. Lots of bubbles. Sunny could barely bring herself to look at it.

'You're probably in a state of mild shock.' He tested the water with one hand and just then Flora appeared with the backpack and hovered by the door.

'I was teaching Sunny how to swim,' she offered.

Stefano shot her a frowning, questioning look. 'She doesn't know how to swim? You're eight and you swim like a champion… We're going to have to have a race one of these days. I can't believe…'

'I know. It's silly.'

'It *is* a little odd.'

'Would you two mind not discussing me as though I'm not here?' Sunny was burning up with embarrassment and even more so when Flora looked at her with an eight-year-old's sympathy.

'You were doing really well until…'

'Yes…well…' There was no way she was going to get into any conversation about how Stefano's sudden appearance at the side of the pool had thrown her into a tailspin. 'If the two of you wouldn't mind, I'll have this bath now…' Not, she wanted to add, that she needed one.

But the bikini, drying on her, was cloying and uncomfortable and she felt horribly exposed in it, her nipples tight from the damp cold, pushing like bullets against the fine, stretchy fabric. When she glanced down she could see her own shadowy cleavage and her bare stomach and her legs.

She wanted to burst into tears but, instead, she stared down at the pale tiled floor and almost collapsed with relief when they both left the bathroom, quietly shutting the door behind them, a door which she made sure to lock.

She sank into the bath, which was blissful because she had been colder than she had thought, and she closed her eyes, letting the warm water wash over her.

What was happening to her? It had been a shock for her to discover, having written off her sexuality, that she could find a man so blindingly attractive. But this wasn't just any man and she knew that even if she might react to those incidental touches, that sort of reaction was purely on her side.

Stefano Gunn was out of her league. Over the past two years, after she and John had broken up, many men had looked at her, made passes at her, some crude, others more subtle, but she had never been interested. None of them had penetrated the hard outer shell she had taken pains to develop around herself and she still couldn't understand how it was that Stefano, without even trying, had managed to do so.

She had always considered herself immune to the superficial tug of lust. She had learned lessons from her flawed parent and then, later, having to always be on guard against the covert, greedy glances of her foster father, she had developed an edge of cynicism that had never left her.

Even the more open, healthy appreciation from the boys she had met when she had been at the boarding school and after, at university, had failed to get past her inherent wariness and when the one man she'd felt she should have been able to really open up to had failed to excite her in that way, she had firmly shut the door on physical attraction.

Stefano didn't look at her at all and yet…flustered her.

When he did look at her, it was as if she was plugged into an electric socket and there was no part of her body that didn't respond.

Was it because he was so out of her league? Because there was no danger of him taking any interest in her?

Was it the sort of silly schoolgirl crush that made teenagers stick posters of pop stars on their bedroom walls? Was that it? Something passing, harmless and hardly surprising?

She uneasily told herself that that was exactly what it was because she knew that when and if she ever tested the waters again, ever felt inclined to go on a date, then it would be with someone safe, someone who wouldn't make her feel vulnerable and out of control. True, John had filled that specification but because that particular relationship hadn't worked out didn't mean that the parameters for all future relationships should change. They shouldn't. Logic decreed that.

And when had she ever not listened to the unwavering voice of logic?

Listening to her head, paying calm heed to what it told her when her own young life had been in such disarray through no fault of her own, had always worked.

Feeling a bit better, she opened the door and there he was, lying on the bed in a pair of faded jeans and an old T-shirt with his computer on his stomach. He snapped it shut and eased himself off the bed.

'I was beginning to think about breaking the door down to make sure you hadn't drowned in the bath...'

Caught on the back foot, Sunny could only stare. He looked so effortlessly elegant. The low-slung jeans did amazing things for his physique and the T-shirt clung in a way that showed off the muscled strength of his arms. And he was barefoot. She hurriedly looked away.

'I'm sorry about that,' Sunny said stiffly. She eyed the

open door and headed towards it. 'Perhaps—' she cleared her throat '—I might have a quick word with you.'

'I'm surprised you haven't asked me why I'm back so early. Did you start floundering because you weren't expecting to see me?'

'I…' They began trotting down the stairs, she quickly, he taking his time but still keeping pace.

'Because I wouldn't like you being so nervous in my presence that it becomes life-threatening.'

Sunny rounded on him, arms folded. 'Are you laughing at me?'

'How is it that you've never had swimming lessons?'

'I… I…' She went red and looked away. 'Where's Flora?'

'Happily ensconced in front of the television in the sitting room. I told her you would probably need a little time to gather yourself after your skirmish in the pool. I thought that swimming lessons were compulsory for all schoolchildren…'

'They probably are!'

'Did you have an early aversion to water?'

Sunny glared. 'I would have loved to have had swimming lessons,' she gritted. 'But that never happened to me.' She spun on her heel, heart beating wildly inside her and made for the kitchen. She would have to hand in her notice. How could she not? What sort of babysitter ended up having to be rescued from a dangerous situation by the young child she was in charge of babysitting? He would never trust her around his daughter again.

And maybe that was for the best, she thought. He did weird things to her, things she didn't like, and if he wasn't around then life would get back to normal without that jumpy, sickening feeling inside her that she'd been carrying around for days.

And maybe, she further thought, she could address

some of his curiosity about her. Curiosity about why she spent all her time working, why she needed money so badly, why she'd never learned how to swim…

Maybe it would be a good thing for those glaring differences between them to be brought out into the open. The way she'd been brought up was something that had been out of her control but maybe vocalising it would be a timely reminder to her of the idiocy of harbouring delusional fantasies about him. It would also kill off his curiosity stone-dead because he certainly wouldn't keep prying for extraneous information when he knew that he might be provided with information that would make him feel uncomfortable. Rich people always, but always, felt uncomfortable when they were treated to tales of hardship, poverty or despair.

But mostly, if her body kept ignoring the fact that he was from a different world, then wasn't it time that her head took control?

'I just want to say…' She turned to him the minute they were in the kitchen, making sure to keep her voice low just in case Flora decided that the television programme she was watching wasn't as much fun as seeking out her nearly drowned babysitter, to whom she'd been giving swimming lessons. 'I just want to say,' she repeated, 'that I'm handing in my resignation.' She tried a laugh. 'It goes down as the shortest job in history.'

'What are you talking about? Why are you handing in your resignation?' She'd washed her hair but already the late-afternoon heat was drying it, throwing blonde strands in stark relief. It hung down her back, almost to her waist. And she didn't wear make-up. He had never known a woman who didn't lather on the war-paint the second she was out of the bath. But her skin was satiny-smooth and clear. His gaze lingered on her ripe, full lips and he looked away because he could already feel his body stirring into life. Once again. Just as it had when he'd been holding her, wet and trembling, against him and as light as a feather despite the fact that she was tall.

He'd had a battle not to stare at the plump thrust of her breasts under the bikini top, not to get trapped by the sight of that tightened nipple poking against the wet cloth. She had been utterly unaware of just how revealing the swimsuit was and, thankfully, just as utterly unaware of the effect it had been having on him.

It seemed his body had decided to raise two fingers to common sense. He'd never had to deal with self-denial and he was finding it difficult.

He wondered whether his mother would have been amused by the fact that the woman she had done her best to set him up with had left him cold while the office junior was sending his blood pressure into the stratosphere.

The difficult, stubborn office junior whom he'd had to cajole into this job. The job she was now talking about ditching.

'Because I think it's safe to say that I failed.' She looked away quickly. 'You didn't pay me to…to…'

'Endanger your life?'

'I should never have gone anywhere near that swimming pool considering I can barely doggy-paddle from one side to the next.'

'You're good for Flora and I wouldn't dream of accepting your resignation.' And that, he reminded himself heavily, was why he couldn't do what he wanted to do. She was good for Flora and, in turn, that was proving to be good for his relationship with his daughter and he wasn't going to risk fooling around with that…

'You don't have to say that,' Sunny said fiercely.

'You're right. I don't. So why don't you just take me at my word?' He ran his fingers through his hair and stood up to pour them both some water. 'You've probably had enough of this stuff for the day. Want something stronger?'

'This is fine. But you don't pay me to get myself in situations where I need rescuing.'

'I haven't rescued a damsel in distress for a while. Maybe it was time that I brushed up on the skill.' He looked at her over the rim of the glass and was surprised at how vulnerable she seemed. Scratch a little under the surface and it was easy to reach the person who didn't spend her every waking moment doing her job and keeping the world at bay.

Was that why he found her so intensely appealing? She made him feel young again for reasons he couldn't quite put his finger on. He was thirty-one and most of the time he felt much older. But something about her...

Was it the same thing that appealed to his daughter?

He fought to stop the senseless speculation.

'I don't need rescuing,' she heard herself say. 'And I've never been a damsel in distress. In fact, I disapprove of all those limp women who think that they need rescuing by some big, strong guy...'

'Is that your way of telling me that you think I'm big and strong?' He caught her eye, raised his eyebrows and grinned crookedly, unable to help himself. 'So tell me why you've never learned to swim.'

Sunny took a deep breath. Would he be amused if he knew her background? Pity she would find hard to tolerate but she somehow didn't think that he would pity her. Certainly, it would reposition the lines between them which, for him, were clear but for her too blurred for comfort.

She was an underling in a company he could buy ten times over. Had he given them the job because of Katherine? She didn't know. What she did know was that Katherine was far more in his league than she was so it was totally out of order for her to even look at him in any way other than someone way down the pecking order who was working for him.

Get the boundary lines back in place, at least in her mind, and maybe she would stop responding like the teenager she no longer was. And he would keep his distance, too.

'I guess you think that I'm like all the other people who work for the company,' she said, tilting her chin and maintaining eye contact, even though she could read nothing on his face.

'Do I? Tell me what you think I think about all the other people who work for the company. I'm all ears…bearing in mind I haven't met most of them…'

Sunny blushed. Explaining about her past was something she had never done. The other kids at the boarding school into which she had been accepted had known that her circumstances had not been like theirs, had known that she had been given a scholarship, one of only three full scholarships awarded to kids from underprivileged backgrounds.

But she had never talked about hers.

There was no reason to talk about it now but something in her head was telling her that she had to recognise the lines drawn in the sand between them because she couldn't understand her response to him and she was desperate to keep it at bay.

She needed to tell him more for her sake than for his.

And part of her…wanted to.

'I didn't have a cosseted childhood,' she said steadily. 'In fact, I had a pretty awful time growing up, although I just accepted it for what it was and never really spent too much time thinking of how it could have been different. I learned early on that what you can't change you just have to accept…'

She remembered the way Flora had, very briefly, communicated with her father and allowed him into her world and she wondered whether her words of advice had been taken on board. *Accept the things you can't change.*

Stefano was listening intently, his head ever so slightly tilted to one side.

When women launched into anecdotes about their past, they did it to try and engage his attention and encourage his interest.

He didn't get the feeling that she was trying to encourage his interest.

There was an underlying defiance to her voice that made him wonder whether she was even trying to engage his attention at all or whether she was, in some obscure way, trying to warn him off.

Surely not.

Surely she couldn't have noticed the effect she had on him. For once, he was in the company of a woman who was…unpredictable. A woman he couldn't read, a woman who wasn't out to impress him.

Throw sexy into the mix and was it any wonder that she turned him on?

'Tell me,' he encouraged huskily and he caught the wary look she shot him from under her lashes.

'Most of the people I work with come from good, solid, middle-class backgrounds.' She stared at her fingers, inspecting her fingernails while talking. 'I don't have a problem with that. It's great, but a good, solid, middle-class background was so far out of my reach when I was a kid…' She sighed and stopped fidgeting to look him squarely in the eyes. 'My mother drank and took drugs. She was weak, easily influenced by men, and I spent my childhood never knowing what life was going to bring from one day to the next. There were times when I was taken into care and other times when there were little periods of stability. My schooling was patchy and then, when I was still far too young, my mother died from an overdose and

I was taken into care permanently. Eventually I was fostered, which was a nightmare, and thankfully I managed to win a scholarship to a prestigious boarding school. In between all of that, there was no opportunity to really crack on with the swimming lessons.' She smiled wryly. 'It was all I could do to make sure I kept ahead with my schoolwork, to be honest.'

'Why did you choose to tell me…?'

'Because you were curious. Hence your question about how it was that I couldn't swim. In your world, there's no such thing as an adult who doesn't know how to swim. I think, in your world, most people don't know what it's like to grow up without their own private swimming pool and holidays abroad by the sea.'

Stefano didn't say anything. She was beginning to make sense to him. He was beginning to understand the layers she had constructed to protect herself and he was also beginning to understand why it was so important for her to work hard and build a career.

A career would be something tangible she could hold onto and he guessed that, after a turbulent childhood, that would mean a lot to her.

And she was right. He'd been curious about her. He'd wanted to find out what made her tick even though it went against his better judgement.

Sunny shrugged. 'I don't share details of my past with people as a rule,' she explained, 'but neither is it some great big secret and it was easier to just fill you in than to have you constantly asking pointed questions. Also, you should know because you might want to change your mind about hiring me as a babysitter for Flora.'

'Why would I change my mind?'

'Because…' Flustered, she looked away.

'Because you think I'm probably a snob…'

'I don't think anything. I was just…giving you the

opportunity… Anyway, it doesn't matter. I'm more than happy to continue working for you until the end of next week. Who will be taking over after I've gone? Have you managed to secure another nanny?'

She was a wrong-side-of-the-tracks girl and she had made sure to tell him that, made sure to point out their differences, because she had picked up something. Probably she hadn't even consciously registered it, but she had picked up something, some vibe he had been giving off, and she was firing a warning shot from the bows.

Except when had he become the sort of guy who got scared at warnings being fired? His learning curve at the hands of his ex-wife had freed him from any hesitations when it came to women. He played fair, he laid out the rules of the game and within those constraints it had never, not once, occurred to him, *ever*, that he might allow anything of himself to get out of control. He'd buried his emotions so deep that he had no idea where they were or if he would ever be able to find them and that suited him.

So if she was trying to warn him off by filling him in on the horrors of her background…

She truly must think him a crashing snob.

'My mother usually helps out. Right now, as I have explained, she's in Scotland but she will pick up the slack until I can secure someone else. Flora gets along with my mother slightly better than she gets along with me, which is not terribly well, but at least she isn't outright rude, as she's enjoyed being with the nannies I've hired in the past. Now, why don't I get Eric to drop you at your flat, just long enough for you to change into something a little more dressy? I intend to take you both out for dinner, as I happen to be home much earlier than expected.'

'No! Thank you. I… If you're here, then I should be getting back.' Which would come as a major blow to Amy, who was probably, right now, in full-blown domestic-goddess mode.

'Nonsense,' Stefano said smoothly. 'I insist.' He stood up and dialled his driver, whose lodgings were in a cottage on the grounds. 'I've tried meals out with my daughter,' he admitted with a trace less of his usual self-assurance, 'and the success rate has been zero. When my mother comes, the situation is slightly less fraught but I've noticed small changes in Flora and I can only thank you for that.' He gave his words time to sink in. 'I think,' he continued honestly, 'if you came there might be a marked change of atmosphere.'

Why did the thought of having a meal out with him make her feel so jumpy? Flora would be there! Yet the thought of getting dressed up…turned it from a casual chat into *an occasion*.

But she'd told him about herself, had mentally reinforced the differences between them. Hadn't she killed off all stupid notions of romance? She wasn't tempted by bridal magazines and she didn't peer at engagement rings in the windows of local jewellers. She'd sharpened up her act over the years and, anyway, she'd been born streetwise. She knew that there was a big difference between finding a guy attractive and knowing that he would be rubbish as a long-term investment and she would never allow herself to get wrapped up in anyone who would turn out to be a rubbish long-term investment. Her financial long-term investments were carefully thought out. Her emotional ones would be the same. She'd made that her life's work.

So she was safe as houses when it came to Stefano Gunn, and sparing him no detail about her background— so very, very different from his—was just another safeguard in place.

Just for one bleak moment she stood back and looked at herself. So tough, so sensible, head always screwed on…

It made sense!

It was important to have full control… She'd lived a life where there had been no control; she'd seen how complete lack of control had destroyed her mother…

So here she was, letting her head work through her life options instead of her emotions…

Yet…

For just a few fleeting seconds she was shaken and disconcerted by a sort of raw *envy* of Amy's trusting outlook on the world, her open, hopeful view of men, the enthusiasm with which she flung herself into relationships which Sunny could see would never work.

For a few fleeting seconds she wondered whether she hadn't sacrificed too much in her quest for stability and her distrust of basic relationships. She'd watched her mother and had sworn from a young age that she'd protect herself from ever getting like that. She'd never let a parade of unsuitable men influence the outcome of her life. She'd never let a weakness for passing fun get the better of her good judgement. She'd never think that salvation could be found at the bottom of a glass or after getting high.

But now it crossed her mind that in her rush to learn her life lessons she'd written off a lot more than just those things.

Had she written off *fun*? Amy pretending to be a domestic goddess for some guy she would get bored with after two minutes…wasn't that *fun*? And how much could you protect yourself from getting hurt? Without becoming a rock, isolated and set apart from the rest of the living, breathing, hurting human race? With John, she'd dipped her toes in the water only to hurriedly yank them out because the temperature hadn't been right. So what happened next? The dry, sterile, clinical life of someone who refused to…*dare*?

'Fine,' Sunny said abruptly, annoyed with herself for the

foolish tangent her thoughts had taken. She smiled stiffly and politely. 'I'm sure Flora will be pleased. What time do you…want me back here or will we be going to somewhere in London? In which case I can meet you both there…'

'Eric will wait for you. Somewhere here, I think. I know a couple of places and it'll be far less tiresome than making the journey into central London, even if Flora and I *can* overnight in my apartment in Mayfair.'

He thought she didn't have fun. Sunny's thoughts were still whirling in her head even though she'd tried to snuff them out with a stern talking-to.

He thought she was an ambitious and probably bitter young woman who didn't know how to do anything else but work. She had no boyfriend, she'd had a sad and challenging life, and now…she worked late every night, did a second job in her free time to earn money and on the weekends caught up on her sleep…when her head wasn't buried in her books.

She recalled him saying that he worked hard but *he played as well…*

She imagined that, deep down, he would expect her to turn up in work clothes if they were going somewhere where the dress code wasn't *jeans and a T-shirt and some trainers.*

Was that why he had kindly warned her that they might be going somewhere *dressy*? Because he feared that she might show up, whatever the occasion, in her stiff little suit and crisp white blouse?

'Okay—' Sunny shrugged '—but I hope he doesn't mind waiting. Girls can be…er…indecisive when it comes to choosing clothes…'

Stefano raised his eyebrows wryly and she flushed because she had the annoying feeling that he could see straight through her—which made her want to carry on protesting.

*Yes...girls take time getting their appearance right! And
that includes me, whatever you might think!*

She was stubbornly determined to prove him wrong
and to prove to herself that she hadn't forgotten what it
was like to dress up and think of something other than
her long-term plans and passing exams.

She'd expected Amy to be horrified at her unexpected arrival but instead the plump, good-natured brunette dim-
pled smugly and pulled her to one side when she was
through the front door.

'The meal was a disaster,' she whispered, giggling.
'Honestly, Sunny, I swear I followed every instruction in
the recipe book, more or less, but it was an absolute disaster!'

'Why are you grinning?'

'Because Jake thought it was hilarious! He said he's a
brilliant cook and he's been looking for a woman who can
be impressed by his culinary skills! Anyway, he's disappeared to the Thai down the road to get us a takeaway and
then we're going to watch a movie. You're not *staying*, are
you? I mean, that's fine, but would it be awful of me to
ask if you could hide out in your bedroom? Just for a bit?'

'I'm not staying!' Sunny laughed. 'But I need you to
do me a favour and I need you to do it before Jake gets
back with your Thai...because I need your undivided
attention...'

Half an hour later, Sunny looked at herself in the full-
length mirror in her friend's bedroom.

Her selection of *dressy clothes* was pitiful. She had
casual and she had work and then, in between those two
polar opposites, she had a paltry array of drab skirts and
jumpers that seemed to be neither one thing nor the other.

She'd become accustomed over the years to playing

down her looks. Her looks had always earned her the sort of unwarranted attention she'd hated. As far as she was concerned, what mattered was what lay beneath the surface and the only way she had ever felt she could be taken seriously was by muting her appearance. Even when she'd been dating John, dear, thoughtful John, she'd made sure not to dress up. She'd always had the sneaking suspicion that he had been a little threatened and overawed by her appearance and so she had unconsciously accommodated his insecurities.

For the first time, she had the crazy urge to make the absolute most of herself and the only person who could help her was Amy.

Amy had the clothes she lacked and, although they weren't really the same size at all, Amy's clothes were tight, small and stretchy. Many of them were a *one size fits all* variety and Sunny, having had her first few picks ruled out as way too boring for a night out on the town, had allowed herself to be led.

'It's not a *night out on the town*,' she had protested, stepping out of one dress and straight into another. 'His daughter is going to be there!'

'You're going out and it's night time. It's a night out in my book, and he's cute, isn't he? You said so before when I asked.'

'He's full of himself.'

'But cute and sexy.'

'Arrogant and way too...too...*much* for my liking.'

'I notice you didn't dispute the *sexy* bit.' Amy had laughed and spun her round to the full-length mirror.

And now Sunny was staring at the young woman she had spent a lifetime making sure to hide.

Her long slender legs seemed to go on for ever and were on full view in the little stretchy skirt which was a demure pale pink in colour with a far from demure cut. She was taller than her friend, so what would have sat a couple of inches above knee level on Amy just about managed to skim Sunny's thighs.

She had a driving urge to tug the skirt down and had to squeeze her hands into fists to stop herself from doing it.

The skirt was accompanied by an equally small stretchy top with a scooped neckline and three-quarter length sleeves. Together, she appeared to be wearing a dress, were it not for the fact that when she moved little slivers of her flat belly were exposed.

'Perfect,' Amy declared with satisfaction. 'You have no idea how long I've been wanting to get my hands on you and do this. You can leave your hair the way it is; just run your fingers through it to make it look a little wilder and if you stay still for a couple of seconds I'll put some eyeshadow, mascara and lipgloss on you.' Amy shot her a sly look. 'I must say you're putting yourself out for some-one who is *arrogant, full of himself and way too...too... much for your liking...*'

Sunny didn't reply because she was too busy staring at the stranger staring back at her.

Despite the disparity in their height, she and Amy both wore the same shoe size and Sunny had been persuaded into a pair of her friend's shoes which weren't particularly high and weren't particularly flamboyant, at least com-pared to the revealing outfit, but which still managed to make her look...

Sexy...

She had a sudden attack of panic. She would never, ever have worn anything like this if she'd been going out with girlfriends. She would have been far too terrified of attracting unwanted attention from all the wrong sorts but she would be going out with Stefano and Flora and she was wickedly excited at the prospect of showing him that, yes, she was a fun girl. She was someone who went out, who did all sorts of exciting things in her free time.

She was a sheep in borrowed clothing but he wasn't to know that, was he?

She teamed the outfit with her own denim jacket and hung onto her casual backpack even though Amy did her best to entice her into something small and sparkly.

'You look fab,' her friend said, practically pushing her out of her door because her legs suddenly felt quite leaden. 'Your arrogant dinner date is going to be bowled over! Now, shoo! I have to work on bowling my own dinner date over! Hurry up so that I have time to spray some more perfume and get myself arranged in a way that makes it look as though I haven't been hanging around waiting for him to get back!' Amy smiled and impulsively stood on tiptoe to kiss Sunny on her cheek. 'And have fun, Sunny. You don't do enough of that...'

CHAPTER FIVE

STEFANO STROLLED OVER to the French doors overlooking the garden and stared in the general direction of the swimming pool. It was darkening outside, the bright turquoise of the sky fading into violet and navy. Upstairs, Flora had taken herself off to change. He hadn't seen her so animated since she had come to live with him. It wasn't to do with *him* or a sudden interest in developing a father-daughter relationship. He wasn't stupid. He knew that. She had been energised by the excitement of the afternoon because, no matter how surly, grown-up and serious she was, she was still too young to really appreciate the potential danger Sunny had been in.

He shoved his hand in the pocket of his beige casual trousers and frowned, recalling every word she had told him of her unfortunate childhood.

When he had told her that he didn't know every person working in the law firm, he hadn't been lying, just as he didn't personally know every single person working in the legal department of his own company, but he knew enough to suspect that the majority of them had not had to struggle to get where they were.

They would mostly be the products of comfortable middle-class families, put through private schools or excellent state schools, brought up on a diet of holidays abroad and generous pocket-money allowances, more than enough to ensure that they didn't have to hold down an extra job in a restaurant to pay the bills.

So what was he to do with this information?

The bottom line was that he fancied her but alongside that elemental physical reaction was the sobering thought that she wasn't like the other women he dated. That, in itself, was inherently disconcerting. Add the relationship she had with his daughter and things moved from disconcerting to downright dangerously foolhardy.

But the more he saw, the more he wanted…

And would she go out with him at all anyway? Was she even interested? Was this physical urge that was making a mockery of his common sense even reciprocated?

She didn't give off all the usual signals. There were no coy looks or glances held for slightly too long or little-girl helplessness designed to bring out his protective instinct. He didn't know any other woman who would have gone into detail about a miserable, deprived childhood because no one would have seen that as the sort of light-hearted chit-chat which formed part and parcel of verbal foreplay.

And the way she always looked as though she couldn't escape his company fast enough…

She wasn't playing hard to get.

But she blushed…and there were times when there was the ghost of a vibe, some electrical current that he could feel passing between them…soft, subtle, barely there but there enough to make his blood run hot…

Was that why he couldn't seem to get her out of his head? He'd wrapped up his work as quickly as he could earlier today, had delegated a great portion of it to Bob Coombes, one of his CEOs…and he knew he had done that because not only had he wanted to take advantage of the thaw in relations with his daughter, but because he had also wanted to see Sunny.

It was a weakness he didn't care to acknowledge because he allowed himself no weaknesses when it came to women. It didn't matter how sexy a woman was or how much he was interested in bedding her, there was always a part of him that knew he could, in the end, take it or leave it.

He'd never rushed work for any woman before. He hadn't even rushed work for Alicia. In fact, had it not been for the pregnancy, Alicia would have been as temporary as all the women he had dated since his divorce.

But he'd found that he couldn't wait to drive back to the house and surprising her in the swimming pool…

He felt the stirrings of an erection as he recalled the softness of her body against his, the teasing temptation of those stiffened nipples…

Deep in thought, he was hardly aware of Flora until she said, standing in the doorway, 'Sunny's here.'

Stefano smiled, turning. 'You look very pretty, Flora.'

Flora frowned and he wondered whether the fragile truce was over now that Sunny was no longer on the scene as a third party and unwitting mediator.

'No, I don't,' she said bluntly. 'I'm too dark-skinned.'

Stefano looked at her narrowly. 'What on earth are you talking about?'

Flora shrugged and it reminded him of those evasive, dismissive shrugs that Sunny often produced when she had no intention of prolonging a conversation she wasn't interested in having.

Had his daughter picked that up from Sunny? But no… he had noticed that trait before. Were there barely discernible similarities just below the surface, similarities that connected them, explained the way they had just *clicked*? And how could a child who had had it all be similar to a woman who had had nothing as a child?

'Who told you that?' he pressed and was met with another shrug.

'Mum mentioned it now and again.'

'Your mother…' He inhaled deeply and held onto his

daughter's serious gaze. 'You're beautiful, Flora, and I'm not just saying that because I'm your…dad…' He had to clear his throat. His voice sounded strangely gruff and he felt a curious lump in his throat when she rolled her eyes but half smiled before leaving the room and heading for the front door.

Dear Alicia, he thought, the corrosive taste of bitterness filling his mouth. She had ensured that their divorce was as acrimonious as possible and, having flown across the ocean with Flora, had made doubly sure that his visiting rights were thwarted at every turn. He had always suspected that she had filled his daughter's head with all sorts of lies and half-truths, even though he had given her every single thing she had requested at the time of the divorce.

But had her machinations gone even further?

Had she taken out her rage and bitterness on their child? Because Flora reminded her of him? Had she made the sort of wilful remarks that had left an impact on Flora? Alicia had been very blonde. He could imagine the ugly twist of her mouth if she'd made a point of criticising Flora's much darker colouring.

If his ex-wife had been standing in front of him right at that very moment, Stefano felt that he would not have been responsible for what he did to her. He could have cheerfully throttled the witch.

Any wonder he'd had his fill of women as long-term investments?

He laughed sourly to himself, heading in his daughter's wake for the front door.

He saw Sunny before she actually saw him because, as he hit the hall, she was turning away, saying something to Eric, laughing.

Stefano stopped dead in his tracks and, eyes narrowed, felt a stab of something like jealousy rip through him.

Gone were the jeans. He'd told her to wear something

dressy. He'd expected a variation on her working-clothes theme. Sensible skirt skimming her knees…neat top… camouflage outfit… The sort of nondescript garb designed to make her blend into the background and not draw attention to her stupendous looks.

He knew he'd been guilty of assuming that she was a girl who made it her business to avoid fun, especially after she had told him about her background, especially when he'd connected the pieces and worked out that security was way more important to her than fun, and financial security was really the one thing for which she was quite happy to sacrifice the business of *going out.*

She didn't want to draw attention to herself. He guessed that she'd had a parent who had done that. What she wanted was to fly under the radar, hence her unassuming work clothes and nondescript casual clothes.

She was fiercely independent and to have been *frothy and flirty* would have gone against the grain.

He'd made all those sweeping assumptions about her.

She had no boyfriend. Another sweeping assumption was that she wasn't interested in looking for one either. That sort of thing could come later and, when it did, it would be in the form of a serious-minded guy with a stable job, who, like her, wasn't interested in the business of having fun.

It was inexplicable why he was so drawn to her, why she had taken root in his head and why she refused to go.

He liked his women to be fun. The last thing he was interested in was a serious woman because it was a short step between the woman who was serious and the woman who wanted a ring on her finger.

Avoid the serious woman and you avoided the whole ring-on-finger killer conversation.

His mother had always mistakenly imagined that he needed a nice, serious young woman to step into the role of wife and mother. She disapproved of the flighty things who came and went like ships in the night.

He liked the flighty ships in the night, though.

Which was why he'd been frankly bewildered at his reaction to Sunny.

Except...

It seemed some of his assumptions had been wildly off target.

Her long, long hair flowed over her shoulders and down her narrow spine in a tide of unruly but utterly sexy curls, and the outfit...

He broke out in a fine film of perspiration. What happened to the girl who *dressed to hide*? Where the hell had *she* gone? Stefano was almost outraged at the appearance of this sex siren to whom his body was responding with rampant enthusiasm.

He scowled at Eric, who caught his eye, reddened and stepped back just as Sunny turned towards him, all long, long legs and long, long hair, and flashing green eyes.

She should have looked tacky in such a short skirt but the casual denim jacket brought the whole temperature of the outfit down, as did the functional backpack carelessly slung over her shoulder.

Flora was staring at her, mouth open, as though an alien had suddenly leaped out of the woodwork. Stefano was on her page.

'Did you forget to finish getting dressed?' he heard himself say, moving forward.

It was hardly the sort of compliment she had been expecting and she stiffened, annoyed with herself for having expected any sort of compliment at all.

She belatedly wondered whether he was looking at the skimpy outfit and wondering what sort of example was being set for Flora.

She swallowed down the urge to tell him that this

wasn't her sort of dress code *at all*. Then she remembered what he thought of her, that she was dull, the sort of all-work-and-no-play sort of young woman who had no boyfriend and never went anywhere.

She tilted her chin at a defiant angle and smiled a challenge. 'Not at all,' she chirruped.

'I *love* it,' Flora piped up with gratifying enthusiasm.

'Thank you very much, Flora!' He might have been sarcastic but she could feel his eyes on her and that dark, intense gaze went to her head like a powerful shot of incense.

'There's not much there to love,' Stefano grated. 'A few square inches of stretchy cloth. I'm surprised you find it comfortable to sit down.'

Actually, she didn't but she wasn't about to tell him that. 'It's…er…what everyone's wearing these days to… er…go out…clubbing…'

'I had no idea you were a clubber,' Stefano muttered disapprovingly, sotto voce, as Flora hopped into the back seat of the car, immediately plugging in her headphones and scrolling through her playlist on her phone.

He was leaning into the car now, his breath warm on her cheek, his dark eyes cool and inscrutable.

'I try and get out whenever I can.' Sunny was beginning to feel horribly uncomfortable in the skimpy outfit, under his accusatory gaze.

What business was it of his anyway? she thought defiantly.

Stefano didn't say anything but he shot a sideways glance at Eric as he slid into the front seat.

He could hardly blame his driver for looking. The outfit was an eye-catcher! She wouldn't be able to walk five steps without drawing stares. Should he revisit his choice of restaurant? Perhaps stay at the house and have one of the caterers he used come in and do the honours? He'd thought of the restaurant in question because it often attracted minor celebrities and he'd thought that might be fun for Flora. Now he had visions of tacky minor celebrities ogling Sunny, maybe trying to slip her their number.

He couldn't even kid himself that he was taking an avuncular interest in her well-being, protecting her from male attention she didn't like. No. He didn't want men staring at her and thinking about making passes because he wanted her for himself. Didn't matter how hard he fought it, that was the base line, wasn't it? He wanted her.

They covered the short distance to the restaurant in silence. Sunny stared through the window while next to her Flora was in a world of her own, listening to music.

When she glanced down, she could see way too much thigh exposed because the skirt had ridden up. He'd seen her in a bikini, had already seen a lot more of her body than was on show now, but this felt *different*.

Not that he was looking. Except in a derogatory way.

She was unusually quiet over the meal, only interacting when pulled into the conversation. The food was delicious and the crowd was interesting. Flora, for once showing her age, got a little excited and bright-eyed at seeing a boy who was, she whispered, the lead singer in a boy band, the name of which neither she nor Stefano recognised.

Wearing this outfit had been a crazy idea. She'd wanted to prove something and the only thing she'd proved was that she had it in her to be just like her mother. Her mother used to dress like this—*worse*, tiny little clothes that left nothing to the imagination and attracted all the wrong attention from all the wrong men.

The more she thought of that, the worse she felt. Instead of seeing her in a different light, Stefano would now see her as someone cheap and easy, someone who stopped being a lawyer the second she could wriggle out of her suit. She worked so hard to project the image she wanted the world to see that it was horrible suspecting that one impulsive decision might have left him with the wrong impression of her.

They stayed at the restaurant far longer than she had expected. Flora, animated and excited at seeing the very young-looking boy band member, dragged her meal out for as long as she could and then insisted on having dessert.

'Why don't you stay the night?' Stefano suggested, turning to look at her from the front seat.

An exhausted Flora had ended up half asleep on Sunny's shoulder but she roused herself sufficiently to sleepily agree with the suggestion.

'It's Sunday tomorrow so, unless you have plans, stay over and have another day out here. It's far nicer than being in London and you can try your hand at swimming again, if you haven't been scared off...'

'Thank you,' Sunny said politely, 'but I couldn't possibly.'

'Why not?'

'Because...' There were a lot of reasons to choose from. *How about*, she wanted to say, *because you make me feel uncomfortable and just the thought of being under the same roof as you overnight sends shivers down my spine? How about the fact that I don't have a change of clothes and I'll die if I have to spend another day in these?* And his suggestion that she try her hand at swimming again? Well, Sunny wanted to laugh out loud at that because there was no way that she was going to parade in her bikini in front of him.

'You heard Flora. She'd like it. Wouldn't you, Flora?'

'I don't think it's very fair to try and coerce your daughter into siding with you.'

'I can play dirty if the occasion demands... Think about it.' He turned back around and within minutes the car was pulling through the stone pillars that heralded the long drive up to the house.

Flora was dead on her feet and was in bed within half an hour and, since it seemed rude to disappear without thanking him properly for the meal, Sunny hovered, feeling more and more conspicuous in the wretched outfit.

'Well? What's your decision to be?' He'd reappeared through one of the side doors, having obviously gone somewhere else after he had dropped his daughter to her bedroom.

Sunny feasted her eyes on him. He hadn't dressed formally for the meal and was wearing a simple pair of black trousers and a cream linen shirt which highlighted his wildly exotic bronzed skin tone. All at once several thoughts raced through her head, clamouring for attention.

'I have a lot to do tomorrow,' she began backtracking but in her head all she could think about was...those fabulous dark eyes coolly assessing her in her borrowed clothes, coolly making judgements, coolly sneering at her.

All her dormant insecurities, ones she had thought she had put to rest a long time ago, wriggled out of their shallow graves.

She remembered the men who had come and gone, chasing behind her mother...she remembered the way her foster father's eyes had followed her even though she had dressed like a nun in his presence...she remembered the boys she had met at boarding school, the way *they* had looked, as though their fingers were itching to touch...

She remembered the way she had never quite managed to fit in, always standing out amongst those well-bred girls with their braying laughs and bone-deep self-confidence.

She thought that if one of that type had dressed in a short skirt and top Stefano would never have dreamed of making awful sarcastic remarks at her expense.

If, say, Katherine had worn an outfit which, quite honestly, was hardly anything out of the ordinary on a girl in her early twenties, Stefano would probably have *complimented* her on it, rather than asking whether she had forgotten to finish putting on her clothes.

'I resent the way you insulted me,' she heard herself burst out.

She honestly hadn't meant to say anything and she couldn't imagine why she had because that sort of remark was a glaring admission of her insecurities—insecurities she didn't want to advertise. Not to him, not to anyone.

Stefano, thrown a curve ball, stared at her in frowning silence.

'Explain,' he said eventually. 'And sit while you explain. You make me feel like a kid called into the principal's office to account for himself.' He turned away and poured them both a glass of wine. They had only drunk a small amount at dinner, which had seemed a good idea with Flora present, and right now he felt as if he needed to make up for the oversight. 'How have I insulted you?' He sat down and dragged a chair over with his foot, pushing it back slightly so that he could extend his long legs on it as a foot rest.

The joys of great wealth, Sunny thought, without a trace of envy but more than a hint of stark realism. Every stick of furniture in the kitchen was handmade. It was obvious. You could feel it in the solidity of the wood and the smoothness of the grain. However, it would never have occurred to Stefano to be precious around any of the furniture because if it got scratched or even destroyed, it could all be replaced with the click of an imperious finger.

'My outfit,' she muttered, already regretting having brought this grievance out into the open because, the second she mentioned what she was wearing, his dark, lazy eyes obligingly roamed over her body, bringing her out in a tingle of excruciating awareness.

'What about it?' Had she noticed the way men had stared covertly at her when they had walked into the airy dining room? Flora would have been mortified had she only noticed that the underage boy-band member had done his fair share of staring at Sunny. Stefano had noticed it all and he hadn't liked any of it.

He'd never cared what the women he dated wore. Indeed, most of them wore less than Sunny was wearing now, hadn't thought twice about displaying their wares, just so that he could be in no doubt as to what he was getting.

Had he ever felt the slightest inclination to demand that any of them change their clothes? Dress in something prissier? Something, preferably, that covered from neck to ankle?

Simple answer…no.

But he'd had to bite back the urge to hurry the meal along this evening so that he could remove an oblivious Sunny from the sideways glances she was commanding from every single male in the room with a pulse.

He could only assume that he was so accustomed to getting exactly what he wanted, when he wanted it, from the opposite sex, that her lack of availability was stirring all sorts of puzzling responses in him. Responses that were unwanted and definitely out of bounds!

Not only was she not making any moves to attract his attention, but she was actively discouraging it.

And it wasn't, as he had assumed, that she actively discouraged *all male attention*. If she did, then she surely wouldn't own an outfit like the one she was wearing.

'I didn't appreciate your insinuating that I looked like… like a tart.' Her voice was barely audible and she was beetroot red, but it had to be said. Considering she'd begun.

Stefano flushed darkly because he could hardly try

and adopt a pious stance when he knew exactly what she was talking about.

Even if she *had* managed to misconstrue the intention behind his words.

'I thought you might have been uncomfortable with the sort of unwarranted attention an outfit like that might attract.'

'I'm not wearing anything any girl in her twenties might not wear.'

'But not many of them have the sort of knockout figure to do justice to it...'

Sunny blinked and then, as the full meaning of his words sank in, she felt her whole body react with just the slightest of trembles. Because those words, huskily spoken, seemed to target every single inappropriate thought she had had about him, ripping them free of the innocent labels she had done her best to attach to them.

He wasn't making a pass at her, she told herself firmly. Maybe he was flirting but, if he was, then he was on a road to nowhere because she didn't do flirting! Especially with someone like Stefano Gunn!

But he'd thrown her off course and she was having trouble marshalling her thoughts.

Stefano watched the way she stiffened, straightening her narrow shoulders. She wasn't quite meeting his eyes, but her mouth had tightened and her expression was shuttered and she was perched on the edge of her chair as though making sure she could leap out of it as fast as possible, should the situation demand.

'I apologise if you found my comment about your outfit...offensive,' he offered gruffly. 'And you're absolutely right, of course. You aren't wearing anything that any other girl your age wouldn't wear. In fact, I know a few who would cheerfully wear half as much and they're twice your age...'

Sunny relaxed a little. She stared at the glass of wine, as if only noticing it for the first time, and took a tentative sip.

Now she felt as if she might have overreacted. He'd hit a nerve, but how was he supposed to have known that? She was struck by another thought…

Had he made that remark, spontaneously and without thinking, because he had felt that she would not have *blended in* with the crowd in the posh restaurant he had taken them to? Had he thought that she would stick out like a sore thumb amongst the upper-middle-class suburban crowd with their cardigans and pearls? When he'd told her that he'd only been thinking about her and the unwarranted attention she might have been exposed to, had he really been saying that he'd been thinking about himself and his embarrassment at being seen with someone who clearly didn't know the dress code for the expensive restaurant he had taken them to…?

In truth, she'd barely noticed who was there at all. She'd been too busy feeling self-conscious. But of course it would have been a wealthy crowd.

A fresh wave of insecurity washed over her, ebbing to leave a sour taste at the back of her mouth.

Now he was being *kind* and she hated that.

'I only reacted because…'

'Because…?'

'My mother used to dress in skimpy clothes,' Sunny burst out, inwardly groaning at the lack of control that seemed to sweep over her whenever he was around. It was as if he could somehow get her to say stuff she wouldn't normally say and he could get her to do that without even trying. She feverishly played with the stem of her wine glass with frowning concentration. 'I always swore that I would never dress in anything that wasn't…wasn't…'

'Buttoned up to the neck? That didn't cover as much as possible without inviting heatstroke…?'

'She had no control,' Sunny said helplessly. 'In and out of drink and drugs and guys...' She felt tears of self-pity sting the back of her eyes and she wanted the ground to open and swallow her up. 'You have no idea...' she said in a muffled voice.

She was hardly aware of him leaving his seat so that he could drag a chair close to her. She was grateful for her hair, which hung across her cheeks, shielding her expression.

'I'm sorry,' Stefano said with urgent sincerity. He reached out to stroke the side of her face and then gently tilted it so that she was looking at him. This was so inappropriate and yet it felt so *right*. He thought about all the reasons why he shouldn't be touching her at all, not even the most innocent of touches, of which this definitely wasn't one, and all that emerged was the stark ferocity of his physical response. It seemed to batter through everything to emerge the victor.

'These aren't even my clothes,' Sunny whispered, even though she had told herself that there was no way she would admit to that because she had been so keen to prove to him that she was capable of *having fun* just like any other girl her age.

'No?' Stefano wondered why he was so relieved to hear that. Her skin, under the roughened pad of his thumb, was velvety-smooth and her eyes, up close like this, were the clearest green he had ever seen, the colour of sea-washed glass.

'They belong to the girl I share the flat with,' Sunny confessed, resisting the urge to lean into the gentle absent-minded strokes of his finger on her cheek. Her heart was racing. This felt very, very dangerous but she told herself that that was purely in her imagination because he was just being kind.

And she didn't want him to be kind... She wanted him to be...a man...

Her breathing became shallow and her eyelids fluttered as the realisation settled like a leaden weight in the pit of her stomach. Finding him attractive had been inexplicable enough but at least that had been a passive situation, something she could deal with, even if it was inconvenient.

But wanting him to carry on touching her *all over*, wanting him to look at her with the hunger of a man looking at a woman he wanted...

She eased back and immediately missed the headiness of being close to him and feeling his skin against hers.

'Amy lent them to me,' she said in a more matter-of-fact voice. 'She thought they might look a bit better than the usual stuff I wear when I go out...'

After that brief moment of intimacy, Stefano could feel her pulling away from him and the need to recapture the lost connection slammed into him with the force of a freight train.

'But I didn't feel comfortable in them, if you want to know the truth.' She gave a careless shrug, hoping to dispel the electric charge between them.

A girl could lose herself in his eyes, she thought a little wildly. So it was no wonder that she was falling victim to all sorts of wobbly legs type feelings!

'Why the name?' Stefano murmured before she could slip away into polite conversation, before she could distance herself from him.

'I beg your pardon?'

'Your name. Is it a nickname? Because, from what you've told me about yourself...about your mother...'

'You're not really interested in that!' Sunny laughed weakly. 'And I'm sorry for being such a wimp and spilling my guts out! I'm sure that's not the sort of thing you bargained for when you asked me to come along with you and Flora tonight…' Hot and bothered by the way he was looking at her, she tried to find something sensible to say about Flora, some observation that would turn the intimacy of this conversation around because her bones were melting, especially because, instead of taking the hint and pulling away from her after she had tactfully drawn back, he had sat forward, once again closing the distance between them.

Nothing sensible came to mind and she licked her lips nervously.

'I'm interested,' Stefano murmured.

Sunny sighed. No big deal. Was it…?

'She was in one of her optimistic windows,' she said sadly. 'That's what she told me many times over the years. She'd come off the drugs and the drink as soon as she found out that she was pregnant with me…'

'And your father?'

Sunny lowered her eyes and felt her breath catch. 'No idea. Probably just another drifter…'

'I'm sorry.'

And he sounded as though he genuinely meant that, which brought a lump to her throat. Her eyes tangled with his and clung. He had, she thought distractedly, the most wickedly long eyelashes…

'You were saying…' Stefano reminded her.

'So I was. I was saying that Mum was off the bad stuff and she just plucked the most hopeful name she could think of…' Sunny smiled wryly '…and I've been stuck with it ever since. I haven't even got a useful middle name I could have reverted to…'

'Your outfit,' Stefano murmured.

Sunny tensed. 'I can't wait to get it off…'

'I didn't say…what I said to be insulting…'

'Maybe you thought I wouldn't fit in with that crowd.'

She forestalled any truths that she knew would cut to the quick.

He looked at her with open puzzlement and she laughed, knowing that she'd at least got that bit wrong. He wasn't the sort to care what other people thought.

'I said what I said because…' he sat back and folded his arms, his eyes not wavering '…the thought of other men looking at you…' He shouldn't be doing this but knowing that didn't help and didn't change anything. He was experiencing that very, very rare feeling of being at the mercy of something bigger and more powerful than his own iron willpower. He allowed his words to sink in, not knowing whether she would respond at all but driven to find out because he *just had to*. 'Well, put it this way… I didn't like the idea and I couldn't see how they could fail to stare in that outfit of yours…'

'You didn't like the idea…' She felt as if she was suddenly walking through thick fog with no signposts in sight.

'Men look…and then they want…' He shrugged in a way that was typically foreign, an overblown gesture that seemed to convey dry amusement and impatient resignation at the same time. 'I didn't like the thought of that…'

'Of what?'

'Of both…' His stomach clenched because, for once, he wasn't staring at a guaranteed outcome. She was quirky and…unpredictable, and both those things added up, for him, to an unknown quantity. And for once the riptide was carrying him. He didn't like it or want it but he was powerless to resist it.

'I didn't like the thought of them looking…and I didn't like the thought of them wanting… I felt that both those things should come from…me…'

CHAPTER SIX

SUNNY STARED AT Stefano in wide-eyed bewilderment, certain that she had somehow got the wrong end of the stick.

'What are you saying?' she stammered.

'Surely I don't have to spell it out in words of one syllable.' His voice was husky and teasing but that thread of uncertain apprehension was still pouring through his veins, investing him with the sort of edge-of-seat feeling he had never had much time for.

His edge-of-seat feelings were all associated with times he would rather not have remembered. The edge-of-seat feelings of waiting for lawyers to try and make progress with resolving custody issues…the edge-of-seat feelings of knowing that his marriage had been a crashing mistake, a disaster that would have to be put right with a messy divorce…the edge-of-seat feelings that had always come whenever he had tried to gain access to see his daughter, half optimistic that this time his ex-wife wouldn't mess him around, half accepting that she probably would…

Catastrophes, he had reflected on more than one bitter occasion, had a way of sharpening up and clarifying the way you looked at things.

Stefano no longer welcomed anything in his life that couldn't be ruthlessly controlled. No situation was ever allowed to deviate from the course he determined. No one was ever allowed to overstep the boundaries he had laid down. And he never allowed himself to flounder… Ever…

Steer a clear route, make sure you didn't stray from it,

and nothing could take you by surprise because surprises were seldom good.

Except, right now, the clear route wasn't as clear as it usually was, when it came to women.

For starters, he had chased her. Not overtly, but did that make a difference? He had noted her Keep Off signs and, instead of shrugging and walking away because the world was full of pretty faces and willing women, he had let himself be hooked in.

He had changed his routine because of her. Having hired her to work nights so that he could focus on several high-powered deals that required long hours, he had caught himself thinking about her, wanting to see her for longer than just in passing…

And when he had shown up unexpectedly and found her in the swimming pool…

That modest black bikini, which was much more her thing than the outfit she had borrowed from her friend, had turned him on more than if she had been wearing nothing but a thong…

Which just went to show the power of the imagination once it broke its leash and decided to fly. He'd been determined not to go near her, to remember that she was connected with his daughter, to not under any circumstances *mix business with pleasure*, so to speak, and yet here he was… Hell, he'd resolved not to venture *near* her in case it jeopardised his fragile truce with Flora…!

Not even her cautionary tale about her background had put him off.

It should have.

He had married a gold-digger and paid the price. Now he had no problem dating beauties who enjoyed the things he could give them, but he was always in control of a relationship, always dictated its course, always dispatched them when they were beginning to outstay their welcome.

Sunny had no money and her background beggared belief. She kept her distance and had made it clear that, given the choice, she would not have chosen to be in his company if she could help it. And yet…he had still chased her.

Which said worrying things about his valued self-control…but he was incapable of backing off. He didn't get it. He didn't *begin* to get it.

Something about the way she was put together… It wasn't just her stupendous and unusual good looks, but the way she tried to conceal them. It wasn't just her sharp intellect, but the soft vulnerability he could see lurking just beneath it. She had somehow gained access to Flora, a feat none of his previous nannies had come close to accomplishing, and she had done so without trying, having made it very clear that she was only in it for the money, which she needed.

On paper, it made no sense for him to be sitting here, waiting for her to come on board with the little journey he was interested in taking with her…

But hell…since when was it written in cement that he had to follow the rules that made sense? Since when was a little deviation something to be banned? And he wouldn't be jeopardising anything. He knew what could be lost and so would also know how to avoid that happening. He'd admitted his own weakness and stepped back to see the situation from all angles.

When it came to the crunch, he would always be in control because that was just the man he was. His concerns, whilst valid, were misplaced. To know what you were dealing with was to be in charge of the situation. He knew what he was dealing with. An itch that begged to be scratched and, once scratched, would disappear. It was a relief to get that straight in his head.

'I fancy you,' he admitted with a slow smile that sent

her senses spinning. It was liberating not to be fighting the unequal fight any longer. 'Don't ask me why but I do...'

Sunny felt as though she were being stroked even though he hadn't laid a finger on her. Her tummy flipped over and for a second every principle she had held dear to her heart disappeared like water down a plughole.

She shook away the mesmeric effect his words were having on her to establish some sanity.

He fancied her!

She'd been fancied before, she scoffed. True, Stefano Gunn was a few notches higher than most but still...

Agitated, she clasped her hands together and looked away. All of that would have been easy to deal with if she didn't, likewise, fancy the man!

'Could the outfit have anything to do with your sudden attack of lust?' She was proud of the casual, dismissive tone of her voice, which didn't seem to have the slightest effect on him.

'Not at all,' Stefano said musingly, as though he'd considered her question and given it a lot of thought. 'Although, in fairness, it did concentrate matters when I realised that I didn't want other men seeing you wearing next to nothing.'

'Well, I... This isn't at all appropriate...' She wanted to stand up but he was sitting so close to her that she would have had to push him back and then clamber over him.

She shrank back as far as she could go into her chair and noted the mild amusement in his eyes when he looked at her.

Why did she have to fancy him? Of all people? Why did those physical responses, which she had assumed she lacked, have to jump out and target a man like Stefano Gunn?

Why couldn't they have targeted someone nice and kind and *ordinary*?

Her skin tingled and prickled with awareness. Now that she knew how he felt, it was as if a Pandora's box had been opened. The silent, shameful charge, which she had thought had just been about her, was out in the open and it was clamouring to be dealt with.

'Tell me why,' Stefano murmured, his antennae picking up her nerves and processing it. She wasn't saying anything he didn't privately think himself but such caution didn't stand a chance next to the demands of his wayward libido.

'Because…I happen to be working for you!'

'In a very temporary capacity,' Stefano dismissed drily. 'I'm not your boss and you're not my employee and there are no office politics to be dealt with.'

'Of course there would be office politics to be dealt with! Not that I intend to…to…to *do anything.*'

'What office politics?'

'This is crazy.' She stood up, nimbly avoiding crashing into him by a whisker and then there was an awkward few seconds while she hovered, waiting for him to shift away from her and wondering whether he intended to at all, before he moved and she slipped past to pace the kitchen floor.

She should go. Of course she should! But something was holding her back, weakening what her head was telling her to do. Temptation. This was what it felt like. She had never experienced it in her life before and after John, who had been just the sort of guy she should have felt tempted by, she had resigned herself to her future being about her career. She felt uncomfortable in her own skin, confused by having her neatly ordered life turned upside down.

'What office politics?'

She paused to stand in front of him, arms folded, mouth pursed. 'You know what I'm talking about!'

'I have no idea and I'm not a mind-reader. If there's some revelation I've been missing, then enlighten me...'

'Katherine,' she muttered, hating herself for what now sounded like office gossip. She couldn't even remember where this particular piece of office gossip had originated.

'Katherine?' His brows knitted into a perplexed frown.

'Nothing. Forget it. It's nothing.'

'You shouldn't start conversations you don't have the courage to finish.' He'd never had to work so hard for a woman. It was as though she had glanced over her shoulder, thrown him a half smile and then proceeded to lay down a bed of nails and burning embers over which he had to walk if he was to follow the glance and the half smile. And where would he get even if he followed the glance and the half smile?

Nowhere much. He wasn't interested in a full-blown relationship. She turned him on and her unattainability was even more of a turn-on but he knew that the second he had her they would both be at the beginning of the end. Since his messy divorce and the bitter disillusionment that had come with it, he had had neither the will nor the stamina to sustain any liaison beyond a couple of months. He didn't jump out of bed with one woman to immediately jump into bed with another, but even after periods of celibacy, sometimes lasting months, he had never had the desire for any relationship with any woman to go beyond its natural course. Which was limited.

So it was puzzling why he was so keen to pursue something that would have a very limited duration.

Sunny could have kicked herself for ever having mentioned Katherine, but wasn't this the man he was? Sexy... powerful...wealthy...a man who thought he could chase whatever woman caught his fancy?

For all she knew, Katherine might have been busy this evening and so he'd thought he'd chance it with her.

That didn't sit quite right but it felt good not to give him the benefit of the doubt.

Because she wasn't going to go to bed with him. It didn't matter whether she fancied him or not or whether he fancied her or not. Did it?

'What about Katherine?' he prompted. 'Are you concerned that if we sleep together, she'll find out and sack you?'

'We're *not* going to be sleeping together!'

But they were. Stefano could read the conflict inside her as if it had been written in neon lettering across her forehead and he felt a kick of pure masculine triumph.

Was this just about winning? He'd never thought of sex in those terms. But, then again, he'd never met a woman who hadn't been eager and willing to fall into bed with him…

'I won't tell if you don't…' he murmured.

Sunny wondered whether he'd just heard what she'd said. His rampant self-confidence was a treacherous turn-on even though she should have found it repellent. She tilted her chin defiantly. 'It's not about whether Katherine finds out…it's just that I wouldn't want to step on any toes…'

'What are you talking about?'

'The rumour mill has it that the only reason the company got your business was because of Katherine…'

'Is that a fact…?'

'I don't suppose I should be telling you any of this, but I just want to make you see why this is crazy and why… well…why…'

'Now you've started telling me…what it is that you shouldn't be telling me…perhaps you should finish… What about Katherine? What's that rumour mill been saying?'

Hoist by my own petard, was what sprang to Sunny's

mind. She hated gossip and yet here she was, repeating it. She couldn't even pretend that it was illuminating work-related gossip, gossip that Stefano might find useful or that he needed to know.

It was cheap tabloid gossip and she cringed with shame but he was looking at her narrowly, waiting for her to carry on. She couldn't suddenly change the subject and start talking about the weather or the state of the economy.

'I don't usually listen to gossip—*I don't*—but it's been impossible to get away from. The minute everyone found out that you were going to be using Marshall, Jones and Jones, the speculation began because…it's new on the scene and it's small. It's not one of the top five…which is where…you know, one might assume…well…' She heard herself tripping over her words and she took a deep breath because now that she'd started this stupid, idiotic story she was committed to finish it.

'One might indeed…' Stefano murmured. He had no time for gossip and even less time for people who had nothing better to do than to spread it but he found the agonising discomfort on her face made her seem impossibly young and vulnerable, especially because she was desperately trying to keep her cool.

He also believed her when she said that she didn't usually listen to gossip. Where two or more people were gathered, gossip became an inevitability and, in a work environment, it was almost impossible to escape it.

Unless, of course, you happened to live in an ivory tower, which, as the head of his sprawling empire, he more or less did.

'So the rumour started that…that…perhaps Katherine was at the heart of it…'

Stefano raised his eyebrows, amazed that wagging tongues could have struck jackpot with nothing to go on but pure speculation. 'Explain,' he said with undisguised curiosity.

Sunny allowed herself a little sigh of relief because at least he wasn't storming around the kitchen, threatening to have her sacked because since when was it part of her job description to gossip to the guy who would be bringing tens of thousands of pounds' worth of business to their company.

'Katherine's very beautiful and someone came to the conclusion that you might have handed some work to the company as a way of…of…of…'

'Shall I help you along with this?'

Sunny stared at him miserably. She wanted to tell him that that *someone* who had come to conclusions hadn't been *her*. She had no idea whether the conclusions were right or wrong, but she hated the thought that he might end up being contemptuous of her. Too much protesting of her innocence, however, would surely end up not ringing true.

'You think,' Stefano said helpfully, 'that I wanted to climb into bed with the very beautiful Katherine and my method of getting her to go along with that was via bringing business to the company…'

'Stupid,' Sunny muttered, mortified.

'A little insulting,' Stefano mused. He thought his mother might have been highly entertained at what her machinations had instigated. 'I mean,' he said softly, 'don't you think that I might, just might, be perfectly capable of wooing the very beautiful Katherine without having to exert a bribe…?'

'I have no idea how that rumour started.' She tried not to fidget in her acute discomfort.

How on earth had they got to this point anyway? It wasn't as though she was going to jump in the sack with him! And yet, if that were the case, shouldn't she just have laughed off his crazy proposition and headed for the door?

It was what any normal, disinterested and frankly appalled person might have done…

Perhaps not appalled, she mentally amended. Who would be appalled at having a pass made at them by Stefano Gunn? He was sex on legs and probably the most eligible bachelor in the country, if not on the planet.

'Although…' he stood up, flexed his muscles and paced the kitchen, finally pouring them both another glass of wine '… I'll admit there's a certain amount of truth behind the rumour so whoever started it must have heard something…'

Sunny felt her insides plummet. She had been shocked when he had told her that he fancied her and she knew that she must have played with the idea of sleeping with him, must have entertained the wicked thought in some small corner of her mind, because to hear him now confirm that Katherine had been the draw for him made her feel slightly queasy.

Had she turned him down? And had his eyes wandered a little further afield until they had alighted on *her*?

'It's none of my business,' she said crisply, standing up so that he got the message that she was leaving.

'Where are you going?'

'Home. It's late.'

'I don't want you to go.'

'Tough.'

'Do you?'

'Do I what?'

'Want to go?' He watched her as she hovered by the door, saw the flicker of indecision on her face, saw the way she took a deep breath, as though steeling herself to clear off. 'I would never make a pass at a woman and then, if I happen to get rejected, scout around for someone else to pick up the slack. I'm not that superficial, Sunny. I don't want Katherine, however beautiful and capable she might be. And I'll tell you something for free…shall I?'

'What?' *He didn't want Katherine. He didn't fancy her.* Relief shot through her and in that moment she knew that she wanted him, that it didn't make sense, not at all, but something in her wanted him and that something was far more powerful than the neat, tidy part of her brain that was telling her not to be a fool.

'What I'm doing right now,' Stefano drawled, his deep, velvety voice curling around her with the seductiveness of the richest, darkest, smoothest chocolate, 'is not what I usually do. I don't usually make passes at women. I don't usually lay my cards on the table and try to persuade a woman to share my bed. But something about you…'

Sunny was beginning to feel faint. 'If you don't fancy Katherine, then what did you mean when you said that there was truth to the rumour…?' She was struggling to think straight because all of a sudden her head was filled with the most erotic images, images that had never formed a part of her life at all. Images of her making love…giving in with wild abandon to a deep vein of passion she had never known existed in her.

Stefano grinned ruefully and she blinked because he no longer looked like the intimidating, ruthless tycoon that he was. He looked *sexy and tantalisingly approachable.*

'I have my mother to thank for engineering my association with your company.'

'Not *my* company,' Sunny automatically said in a distracted voice.

Stefano smiled. 'True. My mother…' he raked his fingers through his hair because this was as intimate a chat with a woman as he could remember having in a very long time indeed '…has taken it upon herself to try and find me a nice wife ever since my daughter came to live with me after Alicia died. She's of the opinion that a girl needs a mother and, in passing, a wife would do me good.'

'Oh…'

'Oh, indeed,' Stefano said wryly. 'When my mother puts her mind to something, she can be a force of nature. She gets convenient hearing loss when I try and explain to her that a wife isn't going to happen.' He hadn't envisaged, when he'd put forward his bold proposal, that he would end up explaining any of this to her but, now that he was, he thought that it might be a good idea.

He'd always made it clear to the women he slept with that he wasn't up for grabs. There wouldn't be long-range plans or meet and greet the relatives or any talk at all about a future that wasn't going to be on the cards.

If any of them decided that they could somehow find a way past those clear, simple clauses then they were destined for disappointment.

But then all those women had been eager and enthusiastic. Sunny hadn't been either of those things and, more importantly, she'd also managed to charm his wilful daughter.

It was doubly important that she didn't see any relationship they might have as a gateway to something meaningful because of her connection to Flora.

Would she anyway? He just didn't know. What he *did* know was that, underneath the veneer, she was peculiarly vulnerable because of her background.

He wondered how it was that he knew so much about her when he hadn't slept with her. He wondered whether instant sexual gratification had always obviated the need for meaningful personal conversations or whether his interest in her had been sparked by the fact that his daughter was part of the equation. Somehow, through her association with Flora, she had managed to find a back door into parts of him no other woman had managed to access after the bitter fallout of his marriage. Was this something that had made him curiously vulnerable to the thought of bedding her? Had the very thing that should have deterred him been the match that had lit the burning flame?

He wondered whether Alicia, the mother of his child, had ever had any real access to him or whether their doomed relationship had generated something that had seemed personal at the time but which, in retrospect, had just been the sort of intimacy that warring partners sometimes had. Intimacy of the wrong kind.

The roundabout cycle of pointless questions was irritating and he focused on the here and now.

'She knows Katherine's mother,' he elaborated with a shrug, 'and she promptly decided that a love match was on the cards.'

'And you went along with it?' Sunny was puzzled because that element of softness was not what she associated with him.

The conversation seemed to be getting more rather than less personal and Stefano hesitated before dismissing the distant sound of alarm bells ringing.

'I am close to my mother,' he told her neutrally. 'I may not agree with her efforts to find me a suitable bride but I thought that it would cost nothing to place some of my business with your company and meet the woman, rather than staging a flat-out refusal and upsetting my mother, who, at the end of the day, is just doing what she feels is best for myself and my daughter. Naturally, I did all the necessary checks to ensure that the company was capable of delivering what I wanted of them. I wasn't about to sacrifice my money for the sake of my mother's whimsy.'

'Naturally.' Sunny cleared her throat. If he had gone full-steam ahead and tried to seduce her with his sheer overwhelming physicality she would have resisted, or at least she *hoped* that she would have resisted. Instead, they were talking and she got the feeling that she had, for whatever reason, been allowed into an inner circle to which not many were invited. She had no idea where that impression came from. Maybe because underneath the casual tone of his voice there was something ever so slightly…hesitant. As though he was picking his words carefully because he was in foreign territory.

It was fanciful, of course. For all she knew, this could be a tried and tested ruse to get what he wanted. State his intentions…switch tactics to persuasive conversation… then stake his claim… It helped to be cynical but not even that could kill her curiosity.

'Your parents must have a very close marriage,' she said wistfully. 'I've always thought that people who are happily married are the ones who recommend marriage…'

'My father's dead but yes, they had a very happy marriage.' He was bemused at the twists and turns their conversation was taking, whilst telling himself that exchanging a few personal details wasn't anything of earth-shattering importance, even if those personal details were not ones he'd ever exchanged with the women who had flitted in and out of his life in the past few years.

'Girls need a mother—' Sunny thought of her own mother and all her tragic failings and she thought of all the allowances she had made for her '—so maybe your mother has a point.' She shrugged, just in case he thought that she was overstepping the mark in giving an opinion.

'In an ideal world—' Stefano thought that this might be the perfect opportunity to get a few things straight '—Flora would have a delightful and adoring mummy, but it isn't an ideal world. A delightful and adoring mummy would necessitate me having a wife and that's a country I've visited once and have no intention of returning to.' He drained his glass, stood up, strolled towards the wide windows that overlooked the extensive back lawns before turning to face her. 'I've been married once,' he said flatly, 'and it was an unmitigated disaster. That's something I need not tell you, but it might explain why there is no Katherine on the face of the earth who could entice me back into thinking that marriage is anything but a train wreck waiting to happen.'

'That's very cynical.'

'You think? I'm surprised we don't share the same sentiment.'

'You mean because of…my background?'

'Yes.' Stefano was curious enough to prolong the conversation. 'Surely you can't tell me that you believe in fairy stories and happy endings when your mother was, from all accounts, a failed and unhappy woman and your father…was a bloke who did a runner before you were born and never looked back…?'

Sunny flushed. He wasn't pulling any punches, was he? But there was nothing disdainful or pitying about his remarks. He was saying it like it was and, weirdly, she didn't seem to mind that.

'I've never thought about it one way or the other.' She felt the nervous beat of the pulse at the base of her neck. His eyes resting lazily on her seemed like the whisper of a promise of things to come and every nerve in her body was on full alert, throbbing with barely contained excitement.

'Are you asking me that because you want to warn me not to get involved with you?'

Stefano shot her a curling smile because there was unspoken acquiescence in that question, although he was certain that she barely realised that herself.

'I'm not looking for involvement with anyone,' Sunny dismissed. She glanced jumpily at him and licked her lips, which were dry and tingly. 'And maybe you're right. Maybe I'm not really interested and haven't actually thought about it because of my background.' She gave him a sad, twisted smile. 'Maybe it's because I don't exactly have the right role models to fall back on. How could I believe in fairy tales and happy endings when I never knew what that sort of thing was like in the first place? Maybe you just can't crave what you've never had or experienced.' She wasn't sure whether she really believed that or not. She knew that when she'd thought she'd found her soulmate she had desperately *wanted* the happy-ever-after ending except the soulmate hadn't quite worked out as planned.

Since then, had she toughened up? Turned into the sort of cynical career woman who had no time for love and romance?

She'd thought she'd given up on having the sort of capacity for a physical response that was necessary for any sort of relationship, but she was wrong, wasn't she? Turned out she did have the capacity for a physical response…

So was she kidding herself that she never thought about the future and what it might hold for her with a guy? Should the right guy come along one day?

If Stefano was warning her off getting ideas about him, as if that would ever happen in a million years, then to tell him that, for all the chaos and heartache of her background, she still believed in the enduring power of love would be a mistake.

He'd get cold feet and run a mile and—why kid herself?—she didn't want that.

'You don't have to warn me off,' she said huskily, daring to step into the unknown and feeling a shiver of molten excitement, 'because, like I said, the last thing I would want would be involvement…' She laughed, heady with the sensation that she was no longer talking to the formidable, feared and respected Stefano Gunn, the man who could make heads of finance quake in their shoes, whose ability to close deals and predict the stock market swings was legendary, who could command immediate attention with the snap of his fingers…

She was talking to a man who fancied her and right now she was no longer the junior in a law firm in the presence of the toughest guy in the concrete jungle. They were both adults working their way towards sleeping with one another.

It was...*thrilling*. It made her realise how predictable her life was. She had spent so long making sure to impose order and control, so that she would never have a runaway future, that somehow the present had become lost in the process, as had *fun*.

'And especially involvement with a guy like you,' she completed with utter honesty.

Stefano, relieved as he was to know that they were both singing from the same song sheet, was a little irked by the speed with which she had established her distance and he was particularly irked by her statement that there was no way she could become involved with someone like him.

Of course he could understand it. If she happened to be someone on the lookout for a committed relationship. But she wasn't and he believed her. Experiences shaped people and hers had been frightful.

'Because I would be unable to return whatever involvement you wanted?'

Sunny laughed and then looked at him with narrowed, amused, speculative eyes. 'You're really arrogant, aren't you...?'

Stefano frowned, taken aback by her blunt criticism. It was rare for him to meet a woman who wasn't either intimidated by him or else desperate to impress him. With the exception of his mother.

'I don't mean to be offensive,' Sunny hurriedly expanded, 'but there's no way I could ever get involved with someone as rich and powerful and driven as you...'

'Since when are money and ambition turn-offs?' he asked incredulously.

'When I was thirteen,' she mused, looking back into the past, 'I got a scholarship to go to one of the top boarding schools in the country. I met lots of girls there who… came from gilded circles, probably just like you. They talked very loudly in cut-glass accents and laughed a lot and flirted like mad with all the boys. What *they* would have wanted to end up with would have been someone rich and powerful and driven. If I ever find my soulmate, he probably won't have much money and he'll be kind and thoughtful and measured…' *And he'll have to be able to do what you're doing now…he'll have to be able to fire me up until I feel like I can't breathe for the excitement…*

'Forgive me while I stifle a yawn.'

Sunny wanted to be angry at the casual way he had dismissed her heartfelt dreams but when she caught those dark, amused eyes she felt her lips twitch.

'Thoughtful and kind can be very sexy traits.' She lowered her eyes, while the heat of their mutual chemistry sizzled around them.

'Maybe,' Stefano murmured. 'But in the meanwhile…' He tugged her to her feet and she bumped against his hard, muscular body.

She knew this was what it must feel like when swooning women said that they *went up in flames*.

Her whole body was burning, on fire. Her nipples, scraping against her bra, felt insanely sensitive and the dampness between her legs was hot and slick, making her want to reach beneath her underwear so that she could rub herself out of her wet discomfort.

'Yes?' she squeaked, as far removed from the efficient and sexless professional she assumed herself to be as was possible.

'Let me show you what someone raw and elemental can do for you…'

CHAPTER SEVEN

'WHAT ABOUT FLORA?' It sounded like a last-ditch chance to back off and Stefano looked at her with a shuttered expression, as though he could read straight into her mind and pull the thoughts from her head.

'Cold feet?' he asked, without bothering to beat around the bush.

'No!'

'Sure about that?'

'One hundred per cent sure.'

'Even though I'm not the sort of person you should get involved with?'

'This isn't about involvement, is it?' Sunny could scarcely believe she was saying this stuff. She'd done a complete U-turn in the space of a heartbeat. She would never have imagined for a second that lust could be this powerful—powerful enough to bring all her well-laid plans crashing to the ground.

But she was safe emotionally and for that she was grateful. Her body might be clamouring for adventure but her heart was still switched on enough to know that the real guy for her would not be Stefano Gunn or anyone like him.

'It's just…a one-night stand…' She thought of her fumbling, embarrassing forays into sex, when she had been going out with John. If she'd had the slightest amount of experience she would have known that the missing link had been…*this*. The missing link had been the wild beating of her heart, the aching of her body, the searing excitement at the thought of being touched…

If she'd had the slightest amount of experience, she would have realised that what made perfect sense on paper didn't necessarily translate into perfect sense in practice.

She was here, barely able to breathe for the excitement, and she knew that *this* would have to be part of the equation when she met any man she felt she could have a long-term relationship with.

It wasn't just about personality but it was about *this* as well, without which the personality on its own didn't stand much of a chance.

They were heading up the staircase, softly and quickly, her hand in his. At the top of the staircase, the broad, airy corridor went right for the wing of rooms in which Flora had her bedroom suite and left where Stefano had his rooms.

In her mind's eye, she could picture his huge super-king-size bed and her heart skipped a beat.

She knew that Flora would be sound asleep. Once her head hit the pillow, she slept the deep sleep of a child but on the one occasion when she had had a broken night and Sunny had asked her, the following evening, what she had done, Flora had simply said that she had read until she had fallen asleep again.

His room was in darkness but, instead of switching on the overhead light, he turned on the lamp by the bay window, leaving the curtains open so that weak moonlight filtered into the room.

In the grip of nervous tension, Sunny hovered by the door, which he had quietly shut behind them.

She thought that she might have forgotten how to have sex. Was that possible? A bubble of hysterical laughter threatened…

Looking at her, Stefano could see that she was as nervous as a kitten. She wasn't the sort of girl who moved from one guy to another with seamless ease and he got a disproportionate kick from knowing that she had been unable to resist *him*. It evened the scales because he hadn't been able to resist *her*. Two controlled people *losing it*.

'You're beautiful,' he said softly, beginning to unbutton his shirt, taking his time, exposing his chest sliver by glorious sliver.

Sunny bit back the temptation to tell him that he was as well. That was something he would know, something countless women had probably told him over the years. How could they not? When he was physically...so *perfect*?

She couldn't stop staring. She didn't care that he was looking at her staring at him, a smile tugging the corners of his beautiful mouth.

He shrugged off the shirt and she drank in the broad shoulders, the six-pack stomach, the ripple of muscle, the small flat brown nipples that she itched to tease with her fingers...

Her mouth went dry when he rested his hand on the zip of his trousers. Even from across the room, she could see the unmistakable bulge of his erection, pulsing under the trousers.

'Having fun?' Stefano shot her a wolfish smile that made her toes curl.

Sunny nodded.

'Care to join me in the striptease or would you rather I took your clothes off for you...? I'm frankly not sure which would turn me on more so...your choice...'

Sunny slipped her fingers under the edge of her stretchy top, feeling as debauched as a stripper in a nightclub, and began slowly tugging it over her breasts and over her head to then toss it onto the ground so that she was now only in her bra and the short controversial skirt.

Stefano walked slowly towards her. There was an in-

nocence in the way she was standing there, hands at her
sides, chin at a defiant angle, as though she was fighting
against folding her arms across her breasts. And her body
was…as spectacular as he had envisaged, long and graceful, with the supple sleekness of a ballet dancer.

His erection was painful, throbbing and pulsing.

'I'm not very experienced at…this sort of thing…'
Sunny whispered.

Stefano was now standing directly in front of her and
he placed his hands on her shoulders and gently massaged
them, relaxing her. 'Me neither…'

Sunny grinned and stole a shy glance at his darkly
amused face. But the little teasing joke and the way he
was ever so gently massaging her shoulders were doing
what they were supposed to do; they were relaxing her.
She could feel her whole body thawing out and her breathing slowing.

She sighed softly as she felt him reach behind her to
unclasp the bra and her small, high breasts popped out,
the rose-pink nipples stiff and pointed.

His low, husky growl of appreciation sent violent ripples of pleasure racing through her.

After a lifetime of playing down her body, it felt incredible to be standing here showing it off and thrilling
in his delight.

He cupped them with his big hands and slowly roused
both nipples with the pads of his thumbs until she was
quivering with excitement, melting, desperate for him to
do so much more than just tease.

He was taking his time, slowing his pace. Sunny could
sense that and she was impressed by the level of thought-
fulness behind that because she could envisage him as a
man who was probably accustomed to taking…fast and
hard.

He backed her gently against the door and she stuck her

hands behind her, flattened against the door as he began to suckle on her nipples.

Head flung back, eyes closed, Sunny could only whimper with pleasure as his moist mouth relentlessly sucked. Her hands balled into fists behind her back and the whimpers were deepening into moans. When he pulled away she wanted to direct his head right back from whence it had come. Her wet nipples were cooling quickly as he tugged down the skirt, allowing her to wriggle out of it, where it joined the little top on the ground.

Stefano stood up. This leisurely business was taking a lot out of him. He was still wearing his trousers, thank God, because if he had been able to press his erection against her bare skin he felt as if the unthinkable might have happened.

Even the squash of her soft breasts against his chest was teeth-clenchingly difficult to bear.

He cupped her between her legs and felt her wetness. Very slowly, applying just the right amount of pressure, he massaged her down there, watching her face as he did so, enjoying her helpless, heated response. Her nostrils flared and she wriggled against his hand, gyrating her hips.

When he pushed his hand underneath her panties, she drew in a sharp breath and held it as he inserted two fingers, feeling and finding her swollen clitoris and playing with it until she was begging him to stop and then begging him not to stop.

He didn't stop. He kissed her, long and deep, tongues meshing.

'You have to stop…' Sunny gave a half-hearted push against his busy hand '…or I'll… I won't be able to stop myself…'

'Good,' Stefano murmured into her ear, which made her shiver. 'I've always had a soft spot for a woman who just can't stop herself…'

It was so unbearably erotic. The fact that he was half dressed…that his hand was there, pushed underneath her knickers…that his breath in her ear was warm and sexy… that her nipples were rubbing against his chest…

She came with a deep shudder that racked her body and then she fell limply against him and curved her arms around his neck. When her breathing was back to normal, she fell against his neck and nibbled it until he laughed and swung her up to carry her over to the bed in a couple of easy strides.

'Very caveman…' She smiled drowsily, replete with contentment and already looking forward to touching him and having him touch her again. She feasted greedy eyes on him as he stood by the bed to remove his trousers and boxers. His legs were long and muscular and she took her time appreciating them, took her time letting her eyes drift higher to rest on his impressive, hard-as-steel, erect manhood. The thatch of dark hair in which it nestled was intimidating in its naked virility. Her tummy flipped and she found that she was holding her breath.

'You like that?' Stefano paused to look at her. She was naked. She'd freed herself from her underwear and she was…spectacular. He'd had beautiful women before but she was…unique in a way he couldn't quite put his finger on. There was something intensely alluring about her mixture of intelligence, savvy streetwise toughness and vulnerability.

'If I'm the last sort of guy you would want to be involved with,' he heard himself say in a roughened undertone as he slipped onto the bed next to her, pulling her into him so that their naked bodies were pressed together, 'then I'm guessing that you've never had a caveman before…' He moved against her and she parted her legs. He nudged his thigh between them and moved it slowly and absently.

Since when did he give a hoot what other men his previous partners had slept with? As far as he was concerned, all of that was an irrelevance.

But he was curious now. Was he the only inappropriate guy she had gone to bed with? Had there been others? She wasn't married, she wasn't engaged and she had no boyfriend so whatever touchy-feely soulmate types she might have encountered clearly hadn't made it past the starting gate.

How come?

Sunny blushed, conscious of her inexperience. 'I haven't,' she said shortly. 'Let's not talk.' She placed a flattened palm on his chest and marvelled at the hardness of his hair-roughened chest. Just the right amount of hair, she thought distractedly, just the right amount to add to that intensely masculine aura.

She wasn't a virgin but she might just as well have been and here she was, with a man with loads of experience and not just experience but experience with some of the most desirable and beautiful women in the world. Sunny wasn't vain but she was honest. Yes, she knew that she had been born with a certain amount of looks, thanks to her gene pool, but she would still be gauche and awkward and she had no inclination to fill him in on her one and only sort of ex-lover. No way.

Why not? Stefano thought irritably, which was such a ridiculous reaction that he almost laughed.

'You're right…there's a time and a place for talking and I've always found that that place isn't in bed…' He licked an erotic trail along her neck while he traced her delicate collarbone with one long brown finger and that finger carried further down to circle a nipple, teasing it with a feathery touch until Sunny could barely lie still in the bed.

She was positively aching for him when his mouth set-

tled at last on one straining, tautened bud, when he pulled
it deep into his mouth, licking the tip with his tongue while
his other hand played with her other nipple, rolling over
it and igniting a blizzard of heated response inside her.

She squirmed, determined that this time she was going
to play with him as much as he was playing with her.

She traced the hard lines of his torso and then circled
his hard length with her hand. The faint shudder that ran
through his body quelled her nerves in a way no amount
of soothing chat could ever have done because it proved
to her just how much he wanted her. Whatever the length
and width and breadth of his experience.

He wanted *her*.

Even though they came from different worlds…even
though he could have had any woman on the planet he
desired…even though she wasn't posh or sophisticated.
He wanted *her*. Right here and right now at this very moment in time.

The strength of their craving was mutual and she could
easily lose herself in that knowledge.

Her body took over and seemed to know what to do
or maybe, she thought, that was just how it worked when
you were really fired up for someone.

Her legs wanted to part and to receive the ministrations
of his mouth as he went down on her, licking and teasing
and sucking, exploring her in a way that was unimaginable and unimaginably wonderful.

For Stefano, nothing had ever tasted this sweet. When
he had begun nuzzling the soft down between her thighs
she had automatically, with some embarrassment, protested, tugging at his hair, even though her legs had remained open, welcoming him to explore between them.

Had she never been caressed and kissed there before?

Curiosity had nudged once again past common sense
and it had increased as he had felt her heated response to

his intimate caresses, had known from the tremble of her slender thighs pressed against his face that she was loving every second of the experience.

Why had no man touched her there before? She'd been strangely shy to start with but there was so much passion there, passion that matched his, and it was like finding a gold mine that just kept on giving.

Had no man roused her to these heights before? It gave him an unholy kick to imagine that he might be the first even though logic told him that the chances of that were frankly non-existent. She was in her twenties and beautiful. She would have had lots of lovers in her past and he wouldn't have been the first to fire her to these heights even though it might feel that he was.

She moved against his mouth and all thoughts vanished from his head as he lost himself in the taste and smell of her, musky…fragrant…perfume to make a man lose his mind…

It was sweet torture to take his time but he did, making sure to explore her and hanging on by a thread as she explored him.

He nudged at her, the blunt head of his penis tantalising her, but that required a level of self-restraint he found he didn't have.

Sunny stilled him. 'I'm not on the Pill.' She was almost at the point of losing control completely. Her body no longer felt like hers. This wasn't the awkward, excruciatingly self-conscious body that had shied away from John's touch, even though she had wanted so badly to be turned on by him. This was another body—a body that seemed to have a will of its own, a body that could melt and go up in flames at the same time. It was a body that excited and amazed and thrilled her.

She dreaded to think that he might pull away from her because she wasn't on any contraception yet why should she be? She'd had no intention of jumping in the sack with anyone any time soon.

'It wouldn't matter if you were.' Stefano reached to the drawer of the bedside cabinet next to the bed and felt for his pack of condoms.

'Wouldn't it?'

'Of course not. Do you honestly think I'd be stupid enough to believe a woman who said that she was on the Pill and couldn't get pregnant?' His lips curled. 'Been there, done that, got the T-shirt. Trust me, you could pop a pill in front of me and I'd still use a condom because if it's one thing I will never again take, it's a chance...'

The depth of his bitterness shocked Sunny and for a split second she saw the man who had locked himself down emotionally, the man who had constructed a fortress of ice around his heart and whilst she knew that none of that should matter a jot to her because she certainly wasn't in it for a relationship, it still was weirdly unsettling. Was this what John had eventually thought when they had both tried their best and come to the conclusion that they had to walk away from one another? That she was locked down emotionally? Frozen where she should have been alive? That she had nothing to give? Not even the generosity of her physical responses?

Stefano sensed just that fleeting second or two when she seemed to disappear, but then she curled her fingers into his hair and arched up to kiss and nibble the side of his mouth, laughing when he pushed her back to kiss her so thoroughly that she wanted to faint.

He was rock-hard as he slipped on the condom in one smooth expert movement, and then he was thrusting in her, loving the warm tightness of her and the motion of her hips as they picked up rhythm, moving under him as though their bodies had been made to do this, to join together in the act of making love.

Sunny clung.

She'd never clung to anyone in her life before. She had learned from an early age that clinging got you nowhere. But she clung now, wishing that she could keep holding him to her for ever, never wanting to let him go and absolutely loving the feel of his lightly perspiring, tightly packed, muscular body under her hands.

Her orgasm was an explosion that took her to another dimension. A slow build, getting faster until she couldn't breathe as he pushed into her, hard, long strokes that drove her wild. She heard someone groaning and realised that it was her.

When they had both finally come back down to earth, with her head resting on his chest, she listened to the steady beat of his heart and the first thing that came to her head was that she didn't want this to be a one-night stand and that was such a scary realisation that she wanted to whimper in panic.

It felt as though someone had pulled a plug she hadn't even known existed and all of a sudden her prized self-control was slipping remorselessly through the plughole.

This wasn't going to do! She'd made love and it felt as though she'd made love for the first time, felt that this was what the fuss was all about, this soaring, wonderful sensation of flying high above the clouds, a feeling of complete and utter union with another human being.

Had that made her vulnerable? Because, if it had, then she was going to have to find a cure pretty damn quick.

She yawned and sat up, slipping her legs over the side of the bed, and he caught her hand and gently tugged her back down.

'Going somewhere?'

Sunny flipped her long hair to one side and glanced at him over her shoulder. 'To get dressed.'

'Why are you going to do that?' He stroked the underside of her wrist lazily.

'Because it's after midnight and I need to get home.'

'You don't need to get home. There are too many bedrooms in this house to count. You can have your pick.'

Sunny noted that he hadn't suggested she share his room with him but he wouldn't, would he? He knew the lines that had to be drawn. Where she suspected she still had the capacity to melt, he was as hard as steel.

'If Eric can't drive me to the station, I can call a taxi.'

Stefano sat up and frowned. 'You don't want to do that…' He tugged her a little bit more so that she fell back against the pillow and he cupped one breast with his hand, teasing the nipple into a stiff, throbbing peak. 'And your nipple agrees with me…'

Sunny wriggled. Of course, this was his great strength, she thought. It wasn't his looks, incredible though they were, or his bank balance or the house he lived in or the helicopter he owned or the cars he drove… It was his searing intelligence and his wicked sense of humour. Both those things could be her undoing.

She smacked his hand and he laughed and caught it and then twisted her to face him so that he could nibble the tips of her fingers one by one.

'I'd bet there are other parts of your body,' he continued in that same devastatingly sexy, low voice, 'that would also be in agreement… Shall we discover which bits?'

'Stefano, this was just meant to be a one-night stand…' But she heard the weakness in her voice with alarm. She sounded as though she was trying to convince herself of what she was saying and she knew that he would be able to see straight through her half-hearted protest.

Her body was responding to his casual touch. She thought, in retrospect, that she should have leaped off the bed in one athletic bound and shoved on her clothes before he had time to reach out and touch her. The second he'd touched her, all her good intentions seemed to have gone up in smoke.

'The road to Hell...' He left the quote unfinished and she made a valiant effort to listen to her head and remove her treacherous body from the equation. 'Don't you want to carry on this process of discovery for longer than just a few hours?' He lowered his dark head to take the same nipple he had been caressing into his mouth and he sucked on it very slowly and very, very erotically, half looking at her so that their eyes were tangling as he continued to nip and suck and flick his tongue over her nipple.

He levered himself up to look down at her seriously and Sunny hated knowing that she just wanted him to return to what he was doing, turning her on.

'It's not a good idea,' she mumbled.

'We're both adults...we both fancy one another... where's the problem?'

'I... I'm not looking for any kind of complicated situation...' Her voice petered out and she worried her lip anxiously.

'Snap.' Stefano pressed her back against the bed, pinning her arms on either side and raking his eyes over her stunning breasts. 'Nor am I...'

'I barely know you...' Sunny felt as though she was running round in circles. Her objections made no sense. He didn't want a relationship and neither did she...and yes, they fancied one another. But surely there should be *something more* than that if they were to continue sleeping with one another?

'You know more about me than anyone else,' he murmured, sifting his long fingers through her hair.

And that was true, he thought with a certain amount of surprise. She knew his motivations, knew his circumstances…*knew his daughter.* And he certainly knew a fair amount about her, or he fancied he did because she was a private person. That was something he *felt* and something he rather *liked*.

'How well do you think you have to know someone in a case like this?' Stefano mused. 'Neither of us predicted that this would happen and yet here we are. It did. Somehow we bypassed all the usual verbal foreplay and ended up in bed because we frankly can't resist one another…but we both share the same pragmatic take on what we have…'

Sunny wasn't sure that *pragmatic* was such a thrilling way to describe what was happening. 'Meaning?'

'We both know that this isn't going to last but we're happy to enjoy it while it does. Neither of us is interested in anything…*complicated*… We're going into it with our eyes wide open and that works for me and I imagine it works for you as well…'

'I just never thought that I'd…be the sort of person to jump into bed with a guy I barely know simply for the sake of sex.'

'Scintillating, mind-blowing sex…'

'You're very egotistic.' But she laughed softly and helplessly.

'It takes two to contribute to scintillating, mind-blowing sex…and, since you're without a boyfriend, I'm guessing that you might have jumped into bed with guys you knew well and yet…ended up in relationships that weren't going anywhere. Am I right?'

'You're so black and white.'

'You see clearer when things are black and white.' He circled her nipple with his finger and then gently flicked a teasing tongue over the tip, before returning his gaze to her face. 'Too much grey has a nasty habit of blurring the lines. And sometimes it pays not to overthink a situation… but just to lie back and enjoy it…'

* * *

'Good job!'

Flora was clapping by the side of the pool. In the shade, Stefano was lying on a lounger, having abandoned the effort of reading the money section of the Sunday broadsheet.

He had tamed his uneasy conscience.

In front of Flora, he and Sunny were simply two adults who communicated and did the occasional joint thing with her, Flora, as the central focus. Flora was basking in it and opening up more and more daily. How could that be a bad thing? In due course, he and Sunny would fizzle out and she would disappear. Of course, should his daughter wish to continue to communicate, there was always email. He would never stop that. As for him…whilst he knew the day they went their separate ways was inevitable, he would enjoy it while it lasted.

The sex was mind-blowing. What was there to worry about? He felt as if he'd recaptured all the self-control he had momentarily lost before they had become lovers.

Sunny was proudly clinging to the side of the pool, having completed her first lap underwater.

Looking down at that summer scene, anyone might have been forgiven for thinking that this was picture-perfect domesticity. Sunny knew better than to allow herself to wallow in such illusions. She and Stefano were now *an item*. An *item* that had been going on for three weeks—an *item* that Flora seemed to accept with the casualness of an eight-year-old, not that Sunny quite knew *what* Flora thought of the situation.

Certainly, Sunny and Stefano *never* exchanged any physical shows of affection in front of his daughter. But, on the other hand, Sunny was at the house a lot. Most evenings, even though there was no longer any need for her to be there and even though she had refused all payment, knowing that it would make her feel cheap should she take money from him while sleeping with him.

'Don't be ridiculous,' Stefano had told her. 'You're here looking after Flora before I return home…you need to differentiate between business and pleasure. Babysitting my daughter is business, for which you deserve payment.'

'If you pay me anything,' Sunny had told him, 'then I'll walk away and never come back.'

Although how easy would that have been? Like an addict, she couldn't seem to control herself when she was around him and when she wasn't around him she was thinking of him. In the space of a heartbeat, she had gone from focusing one hundred per cent on her job to focusing on Stefano.

His face popped up when she was gazing at her computer screen. His voice rang in her head when she was in the office canteen having lunch with the other employees. His smile appeared when she was staring down at columns of legal precedents and then she had to blink for it to disappear.

When Flora was around, they had meals together. Gradually, Sunny could see Flora warming to her father, interacting with him before retreating behind the surliness she had mastered over the months, although now that surliness was half-hearted, the remnants of a habit that was gradually being whittled away, not least because her father was around a lot more than he had ever been.

He hadn't missed the small changes in his daughter and he was generous in laying the reward for that at her door.

'That's down to you,' Stefano had told her two nights before and Sunny's heart had melted at the uneven roughness of his voice, which he had not been able to conceal. 'Let me pay you. I want to. You have done far more than words can say.'

Sunny had refused. Indeed, she could even have said

that, for everything she had done for Flora, Flora had done a great deal for *her*. She had sat and played games on the computer. One afternoon, when Stefano had brought her down to London, they had gone shopping and Sunny had been exposed to a vision of all the clothes an eight-year-old could buy and what a shopping trip might have been like had she had a mother to go on one with. They had, the weekend before, gone to the zoo in Regent's Park so that Flora could see that not all zoos were unethical. It was somewhere Sunny had never visited. She had been enthralled and captivated. There had been a child's party there, a chattering and excitable group of a dozen kids. Was that what normality would have felt like? She'd closed her eyes and tried it on for size in her head. She'd pictured how normality would have felt if she'd been Flora's age.

And this…being by the pool with Flora and Stefano… *felt normal* and that scared her because she knew that it shouldn't.

She just didn't understand what was happening to her. Stefano made no more sense now than he had on day one. He was still utterly inappropriate. Was she just maturing late? Was this the equivalent of a sixteen-year-old's crush? This racing heart, sweaty palms, sweetly aching…*thing*?

Had she made the big mistake of trying to figure everything out, trying to make sure that everything, including emotions, had their rightful place on a spreadsheet… and in the process not allowed for the power of impulse?

If that were the case, then it would be a relief to get this out of her system. What if she had married? Settled down? Only for someone like Stefano to blaze into her life out of nowhere, railroading everything in its path, including her well-thought-out life plan? How much worse would it have been if this sort of reckless craziness had happened later on down the road!

She leaned at the side of the pool and watched him,

stretched out on the lounger, all packed muscle and virile masculine appeal.

She'd stayed the night before but always in a separate room. And before she tiptoed her way there...the memory of their bodies locked together as one could still make her feel a little giddy.

Now, she felt that familiar heat course through her body at what lay ahead. His touch, his mouth, the feel of him... were embedded in her like a burr under her skin, something always there, reminding her of his presence in her life.

Flora was giving her a series of further swimming instructions which included such gems as, 'Try not to breathe underwater!' and, 'Don't sink to the bottom!' or, 'Remember to think like a fish!'

Diving down and holding her breath, Sunny wondered what any self-respecting fish would think if it found itself in a massive turquoise swimming pool in the middle of an English commuter-belt village. Probably die of shock and...drown.

She was smiling, perfectly content, when she surfaced on the other side of the pool to shake water out of her hair, turning around automatically, the way her body seemed to do whenever Stefano was in the vicinity, seeking him out like a heat-guided missile seeking out a source of warmth...

Hair everywhere, water dripping down her face, rubbing her eyes as she levered herself out of the pool, she was expecting nothing more than Flora, who would probably be clapping as though she had invented the art of teaching another person how to swim, and Stefano, who would be looking at them both with that dry amusement that made her want to reach out and touch him.

Instead...

A small dark-haired woman was standing next to Stefano, staring at the pool, mouth open as though the pause button had been pressed at the very moment she had been about to say something.

In fact…when she looked at Stefano…

He looked a little grey round the gills. He looked as though he would quite have liked to have been able to press the delete button…

Only Flora seemed oblivious and Sunny gratefully settled her eyes on her whilst simultaneously wondering…

What the heck's going on?

CHAPTER EIGHT

FEELING AS CONSPICUOUS as a rattlesnake at a tea party, Sunny stood awkwardly at the side of the pool in the ubiquitous black bikini. Never had she felt so underdressed. The woman gaping at her, in her midsixties, was impeccably dressed and impeccably groomed. Although the temperature was in the seventies, she was in a neat skirt and a blouse with a bow at the neck and a jacket that matched the pale yellow skirt. And the shoes, likewise, matched the rest of the outfit.

'Stefano?' The older woman turned to him and Sunny took advantage to dash for her towel, which she secured around her body, and then she remained where she was, not knowing whether she should introduce herself or pretend that she wasn't really there at all.

Because she had worked out who this must be. Stefano's mother.

'She's just back from Scotland,' he had casually dropped into the conversation a couple of evenings before, 'but you needn't fear that she'll unexpectedly turn up. My mother is extremely traditional in most things and that includes what she sees as the annoying habit some people have of showing up unannounced. Appointments should be made so that tea can be prepared.'

'Even with you?' Sunny had laughed, thinking yet again how wildly different their worlds were.

'Even with me,' he had confirmed wryly. 'If I were to

show up on her doorstep she would immediately think that something was wrong.'

'And what about Flora? What if Flora were to show up on her doorstep?'

'She'd be beside herself with joy,' Stefano had admitted honestly. 'Flora has been…difficult with me but only slightly better with my mother. I'm very much hoping things might change on that front… Tea's planned for next weekend.'

And that was a family gathering from which she would be excluded. Sunny knew that and expected nothing different, but it had still hurt somewhere deep inside her.

Nerves gripped her as a pair of dark eyes, very much like Stefano's, once more returned to look at her with eagle-eyed curiosity and interest.

Flora had bounded out of the water and was busily inspecting a tartan skirt that had been brought back for her.

'It'll look great with those black shoes of yours,' Sunny said, if only to break the silence.

'It seems my son hasn't been as forthcoming as he might have been!'

'Mother, this is…'

'I'm Sunny—' she stretched out her hand, determined to set things straight and save both herself and Stefano the awkward embarrassment of trying to sweep her under the carpet '—and I look after Flora now and again. When your son has to work late.'

'For example—' the sharp black eyes were twinkling with humour '—on a weekend? Stefano?' She turned to her son and fixed him with a beady stare. 'What are you working on, lying on a sun lounger by the side of the pool? A tan? Because I don't seem to see that cursed laptop computer of yours anywhere!' She turned back to Sunny. 'Not that I'm not overjoyed to find him without that thing attached to his arm! I am! Now, why don't we all go inside for a nice cup of tea? Here for a reason, Stefano! Quite slipped my mind with all the excitement of finding you out here with a nice young lady you never saw fit to tell your old mother about!' She began striding back towards the house, but not until she had carolled over her shoulder, 'This is not the way I raised my son! I thought... I *thought* I'd raised a respectful young man who would have been the first to tell me that he was in a serious relationship!'

Aghast, Sunny looked around to see whether Flora had heard this telling throwaway remark and, thankfully, she was still too busy burrowing into the package on the poolside table to pay them much notice.

Serious relationship? How much further from the truth could his mother get?

She excused herself as soon as she was inside, mumbling and stuttering something about getting changed. Stefano was as comfortable in his dry swimming trunks and a T-shirt as if he had been dressed in a suit but she, on the other hand, was burning up with mortification.

Flora had scampered upstairs to try on the bundle of clothes and look at the artists' materials that had been presented to her, beautifully wrapped and, Sunny could immediately see, chosen with love and care.

'Coming back down?' Sunny peeped into the room to see her absorbed in one of the colouring books with felt pens neatly laid out on the desk in front of her. 'Your... er...grandmother would be overjoyed to...um...chat with you...'

'Think I'll stay here for a bit,' Flora said chirpily then her smile faded and she chewed her lips thoughtfully. 'It was nice of Nana to bring this stuff back, I guess.'

'Very nice.'

'She says she's got loads of other stuff at her house that she hasn't got round to showing me...'

'She seems very kind,' Sunny said gently and Flora

flushed. 'And you must never worry that you may have offended her if you were a bit confused and quiet when you first came over here,' she continued, 'because she also seems a wise old bird and she'll have understood that everything in life takes time...including getting to know someone... You can't rush stuff like that...'

'I've agreed to go spend the night there.' Flora returned to her colouring. 'So I'll be down in a little while. I'm just going to do a bit more of this and then I'm going to pack a bag.'

Which meant that Sunny was heading back down the stairs without the bolstering support of her little charge. She had no idea what to expect or even where she might find Stefano and his mother but she headed first for the kitchen and, sure enough, there they were. His mother was sitting upright in a chair, with a cup of tea next to her and a little dish of biscuits, while Stefano stood by the French windows, back to the sprawling lawns, the very picture of discomfort.

'My son has not even chosen to introduce us properly,' were her opening words as she briskly stood up, hand outstretched, as though they were being introduced for the first time. 'I am Angela and I know your name is Sunny, but why don't you sit and tell me a bit about yourself?' She shot Stefano a disapproving look. 'Although,' she added, 'I can see for myself that you have had a tremendous influence on the household.' She smiled and Sunny smiled back because under the stern exterior she could sense a genuine innate warmth.

'I...' She looked at Stefano for help and he shot her a rueful, wry smile.

'Stefano tells me that you two have been seeing each other for a little while...'

'He has?' Sunny squeaked, not sure whether to be pleased that he had not tried to erase her out of his life because of her lack of suitability or confused because he hadn't.

'Of course I understand now why he didn't mention you to me...'

'You do?' Sunny sidled over to a chair and sat down because her legs felt like jelly.

'He wanted to be sure...'

'Sure of what?' Sunny asked faintly.

'Sure that you weren't going to be another of those two-week affairs he seems to enjoy having!' She sipped some of her tea and stared thoughtfully at Sunny over the rim of the delicate china cup which he had managed to unearth from somewhere. 'Of course, there was no need for him to tell me that,' she said comfortably. 'I knew the very moment I saw you with Flora...'

'Ah...'

'But we can talk about all this later. For the moment... well...' She turned to Stefano. She was so small and he was so impossibly tall that she had to stare up and up to meet his eyes. 'You will simply have to see about this situation, Stefano. I can't bear the thought of anything precious being ruined and I'm very much afraid that if it's not sorted immediately, that's exactly what will happen. Now, my dear girl—' she patted Sunny on the shoulder and offered another of those wonderfully warm smiles that could melt ice '—I very much look forward to really getting to know you but, for the moment, I'm going to have to hurry off. I only dropped by because this was something of an emergency. My son knows that I absolutely loathe turning up on someone's doorstep when they might be in the middle of doing something and simply can't spare the time...and Flora has agreed to come with me. I can't tell you how overjoyed I am at that. I'll go and fetch her...'

'I'll get her.'

But Angela overruled her son and was already leaving the kitchen, calling behind her that she wanted to see what Flora had in her room so that she could know what sorts of presents to get for her.

'I can't wait to be a proper grandmother,' she said wistfully. 'I never thought the day would come when Flora would actually want to spend time with me. I'll show myself out, Stefano, but I expect you to get back to me about this problem with the house!'

She disappeared, leaving behind her the sort of flat anti-climax that followed a particularly impressive natural event.

Stefano looked at Sunny carefully and cursed himself for the awkward situation in which he now found himself.

Sunny had the stunned look of someone who had been thrown a blinder when they were least expecting it.

'My mother occasionally has that effect on people,' he drawled, leaning on the table, hands gripping the edge. 'She says that's how she managed to get my father. She blew into his life like a whirlwind and, before he knew what was going on, they were blissfully wed. I'm going to change and make sure my mother gets off okay with Flora. I don't want my daughter to suddenly change her mind about going. I'll be back down in ten.'

'Why did she think that we're involved in some kind of *serious relationship*?' was the first thing Sunny asked when, fifteen minutes later, he strolled into the kitchen in a pair of chinos and a white polo shirt.

She'd had a little time to think and it made no sense. He had given her enough cautionary tales about his lack of interest in commitment. He had warned her that he didn't do relationships of any kind. *Once bitten, twice shy* had been his resounding motto since they had started sleeping together.

So why would he have left his mother with the impression that this was something more than it really was? If anything, he should have been keen to make it clear to her that it was nothing of the sort!

'My mother's relationship with Flora, as I may have mentioned to you, has been…fragile. When my ex-wife disappeared to the other side of the world with our daughter, she made it nigh on impossible for me to keep in touch with her and flouted every custody law that had been set in stone as much as she possibly could. As a result, I had very little contact with Flora over the years. Naturally, I employed lawyers to try and remedy the situation but a mother has strong rights to retain custody of children and I had next to no grounds for removing custody from her hands. I was travelling a great deal, rarely in the country for longer than a couple of weeks at a time. Alicia was fully aware of that and used it to her advantage.'

'That must have been awful for you.' She thought that it was heartbreaking for a parent to be denied the opportunity to see his own child. Didn't she know, first-hand, how desperately a child craved the attention of his or her parent?

When she'd accepted this temporary job to babysit Flora, getting past her initial reluctance because the job paid well, little had she known that she would end up engaging like this in their family drama. But then again, she wasn't to know that she would end up sleeping with the guy who had employed her, was she? Against all possible odds. And how could she have guessed that she would have become attached to Flora when she'd never seen herself as particularly interested in children at all?

'Hence the reason why my relationship with my daughter has been understandably strained. The same can be said for my mother, who had even less contact with Flora over the years. Indeed, practically none at all after she was removed to New Zealand.'

'I'm sorry to hear that.'

'She tried hard,' Stefano said, 'and hasn't stopped. Of course, Flora was less…surly with my mother than she has been with me, but there hasn't been any gush of warmth, which my mother has been craving.'

'I guess these things will always take time…er… considering what Flora's been through…'

'And there you have it,' Stefano said in the triumphant voice of a head teacher praising his prized pupil for getting the answer right.

'There you have what?' Sunny was confused.

'The marvel of the breakthrough,' he elaborated with a broad sweep of his hands, a gesture that mesmerised her so that she had to blink herself back to what they were discussing. 'Flora has changed. I have noticed this but the change has not just been with me. It seems that her attitude is changing…that she's beginning to accept that I'm not an evil monster, that this house isn't a loathsome prison, that my mother isn't a wicked witch trying to tempt her with candy canes…and you have been instrumental in this change.'

Sunny flushed with pleasure but hastened to downplay the compliment.

'No!' Stefano halted her in midflow with one raised hand. 'Don't try to deny it! It's the truth.' He tilted his head to one side and looked at her consideringly. 'Before I go any further, you're probably wondering why my mother showed up when I mentioned to you in the past that she's the last person in the world for such displays of spontaneity…'

It dimly occurred to Sunny that they had strayed from the beaten track and her original shock that his mother had misconstrued what was going on, but she nodded in a trance-like way, with the weird feeling of being swept away on a sudden, unexpected and very powerful riptide over which she seemed to have no control.

'There's been a problem with my mother's house in Scotland…'

'I thought your mother lived in London…'

'She does but she hangs onto the family home up there. Sentimental reasons. It's where she and my father lived before he died. She still has many friends there and goes up frequently to visit them.' He waved aside that digression. 'But the house is old and prone to the usual aches and pains of any old property. It seems that there's been something of a flood and certain…possessions have had to be salvaged and moved to another part of the house. At any rate, my mother is now panicked at the thought that things she treasures will be destroyed should the huge leak not be fixed to the right standard.' He shrugged his broad shoulders and relaxed back in the chair. 'She's called on me to take a week off so that I can go up there with her and Flora, of course, to assess the damage and make the workmen know that there's a deadline on doing the job.'

Searing disappointment tore through her but she maintained a bright smile.

This was a 'Dear John' speech. He was off to Scotland and would diplomatically get rid of her before he went so that he could disabuse his mother of whatever misconceptions she was labouring under.

She'd known from the start that longevity wasn't going to be part of what they had—hadn't *wanted* longevity—but she was still…disappointed.

'When do you leave?' she asked politely and Stefano shot her a guarded smile.

'If my mother declares that she wants me to do something, she wants me to do it the day before yesterday. I'll leave first thing tomorrow morning.'

'Of course.' There was an awkward little silence during which Sunny tried to work out how she was going to say what had to be said. 'I'll say goodbye to Flora before I leave and perhaps I could visit her now and again during the holidays? Naturally, when you're not around...'

'What are you talking about?'

'Us...' she said a little tersely, although the smile remained fixed in place. 'This... I do realise that your mother got hold of the wrong end of the stick and you plan on telling her the truth when you have her on your own...'

'And your response to that is to tell me that you're off but you'll visit Flora now and again when I'm not around?'

'You don't have to worry,' Sunny told him stiffly, 'that I'm going to make a nuisance of myself by trying to prolong whatever it is that we have going on between us.'

'I admit my mother was surprised to find...what must have appeared a cosy domestic scene...'

'You should have told her the truth. I felt very awkward at having to act as though this is a proper relationship. I don't believe in lying to people.'

'My mother,' Stefano said bluntly, 'is clearly aware that you have been instrumental in Flora's change of attitude. The last time she and Flora spoke, Flora was, as usual, stiff and unforthcoming. Now, of her own volition, she will be spending the night with my mother...' He allowed a small pause, during which he wondered about the ramifications of what he was on the brink of doing. For every action wasn't there always a *re*action? In other words, *a consequence*?

Sunny didn't say anything. They seemed to be going round in circles, even though she had the uneasy feeling that Stefano's circles made complete sense to him, whilst leaving her totally in the dark.

'This is something she has no desire to jeopardise...'

'I understand that.' Sunny's green eyes were sympathetic although she had no idea what any of this had to do with her.

'And to return to your original question...'

'Yes...about your mother jumping to conclusions...'

'It's not entirely incomprehensible. I've never asked any woman to this house before...'

'You haven't?'

'I tend to keep my private life alive and kicking in London...'

Sunny was beginning to get wild ideas that he had seen something special in her when she remembered, before any stupid wild ideas could take root, that she hadn't come here in the capacity of his girlfriend. She had come here as Flora's babysitter and only after she was here had the whole girlfriend angle come into play.

'And I certainly have never introduced any woman to Flora.'

'Yes, but it was different with me,' Sunny pointed out reasonably. 'I was here *because* of Flora...'

'No matter.' He shrugged while keeping his eyes fixed on her face. 'The scene that presented itself to my mother was not one of the nanny looking after her charge. The three of us were by the pool, which, in my case, is virtually unheard of. Flora was laughing and relaxed, as were you.'

'I can understand that...'

'We're lovers, Sunny,' Stefano interrupted abruptly. 'The order of events might not be quite in line with my mother's conclusions but we're still involved with one another and Flora is part of that equation...'

'So what are you saying?'

'My mother may not have approved of the women I've gone out with but she has trusted me never to allow any of them to overstep the boundaries. In other words, they've been kept in London. She assumes that this relationship is rather more serious because those boundary lines have been overstepped. She's also seeing what she has desperately wanted to see for a while, namely a contender for the role of surrogate mother to Flora and much needed wife for me… Naturally, as we both know, that's not on the agenda…'

'Absolutely not!' Sunny looked appropriately horrified. She thought that his mother might have had a lot more reservations if she knew just how unsuitable she was for her son.

'However…'

'However?' Sunny prompted when he failed to continue and Stefano shot her a speculative look from under his long dark lashes.

'Like I said, the situation, she feels, between herself and her granddaughter is…fragile. And, with a week in Scotland looming, she doesn't want to lose those little gains that have been made…and she feels that the only way that can be assured is if you come.'

It took a few seconds for Sunny to digest what he was saying and then she blinked at him, wondering whether she had misheard what he'd said.

'If *I* come?' Sunny laughed uncertainly. 'I can't come with you to Scotland!'

Stefano banked down a spurt of irritation. This was her way of reminding him that the situation between them was transient and involved nothing beyond having fun in bed. He couldn't stop the flare of his libido when he thought about *just how much fun.*

This was *exactly* the sort of response that should have made his day. A sexy, responsive woman who knew the parameters of what they had and was comfortable with them…a woman who was on precisely the same wavelength as he was. He'd had more than his fair share over the years of women who had ended up wanting more than he was capable of giving and to be with one like Sunny should have heralded the sort of blessed relief that a breeze brought on a stiflingly hot day.

He was annoyed with himself to discover that the blessed breezy relief was absent.

She hadn't even toyed with the thought of coming with him! Hadn't even given it house room! Shouldn't she be *thrilled to death* that he'd asked her? 'If it's about taking time off work, then I'm sure that wouldn't be a problem,' he gritted. 'Even the most dedicated and ambitious of staff need to take time off now and again...'

'It's not about taking time off work,' Sunny said jerkily.

What was it about? Really?

She knew what. It was about the dangers of sinking further and faster into this little family unit that didn't belong to her and never would. She'd never anticipated any of this and she felt as though she'd been taken over, as though her days were now spent in anticipation of the evenings and being with Stefano and Flora. Having spent a lifetime on the outside of family units like this, it scared her just how much she enjoyed being inside one—inside this one. This wasn't her family unit and she was just a stranger peering in through the open door.

The thought of going to Scotland, of getting to know his mother, would be just another dangerous and seductive step closer to finding all of this...indispensable. It was a terrifying prospect because nothing in life should ever be indispensable.

'Then what is it about?' Stefano asked, his voice cooler.

'I don't think it's a good idea if I get any more involved... I mean, this was just supposed to be a one-night stand... wasn't it? Also, it's not fair to your mother, is it? I mean, if she thinks that this is something it isn't...'

'I understand your reservations.' Stefano's voice was more clipped than he had intended and he raked his fingers through his hair. 'Of course, it would be preferable if she wasn't labouring under the illusion that this is anything significant, but there's more at stake here than my mother getting the wrong end of the stick.'

Labouring under the illusion that this is anything significant... Those words got stuck in Sunny's brain and played round and round on a loop. She was *insignificant*. Whichever way you looked at it, that was the upshot. *She was insignificant and didn't mean anything at all outside good sex and a bit of fun.*

'Sorry?' She surfaced to find that she had missed what he'd been saying.

'I can't force you to come to Scotland,' Stefano said heavily. 'If the anticipated one-night stand is in danger of outstaying its welcome, then by all means I will tell my mother that it's over, that it was never anything serious anyway...'

'And it isn't.' Sunny was trying to get her head around the prospect of never seeing Stefano again.

'But if I tell her that this is over, then it's over. No visits to my daughter and no second thoughts. Even when I acknowledged my attraction to you, I was reluctant to act on it because I didn't want to risk a setback in my new-found relationship with Flora. We break up and you disappear, because having you knocking around now and again will only muddy the waters. I can't stop you emailing but that would have to be the size of it. Ready for that?'

And he wouldn't have a problem with that. There hadn't been a hitch in his voice when he had flatly stated that fact. He didn't want it to end just yet but he was a pragmatist first and foremost. If it ended, it ended.

'This is the first time Flora has agreed to do anything with my mother since she came to this country and my mother is anxious that she doesn't pull away when they're in Scotland. Children don't tend to think rationally and they don't look at the bigger picture or necessarily see the consequences of their actions. Your presence, I think, would be of great help…but I can't force you.'

Sunny was feverishly thinking over the gauntlet he had thrown down. Was she ready to go cold turkey? Was she ready to walk away and never look back? 'But surely your mother will find out sooner or later, when this is all over, that it was never serious…'

'Every day, with any luck, her relationship with Flora will strengthen…'

'So she won't really care if I'm no longer around because she will have the sort of relationship she wants with her granddaughter. And I guess, when she finds out the sort of person I am, she'll be mightily relieved that you're no longer involved with me…'

'The *sort of person*?'

'The sort that comes from the wrong side of the tracks.' She hated herself for even mentioning something as silly as that. She had always been determined that she would not carry a chip on her shoulder because of her background. It was true that she kept herself to herself, but that was force of habit, instilled from an early age. Her past had shaped her and for that she would always be grateful.

So why on earth insinuate that she would be seen as not good enough for him?

And why the heck did it matter anyway?

'You're assuming that my mother is a snob,' Stefano said coolly.

'I shouldn't have said that. It honestly doesn't matter anyway,' she tacked on. She took a deep breath and looked him squarely in the face. 'I'll see if I can take the week off work and if I can, then fine, I'll come.'

Stefano only knew that he had been tense when he felt himself relax. Of course, he dismissed, he would be tense. The sudden appearance of his mother and the conclusions she had mistakenly jumped to had altered events and, much as he didn't like the fact that she thought that he and Sunny were in some sort of *serious relationship*, he liked even less thinking that she would be fearful and nervous about Flora being in Scotland and apprehensive in case his daughter did an about-turn and decided to re-treat back into the shell from which she had only so very recently emerged.

He recognised that he wasn't ready to say goodbye to the frankly stupendous sex they shared, but that, he firmly told himself, was not a cause for tension. Had she decided that she couldn't go through with the minor pretence for the sake of his mother, then letting her go would have been regrettable but no more difficult than with any of the women he had slept with in the past.

'Are your reasons purely altruistic?' he murmured, with a slow, lazy smile that made her toes curl and brought hec-tic colour to her cheeks. He hadn't meant to ask that and he grudgingly acknowledged that the question, at least in part, stemmed from the fact that he had been disconcerted and taken aback by the ease with which she appeared to have thought about dumping what they had.

He almost laughed at the notion of a man like him re-quiring reassurance!

'Of course they are!' But she smiled and dipped her eyes, breath catching in her throat as he stood up to pull his chair closer to hers so that their knees were touching.

There were times when just the hot burn of his eyes on her was enough to make her wet for him, was almost enough to start the slow tremor of an orgasm.

This was one of those times.

'So...are you telling me that I don't figure in your decision-making process at all? Because a man could be hurt...'

'Maybe you do figure...a tiny bit...'

'I feel I shall have to show you just how much I actually do figure… We have the house all to ourselves… We could continue the swimming lessons but without the annoying encumbrance of a swimsuit.'

It sounded wildly decadent. Oddly, for someone whose life had been disjointed and challenging, Sunny was not wild or decadent. Her mother had been a steep learning curve in *how not to be*. Short skirts and small clothes and random men…never mind the drugs and the drink… Sunny had rebelled by being the complete opposite. Restraint, self-control and background clothes had been her way of keeping shut the lid of Pandora's box. If she cracked at all, who knew what might happen? She was, after all, her mother's daughter. That, she thought, had been the way her subconscious had worked, which just went to disprove Stefano's theory that black and white was the safest vision to choose. Because she was living in the grey area now and loving it. Swimming naked in a pool wasn't going to turn her into her mother. Swimming naked in a pool was just going to be *fun* and she could see that in closing herself off from anything that could remotely be interpreted as *unsafe* she had also closed herself off from all sorts of experiences that were enjoyable.

She laughed, her bright green eyes gleaming as they met his.

'I've never done anything like that in my life before,' she confided, allowing him to pull her to her feet and then falling against him and staying there, arms around his waist as she stared up at his dangerously handsome face. 'I've always played it safe…'

'Skinny-dipping isn't anything outrageous,' Stefano told her drily, liking the bone-deep sincerity in everything she said and did, the absolute lack of artifice.

'You'd be surprised how outrageous it is for me.' Sunny laughed and he bent his head to kiss the side of her mouth, then covered her mouth with his, deepening the kiss until she was squirming in his embrace.

He could have taken her right here, right now. His erection was rock-hard and he figured that a dip in the pool might take care of that little problem, at least temporarily. Because he wanted to enjoy her at his leisure.

'It turns me on to know that I'm the guy who's going to take you places you've never been,' he confessed in a driven murmur.

And when the trip's over, you'll return to where you belong and...where will that leave me? The sudden prospect of him disappearing out of her life as suddenly as he had entered it gave her a sickening, swooping feeling in the pit of her stomach. She didn't know what it meant and she didn't want to analyse it, but she did know that it was something unwelcome and something he should not suspect. Instinct told her that.

'And I'm glad you are.' Sunny sighed, angling her body so that he could work his hand over her flat stomach to caress between her legs, cupping her over her underwear and rubbing his finger so that the cotton of her briefs pushed into her wetness. 'I mean... I was innocent before I met you...'

'And now?'

'I feel like I've...joined the human race. I feel like I've learned that taking chances isn't always a bad thing and won't always lead to rack and ruin.' She laughed and reached up to kiss him, pulling him into her and pressing hard against him.

'So you're now going to be wild and reckless...' Stefano wasn't sure why he found that concept so deeply unappealing.

'Not wild and reckless,' Sunny said honestly, 'but maybe less careful. I mean...if it can feel this good with you, how will it feel when I'm with my for ever guy...?'

It would be brilliant. Since John, she had resigned herself to the life of being a career woman and had not been
unhappy with her decision, but everything had changed.
Stefano had unlocked the passionate, responsive woman
in her, the woman who could bring the full package to
any relationship she would go on to have, any relationship with a guy who would be her soulmate.

Of course it made sense that if she could feel this good
with Stefano, who was just passing through her life, then
it would be beyond good with the man who would be staying for keeps. She tried to imagine what this guy might
look like and the dark, sexy image of Stefano's face swam
into focus and stayed there.

Stefano thought that there was such a thing as *too much
honesty*. Was it really on to talk about his successor even
though their relationship was still ongoing? He felt the
sharp jab of undiluted *jealousy* towards this non-existent
fictional character who had yet to appear on the scene.

It was laughable.

Except he found that he wasn't laughing.

'Who knows?' he asked in a rough, husky undertone.
'Maybe you'll find that it just won't be as good...' And if
the challenge, stupid though it was, was to prove that to
her, to take her to heights she couldn't conceivably reach
with anyone else, then who was he to back down from
the challenge?

CHAPTER NINE

BEING IN SCOTLAND showed Sunny just how much she had forgotten about the art of pure relaxation.

She'd been apprehensive about the trip. Even when, the day after she had agreed to go, she found herself climbing into the helicopter that would make short work of the trip to Perthshire, she was still questioning the wisdom of sinking even deeper into Stefano and his family.

She'd almost half hoped that she would be told that the company couldn't spare her, but in fact she had talked to Katherine, who had been delighted that she was having some time off.

'Going anywhere nice?' she had asked and Sunny had guiltily been as creative with the truth as she could be without resorting to any outright lies.

Stefano might have said that he wasn't interested in Katherine, but was Katherine interested in *him*? She couldn't see how the other woman could fail to be and she had no desire to step on any toes or instigate any bad feeling between them which would follow her through her career at the company.

Especially when you considered that whatever she and Stefano had, permanence wasn't part of the equation.

She could also understand why his mother might feel apprehensive about the fragile seedlings of the relationship she was building with her granddaughter. Flora had arrived in a new family, full of resentment and dislike, and Angela Gunn was cautious about believing that there had been a turnaround that wouldn't disappear as fast as it had surfaced.

And anyway, she had thought with a spurt of reckless abandon, sleeping with Stefano was the first thing she had ever done on wild impulse and why shouldn't she enjoy it while she could? She'd already thrown caution to the winds when she had climbed into bed with him, so what was the point in trying to play it safe now?

His mother thought that they were involved in something serious, and she was uneasy with that misconception, but they *were* involved and going to Scotland would be…a bit like having a holiday with him. A mini-break.

Of course, he hadn't *planned* it as a mini-break, but still…

She strolled to the window and looked down at the acres upon acres of land that surrounded the country house. It wasn't yet seven and everywhere seemed to breathe with the excitement of a new day dawning.

The helicopter ride had given her a feel for the spectacular natural beauty that belonged to Scotland and a breathtaking first view of Perthshire. Angela had fondly told her that it was nicknamed 'Big Tree Country' and it hadn't been hard to see why.

From above, as the helicopter buzzed and swayed like an angry wasp, all she could see were the rich, varied greens of the verdant forests and rolling, rising hills. There were waterfalls there as well, she had been told, hidden in the depths of the trees, and castles and abbeys and fortresses. It was like looking down at a film set, and she almost expected to see fantastic primeval armies rising up from the undergrowth, surging forward on white stallions, heading for some mythical showdown.

And, over the past five days, it hadn't disappointed. The spaces were vast and open and the scenery was dramatic, shorn of the trappings of civilisation, raw and intensely beautiful. Even the air seemed different, cleaner somehow. London, in comparison, seemed like a tinsel town with too many people chasing too many things that didn't matter very much.

The flooding was in one small wing of the country house and Stefano had taken charge as soon as they had arrived, quizzing the head guy about what was being done, getting in touch with the insurers, bringing in a top chartered surveyor and a team of men who began work almost immediately with ruthless efficiency.

Flora, enchanted by the open spaces, which, she had confided, reminded her of New Zealand, had immersed herself in exploring the woodland, with Angela for company.

'She knows a lot of stuff about plants,' Flora had told Sunny the evening before with a shrug. 'It's interesting. I told her that I could Google all of that on my phone but she said it isn't the same as touching and seeing the real thing. She's going to teach me how to press flowers.'

'Maybe I'll tag along,' Sunny had said, because Stefano tended to work during the day, making sure that he was in the vicinity to check up on the guys working on the plumbing problems, while Sunny couldn't get her head round doing any work at all, even though she had dutifully brought her laptop computer with her.

So she'd done a bit of exploring of her own. She had started with the house, having obtained full permission from Angela to go wherever she wanted to go. She had gone into every room and gaped and gasped at all of them. It was an old house, dating back to the eighteenth century, but it had been very cleverly modernised so the old blended with the new in seamless perfection. Wood panelling combined with soft grey and taupe…antique fine silk rugs did justice to über-comfortable modern Italian

furniture…and the kitchen was a marvel of high-tech mo-
dernity, save for the bottle-green double Aga.

'It's huge for just your mother to visit now and again,
isn't it?' She now turned to Stefano, who was sprawled
on the bed, sheets and blanket half covering his nakedness, leaving just enough on show to remind her of the
night before, when they had spent at least a couple of
hours languorously making love. They had touched one
another everywhere and she quivered as she recalled the
feel of his mouth between her legs, nuzzling and licking
and exciting, taking her to the limits of a wrenching orgasm, shuddering against his mouth as she had arched up.

Wetness pooled between her legs. She still couldn't
credit that she had met someone who could turn her on
just by looking at her.

Stefano grinned. After his divorce, he'd made it a rule
never to sleep the night with any woman and it surprised
him just how comfortable he felt going to sleep with her
next to him and waking up with her next to him.

He liked the fact that he could reach out and touch
her naked body whenever he wanted, whatever the time
of night. He liked cupping her breast, playing with her
nipple, hearing her soft little moans as she enjoyed him
when she was still half asleep. Her legs would open and
it had been hugely arousing a couple of nights previously
when he had slipped his finger along her crease to find
the little bud of her clitoris and she had come against
his hand without really waking up at all, or rather waking up just sufficiently to wriggle close to him, eyes still
closed, where she had promptly settled back into deep
sleep while he had stroked her hair and her back and her
smooth, slender thighs.

'The early morning light is doing incredible things to
your body…' he murmured, eyes flaring as they took in
the long, supple lines of her naked body.

He'd only just recovered from the surprise of being put in the same room as her by his very traditional parent and he certainly hadn't bought the excuse that all the other rooms still needed to be aired. Like hell they did. His mother had convinced herself that Sunny was *the one* and he had been more than happy to go along with that, thereby saving himself a fruitless conversation denying it, plus having the added bonus of Sunny in his bed without having to resort to night-time subterfuge.

'Do you ever think about anything but sex?' But she was grinning back at him as she turned round to perch against the window ledge, resting her bottom on her hands.

It was cold outside but warm in the bedroom, where the heating was timed to come on for an hour every morning to take the early morning chill out of the air.

'I closed a deal yesterday.' He propped himself up on one elbow and gazed at her. Her legs were lightly crossed and her pert little breasts were thrust forward in a pose that was innocent and provocative at the same time. 'I thought about the nuts and bolts of that for a while… Come back to bed…it's too early to be up and about…'

'You once let slip that you're *up and about* by six every morning.'

'That was before I discovered the pleasures of staying in bed when the other occupant of the bed happens to be you.' He patted the space next to him and Sunny strolled back towards the bed but she didn't slip under the covers. Instead, she knelt on the bed, hands pressed between her thighs.

'Let's go for an early-morning walk.'

Stefano looked at the enthusiasm on her face and thought how different it was from the cautious expression she had worn when he had first laid eyes on her, which had been way too adult for her age.

She looked…young, carefree. She laughed. She'd confessed to him that when she'd been told to babysit Flora in the office she'd had no idea what to do with a kid because she herself had bypassed all the normal experiences of childhood, and so she'd stuck her in front of some old legal photocopied cases and let her loose, little knowing that her very lack of effort would provide the glue that would cement her relationship with Flora.

'Is it wise for a workaholic to go on early-morning walks?' He pulled her down so that she toppled onto him, soft breasts squashed against his chest, and then he shifted so that he positioned her lengthwise over him.

Sex, Sunny thought. It really was all he thought about when he was with her. They talked, they laughed but, in the end, the only thing that really mattered to him was the touching that they did.

She tried not to dwell on that but, for some reason, it hurt to think about it now and she immediately shoved the thought to the back of her head. This was all about fun and what *wasn't* fun was wasting time analysing the pros and cons of what they were doing.

'Very wise,' she recommended.

'I'll do a trade…' Stefano caressed the smooth skin of her buttocks, gently easing her legs apart so that his erection was pushed hard against her belly. 'Your glorious body and, yes…I'll give you the early morning walk…'

'So, to get back to your question…' Stefano couldn't remember the last time he had strolled through the woodland that surrounded the country house. Perhaps when he had been a kid, when he'd taken the same pleasure in exploring the woods as his daughter now did, marvelling when he came upon streams and cascading waterfalls.

Actually, he couldn't quite remember when he had taken time out at all… Oh, the odd weekend here and there in the past with a woman, but nothing that had felt as relaxing as these past few days had felt.

He slung his arm over her shoulder. 'Big house for one occasional occupant. You're quite right, of course, and this latest near disaster has finally convinced my mother that the time is right to sell—buy something in the city which she can visit whenever she wants to so that she can keep connected with her friends in the area. Something a lot less high maintenance. She's been reluctant to sell before because not only did she spend her married life here with my father, but the house carries a lot of family history on my father's side. But, at the end of the day, practicality is what matters.'

'Is that why she and Flora are planning on going into Edinburgh for the day?'

'Possibly,' Stefano said drily. 'She claims it's because she wants to treat Flora to lunch in one of the most beautiful cafés in one of the most beautiful cities in the world, but I wouldn't drop dead with shock if she pays a visit to an estate agent. One of her friends owns an agency specialising in upmarket places. She and I have only spoken about this a couple of times but that's been enough to establish that we have very different tastes when it comes to a suitable property for her. I want an apartment. Low maintenance, no land to worry about, no problems with pesky leaks. My mother, on the other hand, would like something, as she calls it, *with character.*'

Sunny laughed. 'That's because she loves this place and probably wants to replicate it but on a much smaller scale.'

Stefano had no need to ask Sunny how she knew how his mother felt about Nevis Manor. She and his mother had clicked. They enjoyed one another's company and, somewhat disconcertingly, Sunny had actually told his mother about her background.

'She asked me about my family,' she had told Stefano

on night number two, 'and I wasn't going to lie to her. It's bad enough that she thinks there's more to us than there actually is without feeding her more half-truths.'

His mother saw Sunny as a candidate for the role of his wife. Maybe she was startled at the choice he had made. Who knew? His long line of transient girlfriends had hardly been intellectually gifted and their charms had certainly never been kept under wraps, hidden beneath faded jeans and old sweats. The mere fact that Sunny was *so different* on every level would have persuaded his mother as to the authenticity of their relationship. Throw his daughter into the mix and you got the perfect scenario.

So she would have been predisposed to love Sunny.

And Sunny? She had told his mother about her painful past and, as he could have told her himself, she had still been accepted, for his mother was anything but one of those shallow snobs who only accepted people according to the elevation of their backgrounds.

Sunny, vulnerable deep inside where no one was allowed to see past the efficient, controlled exterior, would have been predisposed to love his mother for her lack of judgemental criticism.

When you thought about it, it was a match made in Heaven.

But he was not her type, not for any sort of future that was long-term. And she was not his type. Dig a little and you got the soft romantic who really did believe in love, whatever her background and whatever she said to the contrary.

They were having fun and he got a headache when he thought about disappointing his mother eventually with the truth. But by then, he thought, she and Flora would have formed a bond strong enough to withstand the disappearance of the glue that came in the form of Sunny.

He frowned and shoved past the way his mind closed down when he thought about her vanishing out of his life.

'So no mother and no daughter when we get back to the house,' he mused thoughtfully, reverting to the comfort zone that was tried and tested territory. 'I'm beginning to think that I might be inclined to take the entire day off work...'

With the leaks nearly fixed, most of the workmen had left for other jobs and he made sure that the three busily doing the last finishing touches to some copper pipes were firmly engaged in what they were doing and that they had no pressing questions they needed to ask.

'Because I have to work on some important business,' he told them, which made Sunny grin from where she was standing, leaning against the wall, just out of sight, 'and under no circumstances am I to be disturbed.'

There wasn't a workman on the face of the earth who wouldn't have made sure to stay firmly out of sight until otherwise told and, sure enough, they hit the bedroom safe in the knowledge that they were not going to be interrupted.

Morning sex...that would extend to lunchtime sex... and then early afternoon sex...

That was a first for Sunny and she felt heady and decadent when she thought about it.

There had been so many *firsts* with him that she had lost count.

They held hands as they headed up the grand curved staircase and it felt wonderfully intimate. There had been no need to check to see whether his mother and Flora had gone. In fact, they had seen the chauffeur-driven car swing round the bend in the avenue at a little after eight-thirty when they had been returning to the house.

It was easily a two-hour drive to Edinburgh and lunch had been planned.

'The day belongs to us,' Stefano murmured, closing the bedroom door behind them. 'What a shame there are workmen on the grounds or we could have free rein of the house without the inconvenience of having to wear any clothes. Maybe another time.'

'Not if you're planning on selling...' But her heart skipped a treacherous beat because that was possibly the first time he had ever let slip any mention of anything happening at a future date.

'True.' He ushered her towards the bed, bodies shuffling as though they were doing a slow dance to no music.

Had he really told her that he'd bring her back to Nevis Manor? He hadn't even planned on bringing her here the first time! On the other hand, he rather liked playing with images of them strolling round the massive estate and house in nothing but their birthday suits...making love wherever and whenever they chose...

He wondered what it would *feel* like to sit enfolding her in his arms in front of the enormous ancient fireplace in the formal sitting room, in the depth of winter with the snow falling outside and everywhere as silent as an indrawn breath.

He shook his head, clearing it of the fantastical thought.

Instead, he eased her down on the bed, back onto the tangle of sheets they had only just left when they had gone for their early-morning walk.

They made love slowly, taking their time, and then had a bath together in the old-fashioned tub with the clawed feet that could fit them both easily. Without having to surface for anyone or be anywhere, they lingered in there, Sunny quivering as he drew her close to soap her, every last inch of her. Then he towel-dried her, every last inch of her, and undid all the good work by kneeling in front of her, parting her legs and tasting her until she couldn't control the orgasm that left her panting and on fire.

'Breakfast in bed,' he suggested, but stayed her when she would have joined him to make something to bring up to the bedroom. With advance notice, they would have had their usual cook in to prepare meals but his mother, Stefano had told her, had decided that it would be more casual and nicer for Flora if they mucked in and did the cooking themselves, which they had been doing for the past few days.

'You're going to *bring* me breakfast in bed?' Sunny laughed.

'While I'm in the kitchen, I'll make a few calls.'

'So, it's actually about getting a bit of work in,' she teased, reclining on the bed, her vibrant hair spilling over the pillows.

But she still couldn't imagine that he was the type to have ever made breakfast in bed for a woman. Even if he wanted to use the opportunity to slip a few business calls in while the omelette was cooking or the bread was in the toaster… He was making an exception for her and she couldn't staunch the swell of pleasure that gave her.

If she could have bottled the day and sprayed a bit on herself whenever she wanted to feel good then she would have, because the day that passed so quickly was practically perfect.

They drifted into the garden for a picnic lunch, Stefano having dispatched the workmen so that they could have uninterrupted privacy. They shared a bottle of icy-cold white wine and, feeling pleasantly tipsy, Sunny dozed on one of the padded recliners by the pool until she was awakened by Stefano nuzzling her breasts through her T-shirt and they made love right there, outside, which was another first.

'I'm not sure I can walk a straight line,' she giggled when, at a little after four, they made their way back to the house, dumping the lunch remnants in the kitchen before heading upstairs.

'Lunchtime wine can be a killer.' Stefano grinned.

'In which case, why did you bring the bottle? Did you want me to end up not being able to walk a straight line?'

'You won't need to walk a line, straight or otherwise, when you're in bed with me tonight…' He wished they were having the house to themselves for the remainder of the evening. He'd enjoyed the freedom of wandering around semi-clad, knowing that he could reach out and take her whenever he wanted and she, likewise, could do the same.

Their eyes tangled. She was laughing, looking up at him, cheeks flushed, expression drowsy and happy, *unguarded*.

And Stefano felt something sharp tug in the pit of his stomach.

He hadn't signed up for this. In fact, he had made sure to lay down all the rules and regulations that would have warned her against trying to get him to sign up for this. Because what he saw was something he didn't want to see. He didn't want to see that she had fallen in love with him. He didn't want that complication. He'd only ever wanted, from the start, a no-strings-attached affair. It might be an affair with shades of differences to the affairs he usually had, but it was *still an affair*. The *no-strings-attached* aspect was *still* part of the deal.

But her lips were just so damned inviting and, as though recognising some barely visible shift in him, she lowered her eyes and drew back fractionally, although she was still smiling. The unguarded, open expression was no longer there when she looked at him again.

'I should walk my unsteady line to the bathroom and have a shower.' She turned away and began rummaging in a drawer for a change of clothes. 'Your mother and Flora will be back pretty soon,' she threw over her shoulder. 'The last thing I want would be for Flora to come bound-

ing into the bedroom and find me in a state of undress!'
She'd opened herself up, allowed him to see what she had
barely been aware of thinking herself, and now…

She scarpered into the bathroom and braced herself
against the back of the door for a couple of seconds.

When did it happen? When did she go and do the unthinkable? When did she fall in love with him? Was it
when he'd been making her laugh? Making her think?
When he'd been getting under her skin so that she'd been
forced to stretch herself in her outlook on so many things?

She knew it hadn't been when he'd been touching her
because touching her, however expert his touch might be,
would not have got her here, to this place. Of utter, crush-
ing vulnerability. The very place she had spent her life
fighting to steer clear of, the place her mother had spent
a lifetime occupying.

She couldn't think of walking away from him without
something inside her twisting in pain, and she cravenly
wondered whether she had misinterpreted her fleeting
impression that a shutter had dropped over his eyes—
that he'd *noticed*.

Why would he have noticed anything? she feverishly
told herself. Men were notoriously obtuse when it came
to interpreting women's emotions. She knew that. She'd
read it. It was practically common knowledge. And she
wasn't going to test the waters by saying anything. How
on earth could she, without declaring her love? Without
him knowing just how stupid she'd been?

She just wanted to enjoy him for a little bit longer. They
had another day and a half in Scotland. What was wrong
in enjoying that small window before she broke it off?
Because she would have to break it off. She knew that.

She felt scared. Scared of her own feelings, scared of
the way her life had careered off the tracks. The signposts

that had guided her all her life had been snatched away and for the first time in her adult life she felt truly lost.

Because he didn't love her.

He didn't love her and he would never love her and he had kept his head firmly screwed on while she had been carelessly losing hers.

She had gone into this with her eyes wide open, believing herself to be invincible because she knew the lie of the land. She couldn't possibly get wrapped up with him because he wasn't the sort of guy she could ever fall for in a million years. He was a being from another planet. He would be her reckless adventure and that would be that. The theories had all been spot on. It was just that Life had stepped in and screwed everything up.

She expected to find him sprawled on the bed, waiting for her, but in fact he was nowhere in the room when she emerged, fully dressed, from the bathroom half an hour later.

Relieved, because it gave her some time to brace herself for when she next faced him, knowing what she now knew, Sunny headed downstairs to find that Angela and Flora were already home. They had become accustomed to gravitating to the kitchen and they were both there, along with an elderly couple and an elegant woman roughly the same age as Angela. Flora sprang to her feet as soon as Sunny walked into the kitchen so that she could regale her with stories about Edinburgh.

In between, she was introduced to the couple and was vaguely aware that they were something to do with the church but that went over her head because the other woman was the estate agent Stefano had jokingly referred to and Sunny was amused to think that his mother had dragged her friend back to the house as moral support in building her case for a house with a garden instead of a functional apartment.

There was tea—cakes that had been bought from 'the best bakery in the world', according to Flora... Sunny was aware of Stefano walking in at some point but she was busy chatting to Eileen, Angela's friend, asking her about the housing market in Scotland and comparing prices to the property in London.

She was aware of the deep, sexy timbre of Stefano's voice, slightly behind her to one side, and when, after an hour or so, Flora yawned, Sunny leaped to her feet and offered to take her off to bed with some warm milk and a sandwich because they had, as she had heard in great detail, had a fancy lunch in the city.

She wasn't aware of the looks exchanged as she headed out of the kitchen twenty minutes later, a drooping Flora holding her hand.

'Darling, if I've disappeared before you come back down,' Angela trilled, 'then I shall see you in the morning!'

Which initiated a round of goodbyes and 'must see you again soon...'

Standing just behind Stefano, who had also turned and was smiling, seemingly as relaxed as could be, she had to fight the urge to run her fingers lovingly through his hair, to kiss the nape of his neck, to feel the press of his warm skin on her lips. She thought that if she were blindfolded, she would have been able to identify him simply by touch, so well had she committed his body to her mind.

His body and everything else. His laughter, the way he frowned when he was thinking and distracted, the way he slowed right down to accommodate his mother, the patience and interest he took in everything Flora did, the lazy teasing in his eyes that could make her feel on the point of combustion.

How was it that she hadn't recognised the signs of love creeping up behind her, like a thief in the night?

How was it that she hadn't thought to question the way she had found herself being sucked into Stefano's life? A temporary babysitter would have shown up, done what she was being paid to do and left. A temporary babysitter, only in it for the money, would have never become involved in his back story, would never have let herself be moved by his daughter. A disinterested babysitter might have fancied him but wouldn't have taken it further.

Sunny could see now that she might be cynical about a lot and might have had to grow up much faster walking a far tougher road than most of her contemporaries, but when it came to love she still had all her illusions intact. She could see now that she would never have felt inclined to sleep with him *just because he was hot*. For her, lust couldn't be disentangled from feelings. Underneath her frank acceptance of their differences and incompatibilities, there had still been something potent and irresistible that had drawn her to him and that something had not been the way he looked.

What a mess.

For once, she was distracted with Flora, only half listening to her childish ramblings about what they had seen in Edinburgh. She had acquired a thirst for castles now and had Googled a list of them she wanted to visit when they returned to England.

Sunny agreed with everything. She knew that *she* wouldn't be visiting any castles with Flora. She had a day and a half left with her little ward and then…

It was ages before the night-time routine was done and dusted. Flora had been overexcited after her day out and not, as she usually was, happy to settle herself with one of her books. She had wanted to talk and so it was late by the time Sunny eventually headed back down to the kitchen for something light to eat before bed.

She had no idea where Stefano was. Usually, he popped

up to say goodnight to his daughter, a routine to which Flora was gradually warming, but he had not appeared tonight and she wondered whether he had become embroiled in the deal he had been earlier working on.

She found him in the kitchen and she stilled, standing by the door, because he was drinking.

A bottle of whisky was in front of him and he was sprawled over two chairs, reclining in one with his long legs propped up on another. He slanted his head to look at her and took one long, considering mouthful of whisky and then stared at her over the rim of the glass until she smiled nervously and said something about Flora finally getting to sleep after her exciting day, and wasn't she thrilled about all the castles in Scotland…

'Did you know?' Stefano swirled the glass in his hand and stared absently at the brown liquid before taking another mouthful.

Sunny's heart slowed then picked up a pace. 'Did I know…*what*?'

CHAPTER TEN

'THAT MY MOTHER's good friend and overseer of many a wedding ceremony was going to be here for a little informal social visit...'

'No,' Sunny stammered. 'How on earth would I have known that?' She didn't know whether to enter the kitchen or turn tail and run so she remained where she was, dithering and hovering in the doorway.

The man looking at her was not the man she had fallen in love with. This man was a stranger with cool, assessing eyes and a shuttered expression that sent chills racing up and down her spine.

'Well, you do seem to know pretty much everything my mother has been getting up to from one day to the next.'

'I didn't ask to come up here, Stefano!' Sunny shot back defensively. She wrapped her arms around her and walked woodenly into the kitchen to perch on the edge of one of the chairs, her body as stiff. 'You've been working during the days and seeing about the flooding situation in the west wing. What was I supposed to do? Hide out in the bedroom and ignore your mother and Flora?'

Stefano flushed darkly. Of course she had a point. But had he banked on her getting so close to his mother in such a short space of time? Had he anticipated that his mother's assumptions would become so indelibly fixed in the space of a few short days? He had known that his mother was seeing what she wanted to see—a relationship in the making that would give him the wife she felt he needed and the mother figure his daughter probably would need in due course.

But the local parish priest's arrival had come as a shock to the system.

He'd understood very quickly that his mother had gone beyond nurturing fond notions about some fairy-tale, happy-ever-after ending for him, with Sunny in the starring role.

She'd started making concrete plans and that wasn't going to do. He'd been lazy and taken what he wanted and there were consequences attached to that—consequences he would have to eliminate immediately.

He recalled that expression on Sunny's face when she'd looked at him, all flushed and open and drowsily unguarded.

Suddenly restless, he stood up, flexing his stiffened muscles, and scowled down at the empty whisky glass.

The kitchen felt small, oppressive…claustrophobic. He had a very strong urge to hit something—the wall, the granite counter, *anything*.

And he needed to create some physical distance between them because just standing too close to her was an extreme challenge to his willpower and self-control.

'When you left the room with Flora,' he said abruptly, 'I was treated to some not so subtle questions about my intentions towards you.'

'Your intentions?'

'Along the lines of whether I planned on committing to this relationship… Our good parish priest saw fit to wax lyrical on the advantages of marriage.'

Sunny's face was flaming red. Did he think that she had somehow manoeuvred, with his mother, to bring the parish priest to the house so that they could all wage a campaign to get him to commit to her? Was that what he was saying? That his mother had misinterpreted the seriousness of the relationship and she, Sunny, had taken advantage of that to try and wheedle herself into a position he had specifically warned her against?

Anger flared through her in a red-hot wave and she clenched her fists on her lap.

'And you think I had something to do with that?' she queried quietly. The colour had drained from her face and her bright green eyes were blazing with suppressed rage. And he didn't look away. He just carried on staring at her, not backing down one iota with his crazy, misguided assumptions.

Yet why should she be surprised that he had rushed into suspecting the worst of her? He wasn't emotionally invested the way she was. He was in it for the fun and the sex. Sure, they got along, but she suspected that he was the kind of guy who would get along with all the women he slept with. Until he got bored of them or they outstayed their welcome, in which case he would look at them rather like he was looking at her now—coolly, assessingly...with the eyes of a man in retreat.

For a few seconds, Stefano didn't say anything. He knew that there was no option but to pull the plug on this. His mother might be determined that he married but that was not on his agenda and most likely never would be. What was the point of learning curves if you didn't actually learn from them? He didn't have it in him to return the type of emotion a woman like Sunny needed and deserved. He was empty inside.

'Yes,' he said. 'Yes, it did cross my mind because you're in love with me.'

Sunny inhaled sharply. A thousand thoughts rushed through her mind at breakneck speed but she knew that there was no way she could deny the truth of that. There was a certainty in his voice that deprived her of the option of trying to deny what he had said.

'I didn't know your mother would bring Father Leary.' She tilted her chin at a defiant angle and Stefano almost smiled because that just seemed to sum her up. Stubborn, honest, defiant, never walking away from the tricky stuff. She'd fallen in love with him and she hadn't banked on that. Didn't make a difference but he could acknowledge that.

Hell, he'd miss her.

He almost found himself wishing that she'd lied, refuted what he'd said, laughed that laugh of hers and told him that he couldn't have been further from the truth.

He almost found himself wishing that he could have carried on kidding himself that she was as uninvolved emotionally as he was. He looked at her and let the silence gather around them, dense and thick, until she finally sighed and looked away because she didn't want him to see that her eyes had glazed over.

She wasn't going to deny the truth and she wasn't going to pretend that she regretted anything. She didn't.

'I won't apologise,' she said with a little shrug, eyes still firmly averted. She blinked rapidly and took a deep breath before looking him squarely in the face. 'I didn't even think it was a possibility that I could fall for someone like you. You're nothing like the kind of guy I imagined handing my heart to.'

No, that person had been someone like John and she should have put two and two together and realised that John might have been perfect on paper but he had never excited her. Stefano had excited her from the very first second she had laid eyes on him and that had been telling because that spark of physical response, the very spark she had told herself meant nothing, had meant everything. Without it, it didn't matter how much sense a person made, how *theoretically right* they were, it was never going to work because love was so much more than what was *theoretically right*.

'You deserve a guy who can give you what you want.' Stefano felt as though he was swallowing glass but it was the truth. 'That guy isn't me and was never going to be and, for the record, I don't think you had anything to do with the good Father Leary showing up here this evening.'

Sunny thought that this was what was meant by a civilised break-up and she wondered whether this was how it ended up with all his girlfriends. The gentle let-down, the quiet words, the tactful reminder that he'd never promised anything.

Did any of them throw hissy fits?

She wasn't about to do that. The only thing left to her now was her pride and her dignity and she wasn't going to let either of those invaluable assets go.

'Yes, you're right, of course,' she murmured in agreement. 'I do deserve someone who can give me what I want and that guy is out there for me.'

Stefano nodded but the smile felt forced.

'But I don't regret what…what happened between us. I enjoyed it and it opened up a whole new world for me and that was good.' She slapped her thighs and offered him a brittle smile which didn't come close to reaching her eyes. 'I guess this is it.'

'It doesn't have to be,' Stefano heard himself say in a rough, driven undertone.

'What do you mean?'

'I'm not going to be marrying you or anyone else any time soon. I've been burnt once and I won't be stepping too close to the fire again, even if the fire looks harmless.' He had surprised himself because it wasn't his style to try and hold onto anyone. 'But we could carry on…as long as you understand…we could continue to have fun…'

'Until you dump me because you've become bored?'

Sunny almost laughed. 'I don't think so. I won't be clinging to you like some desperate, sad woman who can't do
any better.'

Stefano flushed darkly. What had possessed him to
try and stage an eleventh hour plea bargain? Of course
it would be madness to prolong this. It could only end in
tears for her.

'Naturally, I'd rather not share a bedroom with you tonight.' She thought of Angela and Flora and felt a pang
of desperate unhappiness because she would see neither
of them again.

'You needn't fear that I would make a nuisance of myself but if you're quite adamant about that then it would
be no problem for me to get my man to bring the helicopter here early. He could be here within the next hour
and a half.'

The termination of their relationship hit her in the gut
with the force of a sledgehammer. She nodded mutely
and heard herself winding up the torturous conversation,
telling him that that would probably be for the best, asking him what he would tell his mother, what he would
tell Flora.

Her voice seemed to be coming from a very long way
away. Finally, when there seemed to be nothing left to
say, she stood up and headed towards the kitchen door.

Some pathetic, desperate part of her wanted him to tell
her to stop, wanted him to gather her up in his arms and
tell her that he loved her after all.

It didn't happen and she found her feet taking her up
to the bedroom, where she packed all her clothes back
in her bag and scanned the room to see whether she had
left anything.

How could all this passion and love and soaring heights
and peaks end like this? With him politely seeing her to
the helicopter that, dead on time, arrived an hour later to

return her to the outskirts of London, where his driver would be waiting to ferry her back to her house?

It did.

They didn't kiss and Sunny kept herself together and it was the hardest thing she had ever had to do.

She left and it was over.

Stefano stared at the cellphone lying on his desk. Fighting the urge to dial her number was a daily battle he waged, even after two weeks of silence.

It was tiresome enough that he had had to endure a barrage of questions from his mother, accusatory disappointment from his daughter and the unpleasant sensation of being *persona non grata* in his own house.

And what the hell was going on with *her*?

He had to resist the constant temptation to phone the law firm to try and prise information out of Katherine.

He couldn't concentrate, couldn't focus and, for the first time in living memory, seemed unable to move on. The distraction of another woman held zero appeal. It went without saying that he had done the right thing, that there was no way he could continue a relationship knowing that the pressure to return feelings he couldn't possible have would eventually cause what they had to self-implode.

He'd learned lessons from his ex! He just didn't have the ability to feel the sort of high-drama nonsense she would inevitably want from him!

Surely he had made that clear from the beginning? Why, then, had she pushed him to the point of having to make a decision and shut down a situation before it had reached its natural conclusion?

Thoughts churning like angry wasps in his head, he continued to glare at his cellphone and was startled when it buzzed with, as he glanced at it, a call from Katherine, to whom he had given his mobile number for speed of access and as a token courtesy, bearing in mind their mothers were close friends.

Slight hold-up on the job. A technicality in the legal wording that she would have to run past him. She could drop the paperwork round to him on her way home.

'No—' Stefano made up his mind on the spot and felt a shaft of relief that he was about to do something and had an excuse for doing it '—I'll come over right away.'

'It's really not that urgent.'

He heard the astonishment in her voice and swept it aside. True, it wasn't his style to attend to anything personally that wasn't of the highest importance but since when did he have to stick to the rule book?

'I was about to leave the office anyway.' He was already on his feet, moving towards his jacket, which he had slung over the leather sofa in his office. It was not yet five and a Friday. Unthinkable that he would be contemplating leaving his office so early. 'If you're on your way out, just leave it with someone. Leave it with Sunny. I need to see her anyway… I can kill two birds with one stone.'

He hit the underground car park at a fast trot and was in his Ferrari, heading out towards Marshall, Jones and Jones, before he could give himself time to talk himself out of what he was doing.

He cleared his head of all doubts as he impatiently sat in the Friday afternoon traffic moving out of the city, drumming his fingers on the steering wheel, wondering what he would do if Sunny had disappeared for the weekend.

Hunt her down.

There was parking at the offices and he sprinted in, only slowing his pace as he approached the opaque glass doors, and he was his usual formidable, utterly composed self as he was pointed in the direction of Sunny's office at the back of the building.

People were streaming out. The Friday evening stampede of office workers eager to kick-start their weekend.

Stefano noticed none of them. Nor did he notice the interested stares he garnered as he headed in the direction of her office.

Sunny was alone in her office; the documents which Katherine had given her sat on her desk with the power of an unexploded hand grenade.

Katherine had hurried in. 'Stefano's popping in to collect these papers, Sunny, and I've told him that I'll leave them with you. You're not in a desperate rush to leave, are you?'

No, of course she wasn't. Where would she be rushing to? Back to the flat so that she could pick up where she left off every evening? Thinking about him? Replaying memories in her head like a song on a never-ending loop? Pretending that she was getting a grip when she knew she wasn't?

She'd never put in so much overtime as she was now doing because work, at least, was something of a distraction.

And now…

The last thing Stefano would have wanted would have been to see her but she suspected that Katherine, on her way out, had dumped him in a position from which he could hardly backtrack, having suggested that he come to collect the paperwork from the office himself. The thought of him being cornered into seeing her made her break out in a fine film of perspiration.

She had no idea what he had been up to. Had she been replaced? She didn't want to think about that but think about it she did. On an hourly basis. He'd had his narrow escape with her and she had no doubt that he would have launched himself into finding her replacement with an overwhelming sense of relief.

She heard his footsteps approaching and every nerve in her body tensed up as she waited for him to appear in the doorway of the small office she occupied with all the other juniors who had inconveniently taken themselves off for a weekend of fun.

'I have those papers!' Nerves prompted her to rush into headlong speech but, after that outburst, her mouth went dry and she stared at him.

How was it even possible for her to have forgotten just how powerful, how stupendously sexy he was? How could she have downplayed the devastating effect he had on all her senses? He'd come straight from work and, having not seen him formally dressed for a while, she was driven to keep staring, drinking in the long lines of his muscular body, sheathed in perfect hand-made Italian.

Lounging in the doorway, Stefano couldn't believe it had taken him this long to get in touch with her, couldn't believe that he had been stupid enough to have waited until prompted by a third party.

Couldn't believe that he'd been that stupid, full stop.

Couldn't believe he'd been dumb enough to let her go, had been dumb enough to have fallen back on his well-worn creed of being a guy who no longer had emotions to feel.

And now, the way she was thrusting those papers towards him…it was obvious that she couldn't wait for him to be on his way.

'Where's everyone?'

'They've all gone. It's nearly six.' She knew what that said about her and she didn't care. So what if her social life had dried up? It had never been much anyway because she'd been so damned busy getting her foot on the career ladder and actually believing that that was the most important thing in her life.

Stefano shut the door quietly behind him but then remained where he was, back pressed against the door, searching for words that didn't seem to be at his disposal.

Nerves stretched to screaming point, Sunny began busying herself for leaving. Tidying her desk, stacking some papers under a paperweight, taking her time fetching her blazer from the back of her chair—anything to avoid direct eye contact. He hadn't reached for the papers and they were on her desk and she didn't know whether to just leave them there or hand them to him.

'How are your mother and Flora?' she finally asked to break the tension of the silence stretching between them.

'You're missed. Will you have dinner with me?'

Sunny stilled but didn't look at him. 'I don't think so, Stefano.'

'Please.'

'Why?' She was suddenly angry that he was here, in her space, messing with her head when she should be in the recovery process. 'What for?' she all but yelled. 'I didn't ask you here! You came to get those papers and they're there! On the desk! So why don't you take them and just...leave?'

'I don't want to,' he mumbled, shorn of his natural charm.

'I don't care whether you want to or not!'

'I need to talk to you.'

'What about? We did all the talking we had to do.'

'Do you still...love me?'

'That's not fair,' Sunny wasn't even aware that she had whispered that aloud. The colour had drained from her face and her eyes were huge as she looked at him.

'I've missed you,' was all Stefano could think to say and her heart skipped a beat, then she was angry all over again for pouncing on crumbs like the needy, clingy, pathetic woman she so desperately didn't want to be.

'You'll get over it,' she said cuttingly, although, deep

inside, something flared because did that mean that she hadn't been replaced at top speed?

'I don't think I will,' Stefano muttered, his voice so low that she had to strain to pick up what he had said. He finally pushed himself away from the door, hands shoved deep in his pockets. 'I've been an idiot.'

I should leave... I should just walk out, head held high, because there's no way I'm going to be talked into having some sort of fling... There's no way I'm going to let myself be used by someone because they had the leverage of knowing that I...care...

'What do you mean?' she found herself asking huskily.

'Can we at least sit?' Stefano asked. 'This is pretty hard for me.'

'I'm not going to have an affair with you, Stefano. If that's why you're here... I just can't...'

'I don't want to have an affair with you.'

'Good!' *And it was! Because there was no way she was going to oblige!*

She sat down behind her desk and he dragged a chair over but, instead of sticking it in front of her desk, which would have suited her because it might have given her a jag of much needed confidence to be in the position of interviewer, he positioned it neatly by hers so that their knees were practically touching.

So close that she could breathe in the heady scent of him.

'Then what do you want?' she asked unsteadily.

'I want to marry you.'

Sunny laughed humourlessly. 'If you think that's going to...'

'I mean it,' Stefano stated, deadly serious. He sighed deeply and raked his fingers through his hair. 'After my marriage... I protected myself by shutting down emotionally. It was the safe thing to do. I slept with women but

I had no interest in pursuing anything further than that. Sex. A physical act, devoid of all the messy complications of involvement. I'd had involvement, or maybe I should say that I had involvement thrust upon me and I discovered first-hand how disastrous it could be. Yes, there were happy marriages but they were few and far between and I wasn't about to get anywhere near that place ever again. I was never going to chance it. And then you came along.'

'I did?' Sunny was hanging on to his every word and the shoots of hope that had sprung up the minute he had told her that he'd missed her were growing thick and fast, sprouting their tendrils into every part of her.

For the first time since he'd entered the room, Stefano felt as if he could breathe freely. He fumbled for her hand and their fingers touched and held and he tightened his grip.

'You did.' He kissed her knuckles and then looked at her. 'I fancied the hell out of you,' he confessed, 'and that was no problem. I could deal with that. And when I found myself talking to you, telling you things I'd never told anyone before, I figured it was because you'd entered my life via a slightly different door…'

'Flora.'

'Flora. You knew her. You'd bonded. It was natural that you would occupy a slightly different place to all the other lovers I'd had in the past. And then my mother entered the mix and…things changed. No, things had changed before then. I just didn't realise it. I didn't recognise that what I felt was no longer something I could control, because what I felt was something that was controlling *me*. When I realised that you loved me…I couldn't deal with it. I was still clinging to the theory that I was in charge… that I had my parameters and those parameters couldn't be breached.'

'I didn't plan on falling in love with you either,' Sunny

admitted on a heartfelt sigh. 'I had my parameters, too.' She smiled at the naive self she had been when she, too, thought that she could control what she felt. 'I fought it, you know.'

'But it was a losing battle. I know, my darling. As it was for me. At least you had the courage to admit what you felt and not back away from it. I didn't. But, hell, I missed you, Sunny. I missed the way you laughed; I missed your honesty and your stubbornness. I missed holding you and waking up next to you and knowing that you'd be right there in bed with me every night. There was nothing I didn't miss.'

'Would you have…come if it hadn't been for those papers?'

'It might have taken a bit longer for me to get past my pig-headed idiocy but I couldn't have *not* come because I love you. I love you and need you and want you to be by my side for ever.'

Sunny smiled and she found that she couldn't stop. 'Okay,' she teased, 'so you've talked me into dinner after all.'

'Can I talk you into marrying me as well?'

She tilted her head to one side and looked at him consideringly. 'You know what? Yes, my dearest Stefano. I think you can…'

* * * * *

WEARING THE DE ANGELIS RING

CHAPTER ONE

'YOU'RE NOT GOING to like what I'm about to say.'

The very second Stefano had called his son and told him that he needed to speak with him as a matter of urgency, Theo had dropped everything and taken the first flight over to Italy, to his father's enormous estate just outside Rome.

Stefano De Angelis was not a man given to drama, and both Theo and his brother, Daniel, had spent the past five years worrying about him. He had never really recovered from the death of his wife, their mother, Rose. The power house who had built a personal fortune from scratch had collapsed into himself, retreating to the sanctuary of his den, immune to the efforts of both his sons to pull him out of his grief. He had continued to eat, sleep, talk and walk, but his soul had departed, leaving only a physical shell behind.

What, Theo thought now, was he about to hear?

Cold fear gripped him.

'Have you asked Daniel as well?' He prowled through the huge sitting room, idly gazing through the window to the sprawling lawns, before finally taking a seat opposite his father.

'This situation does not concern your brother,' Stefano returned, his dark eyes sidestepping his son's piercing green ones.

Theo breathed a sigh of relief. If Daniel hadn't been likewise summoned, then at least a health crisis could be discounted. He had been tempted to phone his brother on the back of his father's summons, but had resisted the impulse because he knew that Daniel was in the throes of a balancing act: trying to close a major deal *and* a minor love affair at the same time.

The deal, his brother had confided several days ago, when he had called from his penthouse apartment in Sydney, was a walk in the park compared to the woman who had been making noises about taking what they had *'one step further'*, and didn't show any promise of retreating without putting up a fight.

'So tell me… What am I not going to like to hear?' Theo encouraged.

'As you are well aware, son…' Stefano's hooded dark eyes gazed off into the distance '…things have not been good with me since your mother died. When my beloved Rose went, she took a big part of me with her.'

'Of us all.'

'But you and your brother are young. I, on the other hand, am an old man—and you know what they say about old dogs and new tricks. Perhaps if her death hadn't been so sudden… Perhaps if I had had time to get used to the idea of her absence…' He sighed. 'But this is not why I called you here, Theo. To moan and complain about something that cannot be changed. I called you here because during the time that I was…shall we say mentally not present, certain unfortunate things took place within the company.'

Theo stilled. His keen eyes noted the nervous play of his father's entwined fingers. His father was the least nervous man he had ever known.

'Unfortunate things…?'

'There has been some substantial mismanagement,'

Stefano declared bluntly. 'And worse, I am afraid. Alfredo, my trusted co-director, has been involved in large-scale embezzlement which has only recently been drawn to my attention. It's a wonder the press hasn't got hold of it. The upshot, Theo, is that vast sums of money—including most of the pension funds—have been hijacked.'

Theo sat back, his lean, handsome face revealing nothing of what was going through his mind.

It was a problem, yes—but a serious one? Not really. At any rate nothing that he couldn't handle.

'If you're worried about the man getting what he deserves, then you can leave that to me,' Theo asserted with cold confidence, his sharp, analytical brain already formulating ways in which payback could be duly extracted. 'And if you're worried about the lost money, then likewise. It will be nothing for me to return what's been misappropriated. No one will ever know.'

'It's not that easy, Theo.'

And Theo knew that now they were approaching the heart of the problem—the reason why he had been summoned.

'I would *never* ask either you or Daniel for financial assistance!' Stefano glowered, his fighting spirit temporarily restored as he contemplated the unthinkable. 'You boys have made your own way in the world and my pride would never allow me to run to either of you with my begging bowl...'

Theo shook his head in frustration at his father's pride—which, he had to concede, both he and Daniel had inherited in bucketloads. 'It would not have been a question of—'

'I'm afraid I went to Carlo Caldini,' Stefano said abruptly. 'There was no choice. The bank was not an option—not when there was a significant chance that they would turn down my request. If that had happened, then the business... Well, what can I say? Everything your mother and I built would have been thrown into the public arena to be picked over by hyenas! At least with Carlo we can keep this between us...'

Theo pressed the pads of his thumbs against his eyes.

Carlo Caldini had once been his father's closest friend and now, for longer than he could remember, was his fiercest adversary. The fact that he had seen fit to go to Carlo for help threatened to bring on a raging headache.

There was absolutely no doubt that whatever his father was going to tell him Theo was not going to want to hear it.

'And what's his price?' he asked, because there was no such thing as a free lunch—and when the lunch was with a sworn enemy then it was going to be the opposite of free.

Exorbitant was the word that sprang to mind.

Stefano fidgeted. 'You're not getting any younger, Theo. You're thirty-two years old! Your mother dearly wished that she would see one of you boys settled... It wasn't to be...'

'I'm not following you...'

'All of this unravelled over eight months ago,' Stefano said heavily. 'During that time it proved impossible to repay the loan. It's been an uphill struggle just picking apart the extent of the losses and dealing with Alfredo...'

'And you kept it all to yourself!'

'There seemed little point in worrying you or your brother.'

'Just tell me what ruinous interest rates Carlo has imposed and I'll deal with it.'

'Here is the part you may not like, son...'

'I'm all ears.'

When it came to money there was nothing Theo couldn't buy, and naturally he would pay the bill without complaint—although he was furious with his father for thinking it necessary to seek help outside the direct family circle.

Pride.

'As you know, Carlo has a daughter. An only child. Sadly there were to be no sons for him.'

Even in the thick of disclosing what he knew his son would not want to hear Stefano couldn't quite conceal the smugness in his voice, and Theo raised his eyebrows wryly. He had never known what had caused the enmity between his father and Carlo, but he suspected that the lifelong grudge stemmed from something ridiculously insignificant.

'What has that got to do with anything?' he asked, frankly bewildered at the tangent his father had taken.

'Alexa... I think you may have met her... Or perhaps not... Well, it seems that the girl is not yet married, and Carlo...' Stefano shrugged. 'He is saddened at that—as I would be had I had a daughter... So part of the repayment schedule—which, in fairness to that sly old fox, is more lenient than at any bank—is that you help him out of his predicament with Alexa. In other words, Theo, I have promised him your hand in marriage to the girl...'

Alexa glared down at the outfit her mother had laid out for her to wear.

Something 'suitable' to meet a man she had no wish to meet, far less marry. A wildly ridiculous frothy dress in startling blue that swept down to the ankles with a plunging neckline and an even more ridiculously plunging back.

She was to be paraded in front of Theo De Angelis like a sacrificial lamb.

She wanted to storm out of the house, head for the nearest port and take a boat to the opposite end of the world—where she would hide out for maybe ten years, until this whole ludicrous situation had been sorted out.

Without her involvement.

At first, when her father had sat her down and told her

that she was to be married to a De Angelis, she had thought that he was joking.

An arranged marriage? In this day and age? To a son of the man with whom he had had a stupid, simmering feud for thirty-five years? What else could it have been but a joke?

That had been a week ago—plenty long enough for her to discover that her father had been deadly serious.

'The poor man is in serious financial trouble.' Carlo Caldini had opened up to her in an attempt to pull at her heartstrings. He had looked at her with a sad expression and mournful eyes. 'True, he and I have not seen eye to eye over the years...'

'All thirty-five of them, Papà...'

'But in the end who else does one turn to but a friend? I would have done the same in his position...'

Alexa had been baffled at this show of seemingly heart-wrenching empathy, but if her father had deemed it fit to rush to the rescue of a man he had spent over three decades deriding, then so be it. What did it have to do with her?

Everything, as it had transpired.

She had been bartered like a...a...piece of meat!

She adored her father, but she would still have dug her heels in and point-blank refused had he not pulled out his trump card—in the shape of her mother.

Cora Caldini, recovering from a stroke, was under doctor's orders to take it easy. No stress, her family had been warned. And, more than that, her father had confided, this last stroke had been the most serious of three... Her heart was weak and all her talk was of her mortality, of her dying before she could see her only child married and settled. What if something happened to her? her father had asked. What if she was taken away from them before her only wish could be granted?

Caught in the eye of a hurricane, Alexa had ranted and

raved, had stood her ground with rousing lectures about modern times, about arranged marriages being a thing of the past. She had pointed out, arms folded, that *they* hadn't had their marriage arranged so why should she? She had waxed lyrical about the importance of love, even though she didn't know the first thing about that. She had darkly suggested that the last thing Cora Caldini would want would be a phoney marriage for all the wrong reasons...

In the end she had gained the only concession that she could. *If* she married the man then it would be on her terms. After a year of unhappy enforced marital misery she would be free to divorce and Stefano De Angelis would be released from his debt. Her father had quickly acquiesced.

Now, with the man due to arrive at their mansion within the hour, she gritted her teeth and returned the elaborate blue dress to the wardrobe from which it had been removed.

She wasn't going to dress up like a doll for a man whose reputation as a commitment-phobe womaniser spanned the country and beyond. There had been no need to look him up on the Internet because she knew all about him—and his brother. Theo and Daniel De Angelis, cut from the same cloth, both ruthless tycoons, both far too good-looking for their own good.

Despite her privileged background, Alexa had made it her life's mission to avoid men like them. She had plenty experience with the superficiality of men who had money and power. She had been surrounded with them for years. She had seen the way they always took it as their God-given right that they could do as they pleased and treat women as they liked simply because *they could*.

She disapproved of everything Theo De Angelis stood for. Certainly the sort of men *she* preferred had always been of the thoughtful and considerate variety.

When she thought about love she thought about her

parents—thought about being swept off her feet by someone kind and humorous, with whom she could enjoy the
sort of united happiness her parents enjoyed. When she
contemplated marriage she knew that there would be no
compromises made. She would marry her soulmate—the
man whose hand she would want to hold for the rest of her
life. She had met sufficient idle, arrogant, self-absorbed
and vain rich guys—guys *exactly* like Theo De Angelis—
to know that she would never find her soulmate amongst
them.

And look at her now! So much for all her ideals!

She showered, taking her time because she certainly
wasn't going to scuttle down to the drawing room to wait
for him—like an eager bride-to-be, thrilled to nab a man
the tabloid press had once labelled the most eligible bachelor alive.

And she wasn't going to wear the blue dress—or any
dress, for that matter. In fact she wasn't going to wear anything that displayed her body at all.

She chose a pair of jeans and a loose-fitting blouse that
was buttoned to the neck and then, taut with suppressed
anger at her situation, stared at her reflection in the mirror.

Long, wavy dark hair, pulled back into a no-nonsense
bun, framed an oval face. Like her father, she was olive-
skinned, with dark eyebrows and thick, dark eyelashes,
but from her mother she had inherited her bright turquoise
eyes. Her best feature, as far as she was concerned—
because the rest did little to excite the imagination. She
wasn't long and leggy, and she had stopped being able to fit
into a size eight the second she had hit adolescence. Hers,
to her eternal regret, was an unfashionable five-foot-four
hourglass figure—the sort that personal trainers over the
years had tried and failed to whip into shape.

She heard voices before she reached the drawing room

because the door was open, and was assailed by a sudden attack of nerves.

It was one thing pouring scorn on the likes of Theo De Angelis from the relative safety of her bedroom.

It was quite another holding on to her self-righteous, justifiable fury when he was perched on a chair, metres away from her, just out of sight.

She had never seen him in the flesh. He lived in London, but even if he had lived in Rome she probably wouldn't have seen him anyway, because she made a point of avoiding society dos whenever possible.

Heart beating fast, she took a deep breath and entered the drawing room.

Drinks were being served and her parents were sitting opposite him, their body language indicating that they were delighted with whatever he happened to be saying.

Conversation came to an abrupt halt.

Alexa had never thrived on being the centre of attention. Along with her background of vast wealth, she had grown up in circles where the girls were catty and where looks counted for everything. Trapped in a figure that had always catapulted her in the direction of baggy clothes, she had learned to leave the attention-seeking to others, and once she had left school had turned her back on it completely.

Right now she found herself riveted by the long, lean man, relaxing in a deep velvet chair which he seemed to dwarf.

Photos could say so much, but they had given her very little indication of just how big and muscular he was. They had also not prepared her for the sheer outrageousness of his looks. He was drop-dead gorgeous. His hair was cropped short and black, his features perfectly chiselled, his eyes lazy and the most peculiar shade of green she had ever seen, fringed with the sort of luxurious lashes any woman would have given her eye-teeth for.

He was as beautiful as any human being had a right to be…and yet the air of ruthless power that surrounded him like an invisible cloak removed him from being just an incredible-looking man to being a man who drew stares and held on to them.

For a few seconds Alexa's heart seemed to stop and she lost the ability to blink.

But that only lasted for a few seconds and then reality resurfaced, rescuing her from standing there like a stranded goldfish.

Her parents had stood up to make introductions. She didn't take a step closer to him, and neither did he make any move to rush forward. In fact he remained sitting just long enough for her to wonder whether a complete lack of manners was also part of his personality.

'Why didn't you wear the lovely dress I laid out for you on the bed?' her mother whispered, in clear dismay at her choice of clothes.

'I decided that the casual approach was better than showing up in a Cinderella frock. Have you noticed that the man is wearing jeans? I wouldn't say *he* dressed for the occasion, would you?'

She directed a cool smile at him as one of the staff got busy with a bottle of champagne and the business of polite conversation began.

With her parents there some of the pressure was removed, but she still found herself sitting like a rigid plank of wood, back erect, body screaming with tension. When, after half an hour, her parents rose and informed them that they were going out for dinner, she glanced up at her mother with undisguised panic.

'You two should have some time to enjoy yourselves!' Cora chirruped brightly. 'Elena has prepared something, and you can dine informally in the blue room…'

Alexa wondered whether her mother had taken complete leave of her senses.

Enjoy themselves?

Didn't she realise that this was an absolute nightmare? No, of course she didn't. She thought that, yes, it was an arranged union—but one that had been happily accepted by both parties. And she wouldn't have questioned that any further because it was so much what she wanted. Her daughter married and settled.

The door clicked quietly shut behind them and Alexa stared down at her half-drunk glass of champagne. She could feel those fabulous green eyes looking at her, and it infuriated her that he felt he had no need to say anything at all.

'So...' She finally broke the lengthening silence. She glanced quickly at him and just as fast looked away.

'So...' Theo drawled, stretching out his long legs and linking his fingers loosely on his stomach. 'Here we are. I never imagined two weeks ago that I would now be sitting in the Caldini living room, gazing at the excited, radiant face of my bride-to-be...'

What had he been expecting? he asked himself. The fact that Carlo Caldini—a man with more millions than he knew what to do with—had been unable to source a husband for the daughter he clearly wanted married off had said it all.

Plain beyond belief, with an insanely boring personality—that had been the prediction his brother had made, when he had been told about the catastrophe, and Theo had privately agreed. He and Daniel might no longer live in Italy, but they were rich and powerful enough to garner invitations from everyone who mattered, and neither could remember ever meeting the girl—which, along with her failure to be married off, had also said it all.

But, finding himself locked in the jaws of a steel trap,

Theo had determined to make the best of things. Because, however odious the woman was, no marriage was set in stone. There was always a window for negotiation when it came to an out clause, and Theo had already located it.

In the meanwhile he had imagined someone unappealing and terminally shy, who would make a suitable background spouse while his father's company was patched up from the inside. All things considered, he had come to the conclusion that his life would hardly have to change at all. She would remain in Italy, dutifully keeping the home fires burning, he would visit occasionally, work permitting, and she would not complain.

When Alexa had walked into the drawing room he had been startled to discover that she was nothing like the woman he had conjured up in his head.

She was…

He still wasn't entirely sure—and that was a first for him. For if it was one thing Theo De Angelis excelled in, it was an ability to read a woman in under five seconds.

She had sat in mute silence for most of the half hour during which laboured chit chat had been made, with both Carlo and Cora Caldini making sure to tread very carefully around the giant elephant in the room: namely the matter of an arranged marriage.

Cora, he had been told by her husband, knew that the marriage was to be an arrangement, but she knew nothing of the financial situation that had propelled it into existence and nor should she find out. She could deal with an arranged marriage… Several of her friends had children who had been diplomatically set up with suitable partners. It would be tactful not to go into more details.

Alexa's mute silence hadn't translated into the meek subservience he had been expecting.

And looks-wise…

He tilted his head and noted the mutinous, challenging stare she returned.

'And *I* didn't think that I would be sitting here gazing at my devoted and adoring husband-to-be!' Alexa retorted, because there was no reason for her to pretend that this was anything but a fiasco.

Besides, the man was so good-looking that he might just be arrogant enough to think that she actually *wanted* to be in this position.

She felt she should rid him of any such assumption from the start.

'So I'm assuming...' he rose fluidly from the chair to refill her glass with more champagne before topping his up with more of the whisky he had been drinking '...that we're both singing from the same song sheet?'

'What did you expect?' Alexa threw at him, mouth down-turned.

'I could either answer that question truthfully or else ignore it altogether. Which would you rather?'

Alexa shrugged and tore her eyes away from his long, muscular frame. 'We might just as well lay our cards on the table,' she said.

'In which case,' Theo drawled, 'I should tell you I had reached the conclusion that you might be a little desperate... considering Carlo is prepared to throw you in as part of his financial negotiations with my father...'

Slow, furious colour crawled into her cheeks.

'You are the most arrogant man I think I have ever met in my entire life!' Alexa said through gritted teeth.

She gauged the level of satisfaction she would get from flinging her glass at him, but decided that the only way to handle this disaster would be not to let him get to her.

She wasn't going to lose her cool. She *never* lost her cool. It was what made her so good at what she did. She worked in the offices of a group of pro bono lawyers and daily dealt with people in need of practical and emotional help. Three evenings a week she volunteered at a women's shelter. She was calm personified!

'Since we're about to be joined in happily married bliss, I suggest you take that on board and don't think of implementing any changes.'

Theo was perversely enjoying himself, and he put that down to the sort of man he was. The sort who could deal with whatever was thrown at him, however unexpected.

'And in return,' he continued, in the same lazy dark drawl that made her toes curl, '*I* won't try and turn *you* into someone charming and well behaved...'

Alexa glared and bit down hard on the riposte stinging her lips. She had no idea how she was going to survive twelve hours with this man, never mind twelve months.

'I've spoken to my father,' she gritted, 'and he has agreed that we only have to carry out this crazy charade for twelve months. After that we can part company and you can return to your life of— You can return to your life and I can get back to mine.'

Theo wondered what she had been about to say but let it go. He, in actual fact, had secured a far better deal— because *his* twelve months also included a substantial acquisition of Caldini company shares and a seat on the board. It would tie in very nicely with his current diversion into telecommunications.

After the initial shock of the catastrophe that had been presented to him, he had very quickly reached the perfectly correct conclusion that marrying his daughter off was only one benefit for Carlo Caldini in helping his father.

The other was glaringly obvious.

Carlo Caldini ran a juggernaut of a family business but there was no male family member to whom he could leave his legacy—and, like many traditional Italians, he wanted his business to remain in the family. By marrying his daughter to Theo he netted one of the most wildly respected and formidable businessmen on the globe.

And for Theo, Alexa Caldini came with a considerable dowry.

'So no doubt we should be discussing the mechanics,' he said.

'What do you mean?'

'I mean that to the outside world we must be a loved-up pair about to embark on the greatest adventure of our lives. I will not have a whiff of scandal surrounding this, because under no circumstances is my father to be subjected to any manner of rumour about a convenient match concocted to save his company.' His green eyes had cooled. 'Are we one hundred per cent clear on this?'

'Or else what?'

'That's a road I would seriously advise you not to go down.'

His voice was icy cold, with deadly intent, and Alexa shivered. Theo De Angelis had not reached the dizzy heights by being kind and avuncular. He'd probably never helped a little old lady cross a road in his entire life. She wondered how he would react to her world when they were man and wife...

'When we're in public,' he purred silkily, 'you will withdraw your claws. You can keep them for when we're alone together.'

'You might find that you don't like being scratched.' Alexa tilted her chin mutinously and he smiled—a slow, curling smile that did all sorts of weird and unexpected things to her body.

'And *you* might discover that I'm very good when it comes to subduing wild cats.'

Suddenly confused, and feeling horribly out of her depth, Alexa blinked and gulped down the remainder of her champagne.

She might talk the talk, but how good would she be at walking the walk?

She had virtually no experience when it came to the opposite sex. She had been sent off to England to an all girls' boarding school and from there to university, where she had buried herself in books, determined to get her law degree.

Of course there had been a couple of boyfriends, but neither had excited her and she had always been determined to hold out for the Right One—never to sell herself short. They had both cleared off as soon as they'd realised that she wasn't going to hop into bed with them.

Now, as her bright blue eyes tangled with his cool, unreadable green ones, she knew that this was a predator, born to lead and accustomed to obedience.

Obedience she would give him—but only within the parameters that suited them both. If he didn't want anyone getting wind of the real reason for their union she, in turn, did not want to embarrass her parents, whom she dearly loved.

He wanted her to put up a public front and she would—but the second they closed the door behind them there would be no more game-playing.

And suddenly a thought rippled through her that made her breathing quicken.

When the front door closed…what happened next?

It was something that she would have to broach, and she licked her lips nervously because the mere thought of this big, domineering man touching her sent her whole nervous system into instant meltdown.

He surely wouldn't expect them to sleep together! Not when this was a farce—a marriage of convenience…a union in which there would be no love lost!

Her breathing steadied.

Panic over.

He might be arrogant and ruthless, but he wasn't an idiot—and besides, she knew the sort of women he dated because she had seen pictures in some of the trashy magazines she had flicked through while she was getting her hair done.

Tall, blonde women who wore the minimum of clothing and whose full-time occupation appeared to be personal grooming.

'You said that we need to discuss the mechanics of this…this arrangement…?'

'Shall we do that over dinner—?'

'Why? We might as well hash it out now.'

He stood up, blatantly ignoring her interruption. 'I wouldn't like to kick off our joyous life together on the wrong note,' he drawled, strolling towards the door, which her parents had tactfully shut behind him on their way out.

'What do you mean?' Alexa followed him, disgruntled.

'I mean your mother has had a doubtless delicious meal prepared for us. What kind of guest would I be if I disregarded her invitation?'

'The kind that's marrying me thanks to parental pressure?' Alexa muttered sourly.

He shot her a brief look of appreciation.

'Besides,' she continued, skin tingling from that momentary look, 'you don't strike me as the sort of man who gives a hoot what other people think of him.'

She swept past him, breathing in his clean, woody scent and determinedly ignoring its impact on her senses.

'I find that I'm willing to make an exception for my in-laws-to-be…'

'Why are you taking this so calmly?'

It was the first thing Alexa said as they sat down at the table in the informal dining room. The blue room was still big enough to fit a ten-seater table, but places had been set for them opposite each another at one end. As always, it was a full arrangement, with dinner plates, side plates and separate silver cutlery for every course to be served—in this case salad, soup, main course and dessert.

Alexa could not have felt less hungry, and she looked with uninterest as salads were brought in and placed in front of them.

He, she noted, had no problem with his appetite.

'How else do you imagine I should react?' Theo looked at her, and across the width of the table she felt his overwhelming presence all the more acutely.

There was something intimate about eating together, and she could barely concentrate on her salad as the flutter of nerves threatened to overpower her common sense.

She put that down to her healthy dislike of the man.

'Do you imagine that this is a situation I *enjoy* being in?' he enquired coolly. 'My father dropped this bombshell and I find I've had next to no option but to take the hit.'

'I never thought I'd end up in a marriage with someone who would walk up the aisle only thanks to having to take a hit from a bombshell he couldn't dodge,' Alexa said bitterly—and that was the stark truth.

She had never followed the pattern of her friends, who had believed in sleeping around. She had never assumed that marriage was something to be taken lightly because it could be unpicked without too much difficulty if the going got rough. Her own parents had had a long and extremely happy marriage. Her mother, Irish by heritage, had been a gap-year student when she had met Carlo, and theirs had been a case of love at first sight. Which made it doubly upsetting that her father had seen fit to put her in this position. He had taken advantage of a situation and *she* was going to have to pay the price.

'I don't think that way of thinking will pay dividends in this particular situation…' Theo pushed his salad plate to one side and sprawled back in the chair to look at her coolly. 'We've both been put in an unfortunate position and now we have to deal with it.'

'And you're not angry...?'

'Like I said, there's no point in wasting energy on emotions that won't get either of us anywhere. We're going to present the perfect picture of a couple in love. Naturally there will have to be an engagement and a public announcement. Doubtless there will be cameras. You will smile and gaze adoringly up at me.'

'And what will *you* be doing while I'm smiling and gazing adoringly?'

'Controlling the situation.'

'And this so-called engagement is supposed to last... how long?'

'It'll be brief,' Theo asserted with the sweeping assurance of someone who had given the details a great deal of thought. 'We can't wait to tie the knot.'

'And how is this supposed to make any kind of sense?' Alexa demanded. She lapsed into silence as their salad plates were removed, to be replaced with soup. 'Have you suddenly had a transformation and gone from being a womaniser to a one-woman man who's desperate to get married?'

'And *that*,' Theo said in a hard voice, 'is just the sort of approach I am warning you to avoid.' Then he smiled—a slow, lazy smile that made the breath hitch in her throat. 'I never imagined that you were a spitting cat...' he mused. 'Do you think that's the reason your parents think you'll end up on the shelf...?'

CHAPTER TWO

'I CAN'T BELIEVE you just said that.'

Never had a meal seemed so interminably long. Interrupted by the arrival of their main course—a fish casserole—Alexa could only glare at him with simmering resentment. No one had ever riled her to this extent. His air of superior cool got on her nerves and made her rantings seem childish and petty.

'You have no right to say stuff like that! You don't *know* me!'

Theo dug into his food. She might not be his type, but there was a certain arresting quality to her face. Anger suited her, and he was startled at this reaction—because temper tantrums were things he had always actively discouraged.

Her dig about his womanising had annoyed him, and as far as he was concerned what was good for the goose was likewise good for the gander. If she wanted to throw accusations at him, then her shoulders should be broad enough to take it when he threw a few home truths back at her in return.

Not his style, admittedly, but then again since when had he ever been placed in a situation like this? On every single level she was just the sort of woman he would never naturally be drawn to. Physically, she was nothing like the tall, leggy supermodels he dated and, appearances aside, he liked his women to be obliging and accommodating. His work life was intense enough without having to do battle with a woman.

'Aren't you going to eat?' he asked. 'It's excellent. Maybe I'll get the name of your mother's chef... Do you think she would object if I poached him?'

'Elena isn't a chef,' Alexa muttered. 'She's the house-keeper we've had for centuries. And, yes, I think my mother *would* object if you decided to poach her. For your information, I have never considered myself as *on the shelf*. I'm not one of those women who thinks that the be-all and end-all of life is to get married as fast as you can and start having children.'

'I'm guessing that both your parents *do*.'

Alexa pushed her plate to one side. 'There's no point discussing this. What my parents think or don't think... How long before we get married?'

She was forcibly struck by the surreal situation she was now wading through—and by the fact that her con-tented life had been turned upside down in the space of a few days.

So she hadn't been leading the most thrilling of lives... But it had taken her ages to get used to being back in Italy after first boarding school and then university abroad, fol-lowed by a stint in London, where she had worked for a small law company before her mother's illness had called her back home.

She had spent the past year and a half easing herself into a life that felt foreign. Was it any wonder that excitement and thrills weren't high on her agenda? Once she found her feet, she was sure that the slightly zoned out feeling she lived with much of the time would disappear.

She hadn't banked on excitement landing on her door-step in the form of a forced marriage.

'Max—two months. And, to return to your question

about the plausibility of my settling down at the speed of light... We both need to agree that it's a case of love getting the better of me.' He shrugged elegantly and stood up, tossing his serviette onto the table and prowling through the room as he thought.

Alexa followed him with her eyes. His movements were economical and graceful. He was wearing black jeans, a white linen shirt which was cuffed to the elbows and loafers, and he exuded elegance. He certainly hadn't dressed for the occasion, but he still managed to look every inch the powerful tycoon that he was. He was obviously one of those people who could pull off elegance wearing anything... If he swapped clothes with a tramp he would still manage to look cool and sexy.

'I broke up with my last girlfriend over three months ago—during which time I've been out of the public eye...'

'You're telling me that the press usually follow everything you do?'

Theo paused, leaned against the window ledge, then looked at her and kept looking at her as the dishes were cleared away. He signalled in a barely discernible gesture that they should be left alone for a while, and the door was duly shut as the last dish was removed. The oak table was left with just the wine decanter and a bottle of champagne.

'I'm high-profile,' he agreed. 'I don't ask for it, but it seems that some reporters have little else to do but take pictures of the rich and famous. It's just a fact of life, and I've become accustomed to dealing with it.'

'I would absolutely *hate* that.'

'It's something to which you might find you have to become accustomed—'

'On top of everything else,' Alexa muttered.

Her eyes flickered towards him and she found that she had to tear them away, because he was just so unfairly compelling to look at.

Theo chose to ignore her interruption. He had anticipated someone plain, docile and quite possibly grateful
to be rescued from the prospect of spinsterhood. A traditional Italian woman who would welcome the abundance
of riches suddenly deposited in her lap—because he knew
without a trace of vanity that he was a good catch.

It would have been hard to locate someone *less* grateful
than the girl now glowering at him, and he banked down
a sudden flare of irritation.

'At any rate,' he pressed on, 'no one will raise eyebrows about the timeline, and the fact that at least on paper
this would appear to be the perfect match will certainly
help things along. We both come from prominent Italian
families... I have found the woman of my dreams, someone close to home, and have decided to steer my life in a
different direction... Both families are overjoyed by the
match...'

'Even though our fathers haven't been on speaking
terms for years?'

'All the more touching. Everyone likes a fairy-tale ending.'

'You're so cynical, aren't you?'

'Realistic and practical.'

'And how are we supposed to have met? We don't even
live in the same country.'

'I don't think it will require great feats of the imagination to come up with something.'

Was she going out of her way to get on his nerves? he
wondered. Did she honestly think that *his* life hadn't also
undergone a seismic change? Less than two weeks ago
he had been a free man—free to go where he pleased, to
have whatever woman he wanted. No one was waiting in
the wings, expecting him to put in an appearance. That
freedom had disappeared in a puff of smoke, but was *he*
whining and complaining? No. He was solution-orientated

and, like it or not, plans had to be made so that this pretence could be seamlessly accepted as nothing short of the absolute truth.

'Let's have your thoughts on this,' he said.

An edge of irritation had crept into his voice and, hearing it, Alexa scowled, once again reduced to feeling petty.

'I suppose we could have met here,' she said, a little ungraciously.

'I occasionally *do* come to Italy to see my father. . It's a realistic enough scenario. You happened to be somewhere… Suddenly my life shifted on its axis… If a reporter asks you for details you can always tell him *no comment* and then gaze adoringly at me. Probably safer than getting tangled up in a lie.'

He looked at her glum face, then down to her baggy, unappealing outfit. No doubt she had pointedly dressed down for a confrontation she didn't want, but it was something that would have to be discussed whether she liked it or not. He suspected not, but treading delicately round the issue wasn't going to do.

'Is that how you normally dress?'

'I beg your pardon?'

'Jeans…baggy tops… And what are you wearing on your feet…?'

Alexa looked at him indignantly and stuck her foot out. 'Trainers.'

'Running shoes? To my mind, they're for running. Are you running anywhere? Have you just come from the gym?'

'What are you getting at?' Her voice had risen a notch. His levels of arrogance were in the process of escalating.

'Credibility,' Theo said succinctly. 'We may make the ideal match, and when our engagement hits the news much will be made of our backgrounds, but even the least observant reporter might question the fact that I've fallen head over heels in love with someone who doesn't appear to give a damn how she looks...'

Alexa's mouth dropped open. She contemplated throwing something at him.

'That is the most insulting thing that has ever been said to me in my entire life!'

'It's not meant to be insulting,' Theo informed her drily. 'I'm looking at this situation from all angles and simply bringing one of those angles to your attention. The women I've dated in the past—'

'There's no need to go into that.' Alexa was mortified, and outraged that he should be tactless enough to criticise her choice of clothing. 'I know *exactly* what sort of women you've dated in the past.'

'How so?'

'I've seen the occasional picture in a trashy mag.' She liked the way the words *trashy mag* rolled off her tongue.

'You read "trashy mags"? You surprise me. I thought I might be getting a highbrow intellectual for a wife. I'm disappointed.'

There was a thread of amusement in his voice which she decided to ignore, because it seemed to point to a side of his personality that wasn't part of the package she had conjured up.

'They're the only things to read at the hairdresser,' Alexa told him airily. 'Great big stacks of silly magazines, full of useless gossip. I saw a picture of you in one of them a couple of months ago. A tall, blonde woman was clinging to you as though she might fall flat on her face unless you kept her propped up. Maybe she'd had too much to drink...' Alexa mused, enjoying herself for the first time that evening. 'I hadn't thought of that. But I suppose those society dos usually involve a lot of alcohol. I've been asked to several over the years,' she inserted, truthfully enough, because as the daughter of a prominent Italian family she had occasionally been asked to some event or other in aid of a good cause, 'but I try and avoid them.'

'How virtuous.'

'So, yes, I know that you date tall model-types. A bit like your brother. *He* also pops up in those kinds of magazines, with some drunken supermodel hanging on to him for dear life...'

Theo thought of Daniel and for a second tried to imagine what the mouthy little brunette facing him would have thought of his brother. His brother was the essence of a playboy—which was why he had laughed uproariously when Theo had told him about the situation he was stuck in.

It would have been Daniel's ultimate nightmare, and he had been overjoyed at the prospect of being able to remain free, single and unattached, without having to worry that their father might start making noises about him settling down. One son who had settled down would be plenty good enough.

'I like the way you think the supermodel was drunk...' Theo murmured, temporarily distracted by her digression and thinking that, yes, there was a very high chance that whoever she had seen clinging to him *had* had too much to drink. 'Maybe she was clinging to me because she liked the sensation of being pressed up against me... A lot of women do...'

Alexa blinked and blushed. 'Well...' the conversation had meandered, and she had only herself to blame '...in case you hadn't noticed I'm not six-foot-two and blonde, so you can't turn me into one of your supermodels...'

'You know exactly what I was talking about, Alexa...'

'Do I?' The way he said her name sent little shivers through her, and her eyes glazed over as she tried to fight off the unusual sensation.

'Show up next to me in a pair of jeans, some trainers and

a baggy sweatshirt and people are going to scratch their heads in bewilderment. And show up next to me you're going to have to—because we're going to spend the next couple of months convincing whoever needs convincing that we're a loved-up couple.'

'I have a *job*...' Alexa stared at him in horror.

'I'm not asking you to shadow me twenty-four hours of the day,' Theo clarified. 'In fact I won't even be in Italy for significant periods of time. My work is primarily in London. I will, however, try and arrange my business dealings so that I can be here more often than I normally would. I don't see that I have much choice in the matter. At any rate, when I'm in London you're going to have to drop whatever you're doing and put in an appearance. Two people who are supposed to be madly in love should be madly in love enough that they actually want to spend time in the same country together.'

'Are you telling me that I will have to give up my job?'

Theo looked at her pensively. 'You work in a law office. Am I right?'

'How did you know?'

'Your parents told me before you came down,' Theo said wryly. 'They thought a little background information about you would be a good idea.'

'What else did they say?'

'That you don't seem particularly enthralled by it...'

Alexa was dismayed. She liked what she did well enough, but her liking it only 'well enough' would not have gone unnoticed by her parents. She was their only child, and they could tune in to her moods in ways that were scary.

Was that why they had jumped to the conclusion that she was somehow unhappy with her life?

Like a detective in possession of clue number one, Alexa could begin to see why they might have also come to the conclusion that if she wasn't happy in her job, she wasn't happy in her life—and her mother, traditional as she was, would have instantly decided that it was because there was no guy in the picture. She was now twenty-six years old— at an age when so many Italian girls she had grown up with were married, some with kids. Her mother wouldn't have understood that she was just missing the independence she had had in another country.

'I haven't been there very long.'

'A year and a half is long enough to decide whether you like a job or not. My point being that it won't be any great sacrifice for you to be flexible with it while we indulge in our passionate love affair. And when we do tie the knot it won't be any great sacrifice either for you to jack it in altogether and return to London with me. There's no way I can live out here.'

Alexa's head was spinning. It didn't get worse than this. Not only had her life been overturned, but she felt as if she were on a rollercoaster ride and someone else had complete control of the on/off switch.

'I don't just work at a law firm,' she said tightly, 'I also volunteer three evenings a week at a local women's shelter, and that's something that I *do* happen to like—very much!'

That came as a surprise to Theo. Her parents hadn't mentioned it, and he wondered whether they'd thought it was something he might find a little embarrassing.

He didn't.

In fact he was intrigued. There was no need for her to do anything but enjoy living in the lap of luxury. There was certainly no need for her to have a job, but he could understand her wanting that well enough. However, helping out at a women's shelter was way beyond the call of duty, and he felt a twinge of curiosity about this woman who was going to become his wife.

Since curiosity and women didn't tend to go hand in

hand for him, he allowed himself a few seconds to enjoy the novel sensation.

'Doing what?' he asked with genuine interest.

Alexa hesitated. Determined that total detachment was the only way to deal with a situation she didn't like, convinced anyhow that someone like Theo De Angelis was just the sort of man she could only ever view as an adversary, she was wary of this brief lull in warfare.

He was leaning forward, frowning slightly, his head inclined to one side, waiting for her to reply.

And just for a split second she glimpsed the ferocity of his charm—the charm that drew women like magnets and ensured that his face was always plastered somewhere inside one of those trashy magazines she had told him about.

For a split second it was as if she were the only woman in the universe who interested him. That was how it felt. And even though she knew that it was an illusion, and it didn't change her fundamental opinion of him, she was still...

Sucked in...

'I... You probably don't get this...' she tried for defensive and belligerent but achieved breathless '...but I *am* actually interested in putting back into the community...'

'I'd like to argue that one with you, but go on...'

'I did Law at university, and my experience has been working with pro bono legal teams. I like the thought of being able to help people who need legal aid but haven't got the money to hire some fancy, expensive lawyer. I like thinking that the little guy can get as much from the system as someone with money.' Her voice picked up with enthusiasm. 'One thing led to another, and I found out about a women's shelter that needed volunteers. I thought it would be just the sort of thing I might like—and I do. I help out there on every level...from mucking in with the general work to giving some of the women there legal advice...'

She stopped abruptly, a little embarrassed at the way she had opened up, even though she was hardly divulging state secrets.

'Anyway,' she said, her guard back up and firmly in place, 'there's no need to dress up for my job *or* for my volunteer work—not that I feel comfortable dressing up anyway. You asked me if jeans and baggy jumpers and trainers are the clothes I like wearing and the answer is *yes*.'

Theo didn't say anything for a few seconds. He was still chewing over the picture she had painted of herself and marvelling that he could have been so far off target in his assumptions about this person who had been dumped on him.

Then he shook aside the moment of introspection.

Back to the matter in hand.

'That's as may be,' he said, in a voice that allowed no wriggle room, 'but you'll need a new wardrobe.'

Alexa was happy to fume once again, even though she could see the sense of what he was saying. Who was going to be convinced that he'd fallen in love with a girl who avoided parties and society affairs and whose wardrobe consisted of varying shades of denim? It just demonstrated how far apart they were in everything aside from their backgrounds, and as far as she was concerned similar backgrounds would never be good enough to bridge the gaps.

Thank goodness there was a time limit on this charade!

'And what sort of clothes would you suggest?' she asked politely. 'Do I have a say in what I wear as the radiant bride-to-be, or are you going to take over that aspect of things as well?'

'Would you like me to? I've never been shopping with a woman in my life before, but I'm more than happy to test-drive the experience with you...'

'I'll choose my own clothes,' Alexa said hurriedly as

her head was filled with images of him sitting on a chair in a boutique and looking at her as she paraded different outfits in front of him. Short, over-endowed on the breast front, and lacking in the legs-up-to-her-armpits arena, she could just imagine the comparisons he would make and inwardly cringed.

'And leaving Italy…?'

He let that very important question drop and wondered what ripples it might cause. She was extremely close to her parents. He knew that. Just as he knew that she had returned from working in London post-haste the moment she'd felt she needed to be by her mother's side.

Alexa shrugged. It wasn't a depressing thought. In fact it might be just about the brightest thing on an otherwise nightmarish horizon.

Of course it would entail living with the man now scrutinising her…

Which brought that awkward subject she had shoved aside back to the surface.

What, exactly, would their married life entail? It would be a silly academic question, of course. She wasn't his type any more than he was hers. But she would have to clarify things—draw a line in the sand, so to speak.

'I would want to carry on working wherever I happened to be,' she told him, and he nodded.

'Do you imagine that I'm the sort of dinosaur who would stop you? At any rate…' He shrugged and glanced at his watch, to find that they had been talking for a lot longer than he had imagined. It wouldn't be long before her parents would return. 'At any rate…' he picked up the thread of what he had been saying '…within the constraints of our so-called marriage you would be free to do whatever you wanted to do.'

Alexa nodded, and wondered what sort of woman he would have liked to marry, and what his expectations might have been. Would he have wanted a little stay-at-home wife? She couldn't picture him as a guy who could ever be domesticated. There was something essentially untamed about him. She'd been pushed into this, but so had he. He must have had thoughts about marriage and now he was stuck with her—at least temporarily. His life had been equally disrupted and yet you wouldn't have guessed.

She had noted the way he had looked at his watch. So they might be talking business, but it still felt like an insult to be in a man's company and to find him clock-watching because he wanted to get away.

'Fine,' she said crisply. 'In that case I would look for work as soon as I moved to London. Which…er…brings me to… I feel I ought to get a few things straight…'

'Spit it out.'

'This isn't going to be a *normal* marriage.'

'That's somewhat stating the obvious.'

'We probably won't see much of one another, which suits me just fine, and it'll just be for a few months anyway, but during that time I would appreciate it if you didn't bring women to the house.'

Theo looked at her incredulously. ' *"Bring women to the house…"*?'

'I know…' Alexa felt addled by the way those cool green eyes were resting on her face, making her feel as though she had made one big, enormous gaffe. Which she hadn't. She was just getting things straight. 'I know that behind closed doors…you know…we will be able to drop the act… But I would rather I didn't have to bump into any of your supermodels on the staircase…'

'You think I'm going to bring women back to the house I will be sharing with you? Put them in the room next door for easy access?'

'You're going to be with me for a year. I expect you will have…needs…so to speak…' Her cheeks were flaming red and she licked her lips nervously. 'And of course,' she ploughed on into thick silence, 'our marriage will be for show only. I mean…there will be no question of us… sharing a bedroom…or anything. I just want to make that clear.' She gave a high laugh. 'Just stating the obvious! So, when it comes to…er…' Her voice petered out and she looked at him in helpless frustration.

'To…er…?' he encouraged.

'You know what I'm saying!'

'You're giving me permission to have sex with any woman I want, just so long as I don't bring them into the house I will be sharing with you?'

'Yes!'

'That's very considerate and generous of you, but I'm not the sort of man who believes in fooling around outside marriage.'

'But it won't be a *real* marriage…'

'Are you magnanimously giving me permission because you want me to respond in kind?'

'I—I don't know what you mean,' Alexa stammered.

His eyes were chips of ice. 'Then shall I spell it out for you? Are you telling me that I can have sex with any woman I want because you want me to tell you that you can do likewise with any man?'

Alexa's mouth dropped open.

'You can drop the innocent act,' Theo said drily. 'I may be older than you, but I don't hark back to the Dark Ages. You're in your mid-twenties, and I'm guessing that you have a boyfriend stashed away somewhere. Your parents didn't mention anyone on the scene, in which case he probably isn't socially acceptable…'

'Not *socially acceptable*?' was all Alexa could parrot in bewilderment.

Of course—he was judging her by *his* standards. A bolt of white-hot fury lanced through her. She clamped her lips tightly shut and waited to hear where he would go next with his crazy assumptions.

'If he was the sort of guy you wanted to show off to your parents you would have trotted him back home for a sit-down meal and a meet-and-greet evening by now…'

'Because that's what you've done with your girlfriends in the past?'

'I've always discouraged that.' Theo waved aside her interruption. 'But we're not talking about me. We're talking about you.'

'So he's "socially unacceptable…"?' She stifled a bubble of hysterical laughter.

If only he knew! But to a man like Theo De Angelis the thought of being a twenty-six-year-old virgin would have been unthinkable. It wouldn't even have crossed his radar! It would never have occurred to him that there were some people on the planet who actually weren't interested in jumping into bed *for the fun of it*—people who were willing to hold out for the real thing…people who believed in love and were willing to wait till they found it before they had sex. People who wanted to share the precious gift of their body with the person they truly loved.

'He's not married…?' he mused, for the first time wondering what her social life was like.

His eyes skimmed over her flushed face and, yes…there was definitely something curiously appealing about her— something that would definitely be considered attractive by any number of men.

What would she look like with her clothes off?

Just like that his imagination fired up. Her clothes revealed nothing, but the jut of her breasts suggested that she had more than a generous handful. Big breasts, with big nipples.

He frowned and shifted as his libido, dormant since he had dispatched his last girlfriend, sprang into enthusiastic life. His thick, hard erection pushed against his zipper and he shifted again, annoyed at the way his body was reacting without his permission.

Hell… He had no intention of complicating an already complicated situation by getting curious about a woman who wasn't his type.

But his body was refusing to play ball and he focused on her face, driving inappropriate thoughts from his head.

'What a relief!' Alexa said with thick sarcasm. 'It's nice to know that you think I have *some* morals.'

Theo's eyes narrowed, because the suggestion was there that what she had he obviously lacked in abundance.

What woman had ever insinuated anything like that to him in his life before? It was outrageous. She knew just how to antagonise him, whether deliberately or not, and it took willpower not to waste his energies rising to the bait.

He wondered whether he had touched upon a sensitive issue. Had he hit a home run without even trying? *Was* there some man waiting in the wings? No matter. He would have to be dispatched—and that was certainly something he wasn't going to waste time apologising about.

'I suppose he's one of your do-gooder pals?' Theo asserted flatly. 'Maybe someone working with you at whatever shelter you work at. Am I right? I don't suppose you would want to introduce someone like *that* to your parents. You might enjoy putting the world to rights, but cut to the chase and you're the only child of one of the most important families in the country. You might be allowed freedom of movement to pursue whatever career you want, but when it comes to settling down don't tell me that your parents wouldn't be alarmed if you chose someone who couldn't make ends meet…'

Alexa didn't know whether to be insulted or amused by his freewheeling assumptions. She certainly wasn't going to set him straight—because why should she? She stoutly reminded herself that whilst it was in her nature to be utterly honest this was a novel situation—there was no need for her to account for herself.

'My parents aren't that small-minded,' she told him with saccharine politeness. 'They wouldn't *care* if I brought home someone who couldn't make ends meet.'

'I beg to differ,' Theo said, in just the kind of tone of voice that set her teeth on edge. 'Why do you think your father is so keen for me to marry you?'

'Apparently because he wants to get me down from the shelf before I take up permanent residence there.' Her cheeks were burning and she was clutching the sides of her chair, leaning forward, every muscle in her body rigid with angry tension.

'He sees me as his natural successor,' Theo informed her smoothly. 'He sees me as the perfect match for you— someone who can run his empire. It's what he wants for you…and of course for himself…'

Alexa whitened. It all made sense now, and she suddenly felt like a pawn caught up in a game that was much bigger than her. Their feuding fathers had sealed a bond and all the players had won except her. Theo's father would have his family name kept intact and his company rescued from the threat of public disgrace. Her mother would have her daughter married and, after her stroke, would have what she had wanted for the past few years. She wouldn't see it as an act of selfishness. Arranged marriages were perfectly acceptable in certain social circles. Her father would likewise see his daughter married off, and in return… Yes, he would have the perfect son-in-law.

And Theo would have…

He didn't have to spell it out for her, because it was obvious now that she was putting two and two together. Theo would wangle part-ownership of her father's company. Maybe not all of it, but his portfolio would increase substantially—not that he needed it.

And she, Alexa, would get one year of gnashing her teeth and trying not to commit homicide.

Right now she could dig her heels in and refuse to go along with what everyone else wanted. But she knew that she wasn't going to do that. She wouldn't stress her mother and risk another health problem which might prove far more serious than the last.

Theo could see the play of emotions on her face as comprehension dawned and he squashed the sickening suspicion that he was responsible for that. She was an adult and she had made her choice. True, she hadn't asked to be put in this unenviable position, but neither had he. Tough situations always made a person stronger, more resilient.

Matter sorted, he said bluntly, 'I know this situation isn't ideal, but if you have a boyfriend he's going to have to go into hiding while we're together. I have no intention of sleeping around behind your back. The press follow me like hyenas and I don't plan on giving them any carcasses to chew on—and you're going to do the same.'

He heard a rustle of activity and the distant sound of voices marking the return of her parents.

'There's an event tomorrow evening.' He stood up and raked his fingers through his hair. 'Formal. I've been invited and you'll be my…guest. It will be our first public appearance together and the perfect opportunity to get the gossip mill at work…'

Feeling as though she had been through several wars and only managed to survive by the skin of her teeth, Alexa stood up as well.

'And of course I'm to dress the part…' she muttered, feeling even more powerless standing in front of him, because he was just so…*big*…

'I intend to stay in the country for at least the next fort-night. There will be several high-profile functions.'

'I'll make sure my wardrobe is overflowing with stuff I wouldn't normally wear in a million years!' she snapped.

Theo smiled slowly. 'I look forward to seeing them… I'll pick you up tomorrow evening at seven. Get ready to be the centre of attention…'

CHAPTER THREE

'DARLING, YOU LOOK BEAUTIFUL...'

Alexa tried hard not to grimace. She had spent a restless night. Her entire mind had seemed to be filled with images of Theo, leaving no room for anything else.

First thing in the morning she had telephoned her boss at work to advise him that she would have to take a temporary leave of absence. She hated leaving him in the lurch, but he would find out soon enough the reasons for her abrupt departure. When pressed, she had only muttered that it was of a personal nature.

Then she had spent the day, at her mother's excited instigation, at various beauty parlours and clothes shops.

She had had her nails done, her face done... She had gone to the hairdressers, where they had trimmed her hair, suffused it with highlights and then insisted she look and admire what they had created... She had traipsed from one shop to another and allowed herself to be guided by personal shoppers...

Alexa knew that it was just the sort of day most girls of her background would have taken for granted. But by the end of the afternoon, laden with bags which had quickly been taken to her room, each elaborate dress carefully hung in her wardrobe while her precious casual clothes had got second billing, she had felt utterly spent.

Now, looking at her mother's thin, beaming face, she

reminded herself why she had embarked on this crazy scheme. Her mother was positively radiant.

She hadn't accompanied her shopping, but had greeted the sight of each purchase with gratifying squeals of delight. Alexa was forced to concede that at long last Cora Caldini had managed to get the doll she had wanted rather than the tomboy she had been stuck with.

'I look…' Alexa stole a glance at her reflection and for a few startling seconds, now that she was seeing the complete and finished product, was lost for words '…different…' she eventually managed to croak.

Neither the mirrors she had cursorily glanced in at the various shops nor the face she had politely and very briefly scanned at the hairdressers seemed to have done justice to the person now reflected back at her.

Different was an understatement, and she was honest enough to acknowledge that.

Her curves were still all there, but for some reason the dress took them, held them, shaped them in some way so that she was…*sexy*…

'I know,' her mother said with immense satisfaction. 'Fabulous! And the colour suits you perfectly.'

That colour was a shimmering pale duck-egg-blue that brought out the brightness of her eyes. Perfectly fitted to slightly below the waist, clinging to her torso like a second skin, the dress flared softly to the ground. The neckline was scooped, but not outrageously so, just affording a tantalising glimpse of the soft swell of her breasts, and the back was equally scooped. When she moved, it flowed in gossamer-fine layers of silk around her, so that every movement she made was as graceful as a dancer's.

The highlights she had ignored at the hairdressers picked up rich copper threads in her hair that she had never noticed. Only a fraction of her hair had been trimmed so that, loose, it tumbled down her back and cascaded over her shoulders.

Her mother had brought in some of her jewellery, and the next half an hour was spent trying on several pieces.

Alexa discovered that she actually enjoyed that half an hour...

She was hardly aware of time passing until there was a knock on the door and she was told that Theo had arrived and was waiting for her by the stairs.

Alexa snapped out of her reverie and smiled at her mother. 'This is the most excited I've seen you in ages. Do you think I should have been going around dressed like this for the past few years?'

'You've never been one for dressing up...' Her mother sighed, still smiling. 'And I wouldn't have changed that for the world. But now and again... Well, my darling, you can see for yourself how wonderful it is to just try something new once in a while. Theo is going to be stunned.'

Theo won't notice what I wear unless I turn up in dungarees and trainers, Alexa wanted to retort as she slipped her feet into stilettoes that were precariously high but absolutely suited to the outfit.

'You're going to be *engaged*—and *married*. Such an exciting time... I know you've been nudged a little in that direction—but, darling, a mother knows best, and I just *know* that the two of you are going to be soulmates. When your father told me that Stefano had mentioned his son had seen you, wanted to meet you.., Well, I was over the moon. And, having met him for myself... Well, he's just perfect—and I can tell you feel the same...'

So that's how this little charade is being played out, Alexa thought. Theo had supposedly wanted to set up a meeting with her. Her mother probably had visions of love at first sight, if not at first meeting.

Of course she didn't know of his deal made with the

devil. One year of self-sacrifice and in return shares in their sprawling family company. And, added to that, *his* father's company would be saved from public ruin.

Love and respect for her mother stopped her from prolonging the conversation and hammering the truth home like a battering ram. But it was just so frustrating.

She grabbed a little sequinned bag from the dressing table and then followed her mother along the corridor towards the staircase. Pausing at the top, she looked down to see Theo and her father chatting. Theo's back was to her, but the powerful force of his presence still struck her like a physical blow.

He was dressed as formally as she was. One hand was shoved into the pocket of black hand-tailored trousers, and she could see the pristine white of his shirt-cuff peeping out from beneath his immaculately fitted black jacket.

His body's posture was loose…relaxed. He was a man looking forward to an evening out with the woman he would show off to the world as his wife-to-be.

No wonder her mother thought that the man was the next best thing to sliced bread. Theo had his act down pat. He was so socially adept at handling any situation that anyone looking in would have just seen a prospective son-in-law dedicated to charming his in-laws. Anyone looking in would have probably thought that he had asked her father for her hand in marriage and proposed on bended knee. Which just went to show…

She took a deep breath and began walking down the winding staircase.

Theo turned slowly. Carlo Caldini was proving to be both amusing and intelligent. In fact he reminded Theo of his own father. He could understand why they had been inseparable friends for such a long time. Without much time to spare there had seemed little point in having a drink, so they had remained at the bottom of the staircase, chatting.

It had come as no great surprise that Alexa had not been waiting for him when he arrived. As long as she wasn't hiding out in the broom cupboard in the hope that he would leave without her, then that was all right. He was prepared to wait for as long as it took—whether they arrived on time or not was of little importance to him. In fact the later the better, to some extent, because not only would that limit the hours spent in tedious chatter but it would also ensure that the maximum number of people would witness their arrival, arm in arm.

In Rome, even more than in London, news of the happy couple and their impending nuptials would spread faster than the speed of light.

With his mind toying with the question of how best he could assimilate a wife into his lifestyle without having to alter his day-to-day routine very much, it took Theo a few seconds to focus on the woman gliding with effortless grace down the stairs.

So she'd taken him at his word. He hadn't known what to expect—whether she would actually do what was necessary or else jump aboard her independence bandwagon and don some paint-spattered overalls and hiking boots for the social event to which he had been invited.

Where had that figure come from? She'd hidden it well… With the dress clinging lovingly to her, he could see that she had the perfect hourglass shape. Full breasts narrowed to a slender waist, and even in the floor-length gown he could see that her legs would be shapely. She was the absolute opposite of the stick insects he was accustomed to dating.

Their eyes met and she pursed her lips—just sufficiently to remind him that she was doing this under duress.

If either of her parents had noticed that little show of rebellion they were hiding it well under their broad smiles and proud gazes, but as soon as he had followed her into the chauffeur-driven limousine, Theo turned to her.

'You're going to have to do a bit better than that…' he drawled, making sure that the privacy partition between the driver and the rear seat was firmly up.

She had pressed herself as far away from him as she could physically get without falling out of the car.

'And the evening isn't going to kick off on the right footing if you behave as though I'm carrying the plague,' he went on, keeping his voice even and detached.

'I'll be fine once we get there,' Alexa told him defiantly.

She had noticed that he hadn't complimented her on her outfit. Whilst her father had been holding her at arm's length and showering her with over-the-top compliments Theo had stood back, face impassive. Anyone in that situation would have felt hurt, so it wasn't strange that she had.

Clearly when there was no pressing need to make an impression he wasn't that bothered, so why did he expect her to cosy up against him now? Just in case the driver got suspicious?

'I'm not even sure where we're going,' she said, because yet again his show of good manners had made her feel like a silly kid.

'Art exhibition,' Theo said succinctly. 'Under normal circumstances I would have been in London, but as I happen to be here…'

'An art exhibition…?' She had gone to a couple of those ages ago, with her parents. The art had been incomprehensible and the crowd had been shallow and overdressed.

'There will be no need to stay long,' Theo said mildly. 'Just long enough to create an impression. Although…'

'Although what?' Alexa tensed and looked at him.

In the blue-grey twilight his face was all angles and shadows. She felt a dangerous ripple of response snake through her body and she caught her breath and held it for a few panicked, confused seconds before slowly releasing it.

'Although perhaps we might stay a bit longer than absolutely necessary. After all, it would a shame to waste a dress like that on a forty-minute appearance...'

Alexa was lost for words. He had paid her a compliment, in a backhanded sort of way, and his lazy velvety voice swirled around her like a mind-altering drug. He was leaning against the door, utterly relaxed, and his eyes were broodingly sexy as he watched her, obviously not caring that it was rude to stare.

Of course, she told herself feverishly, what he had *meant* was that it was a dress designed to grab the headlines, so why waste it? Why not stay as long as they could so that it had maximum effect? It hadn't been a compliment directed at her *personally*.

At any rate, it didn't matter one way or the other. This was a business arrangement. They were co-workers, so to speak.

'I've never liked those sorts of things.' Alexa rushed into nervous chatter. 'I think that was the best thing about being away from Italy...not having to go to openings and art shows and film premieres... Not that I was ever forced to, you understand, but I think my parents enjoyed showing me off. The hardship of being the only child of a rich family!'

She was blabbering, but she couldn't seem to stop herself because she knew that if she did she might have to analyse the rush of giddiness that had assailed her on the back of his stupid compliment. And then she would have to link it up with the weird way her body seemed to behave in his presence.

Did it all stem from her lack of experience with the opposite sex?

Blabbering on seemed an easier option than wrestling with those kinds of questions.

'Most people would kill to endure that sort of hardship.'

Cheeks flaming, Alexa turned to look through the window before glancing back at him. The space between them was as big as it could possibly get on the back seat of a very big car, but it still felt tiny. If she reached out she would be able to touch him.

'I get that,' she said stiffly. 'I wasn't complaining. I was talking too much because…'

'Because you're nervous?'

'Aren't you?'

Theo shrugged. He liked the way her hair fell in waves around her. It was much longer than he had originally thought, and it wasn't poker-straight, which seemed to be the only style women below the age of thirty-five wore their hair in the circles he mixed in. A year out from them might be a pleasant break in the monotony. She looked as though she had just climbed out of bed and run her fingers through its length and then left it to its own devices. She was dressed to kill and wearing war paint, but there was still something lacking in artifice about her. She would do those cameras proud.

'Why would I be nervous?'

'Because we're pretending to be something we aren't,' Alexa said bluntly.

'You never did tell me,' he murmured, 'whether you have a boyfriend or not.'

'Because it's none of your business.'

'Of course it's my business,' Theo returned smoothly. Was it? *Really?* Probably not. But he was suddenly curious to find out. 'Reporters will do anything to get background material so that they can flesh out a non-existent story, and you'd be surprised at the efforts they go to to rake up mud. If they uncover a lovelorn pro bono lawyer weeping in a corner somewhere they'll have a field-day. I'm going to have to be prepped with a suitable story.'

'Are you telling me that you're as pure as driven snow when it comes to...to...women? That there are no skeletons in your cupboard that can be uncovered?'

'My love-life is an open book!'

Theo grinned, and she was fascinated at how that open grin could be so engaging. She was as nervous as a kitten and he couldn't have been cooler.

Did *anything* rattle the man?

'We're here.'

Alexa realised that the limo was slowing in front of an impressive white building, fronted with imposing stone columns and a bank of shallow stairs leading up to double doors, which were open. In front of them two uniformed men were checking invitations.

'Boyfriend or no boyfriend?' Theo pressed, circling her wrist with his hand, staying her before she could get out of the car.

'No boyfriend! Okay?'

Theo shot her a smile of such satisfaction that she wanted to smack him. Instead she gritted her teeth and returned his look of satisfaction with one of simmering resentment, which just made him smile a little more.

'No boyfriend. Good. The fewer complications, the better. And stop scowling. Our relationship is too fresh for us to be having arguments in the back seat of a limo. We're still in the honeymoon phase... The way I leave the toothpaste uncovered and forget to put the toilet seat down hasn't started getting on your nerves just yet... So let's smile a lot and face the music...'

He laughed softly at her indignant, helpless expression and gently urged her out of the car as her door was opened for her.

It was a big deal. Cameras flashed at the throng of people clustered outside or making their way in. Even as the car had stopped Alexa had been able to recognise faces. A couple of high-profile politicians, celebrities clinging to other celebrities, as if terrified of moving out of their comfort zones, businessmen in suits, accompanied by wives dripping in diamonds…

Just the sort of crowd she preferred to avoid.

They stepped out of the car and every reporter with every camera seemed to turn, as one, in their direction.

This was the difference between being rich and being rich and newsworthy. The blinding flash of bulbs going off dazzled her, and the steadying arm of Theo, curving around her waist, felt like a solid rock of support in turbulent waters. She knew that she was actually leaning against him. Loathing the man, yet still finding his support strangely comforting.

There was an excited babble of voices and heads turned in their direction.

'You look amazing.'

Theo leant to whisper huskily into her ear and she looked up at him, sensed the popping of cameras taking a picture of their whispered conversation.

'So don't be nervous. I'm right here.'

He felt her automatic protest and his hold on her tightened. He laughed softly under his breath.

'Remember,' he murmured, still pressing close to her, so that no one could overhear what was being said, 'what I told you about retracting those claws in public… Don't forget that we're in love…at the honeymoon stage…you can't get enough of me…'

Alexa had no idea how she managed to deal with the next hour and a half. She drank two glasses of champagne and ate some of the canapés that were passed around. Questions peppered her from various quarters, including from several people—friends of her parents—who wanted to know what was going on.

The gossip mill was in full swing, and they couldn't have announced their togetherness in a more public manner.

Theo didn't leave her side. His arm was around her at all times. She was conscious of that with every step she took.

'Had enough?'

Theo tilted her chin up and their eyes met. Alexa found that she could do little else but stare. His eyes were truly amazing and she felt giddy, sucked in by their green depths. She saw those fabulous, mesmerising eyes flicker and then he was leaning towards her and his mouth was covering hers, grazing it, and then he was delicately teasing his tongue between her lips.

Never in her life had she felt anything like this before. It was as if a series of fireworks had exploded in her head. Every single thought vanished. Indeed, there was no one else in the room—no crowds of people chattering around her, no waiting staff weaving through with trays balanced on hands, no curious eyes boring a hole into her back.

There was just the two of them, and the feel of his tongue meshing with hers, eliciting a soft shudder of response.

Simultaneously the flash of a camera captured the moment, and she knew instantly that Theo had foreseen that.

Everything had been timed to perfection. He had held her with just the right amount of possessiveness, had been attentive to just the right extent, had led the charade, expecting her to follow in his lead—and she had.

They left the still-packed art exhibition and the babble of noise eventually subsided as they moved out into the open foyer outside the room where the main event was taking place, which was far less crowded.

'Well done.'

Theo released her, and without his arm around her reality was re-established.

'What choice did I have?' Alexa asked stiffly as they made their way outside.

The chauffeur had already been summoned and was waiting for them, with the passenger door open and thankfully, no prying cameras to chart their sudden lack of affection.

She was taut with anger. Anger at herself, for having become swept up in that kiss—and not just the kiss. The whispered encouraging compliments…the way he had spent the evening touching her in some way or another… the way he had been the perfect newly loved-up boyfriend.

'About as much as I had.'

The ferocity of his body's response to that well-timed kiss, which would doubtless be in print somewhere by the following morning, had shocked him. He prided himself on being in control of the situation that had been foisted upon him, and he was annoyed with himself for the unrestrained surge in his libido. *Again.*

He propelled her into the waiting car and then slid the partition up so that once again their conversation could not be overheard by their driver.

'Our engagement will be publicly announced in the next few days,' he informed her matter-of-factly. 'So our next bonding session will be at a jeweller's.'

Every trace of affection had disappeared. His cool washed over her like freezing water. He had detached. There was the man who could show one face to the public, and then there was the man who could remove that mask and be someone completely different in private.

This was a lesson she should learn, Alexa thought feverishly. While *her* feelings were all over the place, his had never shifted. He was completely lacking in all emotion—

which was why he had no problem going along with the farce.

Considering she had always thought of herself as a restrained person—someone who could stand back and laugh at the weaknesses of other members of her sex, who got their emotions all tangled up, who ended up being ruled by them—it came as a shock to realise that she wasn't quite the person she had thought herself to be.

She would have to learn fast.

'When shall I pencil that in?' she asked.

'Whenever I tell you to. It will take full precedence over everything else.'

'And I assume there will be some sort of stupid engagement party?'

'I prefer the word *lavish* to *stupid*.'

Alexa glumly pictured the extravagant affair it would no doubt turn out to be. Lots of important people, and among them the friends she had made in her job—who would stick out like elephants in a tea shop.

'I can't see your father having a great time being entertained by my parents,' she said snidely.

'You'd be surprised. They may have their simmering feud, but they have still carried on mixing in the same social circles. You know well enough what it's like over here.'

'Not really. I've spent most of my time abroad. And anyway I never attended those events.' Curiosity got the better of her. 'You've seen our fathers interacting?'

'On a couple of occasions. They bristle in each other's company and yet end up having conversations—like a married couple who can't help fighting but find it hard to stay away from one another. In a room of five hundred people, somehow they'll end up right next to one another. And in between the fraught relations there's usually a fair amount of gossip, which they can't seem to help divulging. Which, in turn, is probably why my father turned to Carlo before heading to the nearest bank. It's a strange case. So I shouldn't worry over-much about your father at our engagement party...it won't be a case of fisticuffs at dusk.'

'Do you know why they fell out?'

'Your guess is as good as mine.'

This lull in hostilities was a temporary soothing balm, but she shook herself free and recalled that this was just a business arrangement with a man she didn't even like.

The limousine was pulling up outside her house, but she remained sitting in the car for a few moments after the car had come to a stop in the courtyard.

'Perhaps you could text me with details of when this visit to the jeweller's is likely to be?' she offered politely.

Theo dragged his thoughts away from the way she was sitting, her body towards him, leaning in so that the soft mounds of her breasts were temptingly on show.

'Let's say I pass by for you at noon tomorrow. The sooner the better, as far as I'm concerned. We can choose a ring and then go somewhere to have lunch.'

Alexa couldn't hide her dismay. 'Lunch? Is that really necessary?'

'Your constant shows of reluctance are really beginning to get on my nerves, Alexa! Yes, *lunch*! What exactly is your dilemma with that? We're newly engaged. Has it occurred to you that as a newly engaged couple we might just want to celebrate together before scuttling off in opposite directions? Scuttling off in opposite directions would be more suited to a couple on the verge of divorce!'

Alexa glared, but this was her life for the time being and she knew that he was right. It was a game that had to be played to the full or not played at all.

She had embarked upon it, and it was too late now to start trying to renegotiate the terms of the contract.

'I can meet you at the jeweller's,' she offered.

'Not good enough. We're browsing together. No need for hiking boots, though…'

'Don't worry,' she sniped in return. 'I know my trainers wouldn't be suitable wear for being seen in public with you.'

'You have to be the most argumentative woman I have ever met in my entire life,' Theo mused in a driven undertone. 'Are you this argumentative with all the men you've been out with?'

Alexa was momentarily caught on the back foot, because the number of men she had dated could be counted on the fingers of one hand and none of them had provoked her the way this man did.

'I've never been out with anyone like you,' she finally gathered enough wit to respond, and Theo grinned.

'Are you telling me that I'm one of a kind?'

'If I'm argumentative, then *you're* downright impossible,' she muttered. 'I should be going in. The lights are on. My parents are probably waiting to hear how our first outing in public went—although judging from the amount of reporters there, they can probably find out in the papers tomorrow.'

'If I've failed to mention it, you handled the evening incredibly well.'

Of their own volition, his eyes dipped to her full and still mutinous mouth.

'Thank you. So did you,' she responded in a stilted voice.

When she glanced down she could see her breasts, too big and too exposed for her liking—especially now that she was in the intimate confines of a car with him—and she surreptitiously adjusted her dress, hoping that he wouldn't notice.

'My mother will ask about this stupid…sorry, this *lavish* engagement party. I expect she'll need time to sort it out. Could you give me an approximate…er…date? And I agree with you—the sooner the better.'

Theo marvelled that here was a woman who, only just engaged to be married to him, was clearly already thinking about the divorce papers being signed. Incredible. The fact that these were not normal circumstances did little to assuage his male pride.

'At the outside…a fortnight.'

'Will your brother attend as well as your father?' she found herself asking, because she knew that his brother lived on the other side of the world and that during these transactions he hadn't been a player on the scene.

Theo frowned. 'All bets are off when it comes to that,' he commented wryly. 'Daniel is in the process of buying himself a toy, and it may remove him from the scene of the action while this drama is being played out.'

'Buying a toy?'

'He has his eye on a small cruise ship.'

Much as he loved his brother, Theo was quietly relieved that Daniel wouldn't be around for the engagement party, such as it would be. Daniel could be counted on to respond with nothing but laughter at the fact that his big brother had found himself tying the knot prematurely. Actually, tying the knot at all.

'I had no idea that cruise ships could be called *toys*…' Alexa was distracted enough to say.

'In which case you don't know my brother.'

Alexa thought that that was just as well, because coping with one was bad enough. Two alpha males didn't bear thinking about.

She pulled open the car door and stepped out into a balmy night. Of course he walked her to the door. No protective arm around her shoulder this time, though! Instead both hands were firmly thrust in his trouser pockets.

'Isn't your chauffeur going to think that we're not behaving the way two nearly married people should be behaving?' she couldn't help but ask sarcastically, reaching into her bag for the house key, even though she knew that her mother was probably hovering very close to the front door so that she could pounce the second it was opened.

Theo lounged indolently against the door frame, looking down at her as she pulled out the key to insert it into the lock.

'Is that an invitation?' he asked softly.

Alexa raised startled eyes to his.

'What—what on earth are you talking about now?' she stammered, as her wide-eyed gaze was caught and held.

She had the oddest sensation that the oxygen was being sucked out of the air she was breathing as she continued to stare up at him. Her heart was fluttering madly, like a caged bird in a desperate bid for escape.

'What do you think?' Theo asked, in that same soft, lazy drawl that gave her goosebumps.

'Are you suggesting that I actually want you to…to…?'

'Kiss you? That's exactly what I'm suggesting…'

'Then you couldn't be further from the mark!' she snapped, blushing furiously and hating him for reminding her of their kiss, which *she* would rather have forgotten. 'I'm fine with you being…being attentive when we're out together, but the last thing I want is to be *kissed* by you! Do you know something, Theo De Angelis? You're the most egotistical, arrogant man I have ever met!'

'I know. I think you've told me already. But you make a valid point… Just in case…'

She sensed what he was about to do and yet it still took her by surprise—and this time there was an urgency to his kiss that hadn't been there before. His mouth assailed hers, his tongue seeking out hers. He curved a big hand behind her back and pulled her towards him.

He could feel the softness of her breasts squashing

against his chest and knew that he was losing his cool. *Again.* But her mouth was nectar-sweet—and after all, he told himself, it was all for the benefit of a driver who might or might not be taking note. Why take chances…?

'I'll see you tomorrow.' He straightened. 'Engagement ring shopping. Who would have thought…?'

With which he headed back to the car and Alexa, thoroughly unnerved, let herself into the house.

CHAPTER FOUR

As PREDICTED, THE next day the centre pages of all the newspapers had been printed with at least half a dozen pictures of the loving couple. Whoever had taken the photos couldn't have done better when it came to capturing angles that actually seemed to *prove* the lie that they were in love.

Theo's arm was always around her. In several pictures Alexa was looking up at him, mouth parted, the very picture of an enraptured girlfriend—as opposed to wearing the teeth-clenched, resentful expression, which was a lot closer to the truth.

Cora Caldini, who was waiting for her when she emerged at a little after eight, had all the papers spread out on the massive dining room table and Alexa stifled a sigh.

'I know this has all been unexpected for you,' her mother said gently, 'but there's so much to be said for a whirlwind romance—and looking at these pictures…my darling, you *sparkle*.'

Alexa helped herself to coffee and a croissant from the basket of fresh bread on the sideboard. Sparkle? Did minnows sparkle in the presence of hungry, prowling sharks?

'He's certainly a force to contend with,' Alexa forced herself to say. 'And you're right. It wasn't…er…exactly what I had in mind when I thought about meeting the man of my dreams. In fact I'm a little dazed—because he's just the sort of guy I never thought I'd...um...fall for. But... well...life is full of surprises, I guess...'

Unable to be more effusive than that, she scanned the photos once more and wondered whether the reporters had bothered with any other guests at all, or whether they had just decided to trail along behind Theo, snapping pictures.

'Isn't it...?' Her mother beamed. 'And sometimes surprises turn out all the better for being unexpected. It reminds me of when I met your father, as a matter of fact. Of course I'd seen him out and about, but at a distance, and when my parents arranged for us to meet face to face... Well, it really was love at first sight. He was nothing like what I'd expected, and I just fell for that rogue on the spot.'

Always mindful of the consultant's warning words several months ago, in the wake of her mother's third stroke, Alexa reluctantly decided to backtrack.

'Theo's...er...certainly not what I expected,' she conceded. 'I suppose he's quite intelligent, and he has a certain amount of...er...charisma...'

'Funny...your father likes him very much.'

Then perhaps *he* should marry Theo, Alexa thought nastily, surprising herself because she wasn't an uncharitable person by nature.

'That's good.'

'And I know you, my darling. You're as headstrong as I was at your age. If you really didn't like Theo I think we'd all know about it by now! You just don't want to jinx anything—which is why you're being reticent—and I completely understand. It took your father and I ages to have you, and I didn't tell a soul I was pregnant until I couldn't hide it any longer! So I won't press you. Now, tell me what your plans are for today.'

Alexa told her mother and could immediately feel her tummy clench at the prospect of a few hours browsing for a ring and then having lunch in a trendy restaurant with him.

The memory of that blistering kiss the night before had preyed on her mind all night, and she had awoken determined to make sure that they kept a cool distance from one another when there was no one around.

Her thoughts drifted while her mother chatted about rings and reflected on how fast she and Carlo had progressed from that first meeting—marrying within three months and never regretting a day of their long and happy marriage.

Naturally Alexa had known that the man was good-looking. But why did he have to be *so* good-looking? Averagely good-looking would have been all right. She felt that she might have been able to cope with that. But something about Theo De Angelis sparked a reaction in her that burned as fierce as a conflagration.

She didn't understand it. It didn't make sense, And it unsettled her. Scared her, even—although what was there to be scared about?

She surfaced to catch the tail-end of her mother informing her that Theo was going to be dashing off to New York—apparently called away on business. Carlo had wanted to show him around the electronics plant later in the week, talk men stuff, but unfortunately it was a visit that would have to wait.

'He never mentioned that,' Alexa murmured, brightening. 'When? Exactly?'

'Tomorrow, I believe. Your father called him first thing this morning about a visit to the plant and it seems that an emergency blew up overnight. So he wouldn't have mentioned anything to you when you were out.'

'I don't suppose you know how long he'll be away, do you, Mother?'

'A week at the very least... I'm sure he'll be most apologetic when he sees you later and will explain it all himself.

If there's one thing I can say for Stefano's son it's that he's an extremely polite young man...'

Good humour restored on the back of the heartening news that she was going to have a break from Theo, Alexa spent the remainder of the morning looking through her law books, making sure her brain was still ticking over. She dealt with a variety of problems at the shelter on a daily basis, and some of them were practical—questions pertaining to government allowances, retrieving cash from runaway partners, applying for social housing. It paid to keep abreast of the law, and it was no great hardship because she enjoyed it anyway.

At precisely eleven-thirty she got dressed, but she didn't rush.

This time, her spirits light because with Theo out of the country for maybe as long as a fortnight she would at least have some respite from his dangerously incendiary personality, choosing what to wear was far less of a chore than it had been the evening before.

Jeans, but smart black ones, a cream silk camisole top, because it was beautifully warm outside, and flat black pumps. Everything was brand-new, and she was in a good mood when, at twelve sharp, the doorbell rang and she forestalled her mother to answer it.

This time there was no driver, which was even better—because with Theo driving she would be spared those intense, speculative green eyes on her.

'You're in a good mood,' he said flatly, starting the engine of a Ferrari and easing it out of the courtyard towards the buzzing town centre. 'Why does that make me instantly suspicious?'

Alexa relaxed against the passenger's door, her head resting on the window, rolled up thanks to the air-conditioning which kept the temperature wonderfully cool. She absently noted his strong jawline and the sharp beauty of his lean face, in profile now as he focused on the road. He was wearing black sunglasses and a navy blue polo shirt and cream trousers. He looked impossibly elegant.

She tugged her eyes away from him, simultaneously deciding that this was just the sort of thing that had to stop—this mindless staring at him—and again applauding the fact that he was going to be away for the next few days. Plenty of time during which she could recover her equilibrium.

'I have no idea,' Alexa said chirpily. 'Doesn't *every* girl like going out shopping for her engagement ring?'

Theo glanced narrowly at her, then relaxed and smiled. 'Indeed. That *would* explain your good mood. You're right. I have yet to meet a woman whose heart doesn't beat faster at the prospect of all things bridal…'

Alexa scowled, because her saccharine-sweet sarcastic rejoinder had clearly backfired. 'I honestly don't think we should waste much time traipsing through shops in search of a diamond ring,' she told him loftily.

'Agreed.' He put the fast car into cruise mode and relaxed in his seat. 'There's no need for us to be seen going from one shop to another in search of the perfect ring. We've already got all the press coverage we need. Speculation is rife that marriage is in the air… If we went to the corner shop and bought a plastic washer it would probably be enough.'

Alexa grimaced as she recalled the spread of newspapers her mother had neatly laid out on the table for her perusal. 'Maybe they'll leave us alone now?' She breathed a sigh of relief at the thought.

'I expect they'll only leave us alone when there's a chunky wedding ring on your finger. Before then there are infinite possibilities for our relationship to crash and burn—and disasters always make better headlines.'

'Why would they assume that it will crash and burn?' How on earth did *real* celebrities survive? she wondered. Without going completely mad? 'And who *cares* if our relationship crashes and burns anyway? Who's interested?'

Alexa was genuinely bewildered, because she might come from a wealthy background but—of her choosing— she was as noticeable as wallpaper. Theo might be similarly rich, with the added bonus of his looks, but he wasn't a *star*...was he...?

Theo shrugged. 'Don't know. Don't care. I just know how the world of media operates and I deal with it. So if you don't want some trigger-happy reporter to shoot you leaving the house without your make-up, be warned.'

'I honestly don't care.'

Theo found an empty space in a crowded square around which designer shops extended outwards in ripples—layers of them, sandwiched between cafés and restaurants. In the centre of the square a trio of mythological creatures figured in bronze cavorted in the centre of an enormous fountain.

He turned to her and said, with utter seriousness, 'You don't, do you?'

'No. Do you?'

'I'm a man. I don't tend to go out wearing make-up. Well, not unless I have to. Sometimes after a long night at work I find a bit of foundation under the eyes...'

Alexa felt her mouth twitch and she grinned shyly and reluctantly at him.

He killed the engine, but she got the impression that there were more questions he wanted to ask her. It felt as if he had been testing her boundary lines...placing one foot over the perimeter of her electric fence, threatening to make inroads. That made her shiver a little.

'Right,' he said briskly. 'Engagement ring.'

In case she started falling behind him he curled his fingers into her hair and pressed his hand to the nape of her neck, gently making sure she kept up with him and slowing his naturally long stride to accommodate her much shorter one.

People turned and looked.

They clearly didn't know exactly who Theo was, but Alexa could almost see their brains churning, trying to figure out why he was famous—because he just *had* to be, looking the way he did.

Something weird rippled through her. A surge of pride. That he was with *her*.

They bypassed the first three jeweller's they came to and went directly to the fourth, which was little more than a nondescript door leading into a shop that was barely visible from the street outside.

'How on earth do you know about this place?'

'You're a woman. How on earth do you *not*?' From behind his dark shades Theo looked down at her upturned face, amused. 'Have you made it your life's mission to avoid leading the sort of life you were expected to lead?'

'I'm not into expensive jewellery. Do you come here with your girlfriends?'

She was acutely conscious of his fingers, still in her hair, absently stroking her neck. It sent shivers racing up and down her spine, and she had to forcibly remind herself just how over the moon she was that he would be disappearing to salvage his business deal and she wouldn't have to put up with these public shows of phoney affection.

Theo paused. 'Quite some time ago a woman I was dating dragged me here and made a point of telling me how exquisite and expensive the jewellery was.'

'So you bought her a diamond ring?' Alexa squeaked.

'Quite some time ago' implied that the woman he had been dating might have been *her* age, and she was struck again at just how sheltered a life she had led—more inter-

ested in her studies than in getting a guy to buy her baubles and trinkets…waiting for love to knock on her door and refusing to spread herself thin in the meanwhile…

'I broke off the relationship,' Theo returned wryly. 'I didn't like the direction it was taking.'

Alexa stopped dead in her tracks. 'You must *hate* this,' she said with sudden force. 'Being trapped into marrying me.'

'The rewards outweigh the inconvenience,' Theo said, fighting an urge to brush the hair blowing softly around her face from her eyes. 'And your dowry is certainly a healthy incentive.'

Feeling like cattle that had been successfully bartered to a new master, Alexa spun round on her heels and pushed open the door to the jewellery shop—which was as unprepossessing on the inside as it was on the outside.

'Take your time,' Theo urged as they were ushered into comfortable chairs and the process of displaying rings began.

The owner of the shop was small, thin and extremely knowledgeable. He seemed to know everything there was to know about diamonds, and tray after tray was brought, with rings nestling in beds of velvet, unpriced and therefore probably priceless.

Since it wasn't a real engagement Alexa didn't care which ring she wore, but it would be ridiculous to choose something that was big and ostentatious.

'What is *your* preference?' She turned to look at Theo, who was lounging in the chair, his long legs stretched out to one side, lightly crossed at the ankles. 'Why don't *you* choose?'

Theo linked his fingers on his washboard-flat stomach and looked at the proprietor with a knowing, man-to-man grin.

'Women!' He shook his head with an expression of rueful indulgence. 'As if *my* opinion would count for anything!'

He stroked her back with one possessive hand and his fingers lingered for fractionally too long on her bra strap. Alexa kept a smile pinned to her face and wriggled a little to dislodge his over-inquisitive hand.

'The women do usually take the lead when it comes to choosing jewellery, sir.'

The proprietor returned Theo's smile and Alexa gritted her teeth as Theo patted her a couple of times on her back and then linked his fingers lightly on his lap once again.

'And this feisty little lady knows that she can have whatever she wants! So what *do* you want?' He looked at her with lazy, sexy bedroom eyes. 'Your wish is my command…'

'If only *that* were true,' Alexa returned pointedly.

She bared her teeth in a smile and hoped that he was sharp enough to read the hidden message, which was along the lines of *If my wish was your command, you would be on the other side of the world…*

Without warning, Theo leaned forward and quickly, but far too effectively, planted a kiss on her mouth.

Their eyes tangled and she realised, heart beating frantically, that he knew exactly what she had been implying and had duly punished her with that kiss.

To add insult to injury, as she returned her attention to the tray in front of her, she felt his big hand rest on her leg and then, shockingly, move upwards, curving over the sensitive skin of her inner thigh and sending a frisson of electric response through her.

Perspiration beaded her upper lip. She snapped her legs shut and pointed to any ring on the tray—she didn't even notice which one she had chosen.

'That'll do!'

Theo's hand on her thigh tightened.

'Perfect choice, if I may say so myself…'

The proprietor reverently removed it from its velvet bed and they listened to his rhapsodies about the purity of the diamond and the rarity of its setting. They were asked to pay attention to the tiny details in the band, which marked it out as a one-off. Alexa was made to try it on. Measurements were painstakingly taken.

The ring cost a small fortune, so it wasn't hard to understand why the whole process was taking for ever.

'That'll do…?' It was the first thing Theo said as they made their way out of the shop.

'Your hand was on my leg,' Alexa said stiffly. And his arm was around her shoulders now. The public face of unity was back in place, although her body was as rigid as a plank of wood.

'Perfectly natural,' Theo purred, giving her shoulder a little squeeze as he guided her to one of the hippest cafés in the area—a place where people went to be seen. 'You're my fiancée. Of course I'm going to want to touch you. Frankly, I can't keep my hands off you…'

It was a load of nonsense, but Alexa still shivered with an illicit little thrill.

Her treacherous mind wondered what it must be like to have this sinfully sexy guy say those words and mean them…

What would it feel like to actually *know* that he couldn't keep his hands off her…?

Her eyes skittered across to him—a quick glance at his face, once again shielded behind his sunglasses. Then, rebelling against all common sense, she noted the width of his shoulders, the lean muscularity of his body, the strength of his forearms and the way his dark hair curled around the dull metal of his watch strap.

She found herself drinking him in and felt her nervous system ratcheting up a notch.

In a couple of days she would be wearing a large dia-mond rock on her finger. Speculation, such as there was, would be over and she would be officially engaged to the guy now attracting stares from every single woman under the age of eighty and over the age of eighteen.

She was short and unspectacular. He was physical per-fection. Even if he did get under her skin in ways that made her want to scream, there was no way that she could deny the sheer beauty of the man.

Was it any wonder that he was taking all this in his stride? He was accustomed to women. A phoney engage-ment wouldn't faze him and he would be particularly incen-tivised by the carrot at the end of the stick. He didn't need yet more money, but since when did the wealthy ever turn down the opportunity to add to their bank vaults? *Never.*

As expected, every head swivelled in their direction, and Alexa saw one very leggy blonde disengage herself from her group of friends and make a beeline in their direction.

She stifled a groan.

The blonde stalked towards them, her sharp bob ex-pertly cut and dropping squarely to her shoulders. Even in flats she was close to six foot, and wearing next to nothing. She was rake-thin, flat as a pancake, and had the longest legs Alexa had ever seen—and most of those long legs were exposed because her skirt barely covered her underwear.

Her body language said it all as she chose to ignore Alexa completely, focusing one hundred per cent of her blue-eyed attention on Theo. *Surely it couldn't be true?* The blonde ran her china blue eyes dismissively over Alexa. *The press had it all wrong, hadn't they?*

'I mean, I just can't believe it!' she squeaked, sliding him a naughty smile that was designed to eliminate Alexa from the conversation.

She placed a flattened palm on his chest and shimmied

a little closer. Her hair was so silky and so unbelievably blonde that Alexa could only stare in wonder.

'Andrea…' Theo caught the blonde's hand, halted it firmly in its tracks and held it slightly at a distance before dropping it. It was a gesture that was cool and indifferent. Alexa would have been mortified. The blonde remained perky and upbeat. 'I'd like you to meet Alexa…'

'You're really *short*, aren't you?'

'Alexa is my fiancée.' Theo's voice was soft, silky, glacial. 'And now, before I start getting annoyed at your interruption, I suggest you take yourself back to your group of friends.'

For a few seconds the blonde was nonplussed. Alexa almost, but not quite, felt sorry for her. In her world she would rule supreme, but with a few words from Theo she was reduced to a woman of no standing.

'You don't mean that…'

She tried for provocative and Alexa, with a stab of pure womanly satisfaction, could have told her that she had made a mistake. One look at Theo's shuttered face should have sent the blonde running for cover.

'I mean it, Andrea. I'm giving you two seconds. You don't leave…you see that big guy, standing on the corner…?'

Andrea left, head held high, long, slim body taut with anger and wounded pride.

'I don't mind leaving if you feel that you might be uncomfortable here…' Alexa hovered, uncertain as to what to say in the wake of that dramatic scene.

Theo looked down at her, bemused. 'Why would I feel uncomfortable?'

He signalled with a nod to a hassled-looking waitress, who immediately patted her hair and plastered a smile on her face when she spotted him. Every other customer apparently forgotten, she dashed over to them and cleared a path to a table at the back of the restaurant.

'It's reserved,' the waitress confided with a giggle, 'but I'll sort something else out for the women who reserved it…'

Alexa automatically opened her mouth to protest, but Theo was already sitting and ordering a bottle of wine for them to share without looking at the menu.

'Why do you think I would feel uncomfortable?' he asked again, as soon as she was seated. 'And stop looking guilty because someone else had reserved this table. That charming little waitress said she'd sort it out—let's let her do her job.'

'Her job isn't to pander to customers who haven't booked a table.'

'Not my problem.' He shrugged. 'Now, moving on…'

Alexa sighed. The man was utterly impossible. The more time she spent in his company, the more cemented that impression became.

'I guess that woman must be one of your girlfriends and I just thought it might be awkward for you to be in the same place as she is when you know she'll probably be gossiping about you to her friends…'

Theo was looking utterly relaxed. 'You guess correctly,' he said, pushing back his chair to accommodate his long body. '*Ex*-girlfriend. Barely lasted a month, if you want the truth. The woman turned out to be a bunny-boiler. What started as a little bit of fun with a reasonably attractive woman turned into a dozen phone calls a day and attempts to get into my diary to make sure I wasn't seeing anyone else…'

Andrea had wanted a hell of a lot more than he had been prepared to give. Big mistake. On the love front… he had *nothing* to give. He'd seen what unrestrained emotions did to a guy—had seen the way his mother's death had destroyed his father...the way it had left a great gaping hole in his and Daniel's lives. No. Frothy, dewy-eyed looks from women were the ultimate turn-off to him, and trying to get anything more out of him than passion was their fastest way to the exit.

Alexa's mind had become stuck on his description of the blonde bombshell as a *'reasonably attractive woman'*.

What on earth did he consider *stunning*? Were his values so much different from everyone else's because of the way he looked? What on earth must he think of *her*?

'Some women are possessive, I guess...' she said.

Wine had been brought to the table and poured into oversized goblets and she took a sip of the chilled liquid and then stared at the glass—which seemed less fraught with potential danger than staring at *him* and getting into a mental muddle.

Theo nodded. He found it amazing that a life of luxury and wealth appeared to have had so little effect on the woman sitting opposite him. The privileges which should have turned her into the sort of vain, self-obsessed young woman he met every day of the week in his social circles seemed to have had the opposite effect. Frankly, and against all odds, she roused his curiosity.

'I've always found it a healthy option to stay away from those,' Theo drawled. 'Life's too short to waste any of it with a woman who wants to micro-manage my life. No, I don't give a damn if Andrea is sitting five inches away from us, gossiping with her friends.The only thing Andrea will tell anyone is that I am now engaged.'

'Engaged to someone short.'

He laughed, and his cool green eyes skirted over her flushed face. 'There's no law about falling in love with someone who doesn't fit the insane prototype other people have come up with,' he murmured.

No, Alexa thought, and as he had pointed out they made

the perfect society match. Two prominent families united in marriage. Who would think to scratch beneath the surface to see two individuals who couldn't have been less suited?

'How is it that you have never settled down?' she asked with blunt curiosity.

It was an extremely personal question—but why not? There would be occasions they spent together away from the spotlight, and they couldn't lapse into silence whenever they were together, could they? It would make living together extremely difficult—even if their living together would be taking place in opposite wings of whatever house they ended up living in…

She wondered whether they might not end up being friends, and then nearly laughed hysterically at that notion—because the man was just too *much*, too *larger than life*, to be considered a potential buddy. Potential buddies didn't make you feel as though you were standing on the edge of a precipice, looking down. Buddies were comfortable to be around, unthreatening, safe…

Theo looked at her consideringly. Out of the corner of his eye he could see his ex-girlfriend shooting venomous looks in their direction. He wanted to grin, because he knew that the single thing that would enrage Andrea and all those women like her—all those beautiful, arrogantly self-assured women he had dated in the past—was the fact that he was engaged to someone they would consider downright plain.

The fact that Alexa had been born to privilege would make little difference. Beautiful women were notoriously superficial when it came to judging other women, by standards that were almost always according to looks.

He felt a sudden surge of protectiveness towards his fake wife-to-be.

He reached forward and stroked the side of her face, linking his fingers through hers at the same time.

Another public display of affection, Alexa thought as her heart picked up a frantic pace. And particularly appropriate given that their actions were being minutely watched by an ex-girlfriend who would be busy spreading the news that the most eligible man on the planet had been caught.

An ex-girlfriend who was probably appalled and stunned that he had been stupid enough to fall for someone *like her*…

Alexa had always known that when it came to looks she could only ever aspire to be average. She didn't have razor-sharp cheekbones or long, thirty-four-inch legs or shiny poker-straight hair. She had never felt comfortable in revealing clothes and largely avoided wearing anything that was too bright or too eye-catching.

And yet here she was. Engaged to a man who could have any woman he wanted with the crook of one imperious finger.

Okay, so it might all be pretend, but just for a moment she felt something wicked steal into her. A purely feminine response kicked into gear. His fingers were still entwined with hers and she slowly lifted them to her lips and grazed his knuckles with her mouth.

Heat flared in Theo's eyes. She could almost hear his sharply indrawn breath.

Alexa felt a rush of unfamiliar daring. She raised her eyes to his and held his stare, watched the way his slow smile transformed his face and tried hard not to panic when he leaned in close to her, creating a little bubble of intense intimacy between them.

Nerves threatened to overtake her, but she could feel the blonde's glassy blue eyes boring into her back and that gave her the impetus she needed to lean right into him. To offer her lips to him.

And when he kissed her she responded with an enthusiastic lack of inhibition. She slid her tongue against his and stifled a little moan as, eyes closed, she indulged in naked, forbidden desire.

This was what was expected of her. She was his fiancée. He had confirmed that to an ex-girlfriend, who would have been surprised if they had continued sitting opposite one another making polite conversation. Theo De Angelis was an intensely physical man. You just had to look at him to know that. So kissing him like this, curling her hand into his hair, was only to be expected.

She was just playing the part she had been commissioned to play!

It was liberating to think that she wasn't doing anything out of the ordinary.

It was permission granted to sink into a kiss that was... *explosive.*

When she pulled back she knew that she was shaking a little, and she licked her lips and forced a smile.

'Just for show,' she mumbled, and Theo raised his eyebrows.

'I like it,' he murmured softly. 'I sense a change from all those other displays of affection you didn't seem to enjoy—or was I wrong about that...? Were you actually burning up and looking for a few encores?'

'Of course not!' Her mouth was still tingling from that searing kiss. 'But...'

'But you thought you'd take the opportunity to get one up on the delectable ex-girlfriend who's been shooting you daggers behind your back...?'

'Of course not!' But she blushed furiously.

Theo grinned. 'Trust me, I don't have a problem with your reasoning.'

'I...I hope you don't think that was anything but acting,' Alexa breathed forcefully. 'It's just that you've announced that we're engaged… I thought it would look odd if we didn't act like a newly engaged couple. I mean… you're the one who's kept telling me that we have to make this stupid charade look real…'

'Of course…' He paused, wondering just how real he would like the charade to be. Complications aside… 'And I'm heartened that you're now in such a positive mindset,' he told her, 'because I should tell you that I've been called away on business. I will be out of the country for a week. Maybe a bit less…maybe a bit longer. It's hard to tell because this is a complex deal…'

'I know.'

'You do?'

'My mother broke the news while she was poring over all the pictures of us together at that art opening we attended last night. Don't worry…' Now, more than ever, Alexa was looking forward to a few days on her own—away from his powerful, charismatic personality and the weirdness of their situation. 'I'll make sure to keep the home fires of the newly engaged couple burning…'

'You won't have to do that,' Theo informed her kindly.

'I won't?'

'Don't be silly. How could you think for a moment that I would want you out of my sight for an hour, never mind a week…? No, there will be no need to keep those home fires burning, because you will be right there with me… by my side…'

CHAPTER FIVE

ALEXA WAS APPALLED. She stared at him in open-mouthed consternation, forgetting that her every move was being watched by an interested party.

'Coming with you?' she stuttered.

'Step one in assimilating into my lifestyle,' Theo said smoothly. He leaned back and slouched elegantly in the chair. 'You may hate premieres and art gallery openings, but there will be a certain amount of socialising that you will have to do—like it or not.'

He signalled for the bill without taking his eyes from her face. 'I'm not a fan of meeting and greeting people I have no intention of forming any sort of relationship with,' Theo said drily, 'but it's all part and parcel of the game.'

'Why do I get the feeling that everything about this arrangement is on *your* terms?'

'Explain.'

'Your father is the one who needed a bail-out,' Alexa muttered, feeling terrible at having to remind him of that little detail, because she liked what little she had seen of Stefano De Angelis and was sorry that he, a proud man, had found himself in the position of having to ask for financial assistance from a man he was not on speaking terms with. Although she was beginning to suspect that their so-called feud had petered out into two old men warring through habit over something both had long forgotten about.

Theo's mouth tightened. His father might have taken his eye off the ball, but he didn't need to rehash that misfortune. And he certainly wasn't interested in anyone rehashing it on his behalf.

'He is—but that's old news now. I don't see the point in moaning about what can't be changed.'

'I'm not moaning.' Alexa fiddled with the stem of her wine glass and wondered where all the contents had gone. She'd barely been aware of drinking. Or eating, for that matter. She raised her eyes to his and struggled to look away. 'I just think that *my* life has been completely disrupted while you continue to carry on as if nothing much has happened...'

'Stop feeling sorry for yourself. It makes sense for you to move to London after we are married. I can't conduct my business from here. And remind me... As far as I am aware you don't currently have many ties to this place. You've quit your job and your only other interest appears to be helping at a shelter somewhere. Nothing that can't be left behind at a moment's notice.'

Alexa felt rage rush through her with tidal wave force. If they'd been anywhere but here she would have been tempted to chuck something at him.

How dared he take her life, sum it up and write it off in a handful of words?

But perhaps that was how he treated all women? she thought with scathing distaste.

'Are you like this with all women?' she asked tightly.

'How do you mean?'

Theo frowned, puzzled. How had they gone from a perfectly rational conversation about the dynamics of their married life to some opaque query about his treatment of women? He realised that never before had he had to hold himself to account with anyone—far less a woman.

Her bright eyes glittered as she waited in silence for a response.

Theo raked his fingers through his hair and muttered an oath under his breath. 'I have no idea where you're going with this...'

'It's a simple question,' Alexa said stubbornly.

'I'm extremely fair in my treatment of women,' he said impatiently. 'Exemplary, some might say.'

'Really?'

'Time to go, I think.'

'Only if you answer my question.' She didn't know why it was important to her. She just had a vague feeling that she had to have some say in what was going on or else he would take control of the reins and she would find life as she knew it disappearing even faster than it already was.

'I already have.'

'I feel like you're bullying me.'

Theo shot her a look of pure incredulity. 'I don't believe I'm hearing this!'

'You expect me to change my whole *life*! You don't even bother pretending that I have any say in the matter!'

'I'm cutting through the red tape,' Theo pointed out, with irrefutable logic as far as he was concerned. 'There's nothing you have here that ties you down.'

'What about my parents?'

'Your parents can come to London any time they want,' Theo pointed out. 'In fact I assume they already do, given that your father has business interests there...'

'That's not the point.'

'It's exactly the point—and if you would stop looking at the big picture with irrational feminine logic you would agree with me.'

'Sometimes,' Alexa gritted, 'I really want to hit you.'

'Who knows…?' he replied without hesitation. 'Maybe you will. Although if you do, it won't be in anger…'

'What are you talking about?'

Colour crawled into her cheeks as he raised his eyebrows and shot her a slow, deliberate smile. Her treacherous body tingled. Try as she might, she couldn't bank down the sudden tightening of her nipples, achingly sensitive as they grazed against her lacy bra. And she was aghast to feel spreading dampness between her legs.

'Never tried a bit of bondage?' Theo asked, enjoying the hectic flush in her cheeks. 'I admit I do prefer my women to fully participate in the action—although who knows…? I'm a man who has always been open to new experiences…'

'I've already told you…' Alexa could barely get the words out because her mouth was so dry. 'We won't be… That won't be part of the deal…'

Did she have *any* idea how much he disliked being told that there was something he couldn't do? Theo thought that if she did she might refrain from that approach.

'Anyway, we're straying off the topic.' She cleared her throat. 'I don't like feeling that I have no input.'

'And you're implying that that's the way I treat women generally? You're telling me that you think I'm a bully who takes advantage of women…?'

Alexa cringed because, put like that, it seemed a crazy accusation. If he was a mean bully who took advantage of women why would they care if they were dumped? That blonde who had sidled up to him still had the hots for him. That had been *very* obvious. And she was the sort of woman who could have any man she wanted. If money had been the only thing keeping her in a relationship with Theo, there was no way she would have looked at him the way a starving man eyed up his next meal.

'I'm just saying—'

'I have never bullied a woman in my life before,' Theo interrupted coldly. 'I have extremely healthy relationships with the opposite sex. I am honest to a fault. I have never pretended that commitment and marriage is a possible destination. I have always told them upfront that I'm in it for fun and that fun doesn't last—that beyond that I have nothing to give. But while they're with me they couldn't be treated better. Andrea, as a case in point, was showered with presents and taken to the sort of glittering social dos that have gone a long way to kick-starting her career in film.'

Alexa didn't say anything, because he seemed to expect congratulations for being the sort of guy most women who wanted something other than a ten-second fling would run a mile from. And she was sure that a lot of those women who had been given his rousing speech on not getting thoughts of permanence wouldn't have been quite as cheerful when they were dispatched as he liked to think.

'What do you mean that you have nothing to give beyond *fun*? Why?'

Theo flushed darkly and immediately decided that he had imparted enough information on the subject of his private life. Inside, where the soul stored love, his soul was empty. No reserves left. That place, instead, stored the pain of his father's reaction to loss and the hurt of his own loss…all the result of that big thing called love.

'I'm not laying down laws,' he said snappily, bringing the conversation back to the matter in hand. 'Feel free to tell me if you think it's feasible for me to set up camp here for the duration of our short marriage… Even when you have no strenuous objections to moving to London aside from the fact that it was a decision you feel you didn't reach of your own free will.'

'I've never had anyone make decisions on my behalf.'

She stuck stubbornly to her guns, but she knew that her moral high ground was being eroded from all directions.

'Then maybe you should sit back and enjoy the novelty.'

Theo knew that that remark was tantamount to waving a red rag at a bull with an axe to grind, but he couldn't help himself. Something about the way she reddened and pursed her lips and glared made for addictive watching.

Alexa refused to rise to the bait. They exchanged a brief look, during which a lot seemed to be said without any words passing between them. She communicated with a slight tilt of her chin that she knew exactly what game he was playing—knew that he was trying to rile her because it amused him—and he, in turn, acknowledged the truth in that.

The moment unnerved her.

'I don't like being told what I can wear and what I can't,' she confessed shortly.

'So I'm taking it that part one of your complaint has been dealt with? You're in agreement with me that London would be the best base for us?' He sighed. 'Decisions have to be made,' he said heavily, 'whether you like it or not. Your parents are more than welcome to come and stay with us whenever they want and let's cut to the chase: we'll only be together for just as long as it takes for the ink to dry on our marriage certificate...'

'It's awful. I never thought that I'd end up getting married for all the wrong reasons...'

It was a sobering thought. An arranged marriage—a marriage of convenience—was a marriage without love, and she had always imagined love and marriage as two words inextricably bound together. Yet to some extent her parents' marriage had started on lines very similar to those she was now having to endure.

This tangent threatened to lead them down all sorts of unfamiliar paths, and meandering chat about emotional issues just wasn't his forte, but when Theo looked at the heartfelt expression on her face he found it hard to feel exasperation.

'Love disappears,' he said gruffly. 'And even when it doesn't it burns so strong that it consumes everything around it and ends up self-imploding.'

They were leaning into one another, unconsciously promoting a space around themselves that excluded everyone else in the restaurant, and for that he was glad—because a bride-to-be with a downcast, near to tears expression could in no way be interpreted as a bride-to-be contemplating the happiest day of her life.

As it looked from the outside, they were two people huddled and whispering sweet nothings to one another.

He entwined his fingers with hers and absently stroked her thumb with his to promote the illusion.

'I prefer not to think that way. I prefer to think that you can really find your soulmate and, yes, live happily ever after without everything "self-imploding", as you say. Or else disappearing like water down a drain. That's not how love works. I might be stupid, but I'd like to think that the man for me, the man who can make me happy, is out there…and I'll find him. *We'll find one another.*'

'And who's to say that won't happen…?'

'What do you mean?' For a few seconds Alexa was genuinely disconcerted. Was he talking about *them*? Insinuating that their marriage of convenience could end up becoming the real thing?

'I mean you will move on from me and find this man of your dreams—maybe a little later than you originally planned, and not quite in the order you might have anticipated, but who knows…?'

'What's made you so cynical?' she asked, flabbergasted at the casual way he was happy to dismiss their marriage and divorce as just something a little inconvenient—

something that could be swept aside in the future as though it had never happened.

Whether they were married for twelve months or twelve minutes, and whether she liked him or not, he would leave an impression. She would not be the same person she had been before.

'Let's leave that thorny subject for another day,' Theo told her wryly. 'I'll let you know when we'll be leaving for the States…'

'I didn't say that I was coming with you.'

'Are you going to argue with each and every small thing until we finally part company and go our separate ways? Because if that's your intention it's going to be a very long twelve months.'

'I'm not being argumentative.' She glared at him mutinously and in return he raised his eyebrows in cynical disagreement. 'But if I'm obliged to fall in line and never complain then I think it's only fair that *you* fall in line a bit as well.'

'Are we about to have another bracing conversation about the "separate bedrooms post-marriage" clause?'

'I'd like you to sample how *I* live,' Alexa continued doggedly. 'You want me to go to all sorts of stupid fancy social dos—'

'Don't write them all off. You might find that you actually *enjoy* some…'

Alexa chose to ignore that interruption. 'The least you could do is try and understand what I'll be sacrificing.'

Theo raised his eyebrows and began standing up. He was at a loss to understand what she was talking about. Of course the 'pause' button would have to be pressed on her fairy-tale love and perfect soulmate, but she was young. Plenty of time for her to find that once their committed spell together was at an end.

Frankly, he could tell her that airy-fairy dreams were a

certain recipe for disappointment—but what would be the point of that? She would find out soon enough. She was an enduring romantic, while he...he had about as much faith or interest in romance as a turkey had in signing up for centrepiece duties next to the carving knife on Christmas Day.

She had asked him why he was cynical. He could have told her that he'd had a close-up view of just the sort of pain love could bring—the sort of pain that no one in their right mind would want inflicted on them.

It tended to turn a guy off marriage. Although, in fairness, he knew the day would come when marriage would make sense, and when that day came he anticipated something very much like what he now had—but without the complication of a partner in search of the impossible. Emotions would not take over, leaving him vulnerable to going through what his father had gone through.

Of course he was a very different man from his father. Stefano had met his wife when they had both been young. They had fallen in love when they had both been green around the ears. Theo was anything *but* green around the ears. The opposite. And he prided himself on having the sort of formidable control that would never see him prey to anything he didn't want to feel.

An arranged marriage with the right woman—a woman who wasn't looking for anything that wasn't on the table—would be the kind of marriage he would eventually subscribe to. It made sense.

'Do tell me what that would be. What great "sacrifices" will you be making? Tell me. I'm all ears...'

They were outside now, walking in the balmy sun. He had a case load of documents to read before his trip to New York, but he didn't think that a few minutes prolonging their conversation would hurt.

'I can show you.'

She hailed a cab and leant forward to give the taxi driver

an address. It was on the tip of his tongue to tell her that time was money, but he desisted. Why provide her with another excuse to stage an argument? He had never met a woman as stubborn and as mulish as she was, and those were traits he had no time for. His life was stressful enough, without having a woman digging her heels in and finding objections to every single thing he said or suggested.

'We're here.'

'Here? Where?' The designer shops and smart cafés had been left behind, to be replaced with dingy shop fronts and fast food outlets. It was the sort of place Theo had only ever passed with the windows of his chauffeur-driven car rolled up.

'The shelter where I volunteer,' Alexa told him.

She pointed to a building next to a pawn shop. A grim concrete block fronted by a no-nonsense black door that would have deterred anyone but the most foolhardy.

'I want you to come in and see it—meet some of the other volunteers I work with.' She sprang out of the car, only realising that he hadn't followed when she had slammed the door behind her, at which point she reopened her door and peered inside at him.

'You're not *scared*, are you?' She smirked, because for the first time since she had boarded the rollercoaster ride that had become her life she felt as if she had the upper hand. 'I promise I won't let anything happen to you...'

Theo looked at her, partly outraged because no one had ever dared accuse him of being scared of anything in his life before, partly amused because she had wrong-footed him and not many had done that either.

'What do you think I might be scared of?' he murmured as they headed into the shelter.

'A new experience?' She blushed, hearing the teasing tone in her voice.

'You've broken the ice on that one,' Theo pointed out

drily. 'When it comes to new experiences, you rank right up there as a first.'

'I'll take that as a compliment,' Alexa threw back at him, because she knew that a compliment it certainly hadn't been meant to be.

He smiled slowly, his amazing eyes skirting over her flushed face and doing a lazy inventory of everything else.

'You should,' he murmured. 'I have a jaded palate, and new experiences are always welcome...'

'Even unpleasant ones?'

'What are we talking about, here? The shelter...or you...?'

He was leaning against the door, towering over her, and she felt her heart begin to race. His voice was as smooth as the finest dark chocolate and his eyes were doing all sorts of weird things to her nervous system, muddling her thoughts and stripping her of that momentary feeling of triumph she'd had moments earlier.

She rang the bell and turned away, although she could still feel him staring at her, and suddenly the memory of all those convenient kisses slammed into her, depriving her of breath.

She didn't like him, she reminded herself fiercely. Not only did she not like him—she didn't like the situation she was in.

But he was so sinfully good-looking. He had the sort of face that made her want to stare with helpless fixation and keep on staring. He had that effect on every woman. She had witnessed it for herself. And, whilst she had thought herself immune to that sort of thing, she had to accept the galling truth that she wasn't as immune as she wanted to be.

That was why she found it so unsettling whenever he got too close to her, and why the thought of those kisses kept her awake at night. She was human, and she lacked the necessary experience to deal with a man like Theo De Angelis.

All her old-fashioned ideas about only ever being attracted to her soulmate had been turned on their head…

Which didn't mean that they had disappeared! No, it just meant that she responded to him on a purely physical level, and it was only now that she was accepting that unpalatable truth. She'd always assumed that, for her, physical attraction would only be possible when it was to the guy who had stolen her heart, but she'd been wrong. She could see that now.

Which was a good thing.

Once you knew your enemy, you knew how to arm yourself—and *her* enemy was her treacherous body. She would just have to make sure that she maintained as much distance as she could and never, ever repeated the mistake she had made at the restaurant, when she had initiated that kiss and totally lost herself in it.

It was great that she was going to introduce him to what she did, because it was the one area in which he would be at sea—and that was something she would really enjoy watching.

'You're smiling…' he leant in to whisper as footsteps were heard on the opposite side of the door. 'Private joke or something you'd care to share?'

'Private joke,' she told him promptly.

She looked away as the door was opened and felt a lump in her throat, because she knew that she was going to miss the shelter beyond words when she disappeared off to London.

The prospect of the lifestyle awaiting her there made her want to burst into tears.

Not that *he* would ever understand.

She sneaked a sideways glance at him and, introductions made, took a background seat to watch the spectacle of the great Theo De Angelis fumbling awkwardly in a situation of which he would have had no experience.

He didn't fumble. He charmed all the women there, Franca and Louisa and Marie and Ndali. He introduced himself to some of the women who came to them for practical and emotional help. He pried and prodded into all the rooms and asked so many questions that anyone would have thought that he was an expert on women's shelters.

He talked finance with the guy who ran the place, and made a show of looking at the books. He even went so far as to make suggestions on how small improvements could be made!

She had hoped to watch him squirm, and instead he had dumbfounded her with lots of phoney interest.

'So what exactly is your role there?' was the first thing he asked when they were back outside an hour and a half later.

The work awaiting his attention would have to wait and he had resigned himself to that. Allowing work to take second place to anything was an alien concept to him, but he had watched her as they walked through the premises, watched her interaction with her colleagues, and the casual, friendly, concerned manner with which she had spoken to the some of the women waiting in queues to be seen or chatting to the other volunteers.

Everything about her had breathed open sincerity. Her laughter with her colleagues had been rich and infectious. Frankly, it was the sort of laughter that had been conspicuously absent between *them*, and he had been irked by that.

He had been tolerant of her hostility, even though he privately thought that she should have taken her cue from him and dealt with the whole unfortunate situation with a bit more aplomb—because why rail against the inevitable? And besides, it wasn't destined to be a lifetime situation. He had gritted his teeth at the patently grudging reluctance in her responses to him and the ease with which she accepted as fact the thought that he was deplorable.

But here he had glimpsed a side to her that he hadn't seen before.

It was rare for any woman not to respond to him. Even when he was uninterested in them they still tried hard around him. He had made exceptions for her because of the circumstances of their forced relationship, but only now was he accepting that her indifference was an offence to his pride.

On a more basic level, he wanted what he had seen of her at that shelter. It was human nature to desire the things that are denied. Fact of life.

Alexa was making sure to keep as much distance between them as was acceptable, considering they were supposed to be madly in love. People who were madly in love didn't necessarily have to hold hands everywhere they went—and besides, no one in these streets knew who they were.

Niggling away at the top of her mind was the uncomfortable thought that she fancied the man, and that her plan of seeing him out of his depth and floundering in unfamiliar surroundings—which she had hoped might put the brakes on her stupid attraction to him—had spectacularly backfired.

She should have guessed. He could pull that charm out when it was needed like a magician pulling a rabbit out of a hat.

'Are you *really* interested?' she asked, then belatedly remembered what he had said about her arguing with everything he said. 'Sorry,' she apologised. 'Even if you're not really interested, it's thoughtful of you to pretend to be.'

She was determined to stop letting him get under her skin and rattle her. If she could reach a higher plane of being cool and controlled when she was around him, then her wayward responses could be harnessed and quickly killed off. Fancying someone because of the way they looked was so superficial that it surely couldn't last longer than two minutes.

'And,' she continued, 'you put on a really good show of being interested in what went on there.'

Theo's mouth tightened. Whatever he said or did, she was determined not to give him the benefit of the doubt and it was really beginning to get on his nerves.

'So what exactly is your role there?' he repeated, keeping his voice even and neutral.

They were heading back in the direction of the bars and shops and cafés, looking out for any passing taxis and walking until they could hail one. They had quickly left behind the insalubrious neighbourhood where they had just been, and the houses to either side of them now were well maintained but small and all exactly alike.

Theo realised that this was a part of town he had never actually visited. He wasn't in the country a lot, and when he was his visits were fleeting, because he far preferred to import his father to London.

Having always considered himself a man of the world—widely travelled, the recipient of far more global experiences than most people could ever dream of achieving in a lifetime—he now wondered when and how he had managed to isolate himself so entirely in a very specific social circle that was accessible only to the very, very wealthy. He was delivered to and from places in chauffeur-driven cars, never flew anything but first class, always had the most expensive seats at the opera or the theatre...

Alexa, having come from a very similar background to his own, should have followed the same route—maybe without the high-powered career—but she hadn't and that roused his curiosity.

'It wasn't quite the sort of thing I was expecting,' he expanded truthfully.

'And what *were* you expecting?'

She turned to him and was dazzled by the glare from the sun, which threw his lean, handsome face into a mosaic of shadows. She shielded her eyes and squinted against the sun. Overcome by a sudden feeling of vertigo, she took a couple of small steps backwards.

'A soup kitchen and people waving begging bowls at you?'

She took a deep breath and told herself that sniping and bristling was just a symptom of the stupid attraction she felt for the man, against all odds. If she carried on like that he would begin to wonder why he got under her skin the way he did, and the last thing she wanted was for him to suspect that he got to her, that she was so horribly alert to him.

'I guess *shelter* might be the wrong word...' She fought to inject polite indifference into her words. 'Most people do think of the homeless when they hear the word *shelter*. It's more of an advice bureau. Women come to us with all sorts of problems. Financial, personal... Often we redirect them to other services, but there are people on hand who are really experienced at listening and getting the desperate off the path they've gone down. We also have contacts with companies who offer jobs wherever possible, to help some of them get back on their feet...'

What she had really wanted to show him, Theo mused, were the sort of people she liked. He hadn't been able to help noticing that the men there had been a 'type'.

Caring, soft-spoken, touchy-feely...

Had she subconsciously wanted to show him the sort of guys she liked—was attracted to? Had her intention been to draw comparisons, so that she could underline how far short he fell of her ideal? Just another way of reinforcing her dislike for the position she was in and the man she would be forced to marry—like a Victorian bride being dragged to the altar, kicking and screaming.

And yet…

When she had pulled him towards her in the restaurant and kissed him… Hell, he knew enough about women to know that loathing and dislike hadn't been behind that kiss. She might not want to admit it, but he had felt an urgency there and it intrigued him.

Why wouldn't it?

'Those are the people I enjoy being around,' she carried on, pausing as his driver cruised up alongside them and stopped.

When had he summoned a driver? But of course that would suit him far better than a normal taxi, because there was the option of sliding up that partition so that their conversation could not be overheard. He was always one step ahead.

'Is that your not so subtle way of telling me that those are the sort of *men* you enjoy being around?' He slid into the seat alongside her and predictably slid up the partition, locking them into complete privacy.

Work hard, play hard. Alexa was beginning to understand that, for Theo, the priority was business and after that came sex. He didn't do love and emotion but he did do *sex*. It was why he could be so cool about the situation they were in. He could detach.

'Yes.'

She took a deep breath and thought she had been gifted a golden opportunity to make it perfectly clear to him that those were just the sort of guys she was attracted to. And by attraction she knew that she meant a lot more than just a passing physical tug.

'Their priorities are all in the right places…'

'Heart-warming,' Theo drawled. 'Not the most aggressive of men, though, are they…? One had his hair in a ponytail. I'm thinking that he might be the type to strum a guitar and sing a haunting ballad by way of entertaining a woman…'

'Jorge is absolutely wonderful! Hugely caring! Besides, I don't like aggressive men!'

'And yet your father didn't get where he is by being the sort of man who gets walked over…'

'He's not ruthless…'

'He bartered you in marriage so that he could get *me* as a bonus prize…' Theo pointed out flatly, because he didn't do well when it came to accepting unfavourable comparisons.

'He did it for Mum,' she contradicted. 'I admit he saw an opportunity and seized it, but are you telling me that you wouldn't do the same thing? He's been desperately worried about my mother and he was convinced that her health and her spirits would improve if…if she had *this* to focus on. And that's why I agreed to…to go along with the pretence.'

'And when the pretence comes to its inevitable crashing halt?'

'A year is a long time,' she mumbled, because that thought had occurred to her as well. 'My mother's health will be in a better place and she'll be able to accept that the marriage didn't work out. She'll no longer spend her days thinking that she's on her way out and will die before she sees me settled down.'

'That's *very* optimistic projecting,' Theo declared, in just the sort of arrogantly self-assured voice that got on her nerves. 'She might have a nervous breakdown when we tell her that, sadly, we're joining the statistics of the happily divorced…'

'That's a risk my father was prepared to take and so am I,' Alexa told him sharply. 'Wouldn't *you* have done the same if it had been *your* mother?'

Theo's face closed down. 'I don't deal in pointless hypotheses.'

But it was *just* the sort of solution his father would have hit upon. Deal with today and let tomorrow be a bridge yet to be crossed. And, yes, Theo would have gone along for the ride. He would have done anything for his mother. He and Daniel both.

'All that's beside the point,' he said, and shrugged elegantly. 'Now, our little detour has eaten a chunk of my time. I'm going to get my driver to deliver you to your house and you can pack your bags for our trip to the States. And no protest-packing please...' he added, for good measure. 'During the day you can amuse yourself, but the evenings will be formal occasions. I expect we will be entertained on a fairly lavish scale.'

'Fine—but I insist that we check in to separate rooms,' Alexa told him.

'Already done,' Theo returned smoothly. 'My person in New York has booked us a penthouse suite. Adjoining rooms...'

'But...'

'But what...? Do you think I might try and break down the door between us so that I can ravish you?'

Alexa felt hot colour rush into her cheeks. She had been so intent on laying down her ground rules that she hadn't even considered the obvious—which was that he didn't even fancy her.

'You're getting a little ahead of yourself,' he said kindly. 'Aren't you?'

'I was just...just...making sure... Of course I don't think that!' She thought of the stunning blonde and the nuisance she had eventually turned into and mortification made her skin tingle.

'Then I'll text you our timings and get my driver to collect you...'

They were pulling up outside her house and Alexa felt physically and emotionally drained. She was gripping the door handle before the car had even pulled to a stop.

'Till tomorrow…' he directed at her as she flipped open the door to step out.

Alexa turned and watched helplessly as the car pulled away. A week in New York, where thankfully their time together would be limited, but then would come their engagement party, and then, in short order, a wedding.

By then she would have to make sure that she…

That she was in control…

CHAPTER SIX

ALEXA KNEW WHAT to expect in New York. She had been there several times before and had always loved the buzz of the city that literally never slept.

She met Theo at the check-in desk at the airport, where he was waiting for her, chatting to the woman who had checked him in, who was trying to ignore the fact that there were two other people impatiently waiting in the queue behind him.

'Is that all you've brought with you?' were his opening words as he strolled towards Alexa, who had joined the back of the queue.

Unlike every other woman he had ever travelled with, Alexa had made absolutely no concession to the fact that they would be travelling first class and he liked that. She was in a pair of loose culottes and a T-shirt, with a cardigan lightly draped over her shoulders and flat ballet shoes. There wasn't a scrap of colour in her outfit, and she had braided her long, untamed hair into a neat French plait which hung over one shoulder.

'I have enough for a week—although you haven't mentioned just how long I will be expected to stay.'

In response to that incendiary way of phrasing her question, Theo slung his arm over her shoulder and felt her tense.

'What are you doing?' Alexa squeaked as the line shuffled forward.

'I'm getting you in the mood.'

'In the mood for what?'

'For being my adoring fiancée… And in answer to your question about how long we will be staying…my plans are fluid.'

'What do you mean…?' she asked, hopeful that his 'fluid' plans might entail a reduction in the time they would end up spending in the city. 'Might we be there for less than a week…?'

Alexa looked up at him, eyes wide, and he shot her a half-smile before lowering his head and kissing her—a delicate kiss that feathered over her lips with just the lightest touch from his tongue. He pulled back and turned to the woman who had checked him in.

'Newly engaged,' he explained, giving Alexa a little squeeze so that she was pulled against him.

'How romantic.' The woman eyed Alexa with a look that shrieked, *Lucky you, how did you manage that…?* 'When is the big day?'

She fiddled on her computer, checking her in and ticketing her bag at the same time.

'Not soon enough,' Theo answered on Alexa's behalf. 'The engagement ring is in the process of being altered. Who knows…? We might tie the knot even before the diamond is on your finger—mightn't we, my darling?'

His low, throaty husk made her blood heat and she stared at the woman with a glassy smile.

'Maybe not,' she said gently. 'I don't think my mother would stand for that. She's a stickler for tradition,' Alexa expanded chirpily, 'and by *tradition* I mean taking her time over the wedding arrangements! None of this crazy sprinting up the aisle!'

But then the sooner they tied the knot, the sooner they

would *un*tie it. It wasn't a case of delaying something in the hope that it might disappear altogether if the delay was long enough. No such luck.

'Speaking of diamonds...' Theo told her as they headed towards the first class lounge and away from the chaos of the tax-free shopping area, which was packed.

'*Were* we speaking of diamonds?' Alexa used the pretence of stopping to peer into one of the shop windows to disengage herself from his embrace.

'I've brought something for you...'

He left that teaser hanging in the air as they reached the lounge and were waved through towards a couple of cosy chairs, with a table in front of them on which a few business magazines were fanned out.

'Have you? Alexa looked at him suspiciously. 'What?'

Theo laughed and crossed his legs. 'When are you going to stop fighting me? I've never met anyone with more of an appetite for arguing.'

'As I've told you before—you're the only one I argue with.'

'Sign of a vibrant, lively relationship...'

'It's a sign of two people who don't get along,' Alexa corrected him. 'Which is probably why you've never argued with any of the women you've been out with. And I'm sure they've *all* been vibrant, lively relationships!'

Theo cocked his head to one side and appeared to give her statement a great deal of serious thought.

'Yes,' he agreed eventually, 'I suppose there's been a certain amount of liveliness in the women I've dated...'

'And no arguments,' Alexa persisted, drawn to prolong the conversation and prove a point. 'I can't imagine *any* of your supermodels arguing with you.'

'It's true.' Theo threw his hand up in a gesture that implied rueful but graceful defeat. 'I don't like argumentative women.'

'So it's a good thing that we don't have to like one another, isn't it?'

She had felt just the merest flash of hurt—because who enjoyed being told that they weren't liked? Especially when his job of pretending that he did indeed like and fancy her was so polished and so convincing. And especially when she had grudgingly been forced to concede that she had become just another member of the long list of women who found him physically compelling.

Who wanted to fancy a guy who didn't even *like* them?

Theo didn't bother to get involved further in a conversation he knew wouldn't end up going anywhere, because he was pretty sure that when it came to arguments there was a mighty one brewing like a storm just over the horizon.

It would certainly pay to broach that thorny subject as soon as possible and get it out of the way. Give her the duration of the flight to assimilate and accept.

He grunted something that might have been anything when it came to a response and Alexa banked down a sigh of frustration.

'What is it that you've brought me?' she reminded him briskly.

'I'll show you when we're on the plane,' Theo said, because there could be no available exit door when they were twenty thousand miles up in the air. 'Your bag looks heavy. What have you got in it? Heavy club for beating me over the head?'

'I'm glad you think this is funny,' Alexa told him coldly.

Theo's lips thinned. 'Lighten up, Alexa. Do you take *everything* in life so seriously?'

'This isn't just any little thing.'

'As I've said to you on a number of occasions, it's inevitable—so why don't you just kick back? Or is that something you don't quite know how to do?'

He watched the slow colour crawl into her face. Hard-working, diligent, involved in the caring profession, pointedly making sure to avoid things she considered frivolous… In her own way, it was a statement of rebellion against her privileged background. She had bucked the tide of every other woman in her social circle, who would have settled into a life of pampered predictability and been married by the age of twenty-one to someone not very different from themselves.

The people he had met where she volunteered her services were all very nice indeed, but none of them had struck him as a bundle of fun.

So *did* she ever kick back?

'I kick back.' Alexa heard defiance in her voice.

'Who with? I haven't met the people you used to work with…what were *they* like?'

'Lots of fun,' she told him edgily. 'But you'd probably think they were dull as dishwater.'

'Why?'

'Because they're not the sort of people who think that "fun" is all about nightclubs and being in the public eye.'

'And have *you*? Ever?'

'Have I ever what?'

They were having a perfectly normal conversation, but Alexa still felt as though she was trying to find a foothold on thin ice. Maybe because when she was in his company, try as she might, she never seemed to *feel* normal.

'Thought nightclubs and being in the public eye are fun? Scrap the being in the public eye. No one in their right mind considers *that* fun.'

Although, if he were to be honest, most of the women he had dated in the past had basked in the glare of paparazzi flashbulbs.

'I'm not a nightclub type of person,' Alexa muttered, wondering how the conversation had managed to get here.

'When I meet up with friends we all prefer to go to places where we can actually hear ourselves think.'

Theo had a vision of a group of earnest individuals, solving the problems of the world over cups of espresso. She was positively the *last* sort of person he would ever have been drawn to normally. Frankly, he had little use for people who solved the world's problems over cups of coffee. If the problem was too big to solve, then why waste time talking about it? And if it was solvable then why not just get out there and solve it? Cut out the middle man, which came in the form of pointless discussion.

On the other hand he had watched her in that shelter place of hers—had seen her interaction with the people there and for a fleeting instant had actually caught himself thinking of the supermodels who had graced his arm in the past with a certain amount of distaste.

'And those friends would be your colleagues at work?'

'I've kept in touch with a couple of school friends,' she admitted. Both were married, and one was the proud mother of a baby boy. 'Why are we talking about this anyway?'

She heard the announcement of their flight over the Tannoy. Travelling first class, she knew they would be the last to board the plane, and sure enough, after a brisk ten-minute walk, they were taking their very comfortable seats in the first class section.

'Books,' she said, and Theo shot her a quizzical look as he made himself comfortable.

Flutes of champagne were brought to them and he sipped the drink while he continued to look at her, waiting for an explanation.

'You asked me what I had in my bag. Books. So that I have something to do on the flight over.'

Theo smiled slowly at her and wondered whether her

definition of *kicking back* might involve having some fun on a long-haul flight...

He'd done that once—a long time ago—and had since come to the conclusion that planes were inappropriate when it came to certain activities for a man as big as he was.

Although *private* planes certainly redefined the options...

His thoughts veered off and he held her gaze steadily. 'Books...?' he murmured. 'Let me guess... Non-fiction for the serious reader?'

'Wrong,' Alexa told him triumphantly. 'Romance and crime! Holiday reading...'

'So you're thinking of this as a *holiday*?' He was quick to pick up her stray remark, although he didn't add to that as their champagne was gathered up by a flight attendant and then, mere seconds later, the plane began its ascent. 'Excellent,' he continued heartily, once they were airborne. 'Big improvement on your lack of enthusiasm! A holiday spirit is just the thing.'

It wouldn't last, but he enjoyed watching the way she blushed at the slightest provocation.

He was almost tempted to swing the conversation back to her mission to read books so that he could ask her whether she had ever done anything more adventurous on a plane...with a man...

She might explode with embarrassment.

'I won't be working.' Alexa rushed into hasty explanation. 'So while I wouldn't call it a holiday in the strict sense of the word...'

'Too much detail, Alexa. Let's stick to the holiday spirit theme. But before you dive into one of your books...' Theo sighed and allowed a telling silence to gather momentum until she chewed her lip with sudden anxiety.

'What?'

'There's been a slight change of plan…'

Sudden scenarios flashed through Alexa's head in Technicolor glory. Change of plan? But they were still en route to New York…

But what if New York for a few days was going to expand into other cities across the globe for an indefinite period of time?

What if her one small suitcase with a few essentials ended up being five large trunks to cater for *a change of plan*…?

What if he was going to surprise her with an impromptu wedding so that the baying nosy press could be satisfied?

What if…? What if…? What if…?

The single certainty she had was that she knew she wasn't going to like his change of plan.

He was looking at her with the expression of someone who truly regretted having to say what they were about to say—except Theo De Angelis was immune to any feelings of true regret about anything. Of that she was *very* sure.

'The hotel we were booked into…'

Alexa exhaled a sigh of silent relief, because hotels could always be changed at the last minute—especially when money was no object. And maybe there wouldn't be a penthouse suite available. In which case they would end up sleeping in separate rooms on separate floors. Fingers crossed…

'Don't worry about it,' she told him kindly. 'It's a great hotel, but there are loads of other hotels in Manhattan if for some reason they've double-booked the suite…'

'Double-booked the suite?' Theo laughed shortly. 'Colin Clark wouldn't *dare* do anything of the sort. I'm a frequent enough guest for him to know which side his bread is buttered. Not only have I used that suite on a number of occasions, I have frequently rented it for members of my staff and have held several conferences at the hotel. No… I'm a valued and cherished customer—as I've been told in the past. And *as* a valued and cherished customer, I know that suite will always be available for my use.'

'Then what's the change of plan?'

'Brace yourself...'

They were briefly interrupted by yet more drinks, and a menu which Alexa didn't even look at.

'My brother is going to be in that part of the world...'

'Your brother? Daniel?'

'Special detour before he buys his toy,' Theo informed her drily. 'So that he can meet the radiant bride-to-be...'

'But he knows that— Well, there won't be any need for us to pretend around *him*, will there?'

Alexa had banked on exploring the art galleries on her own during the day and getting through the evenings as best she could. The pressure to be loved-up would not be nearly so intense as it had been at home, because who in New York really cared?

With Theo's brother on the scene she would have to re-sign herself to a little more than mere polite conversation with people she had no intention of ever seeing again. But no matter. In truth, she was curious about his brother—curious to see whether it really *was* possible for two alpha males to be brothers...

She shrugged and rested back, half closing her eyes. Strangely, she could still see Theo's lean, dynamic face, even though her eyes were closed.

His image was imprinted on her retina with the force of a branding iron. No good fighting it. Sooner or later, once she became accustomed to the inconvenience of fancying the man, indifference would begin to trickle in, and before she knew it she would be able to look at him without a flicker of emotion. He would be just someone she'd happened to share space with for a short period of time—much to her mother's joy and delight.

'Will he be working with you?'

'Oh, no...' Theo drawled. 'My brother is as successful as I am, but his area of expertise is not mine.'

Alexa turned and looked at him. 'You mean *you* wouldn't think about buying a cruise ship as a toy?'

Theo grinned. 'I'm more of a financial guy,' he said. 'I enjoy numbers. Daniel likes the leisure side of things. If he weren't such a successful businessman in the leisure industry there's a strong possibility he would be a beach bum somewhere hot.'

Alexa heard the warmth in Theo's voice and realised that he was in exactly the same position as she was. A devoted child from a close-knit family, willing to make a ridiculously huge sacrifice for the sake of a parent or, in her case, *parents*.

It had been so much easier to pigeonhole him as a one-dimensional cardboard cut-out, and she was shaken at the tangent her thoughts had taken.

'So he'll be there? No big deal.' She closed her eyes once more and tried to block out the silent fizz of electricity radiating from his body.

'Indeed. He will be staying for a matter of just one night, but not, it would only be fair to tell you, at the hotel...'

'That's a shame.' Alexa couldn't stop herself from being just a tiny bit sarcastic. 'You'd think that as you're a *valued and cherished* customer, they would be able to rustle up a room for your brother.'

'Oh, I'm sure they would—if I asked...'

Eyes still closed, Alexa allowed herself a smug little smile. 'But you'd rather he stayed somewhere else? I guess, however close you might be to a sibling, there's still always a part of you that doesn't want them in your pocket...'

'*Not* really where I was going with this conversation,' Theo murmured. 'And, before we get lost in a series of misunderstandings, you should know that Daniel will be staying exactly where *we* will be staying. It just isn't going to be at the hotel, as originally planned…'

Alexa's eyes flew open and she sat up and looked at him. 'Okay… So…?'

'So we'll be going to The Hamptons instead,' Theo told her bluntly. 'Bob, a mutual friend of ours, has something of a mansion there, and I've been persuaded to take him up on his offer to accommodate us…'

'What? *Why?* When did this happen?'

Theo waved his hand in a soothing manner and she only just resisted slapping it away.

Her thoughts were swirling all over the place. None of them were comfortable or pleasant. What was going to happen to her time out, browsing the art galleries, if she was closeted in a house out in The Hamptons? What was going to happen to the peace and quiet she knew she would need just to deal with the wretched man every evening?

She felt physically sick at the unfolding and newly altered scenario.

'Got the call last night. Arrangements were sprung on me. What can a guy do?'

'A guy could have picked up the telephone and called to let me know of the change of plan!' Alexa snapped.

'And risk you bailing on me? No chance. It would have looked very suspect indeed if my beloved fiancée couldn't be bothered to meet her potential brother-in-law, her fiancé's best friend and three top clients who will all be adjusting their schedules for flying visits to the Hamptons to sort out the deal I'm going across to nail…'

'You've told *all of them* that we're engaged…?'

'It would have been peculiar to keep such momentous news to myself—and besides, who knows how far the news has already travelled? You would be surprised how small a world it is, with the internet and Facebook. It would have been downright discourteous for news of my engagement to reach their ears via a third party.'

'I don't have Facebook,' Alexa muttered, feeling well and truly trapped.

'Nor do I. But you can bet that we're in a minority… Bob's wife, Felicity, almost certainly *is* on Facebook—to keep in touch with their daughter in Australia.'

'What am I going to do with myself all day for days on end in a house with people I've never met in my life before?' Alexa was on the verge of undignified sobbing. 'It's just not *fair* that you couldn't even be bothered to tell me until we were in the air…'

'It will be fine,' Theo said. 'Although you might have to adjust your wardrobe a little bit…'

'Meaning…?'

'Those smart outfits might not be appropriate for a house visit.'

'I just can't believe you've done this to me.'

'Let's move on from that. It will be hot in The Hamptons. Outdoor eating is probably going to be the order of the day. Formal long dresses won't work. There's also a swimming pool, and I'm guessing that you didn't pack any swimwear…'

In actual fact Alexa *had* packed a bikini. There was a rooftop pool at the hotel, and she had intended to make use of it during the day when she wasn't out and about busying herself. She hadn't banked on parading in it in front of Theo, and she certainly, even in her wildest nightmares, hadn't envisaged staying at a private house, where she would be expected to hang around a pool with the rest of the guests in nothing but a sheer sarong and the bikini.

'Before we head to Bob's place we can fit in a whirlwind shop in Manhattan…'

'*We…?*'

'I can't say that shopping with a woman is something I
ever do, but I'm willing to make an exception…'

'That's very considerate of you, Theo, but I'll manage
just fine with what I've brought with me.'

Thank heavens for the two big books. She anticipated
doing a *lot* of reading. Although she wouldn't be able to
hide away—not when there would be other people around
whose mission it was to entertain the newly engaged couple.

'I think I'm going to get some sleep now.' She pointedly
turned away and nestled herself into a suitably dormant
position, although her mind was still all over the place.

She didn't want to think about it. What was the point?

'Don't wake me for food,' she muttered, turning her
head, and Theo, who had already extracted his laptop from
his case, grinned at her.

'Are you *sulking*?'

'I don't like plane food.'

'It will be far more relaxing at a house…away from the
noise and chaos of the city…'

Alexa didn't bother to answer, because she just *knew*
that he was having a laugh at her expense. Instead she
snatched the airline blanket and covered herself as much
as she could without ducking under it completely.

Relaxing? How much 'relaxing' did a mouse do in a
lion's den?

But she was far more tired than she had thought. She
had had a sleepless night… The low thrum of the plane's
engine, the dimming of the cabin lights…

She fell asleep for the duration of the seven-hour flight
and was pleasantly surprised to be shaken awake when the
sign flashed on for seat belts to be fastened.

Her mouth was dry, her hair had rebelled against its
restraining braid and was a tousled mess, and she knew
that her skin would look as rumpled as the rest of her did.

Too bad.

'Somehow,' Theo greeted her as she struggled into an upright position and stifled a yawn, 'we got lost in conversation about our change of plan and I forgot to give you my little present...'

The man looked unfairly bright-eyed and bushy-tailed. Had he worked solidly for the entire flight? Alexa hoped that she hadn't flopped against him accidentally, or snored or dribbled, and she hastily undid her plait and sifted her fingers through her hair in an attempt to get it looking a little less like a bird's nest.

'I'm not sure I can deal with any more surprises,' she told him truthfully.

Her nostrils flared as she breathed in his woody aftershave, and when she glanced down she was momentarily mesmerised by the dark sprinkling of hair on his forearm. She could see the strength of muscle and sinew when he flexed his fingers, and she wondered...

Appalled, she tore her eyes away to find him holding a box out to her. He flipped open the lid and there, nestled in a bed of dark blue velvet, was an engagement ring. Not *the* engagement ring, which was currently being altered, but a smaller version.

Alexa had privately thought the original one was a bit on the gaudy side, but she loved the tiny diamond twinkling up at her from this one.

He didn't give her time to protest. Instead he simply stuck the ring on her finger and then looked at it with satisfaction. 'That will do,' he said, holding her finger between his and examining it.

'What on earth is *this* for?'

'Something to wear until the one you chose at the jeweller's is returned.'

'Why do I have to wear something in the meanwhile?' She furtively looked at her finger. It was weird, but this much smaller, less conspicuous ring actually made her feel more *engaged*.

'Humour me. I'm a traditionalist. I like the world knowing that you're my woman…'

Their eyes tangled and he smiled slowly.

Laughing at her again! Yet Alexa couldn't halt the liquid heat pooling between her legs or the tight pinch of her nipples scraping against her lacy bra. She couldn't ignore the effect that low, husky, amused voice had on her weak, weak body.

Her breath caught in her throat and she turned away quickly, hoping that those shrewd, knowing eyes wouldn't gauge her spontaneous reaction.

Thankfully, the plane was descending. She would focus on that, and on checking her bag—which she hadn't opened at all, so there was absolutely no point in making sure that everything was correct and present. But it was a distraction.

They weren't going to be driven to the Hamptons. Instead they would be whooshed there by helicopter, because Bob had extensive gardens—big enough for several helicopters to land and take off, it would seem.

Theo told her all this as they were whisked through Immigration and on to where they could collect their bags.

'I really was looking forward to going to all the art galleries,' Alexa returned wistfully as they were transported like royalty to where the helicopter was waiting for them.

It was hot and sunny and a perfect day for sightseeing.

'Something can be arranged, I'm sure, if you're really desperate. Felicity would probably love to accompany you. If my memory serves me right, she's into that sort of thing… I shall be preoccupied during the day, at any rate…'

Alexa shuddered at the prospect of trekking down to Manhattan in the company of someone else. Strolling through art galleries had always been a pleasurable thing to do on her own—a time for quiet reflection and a bit of peace and quiet.

'How many people are going to be there?' she asked, gazing idly around her as the stretch limo removed them from the main airport,

'A handful.' His phone buzzed and he picked up the call and remained talking, only cutting short his conversation when their helicopter was within sight.

'Work,' he said crisply.

'Is that all you ever think about?' Alexa asked, eyeing the helicopter with trepidation. She had been on a helicopter twice in her life and had hated both experiences.

'Not *all*...'

There was a small, knowing smile on his lips and she shook her head with exasperation.

'Work and flings, then...'

Theo burst out laughing and made a big show of stepping back and helping her into the helicopter. He exchanged a few pleasantries with their pilot and then turned to her, the smile still lingering on his lips.

'Don't knock a good fling. Flings can be very satisfying—as I'm sure you've discovered for yourself, considering you've never married...'

'I can't see anything satisfying in meaningless sex!' Alexa had to half shout as the scream of the rotor blades threatened to drown out conversation.

'I prefer to call it *no strings sex*. And what about *fun*?' Theo prompted. 'Or is that something you disapprove of? Along with kicking back?'

'I just think it must get very boring after a while,' she bristled.

'In which case your "meaningless sex" can't have been very exciting.'

Alexa ignored that. Did he think that she spent her time

hopping in and out of bed with random men? Hadn't he seen for himself that she wasn't like that? She didn't know whether to be relieved or insulted at his one-track mind, but she did know that it was hardly surprising, because he was simply judging her according to his own standards.

He had no problem disengaging his emotions from the act of sexual intercourse. For him it was no more meaningful than a physical workout at the gym. And his relationships, if they could be called that, probably didn't last much longer.

Thankfully, *she* had never been like that—which was some consolation considering she fancied the man.

At least she knew where her priorities were, and would never allow the physical to take over.

She didn't reply to his provocative statement. Instead she stared down at the wispy clouds and thought that in a week's time all of this would be over—and thank goodness for that.

CHAPTER SEVEN

ALEXA HAD NO time to let panic get a grip because the helicopter ride was over practically before it had begun, and then it was buzzing and lowering itself down to a section of lawn which had been converted into a neat helipad.

She had no idea what to expect, but she did know that if Theo had referred to his friend's house as 'a mansion', then it was going to be pretty spectacular—and it was.

She had seen there was a pool from above—a rectangle of pristine bright blue—but the view of the top of the house didn't do justice to its splendour, which only became apparent as they were transported in something resembling a motorised golf buggy to the curving courtyard.

On either side of the drive immaculate lawns stretched towards hedgerows that had been clipped with razor-sharp precision, high enough to ensure perfect privacy. The house was fronted by a series of striking columns that threw the sprawling veranda at the front into cool shade. On the first floor a similar veranda mimicked the one below, but circled the entire house, providing a massive outdoor deck space on which she could spot clusters of shaded furniture. The top floor was more modest, sheltered by an overhanging terracotta roof, and at the four corners of the house massive chimneys advertised indoor fireplaces.

'Huge…' Alexa was duly impressed, even though she

was accustomed to grand houses. 'How many people live here?'

'Four, once upon a time. Now just two, because both kids have left home. As you might gather, they're not my contemporaries. I met them a long time ago, when my father was involved in lending Bob cash to fund his dream of building a golf and country club. The golf and country club is now one of the most frequented by top professional golfers, and he's dabbled in a series of other successful ventures since those heady days.'

'You must have been very young at the time.'

Theo looked down at her and grinned. 'I challenged Bob to a game of golf and whipped him. Since then we've been firm friends...'

'*That's* something else you do,' she couldn't resist murmuring.

'Come again?'

'By way of relaxing... You play golf.'

'Would you like to know which form of relaxation I prefer?'

'No, I wouldn't!'

'You're so predictable in your responses...'

Suddenly he pulled her towards him and tucked her against his body—and, sure enough, waiting in the open doorway was a small blonde woman in her fifties, her face wreathed with smiles.

'Bob never thought you'd do it, you great big lug! But I *knew* that a woman would come along and sweep you off your feet! I'm Felicity, by the way, and you have to excuse my shrieking like a crazy person but we were just so darned *surprised* when we heard that our favourite boy in the *whole wide world* was finally going to settle down!'

In between speaking at rapid-fire speed and introducing herself Felicity managed to plant a friendly kiss on both their cheeks while hustling them into the house and calling out for 'Stanley' to take their bags up.

Alexa had no time to say any of the usual polite things about the house or about their trip or about anything at all.

'Like it or not, you're gonna tell all! *Bob!* Bob's in the middle of one those darned conference calls!'

This to Alexa, with a woman-to-woman wink.

'You make sure when you've got a ring on this guy's finger that you ban all conference calls! And make sure he doesn't take up golf! I've had to start taking lessons or else lose that lug of a husband of mine to fairways and putting greens!'

No concessions were made to the fact that they had been travelling for several hours. Felicity dragged them through the house at breakneck speed, towards a massive kitchen which was the last word in high-tech. Glossy white built-in cupboards concealed everything, and the gleaming marble countertops were bare of all but the essentials. She led them on towards some comfortable seating in a conservatory that overlooked the manicured lawns, and once they were seated offered tall glasses of homemade lemonade whilst promising them that they could 'go freshen up' just as soon as they'd spilled the beans.

'I've got to grab you two kids before the house becomes a hotbed for dull businessmen!' She settled comfortably into one of the chairs and peered at them with lively curiosity.

Alexa could see fine laughter lines around her eyes and mouth. This was a warm, giving woman who loved to laugh and have fun. That was apparent in the way she spoke and the way she punctuated everything she said with a little breathless laugh.

'So, what does it feel like to be in love?' She directed the question to Theo, but her twinkling eyes darted between both of them. She was obviously delighted at their engagement.

Next to her, Theo still had his arm around her shoulders and it took a lot of effort not to shuffle a few inches away. Now that she had faced up to her inconvenient attraction Alexa was finding it impossible to keep her body's responses under control.

'A refreshing change,' he said.

Alexa kept her smile pinned to her face and tried to wax lyrical when Felicity looked at her for more of a gushy explanation. 'Wonderful!' she chirped. 'We never thought in a million years that…er…when we met we would end up…well…'

'In the throes of heady love? Is that what you were going to say, my darling?'

Felicity needed no more encouragement to launch into an impassioned speech about the wonders of love, after which she quizzed Alexa about her family, about what she did, expressing earnest approval of her volunteer work. Everything was interspersed with smug, smiling nods that said Theo had indeed found the perfect woman.

At that point Bob appeared, and there were more introductions and an excited synopsis of everything that had been said in his absence.

These were Theo's good friends and, looking at their interaction, Alexa could see a side of him that had not been in evidence before. He was warm, thoughtful, interested…and utterly, utterly charming. He had ensured that their daughter in Australia was introduced to a social network, thanks to his brother. He had personally chaperoned their youngest daughter when she had travelled to Europe as a sixteen-year-old, making sure that the family to whom she had been sent on an exchange visit was vetted and ticked all the boxes.

She had a new picture of him, and it wasn't the sarcastic, ruthless guy who provoked her and rubbed her up the wrong way.

'I feel like I've been tossed into a cyclone,' she said, when they finally left their hosts to prepare a barbecue for later.

Theo grinned. 'They like you. And you'll get used to their high-octane energy.'

Ahead of them Stanley, one of the staff, had disappeared along the corridor. The house seemed bigger on the inside than it did on the outside, and it was furnished in a beautifully airy, plantation style. The paintings on the walls were bright and eclectic, and the marble flooring on the ground floor gave way to rich, deep wood on the first floor.

She was so preoccupied with admiring the rooms they passed that she only realised that they had arrived at a bedroom when she noticed Stanley disappearing back towards the stairs, and then, as she entered, she looked around her with mounting panic.

'It's a bedroom,' she said in a high voice.

Theo had strolled towards the window, and now he turned to look at her for a few seconds, before moving to quietly close the door behind them. 'Well observed.'

'I'm not *sharing* a bedroom with you.'

Had it crossed her mind that they would be put in the same room? If it had, then the thought hadn't registered long enough to take root. She had glibly assumed that they would be housed in separate rooms... The place must have dozens of rooms, for heaven's sake!

'That is exactly what you'll be doing,' Theo told her, his voice hard.

He stood in front of her, an implacable rock, until she had no choice but to look up at him.

'Furthermore, you're going to compliment Felicity on the room and tell her how fantastic it is being here instead of in a boring, impersonal hotel in Manhattan. Bob and Felicity have bent over backwards to have us here and you're going to be suitably grateful.'

'I'm not sharing a bed with you,' Alexa said, stubbornly holding her ground.

Just thinking about that made the hairs on her hand stand on end. She could imagine his big, muscular body rolling accidentally against hers in the middle of the night and she cringed. She didn't care whether he fancied her or not. She didn't care that she wasn't his type. She cared about the fact that she would combust if they were in the same bed together.

And furthermore... *Did he even sleep with anything on?* He didn't strike her as the flannel pyjamas type...

Theo eyed the chaise longue by the window. 'Fine. In that case the chaise longue is all yours... I'm way too big for that thing.'

'A gentleman would offer to sleep on the floor,' Alexa gritted through pearly white teeth.

'Considering you've already written me off as not being one of those, it's fair to say that I won't be sleeping on the floor. However, you're more than welcome to make *your* bed down there if you like. Now, I'm going to have a shower.'

For a few seconds Alexa remained staring at him in sheer, angry frustration—until it dawned on her that he was beginning to take his clothes off, at which point every nerve in her body was galvanised into horrified action and she spun round to speak with her back to him.

'Do you mind getting undressed in the bathroom?' she hissed, and she heard his throaty chuckle in response.

'Why? Don't tell me that you've never seen a man's naked body before?'

Alexa seethed. 'I won't even bother to answer that!'

Not only did he continue chuckling, he actually *whistled* as he disappeared into the bathroom, thankfully closing

the door behind him and giving her time to unpack her
clothes at the speed of light.

He emerged ten minutes later, a towel casually wrapped
round his waist.

Alexa, about to reach for her bundle of clothing, was
frozen to the spot. Background noises faded and all she
could hear was the frantic thud of her heartbeat.

The man was…*spectacular.*

Bronzed, muscled, broad-shouldered. Not an ounce of
body fat. He was utterly, utterly perfect and she could feel
her skin prickle with heat. It was as if something alien and
unfamiliar had invaded every nook and cranny of her body.

'I'm going to have a bath now!' Her voice was high-
pitched and she cleared her throat. 'I'll meet you downstairs.'

'Oh, I think it would far more fitting if we were to head
down together. Hand in hand.'

Right now *his* hand was reaching to hook the edge of
the towel and she fled, slamming and locking the bathroom door behind her.

She barely noticed the over-the-top luxury of the marble
bathroom suite, or the little touches that had been given
to make it welcoming. The fragrant pot-pourri, the fluffy
white towels, the dinky soaps and shampoos…

She couldn't concentrate on anything but the fact that
Theo was in the next room…*probably strolling around in
his birthday suit while he decided what to wear…*

She took as long a bath as was humanly possible, and
then dressed and applied her make-up in the bathroom,
peering into the steamed-up mirror and finally abandon-
ing the effort because she could barely make out her reflection. Her hair she left just as it was, long and tangled,
and she finally emerged with only her shoes to put on.

He was sprawled on the bed, half naked, just his trousers on, with a book casually propped on his bare stom-

ach. He peered at her over the top of it as she walked into the room.

'How *dare* you go into my bag?'

Theo inspected the book cover and grinned. 'Shall I tell you how it ends or will that spoil the surprise?'

'I thought you might have got dressed!'

'I was about to put my shirt on but this gaudy book jacket grabbed my attention. Of course I figured out who did it by page four, but I thought I'd check to confirm— and, sure enough, I was right.'

He chucked the book and it landed neatly back in her bag, which was on the ground, half open.

'Nice outfit.' Taking his time, he slid his legs over the side of the bed and sauntered towards the wardrobe to extract a shirt. 'The bed's very comfortable. Shame you won't be experiencing it. You'll be trying to find a comfy position on the chaise longue or on the floor...'

'You're... You're...'

'Shall we head down?'

He waited by the door for her, watching as she stepped into some sandals with little wedge heels. He didn't think she realised just how damned sexy she looked in that strappy little sundress, with her long hair tumbling all over the place. Even her scowl couldn't detract from the picture.

Difficult, feisty, mulish and prickly as hell. Who would have thought that *sexy* could come in that package?

He offered his arm and Alexa stormily hooked her hand in the crook as they descended the stairs. He was as cool as the proverbial cucumber, telling her about the history of the house and the antics of the infamous gardener who had landscaped the grounds. Admittedly it was very interesting, and she was big enough to tell him so before Bob and Felicity took over the rest of the evening.

It was relaxed, and they made charming, inquisitive and interesting hosts. Bob had hundreds of amusing anecdotes about the famous golf players he had met over the years…a golf game was arranged…the barbecue was exquisite and informal and champagne flowed. Alexa was even aware that she was laughing at one point as glasses were raised to toast the couple.

But could she relax? Not a bit of it.

Every nerve in her body was stretched to breaking point because all she could think about was that room…that bed…and Theo lying with the duvet half on, half off, possibly clothed but more likely not…

She was spent by the time the evening was at an end. She liked both their hosts, and she could see that they were thrilled at what they considered a wonderful love match. If only they knew!

'So…' Theo flung open the bedroom door and stood aside to let her pass, then shut it behind him and lounged against it, arms folded, a slight smile curving his mouth. 'Did you enjoy the evening?'

The confines of the bedroom and the daunting prospect of the night ahead, not to mention all the other nights ahead, slammed into her with the force of a sledgehammer.

'I…I really did, as a matter of fact,' Alexa replied nervously. She remained standing by the window on the opposite side of the bedroom, with the yawning space of rug-covered floor between them. 'I had no idea what to expect of your friends, but they're incredibly nice and hospitable…'

And that, by association, said something about the man towering in front of her. She relaxed. She had nothing to fear in sharing a bedroom with him. He'd been nothing but decent in accepting her terms and, frankly, putting up with her moods. She'd sniped and argued and fought him every inch of the way when *he* hadn't been the one who had dumped her in this situation. She had used him as a scapegoat for her own frustrations and, arrogant though the man was, he had not retaliated in kind.

'I…er…just want to apologise…'

Theo looked at her in surprise and pushed himself away from the door to kick off his shoes. He began unbuttoning his shirt and Alexa fought to stay calm and hold on to her relaxed frame of mind.

'Apologise for what?'

'I haven't been the easiest person to be around…'

'Really?' Theo said drily. 'I'm glad you brought that to my attention. I wouldn't have noticed otherwise.'

'Not that *you've* been plain sailing!'

Theo burst out laughing and Alexa reluctantly smiled.

'Some men might find your fighting spirit a little challenging, but I admit that I'm growing to rather like it. And now that we've established a fragile truce I wouldn't want to ruin it by forcing you to build your nest on the chaise longue, so I'll take the floor.'

Alexa nodded.

Good.

But it was a super king-sized bed, and the floor was going to be an uncomfortable resting place even for a guy who probably survived on only a couple of hours sleep a night.

She escaped to the bathroom, washed her face and brushed her teeth and changed into her pyjamas. Feverishly she decided that whilst she *could* continue ranting and railing and behaving like a child, she could also just… trust that new side of him she had seen. He wasn't going to make a pass at her just because they happened to be lying on the same mattress, was he? She had been superimposing her own anxieties on to him and it was foolish.

He took the bathroom after her and she pretended not to notice the fact that he was already half naked…that the button to his trousers was undone…that she could see a sliver of his underwear where the trousers dipped down over his lean hips.

In the fifteen minutes during which she heard the whoosh of water and the sounds of him getting ready she tried to get her racing heartbeat under control, and she was burrowed down under the duvet by the time the bathroom door was flung open.

She sneaked a glance and heaved a sigh of relief that he was still in his boxers.

'Well, well, well...' Theo strolled into the room and registered that she was in the bed but that there was no pile of linen on the floor, waiting to be turned into a sleeping area. Instead she had banked some cushions down the middle of the mattress in a neat dividing line.

Alexa flipped over and feigned a yawn of exhaustion. 'It's silly for either of us to sleep on the floor. The bed is huge and there's no reason why we can't share it like two adults.'

'I like your definition of sharing *like two adults...*' He nodded at the military march of cushions along the middle of the bed.

Reluctantly she grinned. 'I thought it might be a good idea to have separated sides.'

'Of course.'

Theo was amused at just how innocent that gesture was. He climbed into bed, his antennae noting the way she shifted ever so slightly away from him. She was clearly awake, but she wasn't reading her book and she certainly wasn't about to engage in conversation. He reached for his laptop, propped it on his lap and casually asked if it would bother her if he worked for a couple of hours. He was even more amused when she didn't answer.

Bother her? It bothered her that he was even *breathing* next to her, far less working.

Her body was rigid. She would never manage to get a

wink of sleep. She knew that. Nor would she be able to toss and turn. If she tossed and turned he would guess that she was awake, plus she would keep *him* up, and then they'd both be awake…in a bed…just the two of them…

Sleep overcame her. It had been a long and tiring day and her exhausted body at last won the battle over her hyperactive mind.

She dreamt that she was skimming over the clouds, looking down. And then, as she looked behind her, over her shoulder, Theo was advancing, getting closer and closer. Part of her wanted desperately to run away, but another, stronger part was holding her fast and *liked* the fact that she couldn't move, that he would get closer and closer, and their bodies would fuse… She would be able to skim her hands over his broad chest and feel the rough surface of muscle and tendon…

The dream was so real that she could almost feel his hands on her, brushing against her thigh and then curving between her legs. She moaned softly.

Her eyes fluttered open and…she wasn't dreaming.

For a few seconds Alexa was completely disorientated. The strategically positioned cushions had hit the floor at some point during the night, and not only had she rolled towards Theo but right now the palm of her hand was flat against his hard chest and he was as awake as she was.

And holding her against him as if it was the most natural thing in the world.

Her limbs felt heavy and lazy and, just like in her dream, whilst a part of her desperately knew that she should pull away, another part of her felt heavy and warm and lazy, utterly incapable of doing anything but revelling in the feel of his equally warm body.

'Shh…' Theo murmured, as if she had spoken.

After lying in complete silence while he had tried to focus on work Alexa had eventually fallen asleep. He had known by the change in the rhythm of her breathing and, oddly enough, having her asleep next to him had made *him* a little jumpy.

He had managed to subdue his disobedient libido when it had reared its head and he had done that by rationalising it out of existence. He was in an unnatural and forced situation—heading down the aisle and not by choice. He was with a woman whose emotionalism was not the kind of thing he sought or appreciated in *any* woman—certainly not in a woman to whom he was to be married. And, physically, since when had he *ever* gone for small, curvy girls? That had always been his brother's domain.

But just knowing that she was next to him in the bed had kept him awake. At one point he had seriously considered slipping out of bed and heading for a cold shower—especially when those cushions had been kicked away and, like a little mouse gravitating towards the source of warmth, she had wriggled closer and closer until she had been touching him.

'You were moaning,' he whispered. 'Having a bad dream? Or a really good one?'

Alexa squeezed her eyes shut and remembered exactly how erotic that dream of hers had been. Heat was still making her want to snap her legs together.

'I'm sorry if I woke you,' she whispered back. 'The cushions…'

'Turns out that soft furnishings don't make very successful fortifications…' He sifted his fingers through her hair. His body was raging, his libido in full surge—a primitive response over which he had no control.

Right now, right here, Theo wanted her in a way he had never wanted any woman in his life before. This wife-to-be he had never asked for and from whom he knew he should keep a safe distance. Because if he slept with her…slept with someone who was looking for a guy who was most certainly *not him*…that single act of passion would make the next year even more impossibly awkward than it was already showing signs of being.

And yet…

'Why did you feel the need to stick a row of cushions between us?'

His hand dipped to the curve of her waist. She wasn't pulling back with a screech of maidenly outrage and more than anything else *that* was a massive turn-on—because it was proof that despite all her protests she wanted him. She didn't *want* to want him…just as *he* didn't want to want *her*…but their bodies were not on the same page as their intellects.

In a life that was formidably controlled this lack of self-control felt good…satisfying…addictive.

How the hell was he going to endure twelve months of wanting her and banking down his desire?

They were both adults, he reasoned. They fancied one another, and he knew from experience that it was a very short journey between fancying a woman and boredom setting in. He had no doubt that if she fancied him it was something she was fighting to ignore, which meant that the same would apply to her. If they slept together they would rid themselves of an inconvenient lust—a bit like taking the right medicine to kill a fever.

'Did you think…?'

His voice was low and soft, and Alexa knew that it was no shock that she was finding it impossible to pull away from him when he was hypnotising her with his deep, dark, sexy drawl.

'Did you think that if it weren't for some scatter cushions you might have found yourself wanting to touch me?'

'No!'

'Liar.' He laughed softly under his breath. 'I've felt the way your body tenses up every time I've touched you and seen the way you slide hot little glances over at me when you don't think I'm watching you… Except I've been watching you a hell of a lot more than you probably thought. In fact a lot more than I ever anticipated…because I'm feeling what you're feeling…'

'I never said…' Her voice was so feeble and unconvincing that she wasn't surprised when he laughed again.

'Sure about that? Because there's a foolproof way of proving whether you're telling little porky-pies…'

He was going to kiss her—and she wasn't going to fight it. Her body was on fire and she wanted him to touch it… she wanted to touch *his*…and she had never wanted to touch any guy like that—hadn't even come close…

She'd never suspected—not for a second—that lust could trample all over her principles and turn them to mush.

She closed her eyes on a sigh, leaned into him, and Theo, trailing the most delicate of caresses along her jaw-bone, simultaneously slipped his finger under the baggy nightie and beneath her underwear and into her wetness to finger her.

It was shocking and unexpected, and Alexa wriggled away from the touch, reaching down to push his hand away, squirming free, but knowing that she didn't want to create space between them—she wanted to abolish it.

She shouldn't want this but she did. She *wanted* his fingers exploring her and she burned with mortification. When he slid his hand along her stomach desire held her fast, stopped her from breaking their connection. It felt like an extension of her dream, weird and surreal and somehow *not really happening*—at least not in a way that felt dangerous or threatening.

Her breathing quickened. She heard herself pant a desperate *'No!'* but it felt so good. She slid her treacherous, trembling hands over his chest, yanked them away, repeated the caress, this time tracing the broad, muscled width of his shoulders.

The sexless nightie felt itchy and uncomfortable, and she wanted to squirm out of her underwear—and was immediately horrified and panicked by the impulse.

So she fancied him. And he, to her amazement, fancied *her*. Maybe it was the strangeness of the situation into which they had both been thrown. In fact that was probably it—because if she had bumped into him under normal circumstances, at one of those social events which *she* hated and which *he* saw as part and parcel of being who he was, then she was sure that she would never, ever, have been attracted to him. And he would have had one of those leggy, supermodel airhead types clinging to him like ivy. He wouldn't have given *her* a second glance.

But here they were…

She tentatively let her hand stray to his waist, and then a bit lower, and she shivered as she felt the massive bulge of his erection pushing against the boxers. It was terrifying, and she withdrew her hand as though she'd suddenly plunged it into an open fire.

But she wanted to touch him *so badly*…

'Theo…this is crazy…'

'Is it? I don't think so. In the whole crazy charade, this feels like the least crazy bit…'

'I don't do this sort of thing.'

'You mean make love to your fiancé?'

'You know what I mean.'

'I know what you mean, my dearest wife-to-be. But do you *want* to…?'

'Yes! No… Oh, I don't know… Theo! I can't think straight…not when you're touching me…'

'Not thinking straight suits me—and what does "Yes! No… I don't know…" mean?'

'It means I find you attractive. Okay?'

'Okay.'

He'd never had to ask a woman if she wanted him, had never received such a grudging response, but hearing her say that put him on top of the world.

He gradually pushed up the nightie. He was as out of control as a horny teenager about to lose his virginity. *Crazy.* He cupped the fullness of her breast and then rubbed his thumb over her stiff nipple, over and over, until she was moaning and moving restlessly against him.

'We shouldn't…' In the grip of the sensations that were bombarding her on all fronts she could barely get the pathetically weak protest out.

'Life is too short for *shouldn't*…'

'That's easy for you to say.'

You're experienced. You haven't spent your life welding sex to love and waiting for them to come along at the same time. You're relaxed and carefree about this sort of thing. Not like me.

And yet for all that she couldn't have shifted out of his reach if she'd tried.

'You've done nothing but fight me,' he moaned softly. 'Now I want you to tell me that you need this as much as I do…'

'I…'

'*Say it*, Alexa…'

'I want this so much,' she confessed shakily, thrilled at the hot urgency in his voice.

'Good.' His voice was thick with satisfaction.

He lowered his head, angling her body so that he could lick and kiss her neck, her shoulders. He nearly lost it completely when he felt the hitch in her breathing as he trailed kisses over her breasts, until finally he clamped his mouth over the big, pink circular disc of her nipple.

Her whole body tensed, and then relaxed into the caress. He was dimly aware of the fluttering of her fingers in his hair as he continued to draw the stiffened bud of her throbbing nipple deep into his mouth, nipping and suckling on it. He was a big man, with big hands, and the abundance of her breasts was a good fit as he cupped her other breast and massaged it.

'Touch me,' he commanded roughly, pulling her hand down and clasping it hard over his erection. 'Just hold me. *Tight*, for God's sake. I don't want to spoil the party prematurely...'

He reared up as she obeyed and took a few deep breaths, fighting to recover some of his lost self-control. When his breathing finally levelled out he resumed where he had left off, this time devoting his attention to her other breast, but not until he had looked at her nakedness, feasting his eyes on the paleness of her skin and the contrasting rosy flush of her nipples.

Alexa gazed up at him through half-closed eyes. He had rid himself of his boxers and his erection was a thick, hard, pulsing rod of steel. There wasn't a shred of self-consciousness in him as he watched her gazing at him. She was scared, thrilled, massively turned on...all at the same time.

'Would you like to sample the fare...?' He asked, and when she frowned in bewilderment he grinned. 'Taste with your mouth what you're busy tasting with your eyes...?'

He couldn't understand her... She was enthusiastic, turned on, and yet curiously shy and hesitant. But, then again, the women he slept with were all so experienced that perhaps he had forgotten what it was like to be with one who didn't see sex as an exercise in impressing him with gymnastics. He liked it. He knew that.

'I... I'm not... I don't... This is all so far out of my comfort zone...'

'Then I'll let you set the pace...'

He was moved by the nervousness in her voice. She

wanted him, but she wasn't going to jump on him, and he got that. She needed to be treated like a delicate piece of porcelain china. He needed to let her have control. And that turned him on.

She covered him with tentative little kisses. She clearly liked him to touch her breasts and he did. But he wanted her to hold his erection, and after a while, after she had trailed delicate little kisses over his stomach—kisses that were driving him mad, had she but known it—she garnered the courage to take those delicate little kisses lower down.

She whimpered softly, and those little whimpers were a turn-on beyond belief. To a man with a fairly jaded palette when it came to the opposite sex and their bedroom antics, this was uniquely refreshing. She was shy. He wanted her to feel comfortable with his body, comfortable to touch him wherever she wanted, but the way she took her time... *agony*. He could barely breathe.

To Alexa, witnessing this big, utterly confident and controlled man lose it a little was as heady as a dose of adrenaline shot straight into her system.

Her faltering self-confidence strengthened into a growing sense of liberation. A guy who was restless and impatient, who took what he wanted whatever the cost—a guy for whom *tomorrow* was not a word in his vocabulary if it could be replaced by *today*—was letting her take charge, and that felt so good to her.

She straightened and looked down at him. She'd never been naked in front of a man in her life before, and her skin tingled and burned as he gazed at her with open, unashamed desire.

When he reached forward to graze his thumbs across her stiff nipples she moaned softly and closed her eyes. Her whole body was trembling.

She wanted more than this. She wanted him inside her, moving inside her, filling her up...

She guided his hand between her legs and even as she did so was shocked at her forwardness. When he began massaging her there she covered his hand with hers, groaned as he slid two fingers inside, unerringly finding her clitoris and sending her into spiralling, ever-increasing zones of sexual pleasure.

She felt like a rag doll. As her pleasure grew...and grew... and grew...she opened dazed eyes and levelled them at him.

'I want more, Theo.' She barely recognised her own voice, which was husky with desire.

'And so do I... You have no idea... But...' He reached for his wallet on the dressing table to extract a condom. 'Life right now,' he murmured, catching her heated gaze and holding it, 'is complicated enough without adding to it...'

CHAPTER EIGHT

HE DROPPED THE condom on the side table and settled over
her, grazing between her legs with his erection, nudging,
but not too much. And then he slid his hands under her
back, arching her up towards him. Nerves mingled with
wicked anticipation, and anticipation won.

She had disposed of her nightie—flung it over the side
of the bed. She knew that she should be feeling timid,
quailing at his frank inspection of her body, but there was
open heat in his lazy gaze. No mistaking the fact that he
was hot for her. She didn't think that his heat could match
her own.

'I'm fat…' she confessed, burning up like straw flung
to a struck match.

'Whoever told you that? Surely not your parents…?'

He didn't normally do pillow talk, but the openness of
her admission touched him. He lay down next to her and
pulled her against him. He could feel the steady beating of
her heart and the squash of her breasts against his chest.

A slight delay to proceedings. There was nothing un-
cool about that. In fact it made sense, gave his body time
to adjust to its normal tempo.

'Gosh, no.'

This intimacy felt good. Not so much sex for the sake
of sex as two people in bed about to make love. She had a
gut feeling that he wasn't the kind of guy who slowed down

to accommodate anyone, and that included the women he took to his bed. But he was slowing down for *her*. And whilst the logical part of her knew that it meant nothing, it still felt good.

Plus… Rushing into sex…

Yes, her body was on fire for him, but her mind was tentative, filled with her own shortcomings and what he might say about them. If he'd made some great big show of trying to get her into bed she might have stood a chance at resistance, but like this…in the dead of night…here in this bed…she was powerless to fight her body's urgings.

Talking like this might relax her…

'The opposite.' She traced the outline of his shoulders, liking its tough ridges and contours. 'My parents always told me that I was beautiful and that I could do anything I wanted.' She laughed a little breathlessly, because confiding wasn't something she was accustomed to doing. She marvelled that she was doing it now, with this man. 'Of course most parents say that, and I wasn't a complete idiot. I knew I wasn't beautiful.'

'And you knew that because…? You had a magic mirror on your wall…?'

Alexa laughed, but there was a telling catch in her laughter and Theo experienced a moment of disorientation during which he felt weirdly tender and possessive towards this prickly, argumentative woman who had given him nothing but a hard time ever since their paths had crossed.

'I overheard a conversation when I was eleven,' she confessed. 'I was in a toilet cubicle at school and I overheard some of my friends giggling about me. I'd never thought I was fat but it seems that I was…and I had also developed way ahead of everyone else. That's a big deal when you're a kid. Whilst all the girls in my year were busy shooting up like beanpoles I was getting…well…*a figure*… It seems I was something of a figure of fun…especially to boys…'

'Boys that age can be idiots,' Theo told her fiercely. He dropped a kiss on her forehead and held her against him, her face pressed against his neck. 'In fact…' he angled her so that he could look down at her seriously '…quite a few idiot boys grow up into idiot men.'

Was that her opinion of him? A guy who judged by appearances only?

He sensed that that was just the sort of introspective question that might not benefit from too much in-depth analysis. Her whole persona now made sense to him. Her defensiveness…her passionate interest in the intellectual as opposed to the physical…her mulish aversion to the sort of high society affairs where she might feel herself judged, yet again, on appearance instead of personality.

The fact that she was here now, playing at a relationship with the sort of man she had probably spent her entire adult life erecting walls to keep out, spoke volumes about her close relationship with her parents.

'I suppose…' She laughed a little self-consciously. 'Thanks for listening…'

Theo was highly offended. 'Of course I listened to you! Why wouldn't I?'

'Because you don't listen a lot when women moan and whine?' she suggested teasingly.

Theo had the grace to flush. 'Maybe that whining and moaning always had a certain predictable flavour…'

'What do you mean?'

'We're having a conversation,' Theo heard himself say.

Alexa nestled against him, nerves temporarily banished. 'Isn't that what you told me we *had* to do, considering we're about to tie the knot?'

'I don't do a lot of that either,' he admitted with a wry smile.

'Talking in bed with a woman?'

Theo thought that it might have been more accurate to

say *talking*, and leave it at that, but of course he *did* talk to women... Regrettably, the conversations were not usually of an inspiring nature and, having never—not once—thought about that, he now wondered whether he had set his standards a little on the low side in the past. At least insofar as intellectual stimulation was concerned.

'There always seem to be far more exciting things to do than chit-chat...' He shoved aside the niggling moment of introspection and returned to the business of making love—his comfort zone.

He curved his hand along her side, smoothing it over her rounded hip and confidently inserting it between her legs, parting them and laughing under his breath at her little pant of anticipation.

This was *definitely* more like it.

'Now it's time for you to lie back and think of England...'

'Is that an order?'

'Of course it is. Haven't we already established that I'm the arrogant sort, who gives orders and expects them to be obeyed...?'

Alexa giggled breathlessly and closed her eyes—although she knew the last thing she would be doing was thinking of England...

He explored her body and took his time doing it, suckling on her swollen nipples, arching her body up so that he could enjoy them all the more. The longer he spent there, the more she frantically wanted him to go further, and her whole body was tingling as he made his way down, inch by inch, until his mouth found the dampness between his legs.

Alexa gave a little yelp and tried to wriggle away, but Theo pinned her down by her hips and glanced up at her.

'What's the problem?'

'There's something you should know...'

She had debated whether to say anything or not. Could

a man tell the difference between a virgin and a woman who was not? Alexa didn't know, but she knew that she would reveal the full extent of her inexperience the very second he started getting too intimate.

As he had just been doing.

'Hasn't anyone been intimate with you like that?' Theo was tickled pink by that. 'Shh… Time for me to show you what you've been missing…'

He didn't want her to think about this. He just wanted her to *enjoy*. He gently parted her legs and felt her tense. He licked the inside of her thigh and she relaxed with a soft moan, and then, so slowly, he began to explore her.

She tasted of musk and honey, fragrant and seductive. He licked her, and then darted his questing tongue, touching the protruding nub of her clitoris. After gently smoothing her thighs he parted the lips concealing her womanhood with his fingers, so that her sensitive clitoris was even more exposed to the erotic dance of his tongue.

Alexa groaned. She could barely breathe, the pleasure was so intense.

She shielded her face with her arm and twisted away. She was so wet down there…melting like candle wax.

The pleasure became more and more intense, spiralling until she was hurtling towards the edge, and only then did Theo slowly ease his rhythm, leaving her begging for more, pleading with him to bring her to orgasm.

By which time he was so shockingly turned on that he could barely steady his hands to apply the condom. More than anything else, he wanted to come inside her, to feel her wet tightness wrap around his erection…

Alexa stayed him with one trembling hand and gulped. 'There's something I should tell you…'

'Alexa… Not now… I want you so much I'm not sure I'm going to be able to withstand another conversation—

not unless we pause for an intermission and I have a cold shower...'

'It's...it's something you really need to know, Theo,' she said with wrenching urgency.

Theo stilled and gazed down at her flushed cheeks. He couldn't imagine what she might have to say that couldn't keep. She was as turned on as he was and he could barely think straight. Add to that the fact that he was highly experienced and you didn't need to join too many dots to work out how explosive her effect on him was.

Was she about to tell him that she was involved with someone else? It was a question he had asked of her before and she had given a negative response—but that might have been a diplomatic denial, intended to halt a sticky conversation.

With a jolt of surprise he realised that he had already formed assumptions about her, and one of them was that he believed she was genuine—and that annoyed him, because he was cynical when it came to members of the opposite sex.

'If you're going to break my heart by telling me you've got the hots for another man, then it's a conversation I have no interest in having.'

He lay back and felt her nestle against him, propping herself up against his chest. Her long hair hung on either side of her heart-shaped face, a jumble of curls.

'What are you talking about?' Alexa was genuinely puzzled. 'If I had the hots for someone else why would I be...? Well...'

Theo dealt her a slashing grin, relieved at the earnestness in her voice. He curled his fingers into her hair and tugged her down to kiss him.

'Then what...?' he murmured huskily. 'Spill the beans...'

'I've... I'm probably not as experienced as you think I am...'

'What are you telling me?'

'I've never...never done this before...' Alexa said bluntly, holding her breath for his appalled reaction.

'You're a *virgin*?'

'And you're shocked.' She miserably filled in the blanks.

Shocked? No. Surprised? Yes. In his experience virgins in their twenties were about as common as sightings of the dodo. But he was also massively turned on at her admission.

He flipped her over so that he was looking down at her. *His woman.* He should have been turned off, but he wasn't. The opposite.

'I'll take my time,' he murmured. 'And by the time I'm ready to enter you, Alexa, you'll be so wet and ready for me...'

Words failed him.

Who needed words? He was going to give her an experience that would live with her for ever.

He explored her body all over again. He nuzzled and licked her nipples until they were warm and throbbing in his mouth. He trailed languorous kisses along her stomach and as he did so slowly rubbed her clitoris with his fingers, readying her for his mouth.

Alexa raised her legs, squirming as he nuzzled between her legs. Just watching his dark head there was the most erotic thing she could ever have imagined. True to his word, he took his time, and she knew, inexperienced as she was, that it would require a lot of willpower for him to do so.

'I don't want to...to come like this...' she gasped, as her body began sweeping her towards the edge.

Theo looked up from where he had been busy and shot her a lazy smile. 'You won't...'

He'd also promised to be gentle, and he was. He nudged his way into her and she felt herself open up for him, and when he began to thrust into her she was crying out for him, her hands curling into his hair, her body arching up so that he could take her completely. Any fleeting discomfort was quickly overwhelmed by a surge of *want* and she came with soaring intensity. It was an out-of-body experience that left her shaking.

She didn't want to let him go. She wanted to cling, to feel his perspiring body pressed up against her. She felt him as he came, shuddering inside her on a broken groan of satisfaction. There were no barriers between them in that moment of total surrender and she wished that she could hang on to the moment for ever.

When he reared up to discard the condom, she *missed* him.

'Did the earth move for you?' Theo teased, settling down next to her and pulling her into position so that they were both on their sides, bodies pressed close together. He could have done it all again, but he would have to exercise restraint even though her nakedness was continuing to drive him crazy.

Alexa lowered her eyes, because the feeling of sudden tenderness confused her. He'd stopped being a cardboard cut-out, and that was worrying, but she felt helpless to do anything about it. She couldn't seem to recover her anger at the situation she was in.

'So, no men before me?' Theo mused. 'Tell me why...'

Alexa shrugged.

'You're not going to get away with that. Didn't you have boyfriends at university?'

'Honestly...?' she mused pensively. 'Like I said, I wasn't all that confident about the way I looked. I have an old-fashioned figure...'

'Hourglass. It's a shape that never goes out of style.'

Alexa laughed, liking the compliment even if it wasn't true. 'I guess I watched what my peer group was getting up to from the age of fifteen and knew that I couldn't compete, so I decided I was just going to find my own path and that was academic. I really threw myself into my degree. Yes, of course I went out—but in a group. I'd already decided that I would only give myself to someone if I was in a loving relationship that was going somewhere...'

With dismay, she heard just how that sounded and was quick to rescue him from any false misconceptions. Marriage or not, he wasn't in this out of any genuine feelings for her and she knew that. It was the same for her!

'I didn't think that I could be physically attracted to a man unless I had deeper feelings for him,' she admitted.

'Are you telling me you don't have deeper feelings for me?' Theo drawled, amused. 'Tut-tut... Any self-respecting husband-to-be might be offended by that! Don't underestimate the power of attraction, Alexa. You'd be surprised how many good intentions get trampled on when two free and consenting adults find that they can't keep their hands off one another...and *I* find that I can't keep my hands off *you*. In fact I'd quite like to take you again. Right now. But I won't. I'm a big man, and you'll be sore down there...'

'Theo!'

She traced the outline of his shoulder blade with her finger. *What happens now?* she wanted to ask, but when she thought about that she knew what would happen... They'd have a lavish engagement party, they'd get married and then they'd get divorced. Why did it seem so muddled when it was actually so straightforward?

'I think we need a little time alone to get this out of our systems...' Theo broke through her soul-searching silence.

'What do you mean?'

'Neither of us signed up for this,' he told her matter-of-factly. 'And I'm not just talking about the arranged marriage scenario. *That* particular bombshell was definitely not on the radar for either of us.' He lay back and stared up at the ceiling. 'Neither of us expected that this attraction would jump out at us, did we? But it has, and it's something we have to deal with.'

'Yes...' Alexa parroted faintly, brow furrowed.

Saying that they would *deal* with it somehow removed the element of emotion—turned an unfortunate situation that had taken them by surprise into one that had a solution. He was right. She knew that. But she couldn't stifle the sudden hollowness that settled in the pit of her stomach.

Theo had paused. *A virgin.* She had just discovered that unbridled lust had an unstoppable momentum of its own but he wasn't a fool. She was an incurable romantic and she had lost her virginity to *him*. And he was destined to marry her. The last thing he needed was for her to get in too deep with him.

He fancied her, but he was all wrong for her—in the same way that *she* was all wrong for him. He could never give her what she wanted. He could never give *any* woman the sort of love that took away the ability to think clearly and behave logically. He just didn't have it in him.

He didn't *do* emotions. He played hard, but he always played with his head. She deserved someone who was willing to give her what she wanted. That man wasn't him, and unless they established some ground rules a year might prove a very long time indeed. For both of them.

Being married to someone who might end up expecting more than he was prepared to give would be a recipe for disaster.

'We get this out of our system,' he said flatly, 'and I see no reason why we won't have a harmonious year together.'

'Get it "out of our system"?'

'We can't fight this. We will be in one another's company all the time...'

'What if we weren't?'

'Then it would run its natural course. Lust fades as fast as it comes. That's always been my experience.'

'And you just walk away when that happens?'

'I'm not looking for deep emotional connections, Alexa,' he told her gently. 'For me, a permanent partner will be someone who is prepared to accept that my work will always come first.' He sighed.

'A marriage of convenience with someone who is emotionally switched off…?'

'I wouldn't necessarily describe it like that…'

'Would you fancy her, or would that not matter?'

'We're veering off topic, here.'

'I hear your warning.'

Her drowsy contentment was fading fast. She knew what he was telling her, but just in case she missed the message he was making sure he spelt it out in words of one syllable. *Don't confuse lust with love.* He could give her lust, but love wasn't on the table, and he was probably horrified at the possibility that he might be stuck with someone who'd fall for him.

He was telling her that his boredom threshold would be reached quickly, and that once that happened they would settle into playing the game they were destined to play, with no nasty surprises along the way.

Like unnecessary emotion.

She knew exactly what she should tell *him*. That this had been a one-off. One of those curiosity things… Something that she had succumbed to but which she did not want to repeat.

She opened her mouth and he smoothed his hand over her, between her thighs, and her body suddenly had other things in mind.

'But…' he said.

'But what?' She tried to inject some defiance into her

voice but she heard the way she sounded—helpless and breathy.

'We have options.'

'What are you talking about?'

He had found the damp patch between her legs and was stroking her, finding her sensitive nub and playing with it so that she couldn't think straight.

'You can either retreat back into fighting with me and put this down as a one-night stand…'

Alexa flushed, because that had been her first thought. She had foolishly betrayed all her principles but maybe she could persuade herself that she had put the lapse behind her—because you didn't have to keep repeating a mistake just because you'd made it once.

But how easy was *that* going to be when he could do this to her?

'I can't…can't think…when you're…'

'Let me do the thinking for you.'

'You're so incredibly bossy. Do you *always* have to take charge?'

'Taking charge suits me. I happen to do it very well.'

But this wasn't a decision he wanted her to make on the back of her arousal—even though watching the dazed heat in her eyes and the hectic flush in her cheeks was immensely satisfying. He reluctantly withdrew his hand and rested it in the curve of her waist.

'You'd like to write this off and pretend in the morning that nothing really happened.'

'You can't say that—'

'I can, because I know the way you think, Alexa. You had a fairy-tale dream wedding and a dream guy all mapped out in your head, but instead here we are…'

It irritated him just to voice that, because playing second fiddle to any man—even a fictitious one—just wasn't his thing, but there was no avoiding the truth.

'You know what those marriage vows say...' he drawled, carefully averting his eyes from the tempting glimpse of one pouting pink nipple peeping at him. 'For better or for worse. Loosely interpreting them, I say we should focus on the better side of things for the moment... We fancy each other, incredible though that might be...'

'Thanks very much, Theo.'

'You'd be the first to agree,' he returned wryly. 'You were *horrified* to find out that you would be walking up the aisle with me.'

Alexa didn't want to turn that flat statement back to him—didn't want to hear that he had likewise been horrified to find himself saddled with an emotional and inexperienced girl who—horror of horrors—didn't even have the decency to look like all his supermodel clones.

Truth hurt, and she had faced too many awkward truths recently—not least being this...her attraction to him.

'I would have been horrified to find myself walking up the aisle with *anyone* who wasn't of my own choosing.'

Theo shrugged, because one way or the other it didn't matter.

'I think that instead of denying what's between us we exhaust it—after which the duration of our time together should be as plain sailing as it can be, given the circumstances.'

'We *exhaust* it...?'

'Correct.'

'And do you have a timeline on that?'

If he got bored with all his beautiful conquests after a couple of months, then she gave herself a couple of *weeks*. Oddly, something inside her twisted.

'I prefer to play things by ear—and that cuts both ways. *You* could be the one who gets tired of me...'

Alexa wasn't dim enough to think that he seriously believed that for a minute, but she nodded in agreement.

This wasn't her at all, but he had cut through all the red tape and produced the bald truth of the matter, shorn of all emotion. They carried on having sex until that side of things dwindled away, at which point they would be able to function in one another's company without that sizzle of electricity—which was something he seemed able to handle but which she had found she just couldn't.

She couldn't imagine ever being around him without the hairs on the back of her neck standing on end and her imagination shaking its reins and running wild. It would be like spending a year doing a high wire act without a safety net. Just thinking about it exhausted her.

He was presenting her with a choice. And why not? She couldn't see herself wanting a man indefinitely when he basically wasn't her type anyway. It *would* fizzle out. Of course it would. In the crazy, surreal world into which she had been catapulted it was the one thing that made sense.

And also...

She would be able to give herself permission to enjoy him.

She felt a guilty rush of pleasure at the thought of that.

'I suppose it makes a weird kind of sense...'

She drew that sentence out and filled it with lots of doubt and uncertainty. She didn't want him to feel that she was a push-over simply because she was inexperienced, or that she had become a member of his worshipful fan club. She wanted—*needed* him to think that it was an arrangement that suited her as much as it suited him...that he was as much a virus in her system which she wanted to dispel as she was in his.

'I suppose we can't help the people we're attracted to—even though I always thought I could. I've been edgy around you...and not just because of the circumstances that threw us together. I haven't *liked* being attracted to you, but I'm honest enough to admit that I am. Stupid, and—as you say—passing.'

Theo wasn't sure he liked the word *stupid*, but he wasn't going to get hung up on detail.

Frankly, the faster it passed, the better for him. She was unreasonably distracting and he didn't like distraction—at least not a distraction that seemed to attack without warning and at any given time.

'I have my guys coming tomorrow,' he said. 'My original plan involved a prolonged stay here, with work taking a bit of a back seat to relaxation. This…change in circumstances…requires a change of plan…'

He accompanied that with a slow, curling smile that reminded her just how dangerous a temptation he could be, so thank heavens it wasn't going to be long-lasting.

'How do you mean?'

'We'll just stay for the day. I'll get my business done and then we'll head to Manhattan—finish our stay there. And no adjoining rooms in a penthouse suite…' He stroked the pink, peeping nipple and the little bud hardened under the abrasive rub of his thumb.

'We can't!' Alexa gasped, responding on cue, pulses racing, her whole body slowly heating up once again and then going into meltdown as he continued to rub her nipple.

'Why not?'

'Because it's *rude*! Your friends…they'll be disappointed…'

'They'll be the first to understand. They think this is a love match and they've been trying to brainwash me into the joys of married life for far too long… They'll be over the moon when I tell them that we have to escape for some private time because we can't get enough of one another… I can already hear the violins in the background…'

Little will they expect that this is just a pretend game, and that this so-called need for private time will just be about sex, Alexa thought, with the sort of cynicism she'd never thought she had.

'And your brother's making a big effort to come over… I was quite looking forward to meeting him, maybe going to one of the local art galleries while you were busy during the day…'

Theo burst out laughing. 'Daniel and art *don't* go hand in hand. I think it stems from the fact that an art teacher once told him when he was a kid that he would be doing the world of art a service by staying as far away from pencils and paintbrushes as he could…'

'Whereas you…?'

'*I* was smart enough to work out that if I couldn't paint anything remotely realistic then I'd paint whatever the hell I wanted and call it abstract… It worked… I'll message my brother—tell him to skip the meet-and-greet detour and head directly to the cruise ship he wants to buy…'

'So we go to New York,' Alexa said slowly, 'spend a week there…after which we should both be over this… this…situation between us. Then we return to Italy as a happy, platonic couple and serve our one year's penance before walking away from one another…' She forced a bright smile to her face. 'You're right, of course. Enjoy one another for a few days…get this inconvenient attraction out of our system…and once that little hiccup's dealt with we'll be able to…to look at one another without any stupid awkwardness…'

Since that was pretty much what Theo had had in mind, he was a little unnerved to hear it stated so bluntly.

'Enough talking…' He tilted her head and when she arched back kissed her neck, worked his way to her breasts and then levered himself up and stared down at her flushed face. 'Now I'm going to give you a little lesson on taking charge…'

He did.

She touched him as he had touched her. She straddled him and worked her way meticulously down his body, loving every inch of muscle and sinew under her exploring hands. She marvelled that her shyness had evaporated. Something about the way he looked at her, with a sort of lazy, lingering, heated intensity, stripped her of her inhibitions and invested her with self-confidence she'd never known she possessed.

When she took him in her mouth and heard his throaty groan a heady sense of power invaded her.

There had been moments in her adult life when she had thought about her virginity. She had never been bothered by it, but there had been a nagging worry that when the time came she would be so nervous that she wouldn't be able to enjoy the experience. Sex would have become a big thing she had built up and would fail to deliver on the night.

The only consolation in that scenario had been the certain knowledge that the guy she fell in love with would be someone kind, thoughtful and patient enough to guide her slowly.

As she felt this big, arrogant, sinfully good-looking man shudder as she continued to caress his erect sheath with her mouth and her tongue a thought flew through her head, as lightning-fast as quicksilver...

He might not be a shining advertisement for kind, thoughtful or patient, but he has been kind and thoughtful and patient with me...

The roughened feel of his thighs under her fingers as she continued to arouse him with her mouth took her own physical response to a level she could barely control, and she drew back from her lingering exploration so that she could rub herself against his erection.

Theo was having to take long, even breaths to keep his control in place. He opened his eyes and inhaled sharply as he looked at her astride him.

With one hand firmly on his erection, she flung her head back as she moved her body sensuously against him. Every shudder of pleasure was reflected in her soft moans as his hardness played against her clitoris.

Her long hair was in utter, sexy disarray and her generous breasts bounced as she moved like ripe fruit, gently shaking, too succulent to pass up.

He tugged her towards him so that those breasts were closer to his mouth, and as she knelt over him, still enjoying his erection against her, eyes still shut, breathing still coming and going in little gasps and groans, he flicked his tongue over one engorged nipple and then stilled her slightly so that he could suckle more thoroughly on it.

Hands on her slender ribcage, he carried on pleasuring himself at her breasts until neither of them could handle the build-up any longer.

They were so hot for one another—but she was still cool enough to fumble through his wallet and extract his last condom, which she took her time stretching over him.

Theo was riveted in a way he had never been with any woman by the sight of her voluptuous nakedness...the satiny smoothness of her shoulders and the soft paleness of her skin in such contrast to the perfect circular deep rose of her nipples.

His feeling of absolute possession was second to none, but he easily explained that away by the fact that she had come to him a virgin.

He was going to enjoy being her teacher, and she was showing all the signs of being an A class student...

Who knows? he thought, before his mind emptied of all thought and the primitive responses of his body took over. *Maybe a week might not be quite long enough after all...*

CHAPTER NINE

LYING ON THE BED, Alexa drowsily watched Theo, sitting at the desk in the hotel bedroom, wearing only his boxers, frowning at whatever he was looking at on his computer.

Their last night in Manhattan.

She couldn't quite believe how fast the time had flown since they had left The Hamptons. As predicted, Bob and Felicity had not been at all fazed at their early departure.

'Completely understand!' Felicity had carolled. 'It's been a while—hasn't it, Bobby?—but I can still remember what it was like to be young and in love…!'

Alexa had had to inwardly admit that she and Theo were certainly giving the impression of two people who couldn't keep their hands off one another, and she could understand how that might have led to the misconception that they were in love.

How ironic that now, when there were no reporters around, furiously snapping pictures, the physical contact between herself and Theo was one hundred per cent genuine.

Every time she glanced at him her imagination took over, and she remembered what it felt like to have those hands all over her body and his mouth kissing every enthusiastic inch of her.

They had checked into the penthouse suite which had originally been booked for them—the adjoining room was now redundant—but, frankly, they could have been anywhere in the world. Any hotel in the world. Just so long as there was a bed, because they spent an inordinate amount of time making love.

For a couple of hours every day Alexa had insisted on going out on her own, so that Theo could work.

'I can work perfectly well with you around,' he had drawled, in the sort of dark, persuasive voice that had made her almost but not quite revise her determination not to submerge herself entirely in him. 'In fact I find I work better, because I can touch you whenever I need a break...'

This was just the sort of heady flattery that she knew could so easily go to her head. It was the stuff she loved hearing—just as she loved hearing him tell her how desirable she was, how irresistible, how he couldn't see the bed without wanting her in it, naked and pressed up close to him.

But flattery was all it was, and Alexa knew that she had to steer clear of reading anything else behind it. Because she was getting seriously hooked on touching him, on hearing all those softly murmured words that did wonders for her self-confidence, making her feel utterly desirable...the most desirable woman on the planet.

He'd swept into her life, bringing with him all his worldly experience, and he had used that worldly experience and his unimaginable charm to captivate her.

He had found fertile ground in her, because nothing in her past had prepared her for the impact of their involvement. Had she had *some* experience with the opposite sex she might have had sufficient ammunition to see his charm for what it was...practised, well-used...the same charm that had turned all those other women's heads...

But she'd lacked the necessary experience. And now...

He was completely oblivious to the fact that she was staring at him. It was still only six fifteen in the morning, but she would have bet that he'd been up for at least an hour—maybe more. He seemed to need very little sleep to function.

She gazed at the way his dark hair curled at the nape of his neck, at the muscled width of his shoulders and the tiny mole on his right shoulder, which she could just about make out in the pool of light from the desk lamp he had switched on. He hadn't yet shaved and there was a definite shadow along his jawline. He was frowning, and she knew that in a second he would gently tap his fountain pen on the desk—a habit he had when he was utterly focused on something.

She had asked him why he had a fountain pen when all his work was done on the computer, and he had twirled it in his fingers and told her that it had been a present from his mother when he was eleven. It was his talisman.

There were so many things she felt she now knew about him, and there were so many physical details she had absorbed too, lodging them in her brain the way information was stored on a computer, lying there, ready to be accessed at the flick of a button.

She could recognise the sound of his soft breathing when he was in deep sleep…could tell from the clipped tone of his voice on the phone when he was talking to someone he wanted to get rid of as fast as possible. She had watched him shave in front of the mirror and had come to realise that, although he must surely know just how good-looking he was, he did very little to enhance his looks. No manly moisturisers. He barely looked in a mirror at all.

Her heart began a steady, anxious thud in her chest.

When exactly had she stopped seeing him as the enemy she was shackled to and started seeing him as someone who was witty, beyond intelligent, wickedly charming…?

She knew when she had owned up to her guilty fascination—when she had acknowledged the chemistry between them. But when, exactly, had that undeniable chemistry turned into something deeper for her?

They had strolled through Manhattan, gone to the famous Museum of Modern Art, walked along the High Line and visited the gallery district. She had forgotten that this wasn't a real-life courtship. She had forgotten that those piercing, lazy eyes that roved over her body with rampant appreciation had no intention of lingering there indefinitely.

What had started out for both of them as a perfectly reasonable way of dealing with the inconvenient attraction between them had morphed into something else—*for her*.

She had…

The steady, nervous thud of her heart picked up pace as the enormity and horror of her realisation hit her with the force of a runaway train.

When had she fallen in love with him?

'You're up. Why are you up?'

His dark drawl made her jump, because she had been so busy being dismayed and horrified at her thoughts that she had blanked him out of her line of vision. Now she sat up and feigned a yawn.

'The light must have woken me…' She burrowed back down into the duvet, so that she could take up where she had left off and carry on chewing over her plight—which couldn't have been worse as far as she was concerned.

'In that case I'll switch it off…'

Theo stood up and stretched, and then headed back to the bed—which was just where, for once, Alexa *didn't* want him. Because she still had so much thinking to do, still had to work out how she had managed to give her heart to a guy who had no intention of looking after it—not in the long term and not, if she were to be honest with herself, in the short term either.

'No—don't!' She tempered the sharpness of her reply

with a little laugh. 'I know you've had a pretty distracted time when it comes to work, and that you get a lot done early in the morning. I'm still very sleepy anyway.' She yawned on cue. 'So I shall try and grab a couple more hours...'

'Sex is very good for guaranteeing restful sleep...' He slid into the bed alongside her and eased her to face him, so that they were both on their sides, looking at one another, perfectly level.

'In which case you should get back to work,' Alexa told him crisply, although her firmness was somewhat undermined by the hand that was now lying between her legs, cupping her down there and moving ever so gently. 'You don't want to fall asleep on the job, do you?'

Theo sighed and reluctantly removed his hand. 'Unfortunately that's the last thing I can afford to do,' he conceded. 'Several million pounds rests on my making sure I stay awake on the job—at least for the next couple of hours...'

He swung his legs over the side of the bed and strolled back towards the desk and the blinking of his computer. When he glanced over his shoulder it was to see that she was on her side, turned away from him, her long hair hiding her face, doubtless on her way back to sleep.

It seemed peculiar that he was going to be marrying a woman who, in the normal scheme of things, would not have excited his interest—and even more peculiar that she had not only excited his interest, but that his interest was showing no signs of petering out just yet.

He wondered what the chances were of a continuing sexual relationship for the duration of their imposed marriage, but dismissed the idea before it had taken root.

He just didn't have it in him to ride the crest of physical attraction for longer than a couple of months, and he knew without the shadow of a doubt, that to sleep with her for any continued period of time would be a big mistake.

He had always been able to deal with broken hearts, but this was a special case. When he and Alexa parted company they would still see one another, because he would have shares in her family company and would, on occasion, be working alongside her father. Her father was a sociable man. There would be instances when he would be invited over for a meal—special occasions, some family do—and there would be instances when she would be there too.

The last thing he wanted was to find himself in the firing line for recriminations should she get more involved with him than necessary. The last thing he wanted was her broken heart. Because she wasn't a tough, sexually experienced woman of the world and her broken heart might not mend quite so easily.

He heard her soft, even breathing and frowned, because thinking of her suffering did something to him.

Which, he concluded, was all the more reason to make sure what they had ended before it could become a problem. No big deal for him, but he might have to gently guide her in the same direction, just to make sure...

Alexa, her thoughts all over the place, actually fell asleep, and woke to the sound of her mobile buzzing next to her on the bedside table.

She could hear the sound of the shower in the bathroom. Predictably, the bathroom door was wide open, because Theo was anything but a shrinking violet when it came to flaunting his nudity.

It was her father, and their conversation was brief and puzzling. She waited until Theo was back in the bedroom, his hair damp and tousled and a towel hooked precariously around his waist.

'That was my dad...' She looked at him anxiously.

'What did he want?'

'He said that he has something to tell me but I'm not to

worry.' She sat up, heels tucked beneath her rear, and she chewed at her lip.

Being told not to worry was the fastest way to make sure that someone got worried—especially when it came to her father, who was the master of understatement.

Had her mother's health scare not been quite as severe as it had been, Alexa was sure that her father would have not deemed it necessary to contact her and ask her to return to Italy sixteen months ago. She'd been protected and sheltered as a child and that was the way it remained.

'What if something's wrong with Mum?' she asked in a quiet, wobbly voice.

Theo crossed over to the bed and looked at her uncertainly for a few seconds. The Alexa he had first met had changed over the brief but intense time they had spent together. Having expected a frumpy little doormat, he had been presented with a firebrand...

A feisty, outspoken, mutinous firebrand, who was also a ridiculous romantic...

Who had been a virgin...

He could sense her making a big effort not to cry, and he fought against his instinct to bracingly tell her to pull herself together.

'He'd tell you,' Theo informed her calmly. 'When it comes to health, people tend to avoid beating around the bush.'

'You don't know my father,' Alexa said ruefully. She suddenly realised that she wasn't wearing anything, and she hurriedly dragged the duvet over her and slumped back against the pillows.

'Fill me in.'

Alexa paused. This was what it meant to be in love, she thought. She could no more fight the urge to confide in him than a starving man could have fought the urge to feast at the banquet. Her head was telling her one thing—telling her to protect herself and back away—but she was drawn to him like a moth to the flame that threatened to kill it.

Being in love meant waving goodbye to common sense—to everything that had been her compass through her life.

'He's always hated the thought of worrying me,' she confessed. 'They wanted more kids, you know, but Mum had a terrible time when she was pregnant with me and was told that to risk having another would be endangering her life.' Alexa sighed. 'You could say that I've lived a pretty sheltered life. Not that I wasn't allowed out of their sight, but I was always protected from what they considered *too much information.* I only found out just how bad Mum's stroke was by cornering the consultant and demanding the details. Left to Dad, he would just have tutted and told me that everything was going to be fine. Which is why for him to call me here and say that he's got something to tell me... Well...'

Theo sat down on the bed, and she toppled a little towards him before steadying herself. For once he was with a woman, in a bed, and sex was not uppermost in his mind.

'I can only think that he's readying me for something big—that it's serious. And the only serious thing I can think of is that Mum... Well...'

Unaccustomed to soothing crying women, Theo pulled her towards him and smoothed her hair clumsily with his hand. She was crying against his chest but trying hard to stifle it, and that more than anything else touched him.

He hadn't had to dig too deep to find the soft-as-mush girl beneath the tough, outspoken exterior. And that was something he felt he should have sensed from the very beginning.

'So chewing over it and coming up with lots of worst-case scenarios...is that going to alter the reality?'

'Well, no...'

'If your mother was seriously ill your father would tell you—however much he didn't want to worry you—and if *he* wouldn't, then my father would call me and say something. You forget—they're back in touch now. And my father, I assure you, has *never* been backward when it comes to being brutally honest...'

'What do you mean?'

She was feeling better already. She liked the way he was holding her—as if she were a piece of fragile porcelain china. It felt good to be held like this, without sex being their final destination. It scared her how much she liked it...

'That art teacher might have been a bit forthright with Daniel,' Theo joked lightly, 'and I may have passed the litmus test with her by painting nonsense and talking my way into an explanation, but I remember my father taking one look at one of my productions and bursting out laughing. He said that it was the biggest load of rubbish he had ever seen, and then he patted me on the shoulder and told me that if *he* couldn't give me a few home truths then who could? So rest assured that he wouldn't shy away from phoning me if there was a crisis over there...'

'And has he?'

Theo looked at her with a frown. 'Has he what? Phoned me? To tell me about a crisis with your family? No.'

Alexa breathed a sigh of relief—because she believed him. It was as simple as that. She would wait and see what the problem was when she returned. Hopefully it would be something to do with the wedding or the engagement party.

Which brought her back to the thoughts that had momentarily taken a back seat.

She edged away from him and shuffled out of bed. Just now, knowing what she knew about her feelings for him, she felt that a bit of distance between them would be a good idea.

'So...' she said, gathering herself. 'It's our last day...'

She was well and truly up and awake now, and the thought of trying to pretend to go back to sleep wasn't going to work.

What happened next? she wondered.

The longer she carried on having sex with him, the more hurt she would be building up for herself. But how on earth was she going to last a year of wanting him and having to hide that want? How was she going to survive when he looked at her with polite indifference because what had started as lust for him had dwindled and disappeared?

The stakes were never going to be even between them, and just thinking about that made her head ache.

More than anything else she wished she could run away and take cover until this crazy love had blown over—except she knew that it never would.

She might no longer be able to keep her heart intact, but she felt she could try and keep her dignity intact—and to do so she would have to guard her expression and never allow him to see just how much he had finally ended up getting to her.

She wondered if this was the fate that had befallen all those women he had dated in the past. Having heard him give them his warning speech about not getting involved, had they, like her, found themselves being sucked into something that was bigger than them?

Had that been the fate of the striking blonde who had confronted him in that restaurant?

Alexa could only hope that, however hard she had fallen for him, she wouldn't be one of those women who kept trying to grab his attention whenever they happened to bump into him—who let him think that what he had once taken from them was still on offer should he decide to pay them another visit.

She had seen the way he had looked at that blonde, with

veiled contempt in his eyes—the same contempt that had been in his voice when he had talked about her.

There was no way Alexa would allow herself to become someone like that.

'I think we should do some sightseeing,' she said lightly. 'I'll just grab a shower and then we can think about heading out…maybe have breakfast at one of those bagel places by the hotel… Or we could go to Central Park… There's still so much to see… The earlier we leave, the better, don't you think?'

Theo inclined his head to one side, his antennae picking up invisible signals and trying to decipher them. 'Don't rush,' he told her with a little shrug, 'I'll have to wrap up these documents. It'll take at least half an hour…'

Alexa took longer than that, and emerged fully dressed an hour later. Theo, likewise, was in a pair of black jeans and a cream polo shirt that did amazing things for his athletic, muscular body.

She licked her lips and tried not to stare. Staring had been permissible when it had been about lust. Now that it was about love, staring was a weakness she could not afford.

Her heart was still beating fast and she frantically wondered how she could carry on sounding normal when everything inside her felt so *abnormal*.

She need not have worried. Theo's charm and the breadth of his knowledge proved irresistible.

She had, of course, travelled—but not nearly as extensively as he had, and he didn't allow her to be introspective as they had breakfast in a noisy bagel café before jumping on the subway—something she had to persuade him into doing—so that they could explore Williamsburg.

At one point he grabbed her hand and continued holding it. She knew that it was just one of those throwaway gestures of his, but also knew that would be one more thing she would store in her memory bank, to be extracted for examination at a later date.

She couldn't resist.

And she couldn't resist when he pulled her towards him and casually dropped a kiss on her parted lips.

She couldn't resist the way he took it for granted that her body belonged to him. Every passing touch was like the heavy brand of possession, but if he'd known the effect he had on her he would have been quailing at the thought of their year-long pretend union.

She hoped she'd kept everything on a light level, and by the time they'd headed back to the hotel and begun packing for their trip back to Italy she even managed to ask the question that had been uppermost in her mind for the past few hours.

'Should we discuss how we…er…move forward now…?'

About to fling the last of his clothing into his suitcase, Theo paused and stared at her. Something was off, but he couldn't quite put his finger on it.

'Come again?'

'Well, the week is up,' Alexa pointed out nervously. 'And I know that was the time limit we both agreed for us to…er…get this thing between us out of our system…'

'I don't recall agreeing to any such thing,' Theo pointed out.

She had come to him a virgin and yet now it seemed that she was keen to draw her experiences with him to a close. He clenched his jaw as it was brought home to him how little they had in common, aside from the obvious bond of their similar backgrounds, and how much, fundamentally, she still disapproved of him. He had the feeling that he'd been used, and it wasn't a feeling that he liked.

His cell phone buzzed and a text message popped up, saying that their limo had arrived to take them to the airport.

She had certainly started a tricky conversation at the

right point in time, he thought drily. Did she think that he would be too embarrassed to continue in the back of a taxi?

'Taxi's here,' he said curtly.

He phoned through to Reception to ask for their bags to be taken down to the limo and then waited until they were inside the spacious car before he picked up their conversation.

'Well…I know we didn't *exactly* set a time and a date,' Alexa said, when he lazily asked her to finish what she had started saying. 'I mean, I do understand that it's hard… impossible…'

'To set a time and a date when it comes to lust?' he interrupted smoothly. 'You're right. It is.'

'But,' she persisted valiantly, 'I do think we need some kind of clarification here…'

'Why?'

They did. He knew that. However, for some reason he had a perverse desire to dig his heels in. He wasn't ready to give up what they had, and there was nothing worse than unfinished business, as far as he was concerned.

True, when it came to women that was pure conjecture, but he couldn't see the point of self-denial and that was precisely the road she was trying to head down right now.

'Because this marriage of ours isn't going to be real,' Alexa mumbled. 'And if it's a business arrangement—'

'You can try.'

'I beg your pardon?'

'You can try to fight this thing between us, but you won't be getting any help from me.'

'What—what do you mean?' Alexa stammered.

'I mean that I'm not ready for this to end yet. And don't forget—we may have had a little respite from the cameras but we're heading back into the lions' den, and with our engagement those pesky reporters are going to be snapping away to capture the happy couple. I just want you to know that when I kiss you it won't be for the cameras...'

'I'd forgotten about them,' Alexa said in dismay.

He grinned wolfishly at her. 'Don't worry. It'll soon come flooding back...'

'So in other words,' Alexa said tightly, 'you want this to carry on until *you* get tired of it?'

'In other words, I have no intention of fighting what's between us.'

The taxi ride was completed in silence. Typically, Alexa thought, he had said what he had to say and then, rather than continue driving his point home, had dismissed the topic by spending the ride to the airport with his laptop open, sifting through dozens of emails and ignoring her completely.

He was just so damned *sure* of himself—just so *convinced* of his own monumental appeal that he didn't envisage her standing a chance of saying *no* to him.

She despaired.

Would she be able to withstand an onslaught? Even though she knew that he was not in it for more than just sex? Even though she knew that she would end up being desperately hurt? That she would turn into one of those clingy, needy women he had no time for? The sort who never forgot him and staged scenes whenever their paths chanced to cross?

All her resentment and anger, her conviction that she could never in a thousand years fall for a guy like him, now seemed like naïve stupidity. She had been able to hate the one-dimensional cardboard cut-out, but the minute the three-dimensional man had emerged she had not been able to resist.

She'd turned into just another one of his conquests, and she shivered at the prospect of those lips touching hers and her knowing that she wanted more. She was terrified of being betrayed—not just by her own weak body, but by her emotions.

Her head buzzed with so many scenarios that she was barely aware of the flight. He left her to stew. In fact she was certain that he wasn't even aware of her presence next to him. He was utterly absorbed in his work, and sex, however compelling, played second fiddle.

Only as they were taxiing on landing, and after having fitfully dozed for part of the trip, did she find other concerns settling—and the main one was whatever it might be that her father had to say to her.

All over again she felt anxiety begin to claw at her insides. Theo had calmed her fears by telling her that if her mother's health was involved *he* would have known about it. Now, Alexa could see all the flaws in that argument. Why would her father advertise something like that to his dad? It was a personal problem and he would surely want to keep it to himself. The fact that his instincts had always been to protect her from anything unpleasant meant that whatever he wanted to say must be of grave concern. It must be something he couldn't keep from her.

'What if something's really wrong with Mum?' she couldn't help asking as they disembarked.

She hated herself for appealing to Theo for reassurance, but she had had time to contemplate the worst and she *needed* to hear the strong conviction in his voice. It was irritating—especially considering she should be trying to erect whatever fragile defences she still had at her disposal to protect her pathetic, foolish heart—but she needed his logical explanation. Even though she had already convinced herself that it made no sense.

'It won't be.'

Theo had had plenty of time on the trip to try and work out why he was in the process of breaking his own self-imposed rule never to chase any woman. She was backing away, and instead of shrugging his shoulders and moving on he was intent on pursuit. Ego and pride, he presumed. Not exactly the most endearing traits in the world, but he wasn't going to pretend that there was anything more to it than that.

'But you don't *know*...'

Theo stared down at her flushed, earnest face and his libido kicked into gear with surprising ferocity. What *was* it about this woman that made him want to drag her off to the nearest empty room and take her?

He actually caught himself doing a brief mental tour of what he could recall of their route towards Immigration, trying to figure out if there were any cubbyholes he could pull her into, so that he could yank down those oh, so prim and proper trousers, taking her underwear with them, and have sex with her in the most basic way possible.

Reluctantly he gave up the idea, but this, he thought, was precisely why he would carry on his pursuit... Because to back off now, when neither of them wanted to, whatever she said to the contrary, would be like having to endure an indefinite erection without the benefit of a cold shower to get rid of it.

'Nor do you,' he said with a hint of impatience. 'Now, don't forget that we're back in the public eye. Try not to trail behind me—and it would help if you wiped that anxious expression off your face.'

With his free hand he massaged the nape of her neck, underneath her silky hair—which Alexa knew was unnecessary because there was no one with a camera around. But he had warned her that he wasn't going to play by her rules... He was just proving to her that he had meant what he said.

And right now, in these crowds, she was powerless to do anything about it.

Even when they were in the back of his chauffer-driven

car—he had called from the airport for it to come for them—she still had an insane urge to close the gap she had studiously put between them.

Like a predator, with all the time in the world to hunt its prey, he made no move to get closer to her, contenting himself with watching her through brooding, speculative eyes that gave her goosebumps.

Finally she hissed, with one eye on the driver, although the screen, as always, was up, 'I wish you'd stop staring at me!'

'Why?' Theo drawled.

'Because I don't like it!'

'Liar. You like it—and so do I.'

His words floated around her like a physical caress. There was lazy intent in his eyes and she looked away hurriedly, her body turned on to screaming point. Because he was one hundred per cent right… *She did like him staring at her—liked the way it made her whole body tingle, as though it had been plugged into an electric socket...*

She heard herself launch into nervous chatter, babbling even while her body recalled how and where it had been touched, and fought against the seductive temptation to think about how and where it would be touched again…

She was surprised that they made it to her house with her nervous system still intact. Of course he hadn't opened his computer once, or checked his phone at all. He'd just leaned against the door, limbs loose, his fabulous green eyes pinned to her face, fully aware that he was unsettling her and amused by it.

'I'll come in with you,' Theo murmured, pressing a button and talking to the driver once the partition was lowered.

'There's no need,' Alexa said hastily.

He didn't bother to answer, instead stepping out of the car and moving round to wait for her as she followed suit.

'There's no need to pretend now that we're here,' she muttered as he neatly tucked her arm into the crook of his.

'Oh, I know *that*,' Theo murmured silkily, 'but remember what I said to you?'

Alexa's breath caught in her throat, because she knew that she just didn't have the weapons for a sustained assault.

'And remember what *I* said to *you*!' But her voice was weak.

He actually laughed under his breath. Laughed and patted her on her arm. 'You want me. Don't fight it, Alexa. Enjoy it while it lasts. Now...' his tone changed from lazy to brisk as he rang the doorbell '...why don't we see what all the fuss is about with your father?'

CHAPTER TEN

NOT ONLY WAS her father waiting for her, so was her mother. And, even more ominous, so was Theo's father. All three were hovering by the door, and she got the uneasy feeling that they had been waiting for their arrival.

Alexa automatically stepped a shade closer to Theo, who had sized up the situation and taken charge, smoothly querying their joint presence by the front door with the quirk of an eyebrow but not commenting on it, instead leading the way into the kitchen while conducting a running commentary on their trip, omitting the salacious details and focusing on filling his father in on Bob and Felicity.

They followed him like sheep.

The man was a born leader, and she could understand why her father had dangled the carrot of shares in the family firm, ensuring that he would oversee holding its reins in the years to come. A true marriage of convenience.

'So…'

Somehow, without her noticing, Theo had managed to pour their collected parents glasses of wine and put the kettle on for coffee for both of them. He sauntered towards the kitchen table, which was a long oak affair that could comfortably seat twelve. He looked perfectly relaxed and utterly in charge.

'Which lucky family member gets to tell us what's

going on…?' he drawled, patting the chair next to him, into which Alexa sank with a sigh of relief, because nervous tension at this new, unsettling situation had piled up on top of the nervous tension already wreaking havoc inside her. He looked narrowly from face to face and his father cleared his throat.

'We have been talking, son—' Stefano said, sitting at the head of the table while the other two followed suit, flanking him on either side. Alexa's mother nervously twirled the stem of her wine glass and looked at her daughter,

'Let *me*, Stefano,' Cora interrupted. 'Now, Alexa, your father's come clean and told me everything. I know you two have been worried sick about me, and I understand that you reached this…this…*arrangement* with poor Theo for the best possible reasons, but I don't need protecting as much as you think.'

She looked lovingly at her husband, who looked away sheepishly.

Alexa's brain had stopped at the description of Theo as 'poor', as in *helpless*, and she wanted to burst into hysterical laughter.

'I've had health problems, all three of you know that, but they've been physical—not emotional. Yes, I'll admit that I may have told your father, Alexa, that I longed for a grandchild—longed to see you settled down with a nice man—but what mother doesn't wish that for her child? There was no need for you to concoct this silly scheme…'

'So what are you saying?' Alexa looked between the three parents in bewilderment. She was trying to follow what her mother was saying, but it was like walking in treacle. When she looked at Theo he was frowning, his brooding eyes speculative. It hit her just how much she had come to admire the silent strength of his personality, and was floored by how much it hurt to love him when her love wasn't returned.

Stefano picked up the thread of the conversation. 'We're saying that there's no need for this charade any longer. Certain things will remain in place...'

'I promised you shares in my company,' Carlo said, addressing Theo, 'and that stays in place. I won't pretend that I didn't...' he cleared his throat '...see certain advantages to helping your father out financially...'

'Because you're a manipulative old man.' Cora smiled indulgently at her husband. 'But, Alexa, darling, I don't understand why you didn't put your foot down and refuse to go through with this silly pretence. No...' She sighed. 'I *do* understand, and for that I have only love for you...'

Alexa's head was swimming. She was now grasping exactly what was being said. She had been looking at the prospect of a year with Theo—a year trying to fight the impulses that were so much bigger than her...a year knowing that every time he crooked his finger it would take all the strength at her disposal not to go running...a year of knowing that she would walk away from their relationship battered and hurt beyond comprehension.

That year wasn't going to happen now. She was being given her *Get Out Of Jail Free* card—and so was Theo.

And the future yawned in front of her like a black, empty void.

'So...' she said slowly.

'Yes, my darling.' Cora reached across the width of the kitchen table to pat her daughter's hand. 'And of course the press have hounded you both. You will simply tell them that the engagement's off and so is the marriage...'

Alexa headed for the most secluded seat in the first class lounge at the airport. She didn't want to be near anyone because she didn't want to be dragged into making small talk. She'd been operating on automatic for the past three weeks and she planned on carrying on doing just that—at least until she reached London, when she was banking on new surroundings and the thrill of her new job to rescue her from the zombie-like torpor into which she had sunk.

Where had Theo gone? She didn't know, and of course she had been too proud to ask her parents. She had moaned and railed against the situation in which she had found herself, and yet when that situation had been whipped out from under her feet she had been lost because she had become so dependent on him.

In the blink of an eye he had gone from being just the sort of guy she would run a mile from to being just the sort of guy she couldn't imagine living without.

But live without him she would, and it hurt more than she could ever have contemplated in those carefree first few days when she had actually disliked him.

The press, predictably, had passed a few days speculating on the break-up of the perfectly matched couple and then, just as predictably, new scandals and gossip had drawn them away.

Now, staring down at the book on her lap, and with two hours of waiting ahead of her because she had been itching to leave, she thought back to the brief conversation she had had with Theo after his father and her parents had fled the scene, leaving them stranded in the kitchen like a couple of castaways, washed up on a beach after being stuck on a raft together but with nothing to say now that the storm had passed.

The passionate lover had gone. He had carefully asked her what her plans were now. One minute he hadn't been able to keep his hands off her—the next minute, freed from the shackles of a union he'd never asked for, he'd been coolly indifferent.

Of course *she* had gone on about the relief of not having to face a marriage neither of them had wanted. The more indifferent he'd seemed, the more she had sparkled, voicing the joys of her newfound freedom.

And then he'd gone, and she'd been left in an empty kitchen contemplating the horror of her newfound freedom.

London. Her parents had an apartment there. It was where she had lived before she had left for Italy and she would go back there. She had phoned her old company, who had remembered her, and after a million calls they had found her a job.

The change of scene would do her good—she knew that. Just being in her parents' house had reminded her of Theo. And in the dead of night, her whole body ached for him.

Right, she thought severely, *think about the good stuff.* No falling deeper and deeper in love with a man who didn't love her. No agonising year together, during which time he would have grown tired of her body and settled back into enduring the time he was forced to spend in her company. He had simply been her lover, and she knew that she would eventually meet someone else—someone she could entrust with her heart.

She forced herself to read a few pages of her book and was totally unaware of anyone approaching her until a shadow fell over her. When she looked down she saw a pair of very expensive loafers and didn't bother to look any higher, because if she didn't then whoever it was wouldn't ask her if she'd mind if he sat next to her.

'Alexa.'

For a few seconds Alexa was convinced that she'd misheard her name being said—and had definitely misconstrued that rich, mellow voice she had come to love.

She hunkered down and ignored whoever it was—because he *hadn't* spoken, and it was just her feverish imagination playing tricks on her.

'Are you going to acknowledge me or are you going to carry on reading...? What are you reading?'

The book was whipped out of her hands and there he was, standing right in front of her, as cool as a cucumber and as devastatingly sexy as every single memory she had of him.

In a pair of cream trousers and a black T-shirt, with a cream linen jacket hooked over one shoulder, he was drop-dead gorgeous.

'Still on the crime novels, I see. Would you like me to predict the end?'

'What are you doing here?'

Her voice was a hoarse whisper and she cleared her throat, then fidgeted as he took the empty chair next to her and pulled it in, so that there was no way she could avoid looking at him.

Theo wished there was an easy answer to that question—something glib that he could pull out from up his sleeve—but there wasn't. He had spent the past three weeks unable to focus, unable to concentrate—unable to do anything but think about her, even though he had told himself that it was great that he had been released from the obligation of a marriage he hadn't wanted...great that he could resume his life as he had always wanted it...great that his routine would be returned to him.

His address book was bulging with names and phone numbers of women, and all of them without exception would have welcomed a call from him. He had known that.

He hadn't called any of them because he'd had too much catching up to do on the work front. That was what he had told himself. Until he'd been forced to face the fact that he missed *her*. Not just her warm, welcoming body, which he had known for such a brief period of time, but he missed the whole package. He missed the way she bristled and glared at him...the way she never obeyed any of his 'No

Trespassing' signs but got stuck in and told him just what she thought of him anyway. He missed her shy, hesitant smiles and the ready way her eyes filled up with tears. He missed the softness underneath the feisty scrapper. Most of all he just missed the woman who had been born to have it all and had chosen to do her own thing and ignore the life she had been conditioned to lead.

Except he had no idea how to put any of that into words, and he could feel her blazing eyes on him—could feel her willing him to just *go away.*

'How have you been?' he asked, in a lame attempt to kick-start the conversation.

'Fine,' Alexa said coldly. 'Are you travelling to London? I had no idea.'

'And if you had you would have checked on to a different flight…?'

Alexa shrugged. 'Probably,' she told him truthfully. 'You can't deny that this situation is a little uncomfortable at the moment. I do realise we'll probably bump into one another in the years to come, but right now…'

'I get it. From being lovers and engaged to…nothing…'

Resting his forearms on his thighs as he leaned forward, Theo raked his fingers through his hair and took some small comfort from the delicate blush that bloomed in her cheeks at the mention of their having been lovers.

'I don't want to talk about that,' Alexa said stiffly. 'In fact I'd rather you left me alone,' she continued, barely able to look at him. 'I have lots of planning to do for my new job in London and I really would like to do that in peace and quiet.'

'No.'

Alexa's mouth dropped open and she stared at him. 'What do you mean, *no*?' she demanded furiously.

'I haven't come here so that I can disappear without telling you what I've come to say.'

'Which is what?'

'I liked being engaged to you.' He looked around him at the crowded lounge. 'I have my driver outside.'

'I *beg* your pardon?'

Alexa was frantically trying to analyse what he had just said about liking being engaged to her. What did *that* mean? She didn't want to dwell on it, because it meant nothing coming from a man who had spent the past three weeks avoiding her and who didn't have a committed bone in his body—a man who had a block of ice for a heart.

'I want to talk to you and I can't do it here.'

'Well, *I* don't want to talk to *you*.' Alexa's body was ramrod-straight and as stiff as a board. She dreaded that one of those hands loosely dangling between his thighs might accidentally brush against her, because if it did then she knew the already uphill task of projecting indifference would be even harder.

'Please.'

That single word was wrenched out of him and for a second she hesitated, because *please* was not a word that passed his lips very often.

'What do you want to talk about?' she asked, relenting a little.

Theo glanced at her and kept his gaze on her face.

'I've missed you,' he said roughly, and Alexa tried to hold on to some of her gritty determination not to melt.

You've missed having sex with me.

'Are you travelling to London as well?'

'I will if I have to. I'm booked on the same flight as you, although I'd rather we didn't have this conversation on a plane or in an airport lounge...'

'Look, I can't think that there's anything to talk about, Theo. I mean, you've got your freedom, and I know that was all you wanted when you thought you'd lost it for a year. So maybe you miss having sex with me? You said that you wanted to carry on sleeping with me until… Well, until you got bored and dispatched me to wherever it is you dispatch women you no longer want hanging around. Some locked cupboard in your head, I expect. Of course, physically I'd have still been around, until the year ran out, but as far as sleeping with me went I guess it would have been separate rooms and you discreetly returning to your diet of leggy blonde supermodels…'

Her voice was brittle and she looked away and stared straight ahead.

'So I'm not going to jump into bed with you again just because you're not bored with me yet, Theo.'

Theo heard what she was saying and knew that she was describing the man he had thought himself to be. Even when they had walked away from one another he had still thought himself to be a guy who worked hard, played hard and avoided commitment.

'And I wouldn't ask you to,' he said quietly. 'Are you sure you won't dump your flight so that we can have this conversation somewhere a little less…frantic?'

'No one's paying us a scrap of attention.' She sighed with heartfelt longing. 'I just want to get to London and begin a new chapter in my life.'

Theo's jaw hardened. He had heard a lot about this wonderful new chapter in her life on the night they had returned from the best time he had ever had with a woman, to discover that the charade was over and they were free to go. She couldn't have waxed more lyrical when it had come to letting him know how relieved she was that the pretence was over.

Pride had turned his responses then to ice, and pride had kept him away for three weeks, but now he had discovered that there was something more powerful than pride and that had been a bitter pill to swallow.

'Your mother tells me that you have a new job lined up.'

'You spoke to her?'

'That's how I knew that you would be leaving for London today. She told me a few days ago...'

'*A few days ago?* Since when have you and my mother been having cosy chats behind my back? She never mentioned a word about talking to you!'

'Because I asked her not to.' Theo flushed darkly.

'You *asked her not to*? Why would you do that?' Alexa was genuinely bewildered.

'I...' He hunkered down.

Never in his life had he felt less cool, more in danger of making a complete fool of himself and more exposed to rejection. Indeed, when it came to women he had *never* felt exposed to rejection, and he loathed the feeling of vulnerability. He had never been vulnerable. He had always had the direction of his life firmly within his controlling hand.

Alexa was even more bewildered at his discomfort. It just wasn't *him*.

'I never thought I wanted involvement with a woman,' Theo surprised her by saying. His eyes met hers and held them. 'Don't interrupt me,' he continued, returning to some of his usual form. 'I...I didn't have any crash-and-burn relationships that turned me off commitment. I never lost my heart to a gold-digger only to find out in the nick of time. I suppose I was simply a product of my background—just as my brother is. I was ambitious, and in my upward climb I enjoyed women but never invited any of them further than the front door, emotionally speaking.'

Alexa gave him an encouraging look. She was all ears.

'I was in no hurry to settle down—in fact it never crossed my mind what sort of woman I would end up with, or even if I would end up with one at all.' He paused and thought about the relationship his parents had had. 'When my mother died Daniel and I watched my father fall apart at the seams. Actually,' he confessed heavily, 'we *all* fell apart. And that was when I realised just how destructive all-consuming love can be.'

'Empowering,' Alexa corrected in a staccato voice. 'I'm sure your father would agree that it was better to have had all those wonderful years with your mother than to have lived the sort of life *you* want to carve out for yourself.'

Theo smiled crookedly at her. 'And that's why I thought that, whether I married you or not, you and I were poles apart. I admit that the only kind of marriage that ever crossed my mind after my mother died was one that would have been very similar to the one we found ourselves pushed into—a marriage of convenience. But not with a woman who was all about romance and love and happy-ever-after endings… What I anticipated was a relationship where I couldn't be hurt—a relationship that was a mutually convenient business arrangement…'

'So you've come here to tell me what I already knew?'

'No. I've come here to tell you that I was wrong.'

Hope flared inside her, suffocating everything else and shooting up blooms that she couldn't squash.

'What do you mean?' Alexa asked in a stifled voice.

'You *know* what I mean,' Theo said drily. 'I was wrong. I might have *wanted* a relationship I could control, but in the end I *needed* the relationship that I couldn't. I needed *you*. I still do…'

Alexa masked her disappointment, because need was very far from love. 'And that's why you're not the man for me,' she said softly. 'You've learned to be cynical and I've learned the opposite. I don't want something that stops at *need* or *desire* or *lust*. I want the full package and I always did.'

'And why can't that be *me*?' Theo demanded with muted belligerence.

He had never had to justify how he felt to anyone in his

life before, and even if he left now, without her, he was driven to lay himself open to that possibility.

'Because—'

'I love you, Alexa. I never expected to, but somehow it just…happened. Without even realising it I let you into my life, and I came here to tell you that I don't want you to leave it. I came here to ask you if you'd be mine for ever. Hell, Alexa, I came here to propose to you now that we're no longer engaged…'

'You *love* me…?'

The words hitched in her throat and she tentatively stroked his knuckles with her finger, wishing now that she had abandoned her flight and gone somewhere else with him for this conversation—but how was she supposed to have known what he had come to say?

'You have no idea how much I've longed to hear you say that,' she whispered tremulously. 'I didn't think I would ever fall in love with you. You didn't make sense. I'd always assumed that the guy I fell for would be…well, just the *opposite* of you, to be honest. And I hated it that I was being forced into marrying you…'

'Tell me about it. I've never known a woman fight me as much as you did…'

Alexa laughed. She believed him. She'd dug her heels in. But even when she'd thought that she was refusing to budge an inch more than necessary she had already been shifting in places she hadn't begun to understand.

'I was so desperate for you to be the horrible, arrogant person I wanted you to be, but it felt like with every day that passed you escaped the box I'd shoved you in just a little bit more—until I realised that I'd fallen in love with the three-dimensional guy I never thought you could ever be.' She frowned as a sudden thought occurred to her. 'Did you tell my mother why you were coming here?'

'It was the only way I could find out what sort of reception I might expect,' he confessed, with such humility that she wanted to kiss him and keep right on kissing him. 'I swore her to secrecy,' he further admitted. 'She was to say nothing if it turned out that you wanted me out of your life for good.'

'I love you so much, Theo,' Alexa whispered, half giggling, because this was such an inappropriate place for such a wildly wonderful marriage proposal.

'So you'll marry me…?'

'Try and stop me…'

* * * * *

THE SURPRISE DE
ANGELIS BABY

CHAPTER ONE

COULD THE DAY get any better?

Daniel De Angelis stepped out from the air-conditioned comfort of his black chauffeur-driven Mercedes and removed his dark sunglasses to scan the scenery around him.

Frankly—perfect. Brilliant sunshine glinted on the calm turquoise water of the Aegean Sea. He'd never made it to Santorini before, and he took a few minutes to appreciate the scenic view of the bowl-shaped harbour from where he stood, looking down on it from a distance. He could even make out the vessel he had come to snap up at a bargain price.

It looked as picture-perfect as everything around it, but that, of course, was an illusion. It was semi-bankrupt, on its last legs—a medium-sized cruise ship which he would add to his already vast portfolio of conquests.

He knew down to the last detail how much money it had lost in the past five years, how much it owed the bank, how much its employees were paid, how discounted their fares were now they were desperate to get customers... He practically knew what the owners had for their breakfast and where they did their food shopping.

As with all deals, big or small, it always paid to do his homework. His brother, Theo, might have laughingly referred to this extravagant purchase as nothing more than a toy—something different to occupy him for a few months—but it was going to be a relatively expensive toy, and he intended to use every trick in the book to make sure he got the best possible deal.

Thinking about his brother brought a grin to his face. Who'd have thought it? Who would have thought that Theo De Angelis would one day be singing the praises of the institution of marriage and waxing lyrical about the joys of love? If he hadn't heard it with his own ears when he had spoken to his brother earlier in the week then *he* wouldn't have believed it.

He looked around him with the shrewd eyes of a man who knew how to make money and wondered what he could do here. Exquisite scenery. Exquisite island, if you could somehow get rid of the hordes of annoying tourists milling around everywhere. Maybe in the future he would think about exploiting this little slice of paradise, but for the moment there was an interesting acquisition at hand, and one which would have the benefit of his very personal input—which was something of a rarity. He was relishing this break from the norm.

Then there was his successful ditching of the last woman he had been dating, who had become a little too clingy for comfort.

And, last but not least on the feel-good spectrum, a sexy little blonde thing would be waiting for him when his time was up on that floating liner so far from paradise...

All in all this was going to be something of a holiday and, bearing in mind the fact that he hadn't had one of those in the longest while, Daniel was in high spirits.

'Sir? Maybe we should head down so that you can board the ship? It's due to leave soon...'

'Shame... I've only been here for a few hours.' Daniel turned to his driver, whom he had brought with him from the other side of the world on an all-expenses-paid, fun in the sun holiday, with only a spot of driving to do here and there. 'I feel Santorini could be just the place for me... Nice exclusive hotel somewhere... Kick back and relax...'

'I didn't think you knew how to do that, sir.'

Daniel laughed. Along with his brother and his father, Antonio Delgado was one of only a few people in whom he had absolute trust, and in fairness his driver probably knew more about his private life than both his brother *and* his father, considering he drove him to his numerous assignations with numerous women and had been doing so for the past decade.

'You're right.' He briskly pulled open the car door and slid inside, appreciating the immediate drop in temperature. 'Nice thought, though...'

In truth, kicking back by the side of a pool with a margarita in one hand and a book in the other wasn't his thing.

He kicked back in the gym occasionally, on the slopes occasionally and far more frequently in bed—and his women all ran to type. Small, blonde, sexy and very, very obliging.

Granted, none of them stayed the course for very long, but he saw that as just an occupational hazard for a man whose primary focus—like his brother's—had always been on work. He thrived on the pressure of a high-octane, fast-paced work-life filled with risk.

He had benefited from the privileges of a wealthy background, but at the age of eighteen, just as he had done with Theo, his father, Stefano De Angelis, had told him that his fortune was his to build or not to build as the case might be. Family money would kick-start his career up to a certain point, but that would be it. He would fly or fall.

And, like Theo, he had flown.

Literally. To the other side of the world, where he had taken the leisure industry by storm, starting small and getting bigger and bigger so that now, at not yet thirty, he owned hotels, casinos and restaurants across Australia and the Far East.

He had acquired so much money that he could spend the remainder of his life taking time out—next to that pool with a book in one hand and a margarita in the other—and *still* live in the sort of style that most people could only ever dream of. But work was his passion and he liked it that way.

And this particular acquisition was going to be novel and interesting.

'Don't forget,' he reminded Antonio, 'you're to drop me off fifteen minutes away from the port.'

'It's boiling out there, sir. Are you sure you wouldn't rather enjoy the air-conditioning in the car for as long as possible?'

'A little discomfort won't kill me, Antonio, but I'm deeply touched by your concern.' He caught his driver's eye in the rearview mirror and grinned. 'No, it's essential that I hit the cruise ship like any other passenger. Arriving in the back seat of a chauffeur-driven Merc isn't part of the plan.'

The plan was to check out the small cruise liner incognito. The thing hadn't made a buck in years, and he wanted to see for himself exactly where the myriad problems lay. Mismanagement, he was thinking. Lazy staff, incompetence on every level...

He would spend a few days checking out the situation and making a note of who he would sack and who he would consider taking on as part of his team when the liner was up and running in its new format.

Judging from the list of airy-fairy scheduled activities, he was thinking that the entire lot would be destined for unemployment.

Five days. That was the time scale he had in mind, at the end of which he would stage his takeover. He didn't anticipate any problems, and he had big plans for the liner. Forget about woolly lectures and cultural visits while on board substandard food was served to passengers who frankly wouldn't expect much more, considering the pittance they were paying for their trips.

He intended to turn the liner into one of unparalleled luxury, for a wealthy elite whose every whim would be indulged as they were ferried from golf course to golf course in some of the most desirable locations in the world. He would decide on the destinations once the purchase was signed, sealed and delivered.

As with every other deal he had successfully completed, Daniel had utter confidence that he would succeed with this one and that the ship would prove to be a valuable asset. He had never failed and he had no reason to assume that this would prove the exception.

At the port, with the shiny black Merc behind him and a battered backpack bought especially for the purpose slung over his shoulder, he cast a jaundiced eye over the motley crew heading onto the liner.

Already he could see that the thing was in a deplorable state. How could Gerry Ockley, who had inherited this potential goldmine from his extremely wealthy father, have managed so thoroughly to turn it into something that no self-respecting pirate would have even considered jumping aboard to plunder? How the hell could he ever have imagined that some wacky cultural cruise would actually turn a profit?

True, it had taken over eight years to run it into the ground, but he would have thought that someone—bank manager...good friend...concerned acquaintance...*wife*— would have pointed him in the right direction at some point.

The liner was equipped to hold two hundred and fifty passengers comfortably, in addition to all the crew

needed. Daniel figured that at present it was half full—
if that.

He would be joining it halfway through its trip and,
ticket at the ready, he joined the chattering groups of
people, mostly in their mid-fifties and early sixties, who
were gathering in preparation for boarding.

Did he blend in? No. When it came to anyone under
the age of thirty-five, as far as he could tell he was in the
minority. And at six foot two he was taller than nearly
everyone else there.

But he was in no doubt that he would be able to fend
off any curious questions, and he was tickled pink that he
would be travelling incognito for the next few days. Was
that really necessary? Possibly not. He could always have
stayed where he was, in his plush offices in Australia, and
formulated a hostile takeover. But this, he thought, would
afford him the opportunity of removing at least some of
the hostility from his takeover.

He would be able to tell Ockley and his wife exactly
why he was taking over and exactly *why* they couldn't refuse him. He would be able to point out all the significant
shortcomings of their business and he would be able to
do that from the advantageous perspective of someone
who had been on board their liner. He was being kind,
and in the process would enjoy the experience. The fact
that the experience would be reflected in his offer would
be a nice bonus.

He could feel inquisitive eyes on him as the crowd of
people narrowed into something resembling an orderly
queue. With the ease born of habit he ignored them all.

His appearance matched his battered backpack. He was
just a broke traveller on a cut-price cultural tour of the
Greek islands and possibly Italy. His hair, a few shades
lighter than his brother's, was slightly longer than he normally wore it, curling at the nape of his neck, and as he

hadn't shaved that morning his face was shadowed with
bristle. His eyes, however, the same unusual shade of
green as his brother's, were shrewd as they skimmed the
crowds. He had tucked his sunglasses into his pocket.

The sun was ferocious. He could feel himself perspiring freely under the faded polo shirt and realised he
shouldn't have worn jeans. Fortunately, he had a few pairs
of khaki shorts in the backpack, along with an assortment
of tee shirts, and those should do the trick in the blistering sun once he was on board the liner.

He switched off the thought, his mind already moving
to work, planning how he would co-ordinate the work to
be done on the liner and the time when it would be ready
to set sail in its new, improved condition. He would charge
outrageous prices for anyone lucky enough to secure a
ticket, and he had no doubt that people would be queu-
ing to pay.

Done deal.

He hadn't felt this relaxed in ages.

Delilah Scott eyed her mobile, which was buzzing furiously at her, and debated whether she should pick it up
or not.

Her sister's name was flashing on the screen, demanding urgent attention.

With a little sigh of resignation she answered, and was
greeted with a flurry of anxious questions.

'Where on earth have you been? I've been trying to
get through to you for the past two days! You know how
I worry, Delly! It's mad here, with the shop… I can't believe you've decided, just like that, to extend your holiday! You *know* I'm depending on you getting back here
to help… I can't do it on my own…'

Delilah felt her stomach churn into instant nervous
knots.

'I—I know, Sarah,' she stammered, gazing through the tiny porthole of her very small cabin, which was just big enough for a single bed, the very barest of furniture, and an absolutely minuscule en-suite shower room. 'But I thought the added experience would come in handy for when I get back to the Cotswolds… It's not like I'm on *holiday*…' she tacked on guiltily.

'You *are* on holiday, Delly!' her sister said accusingly. 'When you said that you'd be doing some teaching for a fortnight, I never expected you to send me an email telling me that you'd decided to extend the fortnight into *six weeks*! I *know* you really needed to get away, Delly…what with that business with Michael…but *still*… It's *manic* here…'

Delilah felt the worry pouring down the phone line and experienced another wave of guilt.

Back home, Sarah was waiting for her. Building work which was costing an absolute arm and a leg was set to begin in two weeks' time, and she knew that her sister had been waiting for her to get back so that they could weather it together.

But was it too much to take a bit of time off before the dreadful drudgery of normal life returned? She had just completed her art degree, and every single free moment during those three years she had been in that tiny cottage with her sister, worrying about how they were going to survive and counting the takings from the gallery downstairs in the certain knowledge that sooner or later Dave Evans from the bank was going to lose patience and foreclose.

And then there had been Michael…

She hated thinking about him—hated the way just remembering how she had fallen for him, how he had messed her around, made her feel sick and foolish at the same time.

She definitely didn't want to hear Sarah rehashing that horrible catastrophe. Delilah loved her sister, but ever since she could remember Sarah had mothered her, had made decisions for her, had worried on her behalf about anything and everything. The business with Michael had just fed into all that concern. Yes, it was always great to have the comfort of someone's love and empathy when you'd just had your heart broken, but it could also be claustrophobic.

Sarah cared so much...always had...

Their parents, Neptune and Moon, both gloriously irresponsible hippies who had been utterly and completely wrapped up in one another, had had little time to spare for their offspring. Both artists, they had scratched a living selling some of their art, and later on a random assortment of crystals and gems after their mother had become interested in alternative healing.

They had converted their cottage into a little gallery and had just about managed to survive because it was slap-bang in the middle of tourist territory. They had always benefited from that. But when they had died—within months of one another, five years previously—sales of local art had already begun to take a nosedive and things had not improved since.

Sarah, five years older than Delilah, had been doing the best she could, making ends meet by doing the books for various people in the small village where they lived, but it had always been understood that once Delilah had completed her art degree she would return and help out.

As things stood, they had taken out a substantial loan to fund renovations to the gallery, in order to create a new space at the back where Delilah would teach art to anyone local who was interested and, more importantly, other people, keen on learning to draw and paint, who would perhaps attend week-long courses, combining sightsee-

ing in the picturesque Cotswolds with painting indoors
and outdoors.

It was all a brilliant if last-ditch idea, and whilst Delilah had been totally in favour of it she had suddenly, when
offered the opportunity to extend her stay on board the
Rambling Rose, been desperate to escape.

A little more time to escape the finality of returning
to the Cotswolds and to breathe a little after her break-
up from Michael.

Just a little more time to feel normal and relaxed.

'It'll be brilliant experience for when I get back,' she
offered weakly. 'And I've transferred most of my earnings
to the account. I'll admit I'm not on a fabulous amount,
but I'm making loads of good contacts here. Some of the
people are really interested in the courses we'll be offering…'

'Really?'

'Honestly, Sarah. In fact, several have promised that
they'll be emailing you for details about prices and stuff
in the next week or so.'

'Adrian's just about finished doing the website. That's
more money we're having to expend…'

Delilah listened and wondered whether these few
weeks on the liner were to be her only window of freedom from worrying. Sarah would not countenance selling the cottage and Delilah, in fairness, would have hated
to leave her family home. But staying required so many
sacrifices that she felt as though her youth would be eaten
up in the process. She was only twenty-one now, but she
could see herself saying goodbye to her twenties in the
never-ending task of just making ends meet.

She had had a vision of having fun, of feeling young
when she had been going out with Michael, but that had
been a very narrow window and in the end it had just
been an idiotic illusion anyway. When she thought about

him now she didn't think of *fun*, she just thought of being stupid and naïve.

She knew that she was playing truant by extending her stay here, but the responsibilities waiting for her wouldn't be going anywhere…and it was nice not being mothered by her sister, not having every move she made frowningly analysed, not having her life prescribed because Sarah knew best…

She hung up, relieved to end the conversation, and decided to spend what remained of the evening in her cabin.

Maybe she would ask a couple of the other teachers on the liner—young girls, like herself—to have something to eat with her in the cabin, maybe play cards and joke about some of the passengers, who mostly reminded her of her parents. Free-spirited ageing hippies, into all sorts of weird and wonderful arty pastimes and hobbies.

Tomorrow, she would be back to teaching, and she had a full schedule ahead of her…

Daniel stretched. Peered through the porthole to a splendid view of deep blue ocean. The night before he had enjoyed an expected below average meal—though not sitting at the captain's table. That sort of formality didn't exist aboard this liner. It seemed to be one big, chattering, happy family of roughly one hundred people, of varying ages, and fifty-odd crew members who all joined in the fun. He had mixed and circulated but he knew that he'd stuck out like a sore thumb.

Now, breakfast…and then he would begin checking out the various classes—all of which seemed destined to make no money. Pottery, poetry writing, art, cookery and a host of others, including some more outlandish ones, like astronomy and palm reading.

Today he ditched the jeans in favour of a pair of low slung khaki shorts, a faded grey polo shirt and deck shoes, which he used on his own sailing boat when he occasionally took to the sea.

He paused, in passing, to glance in the mirror.

He saw what he always saw. A lean, bronzed face, green eyes, thick dark lashes, dirty blond hair streaked from the Australian sun. When he had time for sport he preferred it to be extreme, and his body reflected that. Boxing sessions at the gym, sailing on his own for relaxation, skiing on black runs…

It was after nine, and on the spur of the moment he decided to skip breakfast, pulling a map of the liner from his pocket and, after discarding some of the more outrageous courses, heading for the section of the liner where the slightly less appalling ones were taking place.

He had no idea what to expect. Every single passenger seemed to be an enthusiastic member of some course or other, and as he made his way through the ship, his sharp eyes noting all the signs of dilapidation, he peered into full classes. Some people were on deck, enjoying the sun, but it had to be said that the majority had come for the educational aspect of the cruise.

It took all sorts, he thought as he meandered through the bowels of the liner.

Inside the ship, as outside, it was very hot. The rooms in which the various courses were being taught were all air-conditioned, and for no better reason than because his clothes were beginning to stick to him like glue, he pushed open one of the doors and stepped inside.

In the midst of explaining the technique for drawing perspective, Delilah looked up and…

Her breath caught in her throat.

Lounging indolently by the door was the most stunningly beautiful man she had ever seen in her life. He definitely hadn't joined the cruise when they had started.

He must have embarked in Santorini, a late member of the passenger list.

He was tall. *Very* tall. And built like an athlete. Even wearing the standard gear of nearly every other passenger on the liner—longish shorts and a tee shirt—it was impossible to miss the honed muscularity of his body.

'May I help you?'

Everyone had turned to stare at the new recruit and she smartly called them back to attention, and to the arrangement of various little ceramic pots they had been in the process of trying to sketch.

Daniel had been expecting many things, but he hadn't been expecting this. The girl looking at him questioningly was tall and reed-slender and her hair was a vibrant shade of copper—a thousand different shades from red through to auburn—and had been tugged back into a loose ponytail which hung over one shoulder.

He sauntered into the room and looked around him at the twenty or so people, all seated in front of canvasses. A long shelf at the back held various artists' materials and on the walls several paintings were hanging—presumably efforts from the members of the class.

'If I'm interrupting I can always return later...'

'Not at all, Mr...?'

'Daniel.' He held out his hand and the girl hurried forward and briefly shook it. 'I joined the cruise yesterday,' he expanded, 'and I haven't had time to sign up to any of the courses...'

'But you're interested in art?' That brief meeting of hands had sent a sharp little frisson skittering through her and it was all she could do to maintain eye contact with him. 'I'm Delilah Scott, and I'm in charge of the art course...'

Up close, he was truly spectacular. With an artist's eye she could appreciate the perfect symmetry of his lean face. The brooding amazing eyes, the straight nose and the wide, sensual mouth. His hair looked sun-washed—not quite blond, but nothing as dull as brown—and there was something about him…something strangely charismatic that rescued him from being just another very good-looking guy.

She would love to paint him. But right now…

'I can explain the course that I run…'

She launched into her little set speech and edged slightly away, because standing too close was making her feel jumpy. She'd had enough of men to last a lifetime, and the last thing she needed was to start feeling jumpy around one now.

'Of course I don't know what standard you're at, but I'm sure you'll be able to fit in whether you're a complete beginner or at a more intermediary level. I can also show you my qualifications… You would have to return later to get the proper lowdown, because as you can see I'm in the middle of taking a class and this one will last until lunchtime… But perhaps you'd like to see some of the work my class have been doing…?'

Not really, Daniel thought, but he tilted his head to one side and nodded with a show of interest.

She was as graceful as a ballerina. He liked women curvy and voluptuous. This girl was anything but. She was willowy, and dressed in just the sort of appalling clothes he disliked on a woman. A loose ankle-length skirt in a confusing number of clashing colours and a floaty top that left way too much to the imagination.

Personally, he had never been a big fan of having to work on his imagination when it came to women. He liked to see what he was getting, and he'd never had any trouble in finding beautiful women keen to oblige. Small, tight clothes showing off curves in all the right places… Girls who were in it for fun, no-strings-attached relationships. True, the occasional woman might get a little too wrapped up in planning for a future that wasn't going to happen, but that was fine. He just ditched her. And not once had he ever felt a qualm of guilt or unease about doing that because he was straight with every single one of them upfront.

He wasn't ready for marriage. He wasn't even in it for anything approaching long term. He didn't want a partner to meet his family and close friends and start getting ideas. He didn't do home-cooked meals or watching telly or anything remotely domesticated.

He thought of Kelly Close and his lips thinned. Oh, no, he didn't do *any* of that stuff...

As far as Daniel De Angelis was concerned, at this point in his life work was way more important than women, and when and if he decided to tie the knot— which was nowhere in the near future, especially as Theo was now happily planning a big wedding himself, thereby paving the way for Daniel to take his time getting there— he intended to marry someone who didn't just see the benefits of his bank balance.

He'd had his brush with a scheming gold-digger and once was plenty enough. Kelly Close—an angelic vision with the corrupt heart of a born opportunist. He slammed the door on pointless introspection. Enough that she had been a valuable learning curve. Now he had fun. Uncomplicated fun with sexy little things, like the blonde who would be waiting for him when he jumped ship.

Delilah Scott was showing him around the room, encouraging him to look at what the aspiring artists had already accomplished while they had been on the cruise.

'Fascinating,' he murmured. Then he turned to her before she could conclude the tour. 'So—lunch. Where shall we meet and what time?'

'Sorry?' Delilah asked in confusion.

'You said you wanted to give me the lowdown on the course. Over lunch sounds good. When and where? I'm guessing there's only one restaurant on the liner?'

Delilah felt a rush of heat swamp her and sharply brought herself back down to earth. 'Did I say that? I didn't think I had. You're more than welcome to just turn up tomorrow morning for the class, or you could join in right now if you like… There's lots of paper…pencils…'

Those amazing green eyes, the opaque colour of burnished glass, made her want to stare and keep on staring.

'I intend to spend the morning considering my options,' Daniel inserted smoothly. 'Checking out what the other courses are…whether they're more up my street… I'll meet you for lunch at twelve-thirty in the restaurant. You can tell me all about your course and see whether it fits the bill or not…'

Not his type, but eye-catching all the same. Skin as smooth as satin, sherry-coloured eyes, and she was pale gold after time spent in the sun. And her mouth… Its full lips parted now as she looked at him.

'I don't think there's any need for me to explain the course over *lunch*…'

'You're in the service industry… Surely that implies that you have to serve the customer? I'm just after some information…'

'I know that, but…'

But Michael had left her wary of men like this one. Good-looking men who were a little offbeat, a little off the beaten track…

Eight months ago Michael Connor had sauntered into her life—all long, dark hair and navy blue eyes and a sexy, sexy smile that had blown her away. At twenty-seven, he already had a fledgling career in photography, and he had charmed her with the amazing photos he had taken over the years. He had wined and dined her and talked about taking her to the Amazon, so that she could paint and he could take pictures.

He had swept her away from all her miserable, niggling worries about money and held out a shimmering vision of adventure and excitement. Two free spirits travelling the world. She had fallen in love with him and with those thrilling possibilities. She had dared to think that she had found a soul mate—someone with whom she could spend the rest of her life. They had kissed, but he hadn't pressed her into bed, and now she wondered how long he would have bided his time until deciding that kissing and cuddling wasn't what he was in it for.

Not much longer—because he'd already had a girlfriend. Someone in one of those countries he had visited. She'd chanced upon the fact only because she had happened to see a text message flash up on his screen. When she had confronted him, he'd laughed and shrugged. So he wasn't the settling down type…? He had an open relationship with his girlfriend so what was the big deal…? He had lots of women…he was single, wasn't he? And he'd hung around with *her*, hadn't he? She hadn't *really* thought that they were going to get married and have two point two kids and a dog, had she?

She had misread him utterly. She'd been taken in by a charming facade and by her own longing for a little adventure.

She'd been a fool.

Her sister had always sung the praises of stability and a good old-fashioned guy who could provide, whose feet were firmly planted on the ground. She'd seen no virtue in their parents' chaotic lives, which had left them with debt and financial worries.

She should have paid more attention to those sermons.

'I won't occupy a lot of your time,' Daniel murmured,

intrigued by this woman who didn't jump at the offer of having a meal with him.

Delilah blinked, ready to shake her head in instant refusal.

'There's a bar… We can have something light and you can tell me all about your course. You can sell it to me.' He flung his hands wide in a gesture that was both exotic and self-deprecating at the same time. 'I'm caught on the horns of a dilemma…' Again, he found it weirdly invigorating to actually be in the position of trying to *persuade* a woman to join him for a meal 'You wouldn't want to drive a man into the arms of learning palmistry, would you?'

Delilah swallowed down a responding smile. 'I suppose if you really think it's that important…'

'Great. I'll see you in the bar at twelve-thirty. You can hone your pitch before we meet…'

Delilah watched as he strolled out of the room. She felt as though she had been tossed into a tumble drier with the speed turned to high and she didn't like it. But she'd agreed to meet him and she would keep their meeting brief and businesslike.

She could barely focus on her class for the next three hours. Her mind was zooming ahead to meeting Daniel in the bar. And sure enough when, at a little after twelve-thirty, she hesitantly walked into the small saloon bar, which was already filling up with passengers whose courses had likewise ended for the morning, there he was. Seated at a small table, nursing a drink in front of him.

He was eye-catching—and not just because he was noticeably younger than everyone else. He would have been eye-catching in any crowd. She threaded her way through to him, pausing to chat to some of the other passengers.

Daniel watched her with lazy, deceptive indolence. He hadn't boarded this third-rate liner for adventure. He had boarded it for information.

He looked at her narrowly, thoughts idly playing through his head. She seemed to know everyone and she was popular. He could tell from the way the older passengers laughed in her company, totally at ease. He was sure that she would be equally popular amongst the staff.

Who was worth keeping on? Who would get the sack immediately? He wouldn't need any of the teachers on board, but the crew would be familiar with the liner, would probably have proved themselves over a number of years and might be an asset to him. It would certainly save him having to recruit from scratch and then face the prospect of some of them not being up to the task. When it came to pleasing the wealthy there could be no room for error.

Would *she* be able to help him with the information he needed? Naturally he wouldn't be able to tell her why...

Not for a second did Daniel see this as any form of deception. As far as he was concerned he would merely be making the most of a possible opportunity, no harm done.

He rose as she finally approached him.

'You came,' he said with a slashing smile, indicating the chair next to him. 'I wasn't sure whether you would. You seemed a little reluctant to take me up on my offer.'

'I don't normally fraternise with the passengers,' Delilah said stiffly as she sat down.

'You seemed familiar enough with them just then...'

'Yes, but...'

'What can I get you to drink?'

His eyes roved over her colt-like frame. He watched the way her fingers nervously played with the tip of her ponytail and the way her eyes dipped to avoid his. If he had had the slightest suspicion that she knew who he was he might have wondered whether her shyness was some kind of act to stir his interest—because women, in his company, were usually anything but coy.

'Just some juice, please.' Delilah was flustered by the way he looked at her—as though he could see straight into her head.

Juice in hand, and with a refill of whisky for him, he returned to settle into the chair and looked at her.

'So, you wanted to know about the course…'

Delilah launched into chatter. She found that she was drawn to look at him, even though she didn't want to. It wasn't just that he was a passenger—something about him sent disturbing little chills racing up and down her spine and sent her alarm bells into overdrive.

'I've brought some brochures for you to have a look at…'

She rummaged in her capacious bag and extracted a few photocopied bits of paper, which she self-consciously thrust at him. Several had samples of her work printed inside, and these he inspected, glancing between her face and the paintings she had done at college.

'Impressive,' he mused.

'Have you seen any other courses that interest you? Aside…' She allowed herself a polite smile. 'Aside from the palmistry?'

'I'm tempted by astronomy… When it comes to stars, I feel I could become something of an expert…' Daniel murmured. His last girlfriend had been an actress. Did that count? 'But, no…' He sat back briskly, angling his chair so that he could stretch his legs to one side. 'I'm only here for a week. Probably just to take in a couple of stops. I think I'll go for yours…'

A week? Delilah felt an inexplicable surge of disappointment, but she pinned a smile on her face and kept it there as she sipped some of the orange juice.

'Well, I can't guarantee I can turn you into Picasso at the end of a week… I mean, most of the other passengers are here for the full month, and then we have more join-ing us when we dock at Naples…'

'Seems a bit haphazard,' Daniel said. 'Put it this way—I managed to get a place at the last minute, and for whatever duration I chose…'

'It's…it's a little more informal than most cruises, I guess,' Delilah conceded. 'But that's because it's a fam-ily-run business. Gerry and Christine *like* the fact that people can dip in and out…'

'Gerry and Christine?'

Ockley. He knew their names, knew how far into debt they were. Little wonder people could dip in and out of the cruise at whim. Any business was good business when it came to making ends meet.

'They run the cruise ship. Actually, it's theirs, and they're great.'

She felt herself relax, because he was so clearly inter-ested in what she was saying. He was just another keen passenger, and if his looks made her a bit jittery then that was *her* problem and, after the debacle with Michael, it was one she could easily deal with.

'Are they? In what way?'

'Just very interested in all the passengers—and the crew have been with them for ages.'

'Is that a fact…? And I guess you know all the crew…?'

'They're wonderful. Devoted to their jobs. They all love the fact that they're pretty much allowed free rein with what they do… Of course they all follow the rules, but for instance the chef is allowed to do as he likes and so is the head of entertainment. I've been very lucky to get this job…' She guiltily thought of her sister, but she would be back home soon and all would be fine.

Daniel saw the shadow cross her face and for a few seconds was intrigued enough to want to find out more about the woman sitting in front of him. But there was no time in his busy, compacted schedule for curiosity about a random stranger, however strangely attractive he might find her. He had to cut to the chase.

'So…' He carried the conversation along briskly. 'Tomorrow…what time do we start…?'

CHAPTER TWO

'Now HAVE A look at the jug. George…see how it forms the centre of the arrangement? With the other two pieces in the background? So that the whole forms a geometric shape…? If you could just make the jug a teeny bit smaller, then I think we're getting there!'

For the umpteenth time Delilah's eyes skittered towards the door, waiting for it to be pushed open by Daniel.

Her calm, peaceful enjoyment of her brief window of freedom appeared to have disappeared the moment she had met the man. She had been knocked sideways by his looks, but more than that he had a certain watchfulness about him that she found weirdly compelling…

She was seeing him through the eyes of an *artist*, she had told herself, over and over again. The arrangement of his features, the peculiar aura of authority and power he emanated was quite unlike anything she had ever seen before in anyone.

She had laughingly told herself that she was reading far too much into someone who was probably a drifter, working his way through the continent. Someone who had managed to accumulate sufficient money to buy himself a few days on the liner so that he could pursue a hobby. Most of the passengers were in their fifties or sixties, on the cruise for the whole time, but there were a number who, like him, were on the cruise for a limited period of time, taking advantage of one or other of the many courses offered while enjoying the ports before disembarking so that they could continue travelling.

He was a traveller.

But she still found herself searching out the door every two minutes, and when—an hour after the class had begun—he pushed it open and strolled into the room she drew her breath in sharply.

'Class!' Everyone instantly stopped what they were doing and looked at Daniel. 'I'd like to introduce a new recruit! His name is Daniel and he's an aspiring artist, so I hope you'll welcome him in and show him the ropes if I happen to be busy with someone. Daniel… I've set aside a seat for you, with an easel. You never mentioned what level you feel you might be at…?'

Daniel didn't think that there was *any* level that might apply to him. 'Basic.' He smiled, encompassing every single person in the room, and was met with smiles in return, before their attention reverted to their masterpieces in the making.

'In that case, why don't you start with pencil? You can choose whichever softness you feel comfortable with and perhaps try your hand at reproducing the arrangement on the table in front of the class…'

She was extremely encouraging. She had kind things to say about even the most glaringly amateurish efforts. She took time to help and answered all the questions thrown at her patiently. When he told her, as he stared at the empty paper pinned to his easel, that he was waiting for inspiration to come and that you couldn't rush that sort of thing, she didn't roar with laughter but merely suggested that a single stroke of the pencil might be all the inspiration he needed.

He thought that he might have been a little more interested in art at school if he'd had *her* as his teacher instead of the battleaxe who had told him that the world of art would be better off without his input. Not that she hadn't had a point…

He'd managed something roughly the shape of one of the objects on the table by the time the class drew to an end, but instead of heading out with everyone else he remained exactly where he was, watching as she tidied everything away.

Delilah could feel his eyes on her as she busied herself returning pencils and foam pads and palette knives to the various boxes on the shelf. She'd been so conscious of him sitting there at the back of the class, sprawled out with his body at an angle and doing absolutely nothing, from what she could see. She'd barely been able to focus.

Now she turned to him and smiled politely. 'Won't you be joining the other passengers for some lunch?' she asked as she began the process of dismounting the easels and stacking them away neatly against the wall, where straps had been rigged to secure them in place.

Daniel linked his fingers behind his head and relaxed back into the chair. 'I thought you could give me some pointers on my efforts today…' He swivelled the easel so that it was facing her and Delilah walked slowly towards it.

'I'm sorry you haven't managed to accomplish a bit more,' she said tactfully. 'I was aiming for more of a *realistic* reproduction of the jugs…it's important to really try and *replicate* what you see at this stage of your art career…'

'I don't think I'll be having a career in art,' Daniel pointed out.

'So this is just a hobby for you…? Well, that's good, as well. Hobbies can be very relaxing, and once you become a bit more familiar with the pencil—once your confidence starts growing—you'll find it the most relaxing thing in the world…'

'Is that what *you* do to relax?' he asked, making no move to shift.

'I really must get on and tidy away this stuff…'

'No afternoon classes?'

'The afternoons, generally speaking, are downtime for everyone. The passengers like to go out onto the deck, or else sit in the shade and catch up with their reading or whatever homework's been set…'

'And what do *you* do?'

'I… I do a little painting…sometimes I sit by the pool on the top deck and read…'

Daniel enjoyed the way she blushed. It was a rare occurrence. The women he dated had left their blushing days far behind.

'I thought we might have lunch again today,' he suggested, waiting to see what form her refusal would take. 'As you can see…' he waved in the vague direction of his easel '…my efforts at art are crap.'

'No one's efforts at art are anything but good. You forget that beauty is in the eye of the beholder…'

'How long are you going to be on the liner for?'

'I beg your pardon?'

'Are you here for…?' He whipped out the crumpled cruise brochure from his shorts pocket, twisted it in various directions before finding the bit he wanted. 'For the full duration of a month?'

'I can't see what this has to do with the course, Mr… er… Daniel…'

'If you're going to be on the course for the full duration I *might* be incentivised to stay a bit longer than a week.'

Complete lie—but something about her appealed to him. Yet again she was in an outfit more suitable for one of the middle-aged free spirits on the cruise ship. Another flowing skirt in random colours, and another kind of loose, baggy top that worked hard at concealing her figure—which, he saw as he surreptitiously cast his eye over it, was as slender and as graceful as a gazelle's.

The libido he had planned on resting while he was on the ship stirred into enthusiastic life as he wondered what the body under the unappealing clothes might be like.

He went for big breasts. She was flat-chested—that much he could see. He went for women who were small and curvy—she was long and willowy. He liked them blonde and blue-eyed. She was copper-haired and brown-eyed.

Maybe it was the novelty… But whatever it was he was happy to go with the flow—not forgetting that she could also be a useful conduit to the information he wanted.

'Don't you have the rest of your travel plans already sorted out?' Delilah was irritated to find herself lingering on the possibility that this man she had spent about fifteen seconds with might stay on for longer than he had originally suggested.

'I try not to live my life according to too many prearranged plans,' Daniel murmured, appreciating the delicate bloom of pink in her cheeks. 'I guess we probably have that in common…'

Delilah grimaced. 'I wish that *was* like me,' she said without thinking. 'But unfortunately you couldn't be further from the truth.' She reddened and spun round, away from those piercing unusual eyes. 'Of course,' she said, 'it would be lovely if you stayed on a bit longer. I'm sure you could become an able artist if you put all your efforts into it.'

She knew that the cruise ship was running at a loss. All the crew knew that. Gerry and Christine had not kept it a secret from them at all. In fact on day one they had called a meeting and apologised straight away for the fact that they couldn't be paid more. None of the teachers on board had protested. They were there because they loved what they did, and the fact that there was sun and sea in the mix was enough for all of them.

But the Ockleys had suggested that if they could try and persuade some of the passengers to prolong their stay, or even tempt interested holidaymakers into hopping on board for a couple of days to try their hand at one of the many courses... Well, every little would help.

'Persuade me over lunch,' Daniel suggested. It felt like a challenge to get her to comply—and since when had he ever backed down in the face of a challenge? 'Unless, of course, you find my company objectionable...?'

Realistically, he didn't even countenance that.

'I had lunch with you yesterday because you wanted to find out about the course.'

Delilah did her best to dredge up the memory of her disaster of a relationship with Michael and to listen to the warning voice in her head reminding her that she was still recovering from a broken heart—which, by defini-tion, meant retreating from men, taking time out, paying attention to the value of common sense.

'So? What does that have to do with anything? We've talked about the course and now I'd like to find out whether you think I'm a suitable candidate to be on it. I wouldn't want to be accused of wasting your time...so why the hesitation?'

'Perhaps a quick lunch,' she agreed—for Gerry and Christine's sake.

Daniel smiled slowly. 'Shame the choice of food is so limited,' he said, rising to his feet and giving his effort at drawing the jug a cursory glance.

If he had really been interested in learning how to draw then she would have had to commit to an indefi-nite period of time explaining to him how he might set about improving his skills, because he clearly had none.

Fortunately he had no intention of spending too long on that particular subject.

'And it's below average...'

'Sorry?' Delilah, in the act of washing her hands, turned round and frowned. 'What do you mean?'

'From what I've sampled, the food onboard doesn't exactly set the culinary world alight, does it?'

He moved to stand by the door and watched as she gathered her bag—some sort of tapestry affair that could have held the kitchen table and sink. Again, her hair was pulled back, with strands escaping round her face, and she absently shoved the stray strands behind her ear.

'It's okay...' she said cautiously.

'You don't want to rat on your fellow crew members,' Daniel murmured, with a hint of amusement in his voice. 'I understand that. But just between the two of us, I've been disappointed with what I've been served so far...'

'I don't think the passengers come for the food...'

'It's all part and parcel of the package,' Daniel said expansively. 'You said that the chef is allowed free rein...?'

'But he has to stick to a budget,' Delilah qualified uncomfortably. 'Anyway, it doesn't really matter, does it? I mean, if you're *really* unhappy, then perhaps you should mention something to Christine...'

'Who is the head chef?'

'Stan...and he works really hard to do the best he can with the money he's allotted...' She tripped along behind him, riveted by the long, lean lines of his muscular body.

'Don't worry,' Daniel said in a placating voice.

They had reached the bar and, as usual, people were tucking in to the offerings in a desultory fashion. Salads... baguettes with a variety of fillings...jacket potatoes...

It beggared belief that the owners of the liner had got their mismanagement down to such a fine art. Had they *no* concept of the importance of good food onboard a cruise liner, where the passengers did not have the option of scouting around for alternative restaurants?

'I'm not going to accost your pal in front of the chip-fryer...'

'Can I tell you something?' She reached into her bag for her wallet and insisted that she paid for his drink, as he had paid for hers the day before. This wasn't a date.

Daniel was chuffed. He couldn't remember the last time any woman had offered to pay for anything for him—not that he would have allowed it. But, no...the offer had never been made anyway. And yet this girl, who clearly bought her clothes from charity shops, was offering to buy him a drink. He was oddly touched by that. If only she knew!

His inherent cynicism quickly rose to the surface. If only she knew how much he was worth, then there was no chance in hell that she would be dipping into her wallet to buy him anything.

Once upon a time, in the tragic wake of his mother's death, he had foolishly allowed his emotions their freedom. He had fallen for Kelly Close's sympathetic ear. He had harboured no suspicions about the sweet-natured primary school teacher who had been into doing good and giving back to the community. He'd enjoyed lavishing gifts on her, enjoyed basking in her shyly endearing acceptance of whatever he bought for her.

Until he'd glimpsed the band of pure steel underneath the shyness when she had ditched her job and suggested that they make their arrangement permanent. It had occurred to him then, belatedly, that when you got past all the coy dipping of the eyes and trembling, grateful smiles, she had managed to acquire quite a substantial nest egg of priceless jewellery—not to mention the studio apartment he had bought her because the lease on her own flat had supposedly expired, and the countless weekends away.

At that point he had tried to pull back and bring some common sense to bear on the proceedings. He had discovered then that gold-diggers came in all different shapes and sizes and, his guard temporarily down, had realised that Kelly Close had found her way through the cracks in his armour and staged a clever assault, with her eventual aim being a wedding ring on her finger and a claim to his vast inheritance should they ever divorce. Which, he had seen very quickly, would have happened sooner rather than later.

A clean severing of the ways, however, had turned into a cat fight. Threats of a kiss-and-tell exposé to the tabloids had resulted in money changing hands—a vast sum of money, which had hit him at the worst possible time. In return he had managed to secure a contract with a privacy clause, prohibiting her from ever mentioning his name in public, but the emotional cost to him had also been steep.

With his brother and his father in another country, he had at least been spared the horror of either of *them* knowing about the unholy mess and the financial cost to him because he had taken his eye off the ball. But he had learnt a valuable lesson, and now, whilst it cost him nothing to be generous with his money, he made damn sure not to be generous with his emotions. Those he kept firmly under wraps. Considering his women exited their relationships with him better off by furs and diamonds and cars, he didn't think it was an unfair trade-off.

'What?' he asked.

Their eyes tangled and he didn't look away. But she was desperate to. He could see it in those sherry-coloured eyes and in her sudden flush. She wanted to look away but she was drawn to look at him.

What would she be like under those clothes? What noises did she make when she made love? What would it

*feel like to touch her between her legs...to hold her small
breasts in his big hands...to lick her nipples...?*

He cleared his throat, got a grip. He liked the fact that
he never lost control when he was with a woman. *Never.*
He had no idea why he kept veering off in that direction
now. Was it the salty tang of the sea air? He was here on
a fact-finding mission and yet he felt as though he was
playing truant from real life. Was that it?

'I've known lots of art students...' She tiptoed around
her words, not wanting them to sound offensive. Artists could sometimes be very sensitive souls. 'And you're
nothing like any of them...'

'I'm very glad to hear it,' Daniel drawled. He immediately sideswiped a sudden twinge of guilt at his masquer-
ade. 'I pride myself on being one of a kind.'

'That's what I mean,' Delilah blurted out. 'You'd never
hear an artist come out with something as arrogant as
that.' She pressed the palms of her hands against her
cheeks, mortified. 'I'm so—so sorry...' she stammered.

When Gerry and Catherine had made noises about the
crew trying to persuade their guests into prolonging their
stay, she didn't think that one of the methods they would
have advised using would have been insults. Delilah was
horrified at what she had said. She was not the sort who
ever did anything but encourage.

Having grown up with her wildly unorthodox background, she knew only too well the frailty of human be-
ings—the way they could be lovable and exasperating at
the same time. She had seen the way her sister had made
allowances for their mum and dad, and she, too, had fallen
into line, doing the same. She also knew how hurtful un-
intentionally blunt statements could be. Her mum had
once told Sarah, without meaning to offend at all, that
too much maths was turning her into a very boring person. Delilah didn't think that her sister had ever forgot-

ten that stray remark, which had been accompanied by a merry laugh and a fond ruffling of her hair.

She impulsively rested her hand on his and Daniel looked at her earnestly.

'I think I'll survive,' he said, making no move to remove his hand.

She had beautiful fingers. Long and slim and soft— the fingers of an artist or a musician. He was tempted to ask if she played any instruments...

'In fact, you aren't the first person to have told me that I can sometimes be a little arrogant,' he confessed, with such a rueful, charming, self-deprecating smile that Delilah could feel all her bones begin to melt.

Which made her yank her hand away at the speed of light. Her heart was beating so fast that she would have bet that if everyone in the bar fell silent they would all hear it.

'But I prefer to think of it as being self-confident...' he expanded softly. 'Now, if you insist on buying a drink for me, then I will graciously accept—but on one condition...'

'What's that?' She barely recognised her voice, which sounded high-pitched, girlish and breathless. She cleared her throat. She was a teacher, being paid to do a job. He was her *pupil*. She was also sworn off men.

Her ego had been battered and bruised by her experience with Michael. She wondered whether, instead of toughening her up the way it should have, it had somehow made her more vulnerable to someone like this guy, with his smooth charm and his insanely sexy good looks... Or was he the equivalent of a strong dose of pick-me-up tonic? Was that light, musing, flirtatious banter just a soothing balm, restoring her fragile self-confidence, making her feel good about herself?

And if it was then why should she be nervous around

him? It wasn't as though she was going to actually let him get under her skin, was she? He was nothing more than a passing stranger whose innate charm made her feel better about herself.

She relaxed when she looked at it in that light. It made sense.

'I buy you dinner.'

'What for?'

'Why not?' Daniel frowned.

'You've already bought me lunch. Twice. So that we could talk about the course I offer and your contribution.' She was doggedly determined not to let a couple of non-dates and a dinner invitation—extended because he was obviously a very sociable animal, probably accustomed to an abundance of female company—go to her head. 'I don't see the point of dinner. What do you want to talk about now?'

'Good God…what sort of an answer is *that*?'

Delilah thought it was a very good answer to give a guy who was probably bored by the lack of female eye candy on the ship. A bit of mild flirting might do her the power of good, but it was important for him to realise that she wasn't easy. She was probably over-thinking the whole thing, because she knew that she was no supermodel—and he was good-looking enough to have supermodels banging on his door even if he wasn't made of money. But still…

'How old are you?' Daniel asked, while she was still in the middle of getting her thoughts together.

'Twenty-one, but…'

'We're not at *school*, Delilah… Do you mind if I call you by your first name? We're two adults on a cruise ship. I think it's fair to say that accepting a dinner invitation from me doesn't actually require hours of mental debate and indecision. It's a simple yes or no scenario…'

'Of course, but…' But why did it feel so *dangerous*? Like he said, they were both adults—and why not?

'Besides…' He leaned forward, drawing her into an intimate circle where only the two of them existed. 'I was given a little money before I…er…embarked on this adventure, and I promised myself that I would spend it buying dinner for a beautiful woman…'

Delilah felt a thrill of forbidden pleasure race through her at his blatant flattery. He was so utterly serious that she could feel herself going hot and cold. Gripped with sudden panic and confusion, she tried to remember if she had ever felt like this when she had been with Michael— or had that been more of a slow-burning attraction? The meeting of two minds, connected, she had thought at the time, at the same level? Of course he had been a very attractive man, too, but certainly not in this full-on, sledge-hammer-to-the-ribs kind of way.

Two different situations, she told herself, frowning. This was pure lust—her body reminding her that whilst her emotions had been knocked for six, she could still respond to other men. Reminding her that she would recover from the blow she had taken and that being physically attracted to another man was the first step. This was a healthy and positive reaction to someone with drop-dead good looks.

'Surely you wouldn't insult me by throwing my invitation back in my face? And I thought we could make it something a bit more special than the buffet in the restaurant…'

Daniel hadn't actually tried the buffet, but judging from what he had sampled of the other meals, he didn't think it would be too hard to top it.

'What would that be?' Delilah asked, curiosity getting the better of her.

'I'd like to see you with your hair loose,' he heard

himself say—which surprised him as much as it surprised her.

Delilah's hand flew to her hair and her eyes widened. 'I beg your pardon?'

'Tonight. Have dinner with me. Dress up...wear your hair loose... I have money to blow and I've never been one to hang on to money if I can spend it. I'm going to ask your head chef to prepare a meal especially for us, and I intend to pay him way over the odds for it. Of course I'll make sure I clear it with the captain and his...er... wife first...'

He had no doubt at all that they would accept his offer with alacrity, and it would afford him the opportunity to see exactly what standard the head chef was capable of cooking to. As with all the other members of the crew, he would be more than happy to keep the chef in gainful employment if he was up to scratch. He might be on the verge of staging a hostile takeover, but that didn't mean he couldn't be fair in certain areas.

To his complete mystification she continued to look dubious, even though he could sense that she wanted to take him up on his offer. Even though he could sense that there was a part of her that was drawn to him...

'I'd bet that Stan...that is his name, isn't it?...would love nothing more than to practise the skills he's learnt without having to consider a budget...'

'Isn't it a bit extravagant to blow a lot of money on a meal when you've still got travelling to do...? I mean, I'm assuming this is just a single leg of your journey...'

'I'm very touched by your concern,' Daniel said gently, 'but I'm more than capable of looking after my finances... So what time will you be ready to join me? It's going to be a stunning night. The water is as calm as a sheet of glass. I think I'll get a table laid out for us in a secluded corner of the deck outside... Dining under the stars has always been something of a dream for me, and when else would I be likely to get the chance?'

Delilah wondered how much money he had to spend. She couldn't fight the fact that it was incredibly flattering, and a bit of flattery was just so seductive to her at this point in time. What was the harm in responding to it? As long as she remained in control everything would be fine—and she knew that she was more than capable of remaining in control. She might not be very experienced, but she was experienced enough to know that she would never risk making an idiot of herself again.

'Just dinner,' she said quickly.

'As opposed to dinner and…what?'

Unaccustomed to this sort of sexual banter, Delilah flushed and cleared her throat. 'I don't feel comfortable accepting an invitation from you when I know that it's going to cost the earth,' she offered lamely, only just rescuing herself from launching into a ridiculous speech about sex not being on the agenda because she wasn't looking for any kind of relationship and she wasn't the sort of girl who went in for meaningless flings.

'Hardly *the earth*,' Daniel pointed out drily. 'I'll pay the going rate for a good meal in Sydney. Or London. Or New York. Plus a little extra for the setting, of course…'

He named a figure that made her eyes water.

She had no idea what it felt like to spend that much money on a single meal in one reckless go. Her parents had seldom eaten out. In fact her mother had been a terrible cook and Sarah had usually done the cooking duties in the house. Delilah could remember meals, but they had all been basic, with food bought on a budget, because her parents had never had more than a couple of dimes to rub together. And then later, at art college, she had scraped by and so had everyone else she had known.

Even when she had been going out with Michael they had gone out on the cheap.

This seemed so generous…so impulsive…so *tempting*… Would it be so very wrong to accept? Would a couple of hours of being made to feel better about herself really hurt?

'I would offer to pay half, but there's no way I could afford it,' she said—and if that was the end of that, then so be it, she thought. Though her mind was already leaping ahead to the seductive prospect of being made to feel desirable and attractive by a man like him. 'I mean, I earn… Well, not much, in actual fact…because…'

'Because they're not making much money on this liner…?'

'Times are tough,' she said vaguely. 'The economy isn't booming and cruises aren't the sort of things that people race to throw money at…'

Too true, Daniel thought wryly. Especially ill-conceived cruises with sub-standard food that only seemed to attract ageing hippies with limited disposable incomes…

He was mentally making a note of everything she said and everything he saw, because when it came to putting in an offer there was no way he would allow the Ockley couple to try and pull a fast one by pretending their cruises were anything but loss-making ventures.

'Besides…' Delilah thought of the money she was currently sending to her sister, trying to pull her weight in paying off the interest on the loan they had secured from the bank for their building work.

Daniel tilted his head to one side and looked at her narrowly. 'Besides what…?

'Nothing. Okay. Well, why not? Dinner might be nice… And maybe,' she tacked on dutifully, 'I could persuade you to extend your stay on the ship…?'

'Maybe,' Daniel said, non-committal.

He thought that *that* kind of conversation would hit a roadblock in under thirty seconds. No, this evening would be about finding out about the cruise and her fellow crew members.

And finding out about *her*. She'd been on the verge of saying something about where her limited income went and he had to admit that he was curious. Unlike the women he had dated in the past, she was reluctant to try and engage his attention by bombarding him with every single detail about herself. That in itself fired up his curiosity.

'And you can tell me about your travels,' she said wistfully. 'Where you're planning on heading to next…'

'That's easy. London.'

'Really?'

'I have some…some business to attend to over there…'

'What do you do?' Delilah asked with interest. 'I mean, what's your profession?'

'I work in the leisure industry.'

Which was absolutely true. Although in fairness she probably wouldn't get close to suspecting the role he actually played. Not so much *working* in the industry as running and dominating it…

'That probably explains how you managed to get the time off to do a little drifting,' she said with a smile. 'I guess if you worked in an office your manager mightn't be too thrilled if you told him that you wanted time off to explore the artist in you…'

Daniel laughed. He was rarely bothered by a guilty conscience, but he couldn't help feeling another twinge of guilt at his deliberate manipulation of the truth.

'I don't have a manager,' he murmured. 'Funny, but I've always found it galling to obey someone else's orders.'

Delilah laughed, her eyes tangling with his. He was *so sexy*. He had that indefinable sexiness that came with not caring what other people thought about you. He didn't give a damn if she or anyone else thought that some of the things he said were arrogant. She got the feeling that he wouldn't care what *anyone* thought about him.

Her heart picked up speed. The way he was looking at her, his eyes narrowed and brooding, sent little thrills of pleasure racing up and down her spine.

Why shouldn't she allow herself to feel like a woman again? Surely if she didn't then Michael would end up having the last word?

Yes, Sarah had told her that she had to learn from her experience and *make sensible choices* when it came to men, and Delilah knew that her sister was right. But the sensible choice held as much attraction as a bout of flu, and wicked rebellion flared inside her.

She licked her lips in a gesture that Daniel thought was unconsciously erotic.

'No one likes taking orders from other people,' she said breathlessly. 'I guess we'd all like to be able to do our own thing, but unfortunately that's not how life is.'

Daniel looked around him before settling his gaze back on her flushed face. 'This strikes me as a pretty loose situation for you,' he pointed out. 'Didn't you tell me that you're all allowed to do your own thing on the liner, without constraints?'

'Yes, but I'm only here for a few weeks,' she reminded him.

'And then what? Going to hitch a ride on another cruise ship?'

'If only…'

Daniel leaned forward, intrigued. 'So tell me…?'

'There's nothing to tell.'

From a young age she had learnt that there were just

too many kids who were happy to snigger behind her back. She and Sarah had been the sisters with the weird parents. They'd learned that the less they'd said about their home life, the better, so they had kept themselves to themselves. The habit was so deeply engrained that even now, as a young adult, Delilah automatically shied away from confiding.

So what was it about *this* guy that made her want to open up?

And why did the thought of acting against her better judgement in accepting his invitation feel so appealing?

'I should be heading back to my cabin...' She barely recognised her voice and took a few steadying breaths. 'I... I'm going to do some preparation for my class tomorrow and...and...grab a bit of this beautiful weather... We should be at another port the day after tomorrow... It will be nice to just sit and soak up the sun with my book... You know... It's all go, go, go when we dock...and my students expect me to have clever things to say about all the places of culture that we visit...so...'

Daniel smiled slowly. 'So...' He sat back and thought that he needed to use the afternoon productively himself. Various deals going on required his attention. Time, as they said, was money. 'Seven sharp,' he murmured. 'Out on the deck. Far from the crowds...'

'You haven't got permission yet...' Delilah pointed out.

'Oh, I'll get permission,' he drawled.

'Because everyone listens and obeys when you talk?'

She'd said that jokingly, but there had been a thread of seriousness behind the jest and she wasn't all that surprised when he looked at her, eyebrows raised.

'Without exception...' he replied, deadly serious.

CHAPTER THREE

DELILAH HADN'T CATERED for dining under a starry sky with an Adonis. When she thought of guys at all now she vaguely assumed that the one meant for her would be a little dull, a little staid and a *lot* reliable. She'd had her brush with adventure and had pronounced herself jaded with love, only interested in a guy who would never use her, let her down or make inflated pie-in-the-sky promises he had no intention of keeping because he had girlfriends in every other port.

She hadn't been looking for racing pulses and sweaty excitement, and she couldn't quite believe that racing pulses and sweaty excitement had found *her*.

Consequently she possessed nothing in her wardrobe that was remotely suitable for dining with a man like Daniel. He hadn't talked about his love life, but she imagined him with lots and lots of beautiful women—the female equivalent of him. Head-turning model-types who wouldn't wear long skirts and baggy tops.

Somehow, despite his artistic inclinations, she couldn't picture him actually *going out* with an artist. At least, none of the artists *she* knew.

In the end at precisely six-thirty, after a quick shower in her cramped en-suite bathroom, she extracted the dressiest of her outfits from the single unit wardrobe.

Another long skirt, but black, and a fitted tee shirt with sleeves to the elbows—also black.

At five foot ten, she owned no high shoes at all, so she slipped on a pair of ballet pumps, giving a welcome rest to her flip-flops.

She left her hair loose.

Even in the brief length of time it had been exposed to the blistering sun it had lightened in colour. She was accustomed to tying it back. It was just more practical. Now, staring at her reflection in the mirror, she realised that the long, unruly hair she had always wished she could tame didn't look half bad.

Heart beating madly, she made her way to the outer deck to find him—she had had no idea where exactly he might be.

The sky was velvety black and pricked with tiny glittering stars. As he had said the ocean, dark and fathomless, was as still as a sheet of glass. The air was balmy, salty, indescribably fresh.

The sound of the passengers inside was barely discernible out here. There were a few couples strolling around, but most had confined themselves to the upper deck, which was more brightly lit and allowed easier access to the entertainment taking place inside.

Tonight, someone was doing a cabaret, and Delilah guiltily thought that it was a true indication of the finances of the liner that the person singing was really not terribly good—but then, as with Stan, Alfie, who was in charge of entertainment, was working on a tight budget.

Having managed to secure a charming and very secluded spot on the liner, Daniel was waiting for Delilah to track him down.

As predicted, it had been no bother getting the whole set-up arranged, and it had given him an excellent opportunity to acquaint himself with Gerry Ockley—a genial, bearded guy who clearly lacked any business acumen.

Perhaps his wife was a top-notch accountant, but Daniel doubted it.

The man had been only too happy to accept his very generous offer, and in fact had been more than willing to open up about the general finances of the liner.

Daniel brushed aside a few momentary misgivings about his planned takeover, about the fact that his aim was to get the liner at a knock-down price. When it came to business he had never felt sorry for any of the companies he had taken over. The bottom line was that a company could only be taken over if it was doing badly, and if it was doing badly then it was usually the result of bad management from the top down.

What was there to feel sorry about?

It was a dog-eat-dog world when it came to business. People got their chances, and if they screwed it up then who was to blame the predators for moving in?

But even so… On this particular occasion…

'You've found me…' He stood up, banishing unwelcome thoughts.

Delilah was staring open-mouthed at the table, the chairs, the linen cloth, the wine chilling next to him in an ice-cold bucket.

'Wow…'

'It was the best they could offer,' Daniel murmured as he pulled a chair out for her, 'given the circumstances…'

'It must have cost the earth…' She sat down and thought that it couldn't possibly get more romantic than this.

He was in a pair of dark trousers and a black polo shirt, and in the shadowy darkness he was just impossibly good-looking. When he rested those amazing eyes on her she could feel her skin tingle and her thought processes shut down. She felt like a different person…a person who was

still wonderfully alive and not nursing disillusionment…
She felt young again…

It was heady stuff, and when he poured her a glass of
chilled wine she drank it far too quickly.

'Like I said… I enjoy spending money…' Which was
the absolute truth—and he was generous to a fault when
it came to women.

His eyes roved over her face—the full mouth, the look
of fresh-faced innocence—and all of a sudden he felt impossibly jaded.

'I hope it's not money from…er…ill-gotten gains…'
She could already feel that single glass of wine shoot to
her head.

Daniel pretended to be outraged. 'You're not implying
that I'm a *criminal*, are you?'

'No. I was just…just teasing you. It seems so wildly
extravagant.'

Daniel thought that she had no idea what *wildly extravagant* entailed, and he really liked that.

'Hasn't any man ever been "wildly extravagant" with
you?' he mused, and Delilah laughed.

'No!'

'Why not?'

He'd joined this cruise on a fact-finding mission, but he
decided that he'd found out sufficient facts to be going on
with and that it was much too tempting to find out more
about the woman opposite him, blushingly sipping her
wine, which he had topped up.

'Because…' She lowered her eyes and then laughed
softly. 'Don't tell me you're really interested…?'

'Why wouldn't I be?'

'Because…' This flirty little game felt exotic and daring. 'Because I bet you have loads of girls scampering
behind you. And men who have loads of girls scamper-

ing behind them don't really spend time listening to what
they have to say.'

'I'm offended!' Daniel laughed, enjoying the conversation and the novelty of a woman who didn't care what
she said to him and wasn't trying to impress.

'No, you're not.' She smiled.

'Do you have a boyfriend? And if you have why hasn't
he done anything wildly extravagant for you?'

He fancied her. He didn't know why, because she
wasn't his type, but he didn't intend to question it.

He just knew that he had spent too much of the night
before thinking about her...

And she was jumpy around him—coming close and
then backing away. She fancied him as much as he fancied her, and God knew she was probably wondering
why—just as he was.

He thought of the sexy little number who would be
waiting for him and decided on the spot that he would
have to dispatch her. Right now he couldn't get his head
around any other woman but the one now shyly sneaking glances at him.

'No.' She'd tensed up. 'I don't. And wildly extravagant
gestures wouldn't be what I would look for in a boyfriend,
anyway. I don't go for that sort of thing.'

Daniel raised his eyebrows. 'You're more into the
dull-as-dishwater types? Who always make sure never
to waste a single penny on something unless it has a practical purpose? You shock me, Delilah. I thought, as you're
an artist, you would be wild and reckless...'

'Wild and reckless ends in tears.' She gulped down a
bit more wine and realised that she was on her third glass.
'But you're teasing me, aren't you?'

'Am I?'

'My parents were wild and reckless,' she confessed.

Usually Daniel could spot the incipient beginnings

of a long-winded tale, at which point he would tactfully change the subject—because long-winded tales from women always seemed to ask for similarly long-winded tales from *him*, but this time he had no inclination to do so.

'Were they?' he encouraged.

'Sorry, I don't normally talk about myself…' She started to apologise in advance, breaking off as Stan approached, in full chef garb, to regale them with the various dishes on offer.

Daniel had been right in thinking that the chef would be thrilled to bits to cook something that wasn't dictated by a strict budget. Delilah hadn't seen him this enthusiastic since she had boarded the liner.

Choices made, Daniel sat back and looked at her expectantly.

'You were going to tell me about your wild and reckless parents?' he said.

'They were artists… Neptune and Moon.'

'Come again?' He felt his lips twitch.

'Neptune and Moon. They gave themselves those names before we were born, actually…'

'We…?'

'My sister, Sarah, and me.' She smiled. Sarah had been dismissive of their parents' crazy names, but she, Delilah, had secretly loved them because they'd sounded so ethereal and glamorous.

It suddenly clicked why she loved this cruise so much—loved working aboard the ship. It was full of people just like her parents. The formerly wild and reckless, who had been tamed only by advancing years.

Sarah, five years older, had always preached caution. She had been the mother figure, taking over where Moon had so gaily left off. She had advocated the sensible path, had kept a cautionary eye on the boys who had occasionally come to the house. And Delilah had fallen into line, turning to her sister for practical advice and to her parents for fun.

It should have been the other way around, but it hadn't been. Neither she nor her sister would have changed it for the world, but an unconventional upbringing carried its disadvantages. Maybe a yearning for fun guys was ingrained in her—like those women who just kept falling for bad boys who broke their hearts. Maybe that was why she was here, sitting in this impossibly romantic setting with this impossibly sexy guy.

It was a disturbing thought but she pushed it aside— because she wasn't going out with him. She might be having fun with someone inappropriate but she was tougher now, and not about to make the same mistake twice.

Besides, Michael had never shown any real interest in *her*—had never asked any questions about her childhood or her past. He had been a 'live for the moment' type of guy, which she could now see was part and parcel of his egocentric personality. Their conversations had all revolved around *him*—*his* exploits, *his* big plans.

'Are you going to tell me that they're on this cruise with you?' he asked drily, and she shook her head.

'My mother died five years ago,' she said quietly, 'and my father within six months afterwards. Sarah and I think it was from a broken heart. They were so attached to one another it was just inconceivable that one could exist without the other.'

'A lonely life for you kids—having parents who were so wrapped up in one another…'

She looked at him, startled. 'That's what my sister thinks, but I've never looked at it that way.'

She told him about some of the ventures her parents had been involved in, about the friends who had dropped by and remained in the cottage for weeks on end. Sum-

mer evenings when a party of three had turned into a
party of ten, with someone fetching a guitar. She missed
all that, even though at the time she had found it a little
embarrassing—at least when compared to the very staid
behaviour of her friends' parents.

She barely noticed their starters being brought for
them, although she *was* aware of really enjoying what
she ate.

'It's nothing *like* the stuff he cooks for the masses!'

She was relieved to get on to a less personal topic, because she found that she could have carried on blathering
about herself till the cows came home. He made a good
listener. *Too* good.

Too good a listener. Too good-looking a specimen.
And he seemed to reach parts of her that she'd never
even known existed. Sitting here, close to him, it felt as
if every inch of her body was tuned in to him—as if she'd
been plugged into a socket and been wired. Everything
was amplified. Her breathing…the staccato beats of her
heart…the little pulse in her neck… And between her legs
there was a place that tingled and throbbed… It was crazy.

Daniel's keen eyes noted every minuscule reaction.
She had a face that was as transparent as glass, and she
was too inexperienced to have absorbed the ability to
hide her emotions.

Her pupils were dilated, her full lips half parted.

Did he want to get tangled up with someone who was
inexperienced? It made no sense. In fact, it defied all
common sense.

But they were adults. *She* was an adult. And the way
she had been looking at him for the past hour…

'What did you think of the starter?' she asked quickly,
because her whole body was in danger of going up in
flames.

She wondered whether it hadn't been a gigantic error

of judgement to accept this date with him. It was one thing to opt for daring and reckless and to tell herself that it was okay—because why should she continue in a deep freeze just because she had been hurt once?—but it was quite another when she had no idea what the repercussions might be.

She was vulnerable and he was dangerous.

Did that make him more exciting or less so?

Daniel sat forward, temporarily breaking the spell.

'Excellent,' he said truthfully. 'And I'm expecting the main course to be just as good. The guy obviously has a great deal of skill, even if he can't display any of it because he can't afford good ingredients...'

'It's the same with Alfie, the head of entertainment,' Delilah confided, leaning forward with a soft smile. 'He's hired a young girl to sing. Maria. But she's actually only here so that she can get in a bit of travelling before she goes to university. He plucked her when we docked in the port before Santorini. I don't think he auditioned anyone else. He doesn't have much money to play with, and I think he felt that people wanted more than just to listen to him every night on the piano... She's decorative, but way out of her depth when it comes to doing cabaret...'

'And the other teachers on the cruise? Are they as inspired as you?'

'That compliment sounds a little overblown,' she said drily, and Daniel laughed.

'You're a brilliant artist.'

'Thank you very much. I'm also very cheap, because I've only just graduated. As have a couple of the others. The rest are doing it because they love what they're teaching and don't really need the money because they're retired.'

Their main courses were brought and, as he had predicted, they were as delicious as his starter had been.

Stan, he thought, was *not* going to hit the dole queue. Little did he know it, but Stan—the chef on a budget— was about to hit the jackpot instead. Fat pay cheque and guaranteed work on the liner once it had been updated, modernised and restored to fully operational opulence.

He would find out about the remainder of the crew in his own good time. Right now he was far too absorbed in present company.

'And what are you going to do once you're through with your stint here?' he asked.

Delilah shrugged, suddenly shy of continuing the conversation, suddenly wanting him to stop right there. She was a talented artist who should be finding that the world was her oyster. Not a talented artist who would be returning to the middle of nowhere to bury herself in country life, trying to make ends meet so that the she and her sister could keep the cottage on, walking the sensible path because she had been burnt once.

'Who knows?' she said gaily. 'What about you?'

'I told you... London for me. At least for a month or so. I have a family visit to make...and work to be done... and then Australia...'

'What family visit?' she asked with interest.

London... He would bum around and make some money there, she reckoned, before taking an adventurous path to the other side of the world, seeing lots of exotic and interesting places in between.

'My brother has just found true love and become engaged...'

For a second she frowned at the tone of his voice. 'Why do you sound so cynical?'

'Learning curve...' he said neutrally. 'It's a beautiful thing.'

Theo was about to marry a girl from a similar background and so, Daniel knew, would he. Not because he was in any danger of having his relationship arranged for him, as his brother's had been—against his will—but because he knew what it felt like to get involved with someone who only had your bank balance in mind. A wealthy woman was an independent woman. There would be no danger of opportunism. Which was why it was fine for him to fool around with sexy little starlets and aspiring glamour models—there was no way any of them would make it past the starting post.

He'd loved and been hurt, Delilah thought with a little stab. And he wasn't about to launch into an emotional explanation. The shutters had dropped and for a second she'd been locked out. She'd just finished telling him all about herself and now she realised that she barely knew a thing about *him.*

'Are you close to your brother?' she asked, reluctantly eating the last tasty morsel of steak on her plate. 'What about your parents? Do they worry about you having such a nomadic lifestyle?'

Daniel had the grace to flush. 'Close to my brother? Yes. Always have been. Parents? Just my father. My mother died several years ago.'

He didn't bother with the *nomadic lifestyle* assumption because he had to have the least nomadic lifestyle on the planet. Yes, he travelled—but rarely simply for pleasure. And when he did travel for pleasure it was for very brief windows of time during which he didn't laze around and relax. He stretched himself and his body to the max.

'And what does your brother do?' She tried and failed to imagine what his brother looked like. Surely not nearly as drop-dead gorgeous?

'He's…er…in business…'

Delilah laughed that melodic laugh that made him want to smile.

'Sounds like your family is the exact opposite of my

own,' she said, waving aside the coffee that had been brought to them but tucking in to some of the chocolates. 'Although Sarah's very traditional.'

She leant in to confide in him.

'Right now she's supervising some work that's due to begin on the cottage where we live. Where we've always lived, actually. Our parents were hopeless with all things financial, and since they died we've been struggling just to make ends meet. Thank goodness Sarah is practical. She studied business at college, and if it weren't for the money she makes doing the books for some of the local businesses, well… Of course I send as much money back to her as I can, and it's been brilliant that I've managed to get hold of some work so soon after leaving art college…'

Daniel said nothing. What was there to say? He was here to buy the liner on which she worked in order to send money back to keep her home fires from being snuffed out.

'I'm talking too much about myself…' Delilah reddened. How could she have let herself get so carried away? Why would this gorgeous guy, travelling the world with only his backpack for company, be interested in *her* mundane family history? 'Can I ask you something?'

Daniel fixed watchful eyes on her. She knew nothing about his background, the immense wealth that was attached to the De Angelis name, but he was always wary of the unexpected. He had a feeling that she would not conform to type. He could economise with the truth, but it would be a harder task to lie to her outright.

'You can ask whatever you like,' he drawled. 'Just so long as I reserve the right to say *no comment*.'

Her brows pleated in a frown, because that seemed a peculiar response, but she shrugged it aside and smiled. 'I know we've only just met, but…'

She hesitated on an indrawn breath and for a second Daniel felt a twinge of disappointment.

He'd liked her shyness, the way she blushed and looked away when he stared at her for too long. He'd liked the way she didn't advertise her availability. He was so accustomed to women coming on to him that it had appealed to him that she hadn't. It had nothing to do with money. She thought he was some kind of loser—a drifter bumming around from one destination to the next with no discernible income.

No, she hadn't come on to him even though he knew without a trace of vanity that he was good-looking. Now he wondered if it had all been a ploy she would use to seduce him.

'But…?' he queried, his voice a shade cooler.

'I wondered whether I could paint you.'

Surprise deprived him of an immediate answer, allowing her time to rush into hasty speech.

'I don't mean that I want you to sit for the class,' she elaborated.

Daniel immediately relaxed. 'I'm breathing a sigh of relief even as you say that.'

'And it would have to be out of my working hours, of course. It's a huge imposition, but I think you'd make an amazing…er…subject to try and capture on canvas…'

'I'm flattered,' Daniel murmured, enjoying her obvious discomfort over making the simple request.

'You have very good bone structure,' she informed him quickly.

'I don't think any woman's ever used *that* as a chat-up line with me before…'

'I wasn't chatting you up.'

Hot and flustered, Delilah dived into the remainder of her wine and wondered whether she would be able to walk in a straight line by the time they left the table.

'Please feel free to say no. It was just an idea, but it would entail you having to waste some of the gorgeous sunshine while you pose for me. I know that you only plan on being on this cruise for a few days, and you probably don't want to waste your precious time sitting still…'

'I've always found sitting still difficult,' Daniel agreed. 'But in this instance I'm willing to make an exception.'

She smiled at him with open delight.

'But of course,' he said slowly, watching her face with leisurely thoroughness, 'there is such a thing as quid pro quo. I sit for you and in return you do something for me…'

'If it's to return your dinner invitation in a similar fashion, then there's no chance of that happening.' She laughed.

'I really like the way you laugh,' Daniel said, distracted. 'Your face lights up.'

'I don't think any man has ever used *that* chat-up line with me before…' She parroted what he had said earlier, at which point she realised that she had definitely drunk too much. She *had* to have drunk too much, because this was outrageous flirting—and outrageous flirting was something she had never done…not even with Michael…and it was something she definitely shouldn't be doing now.

Daniel looked at her with lazy intensity. She was as skittish as a cat on a hot tin roof and the urge to take her, to make love to her, ripped through him with astounding force.

He was used to getting what he wanted without putting much effort in. Women went to ridiculous lengths to get his attention. They threw themselves at him with shameful abandon. He couldn't remember the last time he'd had to work at trying to get a woman into bed, but right now, even knowing from the blush on her cheeks that she fancied him, he still hesitated.

He was almost tempted to indulge in that rarely practised art form known as *courting*, but time wasn't on his side and he wasn't even sure if he could subdue the force of his desire in order to take things slowly, one step at a time.

'What do you want me to do?' she pressed on.

The sultry night air… The black ocean all around them… The stars above… She was on a high.

'I'll tell you in a little while.'

He tossed his linen napkin on to his plate and looked around to see Stan, peering at them anxiously from behind the glass windows.

Delilah could only gape as he beckoned the chef across with a practically invisible inclination of his head, but she was thrilled when he proceeded to compliment him on everything they had been served. Thrilled when he quizzed him about his background in cooking, apparently interested in hearing all about where Stan had trained and what had brought him to the liner.

Dnaiel might not divulge a lot about himself, but somehow his restraint was a…

A turn-on…

Compared to him, Michael—who had always been eager to promote himself and had never tired of talking about the exciting life he'd lived, taking photographs in exotic places—seemed immature and empty.

Somehow Daniel didn't glory in his exploits.

He was clearly used to dealing with different people of different cultures and in different situations, but his anecdotes weren't laced with self-praise. It was odd that she was only now fully recognising that trait in Michael, seeing him for what he really was, and it felt good—like an achievement.

'Are you *sure* you can afford this?' she whispered, when Stan had eventually cleared the table and left, visibly puffed up by Daniel's effusive praise.

'Have you *never* been wined and dined before?' He laughed, standing up and waiting for her to get to her feet.

'Do fast food restaurants count?'

He laughed, reached for her hand and tucked it into the crook of his elbow.

Delilah's state of heightened excitement escalated a couple of notches. She could feel the ripple of sinew and muscle in his forearm and the outside lights danced over his face, throwing it into wildly exotic angles.

They strolled towards the railings and peered down at the endless ocean.

This had been a bloody good idea, Daniel thought, with a feeling of wellbeing. *Inspired*, in fact. He hadn't banked on any sort of sexual entanglement, but now that the possibility had surfaced he certainly wasn't going to run away from it.

But first things first…

He turned round so that he was leaning against the railing, with his back to the ocean, and pulled her gently towards him. He registered an initial resistance before she yielded, although her body remained stiff.

'Relax,' he urged, with a smile in his voice.

'You should know something,' Delilah said in a rush. 'I've just come out of a relationship and it didn't end very well. So I'm not… I'm not looking for anything… I shouldn't be doing this at all…'

'You're not doing anything.'

'I'm here…on a date…with *you*…'

'What did he do?'

'He strung me along,' she said painfully.

'That,' said Daniel, 'is something I would never do. I've always made it a policy to lay my cards on the table, and when it comes to women I don't string them along. If you're not looking for a relationship, trust me—neither am I. This is a harmless attraction.'

He was right—*so why didn't it feel that way?* she wondered.

'Harmless?'

'No strings attached,' he soothed. 'And without strings attached there's no emotional involvement. It's only when emotions are in the mix that complications begin. I've been there, done that, and I'm a convert to the uncomplicated arrangement…'

He made it sound so easy, and his conviction liberated her from her misgivings. Who cared whether it was a good idea or a bad idea? She could spend all night analysing the rights and wrongs and then he'd be gone, and she knew that she would regret not having had the courage to take what he was offering.

And wasn't he just echoing what she had been thinking anyway? He'd been upfront and honest with her. He was passing through and she was here, in a bubble, with no one looking over her shoulder.

She tentatively wrapped her arms around him, glad that it was deserted on this section of the deck.

'I'm only here for a few days, Delilah…'

'I know that.'

'You'll only be able to paint me for those few days.'

'I know that, too.'

'And here's where I get to the thing I want from you in return for sitting for you…'

'Yes?' Her voice was a breathy whisper.

'You. I want *you*, Delilah…'

There was just no way that bluntly spoken statement could be invested with anything romantic at all, and yet…

It went to her head with like an injection of adrenaline directly into her bloodstream.

'That's the trade?' she framed in a shaky voice.

'Never let it be said that I don't know how to strike a deal while the iron's hot…'

He dipped his head and his lips met hers in an unhurried, all-consuming kiss. His tongue meshed with hers and it was the most erotic experience she had ever had. Even though his hands remained clasping the rail on either side of him...even though it was only that long, lazy kiss that was doing the damage.

Delilah stroked the side of his lean, beautiful face and heard herself say, *'Okay...'*

CHAPTER FOUR

DELILAH HAD NO idea how she managed to focus at all the following day. Her routine had been disrupted by the liner putting in to dock at Olympia.

Before Daniel had boarded the cruise ship she had diligently looked at the itinerary and made copious notes about all the exciting places of cultural interest they would be visiting. Part of her responsibilities covered introducing interested passengers to new experiences. Bearing in mind she had not travelled at all, and that every single sight would be as fresh to her as to them, she had worked doubly hard to make sure that she had all the relevant facts and figures at her disposal.

Olympia...site of the Olympic Games in classical times...held every four years from the eighth century BC to the fourth century AD...all in honour of the great god Zeus...

She had done all her homework on the Greek gods and Greek mythology. She could have passed an exam.

But as it was, the only thing filling her head as they disembarked was the guy who had allowed her to scuttle back to her cabin the evening before alone, with just a chaste kiss on her cheek as a reminder of his lips.

'You need to think about my proposal...' he had

drawled in his dark, sexy voice, while his eyes had remained fastened to her face, draining her of all her willpower. 'I need to know that we're going to be on the same page…'

He didn't do long-term. He didn't do commitment. He wasn't looking for a relationship. He was looking for a bit of fun and he wanted his fun to be with *her*…

The thought of the *having fun and clearing off* situation he was proposing should have left her stricken with terror after Michael, but she had squared away her misgivings. Daniel had been right when he'd said that no one could get hurt when emotions weren't involved—that was true.

Desire, as she was finding out fast, was a stand-alone emotion. That had come as a revelation to someone who had always thought of love and desire in the same breath. She wanted him, he wanted her, and there was something so wonderfully clean and clear-cut about that. It was nothing like the muddle of hopes and dreams and forward-planning she had so foolishly felt with Michael.

Right here and right now this was liberating.

Now, in the bright, burning sun, Daniel was part of the group she had opted to show around the ancient ruins. How was she supposed to deliver her spiel when she could feel his eyes following her every move? Could see him listening to every word she said with his head tilted?

He was the very picture of keen amateur interest—even though, unlike some of the others, he had not brought his sketchpad with him. Notwithstanding that, she knew what was running through his head. She could just *tell* whenever their eyes met and his gaze lingered on her.

She and Daniel would share a cabin bed for a few days and then he would disappear for ever.

He hadn't even tried to package up the deal in attractive wrapping paper.

He had told it like it was—told her to expect nothing more.

He was a textbook example of just the sort of guy she should be avoiding. No promise of anything long-term. No mention of love.

But she had underestimated the force of her own body and the way it was capable of responding to something that made no sense.

She would return to the Cotswolds, where she could count eligible guys on the fingers of one hand, and she would settle down with someone more suitable. Of course she would. There would be all the time in the world for her to invest her love in Mr Right. But how would she feel if she did that and always thought about the Mr Wrong she had decided to avoid? The Mr Wrong who would be just the sort of replacement therapy she was in need of?

The group lunched at a charming little café close to the site they had been exploring and later, with the sun still burning down, late in the afternoon, made their way back to the liner.

'I'm disappointed you didn't take your sketchpad with you.' She turned to Daniel once they were back on the liner, joining all the others also making their way back on and then dispersing into various groups, or going to one of the bars to relax before the evening meal.

It had been a hot, tiring day, but he still managed to look amazing. In a plain white tee shirt, some khaki shorts, loafers and sunglasses, he looked like one of the Greek statues come to beautiful life.

'I thought about it, but then concluded that I would have much more fun watching you.'

He couldn't credit the level of his excitement at the prospect of sleeping with her. The detailed report he had been putting together, which would highlight all the reasons why the Ockley couple would find themselves without an option when it came to selling to him, had taken a back seat.

For the first time in living memory work wasn't uppermost in his mind.

Delilah, captivated by the slow-burning desire she could see in the depths of his green eyes, was finding it hard to tear her gaze away.

'I… I should go and change… Have a look at some of the sketches my class have done…'

'Boring.'

'I beg your pardon?'

'Give me the sketches and I'll mark them out of ten. Even without the benefit of a degree in art I could tell you that Miranda and Lee need to pay more attention in perspective class…'

Her lips twitched and she struggled not to laugh. 'Maybe I could meet you…later…?'

Daniel leant against the wall, drawing her into an intimate circle that enclosed just the two of them, and Delilah looked shiftily around her.

'We're not breaking any laws,' he said, with an edge of impatience.

'Yes, I know. But…'

'But what? So *what* if some of the people in your class think that we're having a fling? What do you think they're going to do? Report you to the principal?'

'It's not that,' she said sharply. 'The fact is that I'll be staying on after you leave this liner, and I don't want to have people whispering about me behind my back.'

Daniel raked his fingers through his hair and shook his head. 'Why do you care what people think?'

'Don't you?'

'Of course not. No, I tell a lie. I care about what my father and my brother think of me, but beyond that why should I?' Their eyes met, and when she dipped her head to look away he tilted it back so that she was looking at him, his finger gently on her chin. 'Okay,' he conceded, 'why don't you tell me where you are and I'll come to you under cover of darkness…like a thief in the night…'

'Tell you where I am…?' Her mouth went dry at the thought of that, in a mixture of excitement and nervousness.

'Your cabin?' he said drily. 'Unless you're bunking down in a sleeping bag out on the deck?'

'I…'

'Are you having second thoughts?' *Because,* he might have added, *there's a limit to the amount of chasing I intend to do.* He'd never had to chase. Frankly, an attack of nerves—the whole three steps forward, two steps back thing—was something he could do without.

But he wasn't sure whether his rampant libido was capable of walking away.

'No, I'm not having second thoughts.' Delilah had made up her mind and she wasn't going to backtrack.

He smiled and found himself relaxing, which only made him realise that he'd tensed up at the thought of her changing her mind.

'But…' She sighed.

'You're nervous?' he intuited, and she looked at him sheepishly. 'You're not the kind of girl who accepts propositions from strange men you meet on cruise liners…? And especially not when you're supposedly recovering from a broken heart…'

'I was in love with the idea of *being* in love,' she said slowly. 'I wanted excitement and adventure, and when Michael came along it felt like I'd found that…'

'Rule number one,' Daniel drawled, 'is that you don't talk about your ex when you're with me. He's history— and good riddance from the sound of it.'

'Is that the approach you took when *your* heart was broken?' she asked tentatively.

'Another rule—we don't talk about my exes either. But, just for your information, my heart wasn't broken. The bottom line is that whatever doesn't kill you makes you stronger.'

'You're so…so *confident*…' Delilah was frankly in awe of his pragmatic approach.

Daniel shrugged coolly. 'You don't get anywhere by dithering or dwelling on past errors of judgement. You learn and you move on.'

'When you say stuff like that it shows me how much I don't know about you… I mean, I don't know anything other than you're travelling and your next stop is London before you head off to the other side of the world…'

But then she'd thought she'd known Michael because he had talked a lot about himself, and she hadn't at all, had she?

'What else do you want to know? And do you want to have this long and meaningful conversation over there?' He nodded to the outer deck and to a clump of deckchairs, all of which were empty.

Did she want more facts about him? Delilah felt that she knew *the essence* of the man, and knew that she had been drawn to him not just because of the way he looked but because he was incredibly funny, incredibly intelligent and so thoughtful and considerate in the way he had listened to her without interruption. The way he was interested in everything she had to say.

'I have a very small cabin,' she said shyly. 'All of the crew do…'

'Then come to me,' Daniel murmured. 'I can't say it's a palatial suite, but there's a double bed… My feet have a tendency to hang over the edge, but they probably don't cater for men as big as me… And don't be nervous. Who says I'm accustomed to picking up strange girls I meet on cruise liners...?'

'Are you telling me that *you're* nervous?'

'I can say with my hand on my heart that I have never been nervous when it comes to sex...'

'You're so...so...'

'I know what you're going to say. You're going to tell me that I'm so *arrogant*—I prefer the *confident* description.'

Delilah laughed, and just like that he kissed her. And this time his kiss wasn't lingering and explorative. This time it was hungry and demanding.

He manoeuvred her so that they had stepped outside onto the deck and his mouth never left hers.

She'd been kissed before, but never like this, and she'd never felt like this before either. His hunger matched hers and she whimpered and coiled her fingers into his hair, pulling him into her and then arching her head back so that he could kiss her neck, the side of her face, the tender spot by her jawline.

Her whole body was on fire, and right here, right now, she couldn't have cared less who saw her.

She lost the ability to think, and along with her ability to think, she also lost her inhibitions. She'd taken her time with Michael, wanting to make sure that they had something really lasting and special before she slept with him, and it was puzzling that she just wanted to fly into bed with Daniel even though there was nothing between them but lust.

She couldn't get enough of him, of his mouth on her mouth, on her bare skin, setting her aflame. She wanted to touch. Was *desperate* to touch. Not just his beautiful face but all of him. And she was shocked by the need pouring through her in a tidal wave that eclipsed every preconceived notion she had ever had about the nature of relationships.

When he pulled away she actually moaned—a soft little broken moan—before reluctantly opening her eyes and staring right up at him.

'You're beautiful,' Daniel told her roughly, and Delilah laughed shakily.

'I bet you say that to all the women you chase…'

'I don't chase women.'

'Because they chase *you*?'

Daniel smiled slowly, his silence telling her that she had hit the nail on the head. He was a man who didn't have to run after women. He was a guy who didn't have to try.

He was a guy who probably needed someone who played hard to get—but she wasn't good at playing games, and besides this wasn't a normal relationship…was it?

This wasn't one of those relationships that was built to last from its foundations up. There wasn't going to be a slow burn, or a gradual process of discovering one another and really getting to know one another. That had been *her* learning curve, and what a fool she'd been.

This wasn't what she had spent her formative years expecting.

This was a blast of the unexpected, powering through her and obliterating all the signposts she had always taken for granted when it came to relationships.

'And you wonder why I'm nervous…' she sighed on a heartfelt whisper.

If he knew that she had never slept with a man before then he would run a mile. Men who were in danger of being knocked down by the stampede of women eager to climb into bed with him would have no concept of an inexperienced woman, and they wouldn't have any patience with one.

She didn't want him to run a mile.

Just acknowledging that shocked her, but she was honest enough not to flinch from the truth.

This was pure lust, and sleeping with him felt necessary and inevitable.

'Don't be,' he told her softly. 'Just because women chase me it doesn't mean that I make comparisons... Now, I'm going to go and have a much needed shower, and my cabin number is...'

He whispered it into her ear and she shivered.

Just the fact that they were pre-planning this sent a delicious frisson rippling through her.

She almost didn't want him to leave, but she was hot and sticky as well.

She watched him disappear back into the body of the liner and her heart was thudding so hard in her chest that she wanted to swoon like a Victorian maiden.

Delilah had no idea what a man who looked like Daniel saw in her, but she made sure to do her utmost to look her very best before she joined him in his cabin.

He liked her hair, so she left it loose and blow-dried it into glossy waves. She wore no make-up aside from some mascara and a little lip gloss, and thankfully the sun had turned her skin a pale biscuit-brown. As for clothes...

Instead of her usual long skirts she wore one of the only two pairs of trousers she had brought with her. Having anticipated a shorter stay on the liner, she'd found her scant supply of clothes had had to stretch for far longer than she'd bargained for, but these tan trousers hadn't yet seen the light of day and they looked okay, twinned with a cropped vest that showed off her slender arms and just a sliver of tanned belly.

When she stood back from the mirror she realised that

the artist had gone—at least for the night. She briefly wondered whether he might have preferred her artist image, but swatted that temporary misgiving away.

Nerves took hold of her as she made her convoluted way to his cabin. Many of the rooms were empty, waiting for the occasional new passenger who might want to hop on board—not that there had been very many of those, despite the brilliant deals advertised. And she knew, as she wound her way to his section of the ship, that he was in one of the best cabins—probably an upgrade.

Gerry and Christine were generous to a fault, and most of the passengers had been offered upgrades at very little extra cost.

She could barely breathe as she tentatively knocked on the door, pushing it open as he told her to enter.

Outside, darkness had abruptly fallen, another starry, moonlit night, and through the portholes of his cabin she could see the stars twinkling in the sky and the whisper of a crescent moon illuminating the sea with a ghostly radiance.

He'd changed into cream trousers, low slung on his lean hips, and a cream tee shirt, and he was barefoot.

Delilah discovered that she was finding it hard to catch her breath and the Victorian maiden swoony feeling was beginning to get hold of her again.

She inhaled deeply and made a conscious effort not to twist her hands together in a giveaway gesture of nervousness.

God, he was beautiful. That streaky dirty blond hair was slightly too long but somehow emphasised the sharp contours of his face, adding depth to the fabulous green eyes and accentuating the bronzed skin tone that spoke of some exotic heritage in his gene pool. No wonder he needed to carry a large stick with him at all times to fight the women off.

'Are you going to tear yourself away from the door any time soon?' Daniel strolled towards her and gently propelled her into the cabin and closed the door behind her.

He'd taken one very long, very cold shower, and even that hadn't been able to stanch the unfamiliar excitement of anticipation. Always in control, he had now surrendered to the novelty of *not* being in control. The unread email messages on his computer remained unread. His mobile phone was switched off so that he wouldn't be interrupted by someone wanting something from him. His attraction to her had happened so fast and hit him so hard that he could only blame the fact that he was far removed from his comfort zone of wealth and luxury.

'You've ordered room service?' Delilah finally managed to croak as she stared down at the table, which had been set for two.

'Stan again rose to the occasion. Of course I could have just ordered something from the room service menu. but...' He shrugged, unable to tear his eyes away from her.

She'd always hidden the glorious figure he'd glimpsed beneath her baggy clothes. Even earlier, when they had visited the site of the ruins, she had worn a long skirt and flip-flops and yet another loose, floaty top. 'It's the best thing if you want to keep cool,' she had told him when he had asked her whether she wasn't scared of tripping over her skirt and doing untold damage as they clambered around.

She wasn't wearing camouflage gear now.

Caramel skin...those strangely captivating eyes... long russet hair tamed into sexy waves...so, so...long. Way too long to be fashionable, but incredibly, *incredibly* spectacular...

And she wasn't wearing a bra. He could see the firm roundness of her small breasts pushing against the thin, tight vest. Could practically see the circular outline of her nipples...

Feeling as hot and bothered as a horny teenager on his first date, he spun away and reached for the bottle of champagne which was chilling in an ice bucket.

'And—and bubbly,' she stammered, watching him expertly open the bottle. 'You didn't have to...to go to all this trouble...' She fiddled with the thin gold chain she wore round her neck—a birthday present from her parents a million years ago.

'Allow a man to be indulgent...' He held out a champagne flute to her, but before she could drink he curved his hand over her satin-smooth cheek and watched her for a few seconds without saying anything.

'You're staring...' Delilah breathed, but the feel of his hand on her was strangely calming.

'You do that to me,' Daniel husked. 'You make me want to stare.'

He'd always gone for the obvious in women—much to his brother's perpetual amusement. Plenty of time to settle for the prissy, classy clothes of the wealthy, well-bred woman of means he would eventually marry. Prissy and classy wasn't fun, and in the meanwhile he intended to have a fun-filled diet.

This woman couldn't have been more restrained in her choice of clothing, but the effect on him was dramatic.

Delilah sipped the champagne and watched him warily over the rim of her glass. Wanting to be here didn't mean that she had the courage to match her desire.

'I thought we'd have something light to eat.' Daniel broke the bubble of heightened silence and pulled out a chair for her. 'Unless you've already grabbed something? No? Thought not...'

She was still nervous. That in itself was a bad sign, because it meant that she wasn't exactly into transitory

sex—which was what he wanted—despite what she'd
said. But he had given her his speech and that had been
sufficient to ease his conscience.

Both adults and due warning. Job done.

Which nevertheless still left the fact that she was nervous, and he found that he was willing to go against the
grain, willing to move at her pace within reason. In a peculiar way, he was willing to court her...

'Stan has prepared salad stuff...crayfish and lobster...
two things that go perfectly with champagne...'

Delilah sat. Her eyes were fairly popping. What had
she expected? Not this. Maybe she'd thought that he
would greet her half naked at the door, Tarzan-style, before slinging her over his shoulder and heaving her off
to his bed. There was, after all, something raw and elemental about him.

He might not be on the lookout for any kind of relationship, but he was putting a lot of effort in, and she knew
instinctively that he was taking things slowly because he
sensed that she was nervous.

And that warmed her, because it said so much about
him.

'He'll miss you when you go,' she said lightly, helping herself to salad, the little pulse in her neck fluttering
with awareness as he sat down opposite her.

His cabin was at least five times the size of hers. It
was comfortable, but not luxurious, and even with her
untrained eyes she could see the hallmarks of Gerry and
Christine's straitened financial circumstances. The room
needed a good overhaul.

Through the doorway she could glimpse the bed, and
she quickly averted her eyes, determined not to become
a victim of stage fright.

'You've spoiled him by letting him cook whatever he
wants, no expense spared...'

'Are you going to deliver another sermon on my extravagance?'

Delilah blushed. 'No, I'm not. You're not careful, and that's nice. My sister and I have spent so long just trying to make ends meet that I've become accustomed to being careful all the time when it comes to money.'

'You spend a lot of time talking about your sister...'

Excellent salad, he mentally noted. Another point in Stan's favour—and his sous chef as well. Two jobs safe. And from what he'd seen some of the rest of the crew were diligent and efficient and, having spoken to them, he'd seen they knew the ropes.

'She brought me up,' Delilah said simply.

'And where were your parents when this sisterly bringing up was taking place?'

He was fascinated by the guileless transparency of her face. She smiled, dipped her eyes, blushed, fiddled with her champagne flute... Her broken heart hadn't been able to kill off her naturally warm, shy disposition.

Was it unreasonable to expect his next woman to have those appealing traits?

Then he remembered that this woman knew nothing about him. She wasn't out to impress him. He felt that had she known just how wealthy, how powerful, how influential he was, she would probably be a lot more forward in trying to grab his attention and hold it.

'Like I said, our parents were so wrapped up in one another that they didn't have a lot of time for us. I mean, they were fabulous parents, and very, very loving in their own scatty way, but they were unconventional. They really didn't see the point of school.' Delilah smiled. 'Despite the fact that they both went to art college. They had a lot of faith in the University of Life.'

'But they were fun?' Daniel guessed.

'Gosh—absolutely. On the one hand it was embarrassing when I was a kid, because of the way they dressed, but on the other hand they weren't all buttoned up like the rest of the parents…and that was kind of great…'

Daniel pushed back his chair and linked his fingers behind his head.

Every scrap of his attention was focused on her and Delilah could feel herself wanting to open up, like a bud blossoming under the warmth of sudden sunshine.

'And you're looking for the same kind of overpowering love…? You thought you'd found it, and it turned out that you hadn't, but that hasn't really put you off, has it?'

'Security, stability…those are the things that are important in a relationship…'

'Because you fell for the wrong guy? Because your sister told you so?'

'No! Maybe… Well, not in so many words…'

'But deep down you're not falling for it. That's why you're here with me. Deep down you don't see why you shouldn't have the fireworks and the explosions…which is what your parents had…'

'You don't understand. They really were *so* involved in one another. There'd be days when Mum would just forget to shop for food, and Sarah was always the one who shouldered the responsibility for bringing a bit of normality into the house… Sometimes, they would get one of their friends to babysit us for a week or so, while they went on a hunting mission for crystals or artefacts, and at least once a year they blew what little money they'd managed to make on a trip to India…you know, to bring stuff over for the shop…'

Neptune and Moon, Daniel thought wryly. The names said it all.

But the sisters had seen the situation through different eyes. It was obvious that sister number one was a practical bore, who had drilled into sister number two the importance of being earnest and then really hammered it home when Delilah had strayed off the tracks...

And then quite suddenly he thought about his own situation.

Theo, he knew, had been affected by the relationship of their parents and by their mother's death in ways that he, Daniel, perhaps hadn't. They'd both been devastated, had both witnessed their father's slow, inexorable decline—the way the energy had been sapped out of him, the way he had withdrawn from active life, unable or unwilling to cope after the rock on whom he had depended had been taken from him.

That had toughened Theo and shown him a road he would make sure to avoid—the road that led to any sort of emotional commitment.

Daniel couldn't help grinning at the way *that* particular situation had eventually played out, considering his brother was now loved up, locked down and proud of it.

He, Daniel, had found solace in the wake of their mother's death and the sudden upheaval in their household in another way. He had buried his emotions so deeply after Kelly Close that he doubted he would ever be able to find them again. That suited him.

Taken aback by that rare bout of introspection, he closed his hand over Delilah's and slanted her a devastating smile.

'Word to the wise?' he said wryly. 'Your sister's probably got the hang of it by steering you clear of all those fairytale stories of Prince Charmings sweeping lonesome Cinderellas off their feet so that they can live happily ever after in that mythical place known as cloud nine... Have fun and then marry the guy who makes sense.'

Was that his way of reiterating his warning? Of telling her that she had to look elsewhere for romance? She'd already got that message, and there was no way she would be idiotic enough to look for it with someone like *him*. Oh, no.

But, yes, she *did* believe in all that burning fireworks and explosions stuff—even if her sister didn't… It might be called lust, and not love, but she still wanted it and he was right—that was why she was here with him now.

Surprised by just how much she had confided in him, and made uneasy by her lack of restraint, she took a deep breath and caught his eyes.

'I didn't come here to talk,' she murmured huskily.

This, Daniel thought, was more like it. This was the kind of language he understood.

He stood up, pulled her to her feet and slowly drew her against him. 'I like the outfit, by the way…'

He kissed her long and slow, until her whole body was melting. His tongue, meshing lazily with hers, was doing wonderful things, making her want to press herself against him so that there wasn't an inch of space between their bodies. He curved his hand over her bottom and then loosely slipped it underneath the waistband of her trousers, just a few delicate fingers running against her skin.

'And I'm going to like it even more when you're out of it and it's lying on the ground…'

CHAPTER FIVE

SHE FALTERED AS he led her towards the bed she had glimpsed through the door that separated the small sitting area from the sleeping area.

Her mouth went dry and she hesitated—watched, fascinated by his complete lack of inhibition, as he began to undress.

He'd done this lots of times. There was certainty in the way he pulled the tee shirt over his head, exposing his hard, muscled torso, and self-confidence in the way he kept his eyes on her, a half smile playing on his mouth. He was a man who, as he had told her, had never been nervous when it came to sex.

This was his playing ground and he was the uncontested master of it.

Her eyes followed his hand as it reached for the zipper of his trousers and rested there for a few seconds.

'This,' he drawled, strolling towards her, 'is beginning to feel a little one-sided...'

Her courage disappearing faster than water draining down a plughole, Delilah gulped.

'Shall we get into bed?' she whispered, by which she meant under the covers, where she could wriggle out of her clothes in as inconspicuous a manner as possible.

Daniel raised his eyebrows and placed both hands on her shoulders.

They'd spent so much time talking—way more than

he had ever spent talking with any woman, and certainly way more than he had ever spent with any woman before sex. In fact, when he thought about it, conversation rarely served as an appetiser before the main course. Usually by the time he and whatever hot date he happened to be with hit the bedroom clothes would have been off and action would be about to happen—no exchange of words needed.

Hot, hard and urgent.

When, he wondered, were her nerves going to be banished? He'd had an erection from the second she'd walked into the cabin and he was in danger of having to have a very cold shower if he was to get into anything resembling a comfortable state.

'I like my women to be naked *before* we get into bed,' he said gently. 'Jumping into the sack with someone who's fully clothed, right down to her shoes, somehow takes the edge off the whole business... In other words it's a mood-killer...'

He slipped his hands under her tee shirt and Delilah tensed.

'I don't like games when it comes to sex,' he told her, his voice cooling by the second, because her body was as rigid as a plank of wood. 'I have no time for any woman who thinks that she can tease me and then pull away...'

'That's not what I'm doing.'

'Then would you care to explain why you've suddenly turned into a statue?'

Delilah dropped her head and was grateful for her long, loose hair, because it shielded her face from his piercing eyes.

'I've never done this before...' She reluctantly looked up at him with clear eyes and Daniel frowned.

'When you say that you've *never* done this before...'

'You're my first,' she told him bluntly, waiting for him to recoil in horror—but he didn't. Although she had no idea what he was thinking, because when their eyes tangled again she could see that the shutters had dropped.

'You're telling me that you're a virgin?'

'It's not *that* unusual,' she flared defiantly.

'But you were involved with someone…'

'I… We…we were taking it slowly. Look, I don't want to talk about this—'

'Too bad. You're a virgin, Delilah.' He raked frustrated fingers through his hair. 'I don't do virgins.'

'You don't *do* a lot of stuff, do you?' She found that she couldn't bear the thought of him walking away from her—not after she had convinced herself that this was the right thing to do, the thing she wanted and needed to do. 'Why don't you just come right out and say it? You're just not attracted to me now!'

She made to turn away but his grip was holding her in place. He was holding her very gently, applying almost no pressure, but he was strong. *Very* strong.

'Touch me and you'll see that for the nonsense it is,' he told her roughly.

She fixed her eyes on his hard chest—his small, flat brown nipples, the dark gold hair spiralling down to where he had begun unbuttoning his trousers before stopping.

Heat poured through her, settling damply between her legs.

Her eyes flared and, feeling her very slight tremble, Daniel knew that what he should do right now was gently let her go. Perhaps give her a rousing pep talk on waiting for the right guy to come along, with whom she could share the precious gift of her virginity.

It wasn't in his brief to take it—even if it had been offered to him. Virginity equalled vulnerability, and that equalled all sorts of unknown complications.

He had laid out the ground rules but she was a novice

to the game, so how was she supposed to know where he was coming from? She already thought him to be someone he wasn't. The situation was complicated enough as it stood, without her finding that she had got in over her head because of the sex.

He'd never had a problem jettisoning any of the women he had dated in the past. They had all been experienced, had all known the score. If some of them had been disappointed that they hadn't been able to convert him, then tough. All was fair in love and war.

His gut instinct told him that it would be different with Delilah if she turned sex into something it wasn't and would never be.

'You're not saying anything,' she muttered. 'I suppose you're horrified…'

Tears of humiliation sprang to her eyes and she gulped them back. She only had herself to blame. She had punched above her weight and this was where it had got her. It was to be expected. Any man who looked like a Greek god with a wealth of sexual experience behind him…any man who kicked off his affairs by telling the woman involved that he wasn't in it for the long term… was a man who would have no time for virgins.

'Not horrified…' Daniel corrected. 'Flattered. Turned on. Why would I be horrified?'

The more he thought about it, the more turned on he became. Her first… He physically ached to touch her, to show her just how fantastic sex could be… Even though the downside still continued to niggle away at the back of his mind…

He guided her hand to his bulging erection and grinned with a ridiculous surge of satisfaction as her eyes widened and her breathing hitched.

He was a big boy—a *very* big boy—and she was touching the evidence of just how turned on he was.

'But…' His voice was unsteady as he ploughed on with a conversation he knew he had to have. He'd had it before, but this time he had to make sure that she understood and accepted where he was coming from.

'But…?' Delilah whispered.

'You have no idea what you're doing to me right now,' he told her shakily.

He raked his fingers through his hair and shook his head, as though he might be able to clear it and regain some control over the situation. He'd never felt so out of control in his life before. It was as if he'd suddenly found himself stranded on foreign soil, with no landmarks to show him the direction he needed to take.

'Why me?' he asked flatly.

Delilah's breath hitched. 'If it's going to be a question-and-answer session about the fact that I didn't sleep with Michael, then I get the picture. I'm going to go now, and we can both pretend that this never happened. I told you I don't want to talk about it and I don't.'

She turned away. She'd had her reasons for keeping Michael at bay, even though she had supposedly been head over heels in love with him and planning their future, but she couldn't remember what they were now. Daniel's blunt incredulity made her decision to hold off sleeping with her ex feel freakish.

Daniel didn't answer. Instead he propelled her towards the bed and urged her down. Like a rag doll, she flopped onto it before sitting upright and drawing her knees to her chin, wrapping her arms around herself.

'It's not the most difficult question in the world to answer, Delilah.'

The dark, velvety tones of his voice washed over her soothingly, but she was still as tense as a bowstring and she huddled into herself as he, too, sat on the bed, though not within touching distance of her.

'I just don't see what that has to do with anything,' she told him mutinously.

'I'm not your Prince Charming,' Daniel said, without bothering to mince his words. Tough love. Or something like that. At any rate the laying of cards on the table, so that all misunderstandings could be avoided.

He was giving her a choice, and he couldn't be fairer than that, could he?

The mere fact that he was giving her a choice at all, when really he should be extricating himself from a possibly awkward situation in the making, was a little unnerving, but he fought down that unwelcome thought.

'Why would you think that you are?' Understanding dawned. 'Because I've chosen to sleep with you?' she said slowly. 'And you're so big-headed that you think the only reason I would do that is because I'm the sort of idiot who wants her fairytale ending to be with you...'

She swung her legs over the side of the bed before he could reach out to stop her and stood, shaking, arms tightly folded, staring at him and glaring.

'Of all the conceited, smug and, yes, *arrogant* men in the world, you just about have to take the biscuit!'

Taken aback by her anger, Daniel likewise vaulted upright, and they stood facing one another with the width of the bed separating them.

'What's a man supposed to think?' he demanded gruffly.

'Do you want to know *why* I chose to sleep with you?'

'You mean aside from the sizzling, irresistible attraction to me that you're powerless to fight...? The sort of sizzling, irresistible attraction you never felt for your loser ex...?'

Delilah blinked, because just like that the atmosphere between them had shifted.

Her whole body tightened and tensed, hyper-aware of

him, of his glorious masculine beauty, as he stood there, looking steadily at her, his thumbs hooked into the waist-band of the trousers he hadn't got around to removing.

Antennae on red-hot alert, Daniel could almost feel something physical in the change in the air. Her eyes were still angry and accusing, but she was clutching her-self just a little bit tighter, and her body was just a little bit more rigid—as though she had to use every ounce of willpower not to shatter into a thousand pieces.

'Did it never occur to you that you might be my ad-venture? The sort of adventure I need right now...at this point in time?' she flung at him.

He frowned. 'Explain.'

'Why should I? This was a big mistake...'

'Physical attraction is never a big mistake,' he said, in complete contradiction to what he had been think-ing earlier.

Covering the small cabin in a couple of strides, he was looming over her before she had time to take evasive ac-tion. Not that her legs felt as though they could do any such thing. In fact, her legs were being very uncoópera-tive at the moment, seemingly nailed to the floor, unable to move an inch, never mind take evasive action.

'Tell me what you meant when you said that I was your adventure.'

Delilah's heart was beating so fast and so hard that she could scarcely catch her breath, and she inhaled deeply in an attempt to establish some calm inside. Everywhere she looked her eyes ran slap-bang into something that set her nervous system hurtling towards meltdown.

Stare straight ahead and her vision was filled with the sight of his steel-hard, bronzed torso... Raise her eyes and she met his green, sexy ones... Look past him and what did she see? The bed. At which point the images that cluttered her head were enough to make her breathing go funny all over again.

'I went through something I thought was right, but it was only because I wanted it so badly to *be* right,' she whispered.

She found the safest point in the cabin and stared at it—it happened to be her feet. Not for long, though, because he raised her head so that she couldn't avoid looking at him.

'I felt like I'd spent my youth worrying about keeping the gallery afloat and worrying about Sarah working just to stand still. Michael was like a blast of fresh air, and it felt like he brought all sorts of exciting possibilities to my life. Maybe that was what I fell in love with. Maybe I was just desperate for a future that wasn't so...*predictable*. I'm only twenty-one, for heaven's sake! But it didn't work out, and I came here just to get away from...from everything. It was supposed to be just for a couple of weeks, but my art course proved so popular that I couldn't resist staying on—because when I return to the Cotswolds all I'm going to be doing is helping my sister in a last-ditch attempt to get the shop going, so that we have sufficient income to live on without having to worry about money all the time.'

Daniel had never had to worry about money. He and Theo had been born into privilege. Sure, his father had sent them both on their way to make their fortune, but they hadn't left the nest empty-handed. He had no doubt that both he and his brother would have succeeded whatever their backgrounds, because they both had the same drive, the same high-octane ambition that had fuelled their father and propelled him into making his fortune, but the fact remained that they had been born with silver spoons in their mouths.

Golden spoons, if he were to be perfectly honest.

He'd never delved into the details of any of his girl-friends' backgrounds, preferring to live in an uncluttered present which was mostly about sex, and of course the expensive fripperies that accompanied his very brief liaisons. Hearing about the sort of life Delilah was returning to brought into sharp relief the great big space between them.

It wasn't just the fact that she was green for her years, an innocent compared to his vastly more experienced self, but she was also, from the sound of it, broke.

Their worlds were so completely different that he might have been looking down at someone from another planet.

Under normal circumstances their paths would never have crossed, and yet now that they *had* crossed something about her had got to him and wasn't letting him go—wasn't allowing the voice of logic and reason to have a say.

'Have you ever been to the Cotswolds, Daniel?'

'I can't say that the countryside has ever done much for me...' he murmured.

'It's very beautiful. But very quiet. In winter, people hibernate. I love it there, but it's so quiet. It's a place where adventure would never happen to someone of my age.'

'You can't be the only young person there...'

'You'd be surprised how many of them move down to London to see a bit of the bright city lights before they return to the country to have kids and raise families.' She sighed. 'I wouldn't be able to do that because I have a duty to help Sarah, and that's something I want to do anyway, but...'

'But here you are, with one bad experience behind you—although from the sounds of it you don't need any sticking plaster—and here *I* am. And before you return to fulfil your sisterly obligations you don't see why you can't sleep with me on the rebound—have yourself a little fun and excitement before you take up your responsibilities with your sister... *I'm* your bright city lights before you return to the country...'

Did he like that? Daniel wasn't sure.

'That's more or less it.' She squashed the hint of defiance trying to creep into her voice. 'So if you think that I'm in any danger of falling for you, turning you into my Prince Charming, then you're way off track. That's not it at all. I've decided to...to... That you could be the one to...'

'To teach you the many and varying ways of enjoying love...?'

Delilah's mouth tightened, but her heart flipped at the slow smile playing on his lips.

The man was utterly incorrigible—and she had to admit, grudgingly, that that was just part and parcel of his overwhelming appeal.

'I may not be experienced,' she muttered, 'but that doesn't mean I don't have my head well and truly screwed on.'

'By which you mean...?'

Without her even realising he had taken her hand and led her back to the bed, and Delilah sank back against the pillows, not knowing whether she was relieved that this adventure was going to happen or terrified that this adventure was going to happen.

She was still fully clothed, her feet dangling off the bed, and before he joined her he knelt and removed her sandals, easing them off her feet in a gesture that was curiously delicate and erotic at the same time.

How odd that it was just the sort of thing a real-life Prince Charming might have done...

'...that I'm not the sort of catch you have in mind for yourself...?'

Daniel raised his eyes to hers and she shrugged and smiled and nodded all at the same time.

He was her adventure—someone she was prepared to have fun with, but certainly not the sort of man she would ever want as a permanent fixture in her life.

It couldn't be better. Could it? They were singing from the same song sheet and there was no way he should now be feeling as though his nose had been put out of joint by her admission.

'That's right,' she whispered.

She took a deep breath and held it, watching as he lowered his head to hers in slow motion. His kiss feathered her mouth, lingered, deepened, and at the same time he began removing her top. He cupped one small breast and then gently eased his hand underneath her stretchy bra. She shuddered against him.

'Feel good...?'

He breathed the question into her ear and Delilah gasped out a response, because now he was playing with her nipple and sending delicious shivers straight down from her breasts to the place between her legs which was growing wetter by the second.

'Want me...?' he asked. 'Because if I'm to be your rebound adventure, then I need to know that it's an adventure that you really want...'

'I want you, Daniel...' Her eyes fluttered open to meet his. He had the most amazing lashes. Dark and long and in striking contrast to his light hair.

'Good,' Daniel murmured with intense satisfaction. 'Now, I want you to relax. Don't worry. I'm not going to hurt you.'

Aren't you? she thought in sudden confusion. But the thought vanished as quickly as it had come and she settled back into the soft duvet with a sigh as he hoiked up the top, taking the bra with it so that her breasts were pushed free of the restricting fabric.

Her whole body shrieked in urgent response as he clamped his mouth over her nipple and began teasing it with his tongue, drawing it into his mouth, tasting the stiffened bud.

She had exquisite breasts. Small and neat, the nipples perfectly defined rosy-pink discs. Sexy breasts. Breasts a man could lose himself in.

Rampant desire was flooding through him, making him uncomfortable, making him wonder how the hell he was going to keep a lid on his natural urge to take her, fast and hard.

He straightened to pull her free of the top and the bra, and then for a few seconds stared down at her pale nudity, at the perfection of her slender body—the way the golden tan gave way to the paleness where her swimsuit had prevented the sun from touching her bare skin.

Her hair flowed over the pillow in an unruly mass and she had twisted her head to one side, squeezed her eyes shut, clenched her small fists at her sides.

He eased open her hands and she turned, opened her eyes, looked at him.

His erection was prominent against his trousers, pushing into a massive bulge that sent her senses spinning.

'Now we're both half naked,' he growled, 'shall we be really, really daring and go the whole way?'

Delilah smiled, and then nodded. Her natural instinct was to shield herself from his hungry gaze, but for some reason she wasn't feeling shy in front of him—something about the way he was looking at her...with blatant, open appreciation.

She wriggled sinuously and his nostrils flared. 'You

have no idea what you're doing to me,' he muttered in a wrenching undertone, and Delilah decided that she could happily cope with having that effect on him.

He vaulted upright and removed his trousers, and as he did so she propped herself up on one elbow and just... *stared*.

In fact, she found that she couldn't stop staring.

He removed his underwear, silky boxers, and she stilled. Although his erection had been visible underneath his trousers, now she could appreciate it in all its magnificent glory—and magnificent it really and truly was.

'I know I'm big...' He correctly interpreted her wide-eyed stare of apprehension. He perched on the side of the bed and grinned. 'But I won't hurt you. Promise. I'll be very, very gentle, and in the end you'll be begging me to go harder...'

He began easing off her silky trousers, tugging them down until she was left in just her underwear. Simple cotton pants that made him smile, because they was a world apart from the lacy lingerie women always but *always* wore for him.

But then there wasn't a single bone in her body that advertised herself, was there?

Underneath her clothes she was as unaffected as she was everywhere else, and he liked that. A lot.

He didn't immediately tug down her underwear, even though she was squirming, her own hands reaching to do the job for him. Instead he pressed the flat of his hand between her legs, feeling the dampness spreading through the cotton, and firmly began to massage her, knowing just where to apply pressure so that her squirming was now accompanied by soft groans and whimpers.

He didn't stop. He wanted her on the brink of tipping over the edge. He wanted her so wet for him that he would slide into her, and she would stretch and take all of him, and love every second of the experience.

He was going to make sure that nothing hurt.

Even if he had to dig deep to find the self-restraint he would need.

'Please, Daniel…' His hand down there was sweet, sweet torture. Her body was on fire and he just kept on rubbing, until she thought she was going out of her mind. 'If you don't stop…'

'If I don't stop what…? You'll come against my hand?'

'You know I will,' she panted. 'And I don't want it to be like this… It should…should…'

'There are no *shoulds* when it comes to making love,' Daniel admonished teasingly. 'It's all about what makes you feel good. Does this feel good?'

'Better than good…'

She could barely get the words out, and when he slipped that questing hand under her panties, so that he was rubbing her properly, finding the throbbing bud of her clitoris and teasing it remorselessly, she wanted to faint.

She spread apart her legs and her body found its own rhythm as she began to move, angling herself so that he could slip one finger, then two, into her, while making sure to keep pressure on her clitoris. Straining under the bombardment of sensation, unable to hold off any longer, even though she wanted to, Delilah tensed, arched, and with a keening cry came against his fingers.

It was beautiful, he thought, dazed at the ferocity of his reaction to seeing her reach orgasm. Colour flooded her cheeks and she was breathing fast and shallow, and as she raised her body off the bed he thrust his fingers deeper into her, extending her orgasm and deepening it. Her face was shiny with perspiration.

If he could stop himself from ejaculating like a bloody

horny teenager, then he could do anything, he figured—because right now that felt like the hardest thing in the world to achieve.

'It shouldn't have been like that.' Delilah was dismayed, because this was just more evidence of her inexperience, but he was smiling as he lowered himself alongside her.

'Shh...'

'But I want to...to give you pleasure as well...'

'You are.'

'Tell me what to do.'

'You can hold me,' he suggested. 'But just hold me,' he warned. 'Because I might come if you do much more. I'm *that* close to losing control...'

'I bet you never do.'

'Lose control? Never. You, however, are turning out to be the exception to the rule when it comes to getting me to that point. Now, I'm going to touch you everywhere... with my mouth...with my hands...very, very slowly. I just want you to enjoy the experience, Delilah, and stop thinking that there should be a certain way of doing things...'

'Is that an order?' she whispered. She raised herself up to plant feathery kisses all over his face, ending with his beautiful mouth, but that was as far as he would allow her to go.

Masterful.

That was the word that sprang to mind, and his mastery thrilled her to her very core.

He kissed her neck and then spent time on her breasts, giving her body time to subside from its orgasm, time to find its way to building back up to a new peak. He kissed her flat stomach and felt her suck in her breath, then trailed lower, gently parting her legs to accommodate him.

He settled himself between her legs and then rested

them over his shoulders, and then he kissed and licked and teased her in her most intimate spot—and she loved every second of it. She gave herself to his exploration with an abandonment she would never have believed possible. His tongue flicked over her clitoris and she stiffened as she began to melt.

But this time he didn't let her build up the momentum that would take her over the edge. Instead, he teased her. He aroused her. He took her so far and then away, so that she had time to catch her breath, and the more he did that, the more she pleaded with him to come into her.

And in the end he just had to—because he was losing too much of his self-control to do anything else...

His wallet was on the ground and he barely looked as he flipped a condom over his rock-hard erection.

She was tight and wet and he eased himself inside her gently, in a two steps forward, one step back process that gradually allowed her to relax, so that he could fit into her without her tensing.

When he was ready to sink deeper into her, to have his shaft fill her, so was she, and as he thrust in, pushing her up the bed, taking his time and being as gentle as he could, he heard and felt the long, low shudder of her reaching orgasm.

It took her over.

Delilah hadn't thought that this depth of pure, unfiltered sensation could even exist. It did. She had stretched for him and moulded around his bigness as though their bodies had been made for one another. She came over and over and over, just as he reared up, the tendons in his neck straining, and came into her.

Time stood still. When finally they were back on Planet Earth she curved into him with a sigh of pure contentment. 'That was... Thank you...'

The disarming charm of her words distracted him from

the pressing concern that his condom appeared to have split. He chucked it onto the pile of clothes on the ground and wrapped his arms around her, drew her against him.

Mind-blowing. That was the only way he could describe the experience. Had it been because of the situation? Because she'd come to him a virgin? Or had it been because she had no idea of his identity? No idea of who he really was and how much he was really worth?

For just the briefest of moments he was disconcerted by that—by the very thing that had turned him on: namely her ignorance of his monetary value. He was disconcerted by the fact that she didn't know the truth about him.

'There's no need to thank me,' he told her huskily. He pushed back some wayward strands of hair. 'But there's something just a little bit worrying I have to say…'

'What's that?'

'I think the condom may have split…is that a problem? By which I mean are you in a safe period? It's highly unlikely that anything unfortunate will happen, but I thought I'd mention it…'

Delilah thought quickly and decided that she was perfectly safe, even though there *had* been a little hiccup—what with the travel and the stress and the sheer excitement of being on the cruise liner.

'Perfectly safe,' she told him firmly, nestling into him and smiling as she felt him stir against her naked thighs.

Daniel couldn't credit that his body was already gearing up for a repeat performance—one which it would not have…not just yet…because chances were that she would be sore.

The surprising urgency of his response settled his mind on the very pleasant prospect of what remained of the rest of his incognito holiday aboard the liner.

'Good,' he murmured, although he was already thinking ahead, wanting her in ways he couldn't remember wanting any other woman for a very long time. 'Glad to hear it.'

Delilah didn't add the reassurance that it was rare for a woman to fall pregnant on her first sexual encounter. She had read enough magazines to know that that was a myth.

'Now, how do you think we should spend the rest of the evening?' he asked.

She giggled and moved against him, and he grinned.

'Your body will need to take a little rest. I'd suggest we share a shower, but the facilities here leave a lot to be desired when it comes to joint showers... All cabins should cater for couples who want to have sex in the bathroom, don't you agree?'

'I don't think I've ever been in a shower that can fit more than one very skinny person.' She couldn't stop herself from touching him. She touched his hair, stroked his cheek, drew over the fine lines at the corners of his eyes with her fingers...

Daniel thought of the vast bathroom at his house in Sydney. The vast bathrooms at all the places he owned. He liked big bathrooms. Small, cosy spaces didn't do it for him.

What would she think if she knew the truth about him?

Just like that the question sprang from nowhere, and he frowned. She'd turn into just someone else who was desperate to please him, he decided, which was why it was refreshing that she didn't know.

'One shower at a time,' he said, with audible regret in his voice. 'Then what about you telling me about *my* half of this deal...?'

'Deal?' Delilah looked at him, perplexed, and he burst out laughing.

'I like the compliment,' he said with satisfaction. 'You've forgotten that, in return for me getting my wicked and very, very enjoyable way with you, you get to paint me... Talk to me about that. You can even put me in whatever sexy pose you want, and I guarantee that by the time we're finished talking about that we'll both be ready to make love all over again...'

CHAPTER SIX

'IT LOOKS GOOD...' Lying on his bed, arms folded behind his head, Daniel looked at the half-finished portrait of himself.

Somehow Delilah had managed to squeeze an easel into a corner of the cabin, so that she could paint him without being observed by all and sundry.

Daniel thought that had been an inspired idea, considering the portrait of him showed him in the position he was in now—reclining half naked on the bed, with a swirl of duvet blatantly advertising the fact that underneath it he was wearing nothing at all.

'You're not supposed to talk.'

But she smiled, because they did a lot of talking while he was posing for her and she liked that. They didn't talk about anything in particular. The conversation ebbed and flowed, drifted in and out of topics, and although there were vast swathes of his life which she felt she knew precious little about, she still felt that she knew the whole man, the complete package—knew the things that made him laugh and the things that pissed him off.

For three hours every day, for a week and a half now, he had been her captive audience, and it had bred an easy familiarity between them that thrilled her to the bone. If this was what successful therapy was all about then she was a fervent fan, because she hadn't thought about

Michael once, and she hadn't thought about the gallery either.

And she still hadn't tired of just *looking* at him. She knew every angle of his face and every muscle and sinew of his beautiful, strong body.

'It's utterly boring, trying to maintain this pose, if I can't talk at the same time.'

Or work. Or make the important business calls that needed to be made. Or do any of the other things around which his life was normally focused.

The truth was that he had shoved work commitments to one side, only really catching up after she had left him late in the night to return to her cabin. It was a fairly hellish routine when it came to grabbing much sleep, but frankly he didn't care. He was having a good time, and he saw no reason why he shouldn't indulge himself a little. The world wasn't going to stop turning on its axis just because he didn't clock in for a conference call at a prearranged time, or because he delegated a call to one of his guys at Head Office.

He was enjoying her.

And after that first time, when nerves had almost got the better of her, she had opened up to him like a peach.

His eyes flared now as he watched her painting him, her expression one of ferocious concentration.

That ferocious concentration was somewhat diluted by the fact that she wore nothing as she sat at her easel painting him. That was part of *his* side of the deal—a little addendum he had tacked on, and one which she had agreed to without, it had to be said, much persuasion.

She had a glorious body. Having previously only gone for women who were curvy and big-breasted, like pocket-sized Barbie dolls, he found that he couldn't get enough of her slender length, her long, shapely legs, her colt-like grace, the sweep of her hair…

Jarring at the back of his mind was the thought that all too soon it would have to come to an end. He'd already outstayed his original allotted time. He'd visited two countries more than he'd planned on doing. He'd produced more laughable attempts at still-life painting than any man should ever have to do. And he'd had the most mind-blowing sex…

Every day. Every night. More than once a night.

Just thinking about that mind-blowing sex was making him harden, and he knew that very shortly he would have to have her.

Delilah could sense where his thoughts were going without even having to look at the darkening in his eyes. It was as if they were connected by some kind of invisible umbilical cord to one another. He wanted her. And she wanted him.

Her nipples pinched at the thought of it and she wasn't shocked when he levered himself off the bed and strolled towards her.

Their routine of painting took place after lunch, when her classes were over. A lazy time for both of them. The sun continued to shine outside and the deep blue ocean continued to spread around them like a never-ending swathe of navy blue silk, but the only thing she had room for in her head was *him*.

He occupied every waking moment of her thoughts and most of her sleeping ones, as well.

'This portrait will never get finished if you keep interrupting me like this…' She looked up at him and grinned, her body already gearing up to unite with his, liquid pooling between her legs in anticipation.

Her breath hitched as he touched himself, touched his big, hard erection.

'My muscles were seizing up,' he drawled. 'I'm a man who enjoys lots of exercise. Physical activity.'

'I can point you in the direction of the squash courts,' she suggested helpfully. 'They could do with a lick of paint, but they function fine, and I'm sure you could rustle up a suitable partner if you want to get some much needed exercise...'

'I have a feeling that the way I play might spell certain death for whoever happens to be playing against me. Some of the guys here look as though they may have dodgy tickers...'

Delilah laughed, on a breathless high. So much for getting that bit of his arm just right... She could barely concentrate when he was posing for her, and when he was standing in front of her as he was doing now, butt naked and aroused, it was impossible.

She swivelled on the chair so that she was facing him, and then she stood on her tiptoes and kissed him—a lingering kiss that was as sweet and seductive as honey.

You thrill me, she would have liked to have told him, but that was off-limits. She knew that without having to be told. That sort of thing was taboo. Words of endearment or any hint at all that this might be deeper and more significant than either of them had bargained for were never spoken.

It wasn't love—of course it wasn't—but it *felt* as if it should be more than just a two-week fling...

When she thought about him disappearing she felt physically sick, so she tried not to think about it.

Instead, she thought about the fact that he had already stayed on for longer than he had first said he would, and she couldn't help pathetically wondering what that meant.

'Nice...' Daniel murmured, smiling down at her. 'Much better than lying on a bed pretending to be a statue.'

'You make a terrible model.'

'And here I was thinking that you found me good-looking...'

'Lord, but you're conceited. And that's not what I meant. You're far too restless to make a good model. Even when you're trying to stay perfectly still I can *hear* your brain whirring and I know you're itching to get up...'

'How well you know me, my little artist. Now, shall we put that to the test?'

'Put what to the test?'

'Your knowledge of me... Tell me what I'm thinking I'd like you to do now...'

Afterwards, lying on his bed, both on their backs, with her head resting on his shoulder, the pressing question of his imminent departure again began playing on his mind.

This wasn't going to do.

He couldn't play truant from reality for ever, and that was what he'd been doing. Good fun, but the time to say goodbye had come.

Conference calls had been cancelled, delegated, postponed...in one instance flatly avoided...but the final grain of sand had sifted through the upturned egg timer and now he had to leave.

A new acquisition required his urgent attention, and decisions had to be made about an office block he intended to refurbish in Mayfair. He couldn't duck low for ever.

However sweet the temptation was.

He turned to the sweet temptation and stroked her breast, looking down and smiling with male appreciation at the way her nipple tightened under the brush of his finger.

Propping himself up on his elbow, he continued to feather his finger over the stiffened pink bud before lowering his head to tease it with his tongue, then his mouth, suckling on it, but not touching her anywhere else at all.

Driving her crazy with just his mouth clamped to her nipple.

She squirmed and fidgeted, her whole body yearning for his—a physical ache that needed to be sated.

She'd learned how to touch him, where to touch him, the places that turned him on, and she reached down to close her hand over his erection, moving it slowly but firmly, building a little pace until she could tell from the change in his breathing that he was as turned on as she was.

And this, Daniel thought, was how things had ended up where they had—how he had ended up staying far longer than he had anticipated or planned.

This senseless drive to have more and more of her.

He laid his hand over hers and gritted his teeth, willing his erection to subside, because he couldn't think straight when he was aroused. It was as if she took over his whole mind.

After a couple of minutes he flipped onto his back and stared for a few seconds at the ceiling of the cabin.

If he looked through the circular window he would see the clear turquoise sky and the sun shining down on the navy blue ocean. When he took to the water in Australia he sailed with purpose, pitting his skill against nature. He got up close and personal with the sea, felt the whip of breeze on his face, challenged the ocean's depths to do their worst.

It was nothing like this. He thought that perhaps this was what people meant when they said that they'd had a 'relaxing' holiday. This was what doing nothing was all about, and he realised that it was something he rarely did. He hadn't even suspected how enjoyable it could be.

'We need to talk.'

In one easy, fluid movement Daniel slipped out of bed

and stood by the side for a few seconds, looking at her flushed face, at the flare of dismay in her eyes.

Was he going to tell her everything?

When they'd started their fling he'd presumed that he would leave the ship, wave goodbye and she would never be any the wiser as to his true identity. A few hot nights of passion and then a parting of ways.

He would conduct his business transaction with the Ockleys either from London or Sydney. He'd got the information he needed about the liner, had seen for himself what the crew were like. He even had his offer formulated in his head. It was low, but then the liner was fairly run down and would hit the metaphorical rocks within the next year or so. It was an offer he knew they might resent, but would be compelled to accept. In his eyes, that amounted to what was *fair*.

He hadn't planned on staying for as long as he had.

He hadn't planned on a number of things.

He frowned and had a quick mental flashback of her laughing, head thrown back…her concentration in her art classes, patiently giving encouragement to everyone… her blushing and laughing whenever he touched her or whenever she touched him…

'You might want to get dressed…'

He knew that this was for his benefit rather than hers. He couldn't think straight when she was naked, and he needed to think straight. This was just another woman he was going to leave behind, and he tightened his jaw in preparation for his parting speech.

Delilah sprang out of the bed. Her heart was beating so hard that it felt as though it might explode right out of her chest.

It was going to end.

He'd never promised otherwise. Had never hinted at it. Now, however, she realised just how much she had hoped that there might be a future for them. She'd somehow become needy and clingy and it appalled her.

What had happened to all her grand theories about the nature of lust? What had happened to her conviction that she couldn't be hurt if she slept with him because you could only be hurt when you were in love? What had happened to her assumption that love could never enter the equation because he was just a bit of fun to take her mind off the bad time she'd had with Michael and the worrying time that lay ahead with all their money problems?

Thoughts swarming in her head like angry bees, she fought against the realisation that she had fallen in love with him.

With beautiful, intelligent, utterly charismatic Daniel —who was a commitment-phobe, who didn't want to put down roots, who was just taking a breather with her in between his travels…

Just by being himself he had made her see how shallow Michael had been and how unsuitable as a partner.

She dressed quickly, barely able to look at him, already bracing herself for his 'Dear John' speech.

And the worst of it was that she wanted to beg him not to deliver the speech—wanted to tell him that they worked so well together, that they should try and continue what they had…that they had something special.

Except it was only special *for her*, wasn't it…?

'I know what you're going to say.'

'Do you?'

He didn't think so.

'You're going to tell me that you're moving on…that you have places to go, people to see…' She gave a brittle laugh and stared at him, chin tilted at a defiant angle.

Daniel thought that he might miss those shapeless long skirts and baggy tops.

'I never led you to believe that this would be a permanent arrangement.' He shoved his hands into his trouser pockets and then ran his fingers through his hair. He wanted to walk…to burn off some of his restless energy… but the cabin was the size of a matchbox so he settled for dragging the chair from the fitted dressing table by the wall and sitting down heavily.

'I know,' Delilah said tightly.

She badly wanted to beg him to reconsider. Her hands were shaking and she pushed them into the deep pockets of her skirt and perched on the edge of the bed.

'I don't do long-term,' he told her in the sort of gentle voice that set her teeth on edge. 'And there's a reason for that.'

'You've had your heart broken.'

'I've had my heart *hardened*.' He sighed. 'What do you think of this cruise liner?'

'Sorry?' She raised startled eyes to his and wondered where this was going. Was that *it* for his goodbye speech? Didn't she deserve more? Maybe just a tiny bit of remorse?

'What do you think of this cruise liner? I mean the way it's run…its condition…the general state of its health?'

'I… Well… I don't know where you're going with this, Daniel.' When he didn't answer, she gave a little shrug and looked around her. 'It could do with some work,' she said, still bewildered. 'Everyone knows that. All the crew know that Gerry and Christine have been having a few financial problems…'

'They're heavily in debt. Your eyes would water if you knew how much they owed the bank. They inherited this liner from Gerry's parents. A very wealthy family, as it happens. Lots of fingers in lots of pies. This was just one of their concerns. Unfortunately Gerry Ockley may have inherited their wealth—which, frankly, was already dwindling by the time John Ockley kicked the bucket—

but he has failed to inherit his father's business acumen. The estate was evenly divided between three sons and he got the liner as part of his legacy. He turned a niche and nicely profitable service into something equally niche but sadly not nearly as profitable.'

Her mouth had dropped open. He knew every single illusion she had had about him was slowly being shattered, but he had to continue, and he told himself that shattered illusions weren't such a bad thing.

He'd grown from his, hadn't he? Shattered illusions allowed you to develop the sort of tough strength that helped you get through life. That was how it had worked for him. She would move on from this a much stronger person.

He banked down the tide of savage guilt that *he* was the one responsible for giving her this learning curve.

'I am Daniel De Angelis,' he told her softly. 'You think that I'm a traveller, interested in dabbling in a spot of art, but that's not strictly speaking the truth…'

'I don't know what you're telling me…' Delilah shook her head in utter bewilderment. She felt as though she had suddenly been transported into a parallel universe, where everything looked the same but nothing actually was.

Her warm, teasing, sexy guy had vanished and in his place was this stranger, with his remote, guarded eyes, saying stuff that she didn't understand.

'I didn't come here to do a course on art,' he ploughed on—relentless, remorseless.

She wished she could just put her hand over his beautiful mouth and stop the flow of words.

'I came here to inspect this liner…to find out where its failings lay…to see its condition first-hand and to do it without anyone knowing who I was… I wanted the element of surprise—no superficial tidying or paint jobs. I wanted to see it in all its downtrodden glory…'

'But *why*?' Delilah whispered, her voice barely audible.

'Because I intend to buy it.'

That flatly spoken statement swirled around her like thick toxic waste, penetrating her consciousness, and then she was tying up all the things that hadn't made sense about him—starting with that ridiculously extravagant dinner on the deck…their first *date*. What a joke!

Anger began a slow, poisonous burn.

'You're not poor at all, are you?' She knew that she was stating the obvious, but there was still a pathetic part of her that was clinging to the hope that this was all some kind of big joke.

'I am a billionaire,' Daniel said.

No beating around the bush. He looked for the signs he secretly expected to see. The flare of certain interest as her preconceived notions gave way to far more tempting prospects.

They failed to materialise.

And along with that realisation came another one.

He wasn't ready to let her go. Not yet. Eventually, yes. But not yet. He still wanted her.

So now she would know the truth about him—but the bottom line was that he was very, very, *very* rich, and that, in the end, would be the deciding factor.

Women were always predictable in their reactions to extreme wealth. They gravitated towards it like bears to a pot of honey. Once she'd recovered from the shock of his revelations she would surely see the advantages of continuing what they had—not least because it was what she wanted.

He still desired her, and she still desired him—it was simple as that when you cut through all the murky red tape.

Goodbye speeches weren't set in cement, were they? And he didn't want to walk away leaving behind unfinished business. He didn't want to find himself missing those long, shapeless skirts and baggy tops and wondering whether he should have continued what they had.

Practical to the very last drop of blood in his body, Daniel knew that the fact that she was broke would work in his favour. He wondered whether she would be insulted if he offered to help her and her sister out of their dire financial situation...

'Why did you get involved with me?' Delilah asked bluntly. She had to clench her fists to stop her hands from shaking uncontrollably. Like a jigsaw puzzle, the pieces were all coming together, thick and fast, and what she was beginning to see of the finished picture made her feel sick.

'I didn't intend to get involved with *anyone*,' Daniel told her truthfully.

'But here I was and so you decided *why not*? Because I guess you're the kind of guy who always takes what he wants, and I'm thinking that you maybe decided you could kill two birds with one stone. You wanted all sorts of information about the ship and the people who worked on it, and you decided that I might be able to help you out with some of that information.'

Her voice was rising, even though she was trying to keep it calm and controlled. She just knew that if she really let what he had just told her overwhelm her then she would fly at him, and she wasn't going to do that. She was going to walk away and leave him with the contempt he deserved.

But underneath it all she could feel her heart breaking in two.

She'd been the biggest idiot in the world. She'd wanted adventure and she'd got a hell of a lot more than she'd bargained for. She'd got a nightmare.

She should have listened to her sister and to her own common sense. You couldn't clear your head of one stupid mistake with a guy by jumping into bed the second someone else came around.

Daniel flushed darkly. Strictly speaking, there was an element of truth there... But hadn't events put a different spin on it? Things had changed. But he couldn't deny that he *had* seen her as a good conduit of information for him and now, thinking about that, he was prey to a certain amount of guilt.

'You lied to me all along,' she said tautly. 'You lied about who you were, and you lied about what you wanted from me... The only thing you said to me that was true was that you weren't going to be sticking around and that you weren't interested in long-lasting relationships... Aside from that, every single thing you said to me was a lie. All lies!'

'I didn't lie to you about wanting you.'

His husky voice penetrated her anger and she hated herself for the way her body weakened. Even hating him, he could still do that—still make her insides go to mush—and she hated him even more for being able to do that.

Keep it cold, and hang on to your self-control...

'So what do you intend to do now?' she demanded. 'Throw everyone overboard and take over the liner? Like some kind of pirate?'

He *looked* like a pirate. She should have listened to her instincts and followed them... Should have realised early on that he just didn't fit the profile of an itinerant traveller, aimlessly seeing the world and stopping off to indulge his love of art.

No wonder his efforts at drawing and painting had been so poorly executed. In fact little wonder that he had barely put paint to canvas in all the classes he had so dutifully attended.

'I'm not the bad guy here,' Daniel told her, outraged

at the attacks being levelled against him, even though he could understand some of her justifiable fury.

Hell, if she looked at the bigger picture she would see that he would be doing the hapless Ockleys a favour by buying them out!

'Oh, you're an absolute saint.' Delilah's voice dripped sarcasm.

'The Ockleys are going under,' Daniel informed her, even though he was distracted by her glorious beauty—all rage and tousled hair and pursed lips. 'They're on a fast track to bankruptcy and when that happens they'll get nothing for this ship. It'll be taken off their hands for a song. I intend to buy it and bring it back up to spec...'

'And you think that I'm supposed to *congratulate* you for that? You *used* me.'

'You're overreacting.'

Delilah resisted the strong temptation to throw something at him. His stupid portrait would do the trick.

But even as she thought that another treacherous thought crossed her mind.

That portrait would be all she had left of him when they parted ways. And she hated herself for wanting to hang on to it.

'So what happens to all the people who depend on this liner for their livelihoods?' she flung at him, slamming the door on her weakness.

'I'm not going to throw them overboard!' Daniel thundered. 'You're being dramatic! I... Okay, so I apologise if you think that you were used...' Dull colour highlighted his cheekbones. Apologies were something else he didn't do. 'I intend to keep the staff who are up to the job. They'll find that they're richly rewarded and working on a ship that's actually not hanging on to survival by the skin of its pants!'

'I hate you.'

'You don't hate me,' he said huskily. 'You want me. If I came over there right now and kissed you, you'd kiss me back and you'd want more…'

'You wouldn't dare…' She glared at him.

'You should know better than to lay down challenges like that to a man like me.'

The air was charged as they stared at one another in electric silence.

'I should have seen the signs,' she muttered. 'I should have known from the very first moment you had that meal arranged on deck and paid poor Stan extra money that you weren't who you said you were!'

'*Poor Stan* will be singing my praises when I tell him what sort of money he'll be getting when he works for *me*.'

'And I suppose you'll turn this ship into some awful, rowdy, drink-all-you-can cruiser for the under-thirties…?' she said scathingly.

'The opposite—'

'And all that rubbish you told me about not being the sort of guy who wants long-term relationships… I suppose you were just referring to *me*…' Hurt and bitterness had crept into her voice as she dispassionately joined up all the dots. 'You're just an opportunist who decided to take advantage of a vulnerable woman. And you knew I was vulnerable… You knew I'd just come out of a bad relationship—that I wasn't looking forward to going back to the Cotswolds and facing all those financial problems…'

Considering he had spent his life making sure to avoid opportunists, Daniel was enraged that she had flung him into that category.

'I don't *do* relationships,' he told her flatly. 'Nothing to do with you. And I didn't drag you kicking and screaming against your will into the nearest bed because you were *vulnerable*!'

'But you knew that I *was*!'

'I didn't take you for a coward, Delilah.'

'What does *that* mean?'

'Face up to the choices you made. You knew what you were getting into. You knew I wasn't in it for the long haul. You *chose* to sleep with me. That was the decision *you* made—and, trust me, if you'd decided against it I would never have tried to force your hand. So do me a favour and take responsibility for your decisions!'

'I just never thought that I was going to end up in bed with a liar! I thought I'd been there, done that. I thought you were *different*.'

Daniel's teeth snapped, but there was nothing he could say to that.

'And if you *were* to "do" a relationship,' Delilah inserted in a driven voice, 'then it certainly wouldn't be with someone like *me,* would it? Someone without money? Not when you're a billionaire who can buy a cruise ship the way someone might buy a pair of shoes!'

His silence was telling.

'I'm careful,' he gritted. 'I'm a target for gold-diggers. That's just the way it is.'

'I think I've heard enough now,' Delilah said quietly. She felt utterly drained, exhausted on every level. Her legs were like jelly and she hoped that when she stood up she wouldn't go crashing to the ground. 'I'm going to take my painting with me, if you don't mind.'

She began easing the canvas from the easel, her back to him, not looking at him, although she was aware of his presence with every atom of her body.

If he touched her now…

She knew that she had to get out of the cabin as fast as she could—because she didn't trust herself…didn't know what she would do if he touched her now…and the last thing she wanted was to give him any excuse for thinking that she was the kind of mug who was so smitten with him that she would melt in his arms like the fool she'd been.

No way.

'This doesn't have to end here,' Daniel said gruffly.

She spun round to look at him with an expression of scorn.

He *never* pursued a woman. And especially in a situation like this, when he was staring at a woman who wanted no more to do with him... Pursuit should *definitely* be off the agenda. But, hell, he still wanted her, and he was driven by his own physical impulse.

'I still want you,' he told her.

'So you said. But we can't always have what we want.'

'You have no idea what I could give you.'

'A brief fling?' she enquired with saccharine sweetness. 'A couple more weeks until you get tired of me?'

'You could have anything you want,' he intoned, shocked that he was going down this road. 'You say that you and your sister are short of cash? Struggling to make ends meet? I could help you with that. I could inject money into your business, pull out all the stops, get it to a place where you'd never have to worry about money again...'

Considering her sister didn't know a thing about Daniel,—thank heavens—Delilah wondered what she would think if she brought him home and produced him as their knight in shining armour.

What a laugh.

As if he could *ever* be her knight in shining armour.

And 'pull out all the stops'? Rescue them from their financial situation? How long before he started thinking that she was just another one of those gold-diggers who saw him as a target?

She walked towards the door and said cuttingly, 'I don't think so. I don't want you *or* your money. I'd appreciate it if you just left me alone for the remainder of your time on this liner. I don't want you to come to my classes, and if you see me in the bar or the restaurant feel free to ignore me.'

She couldn't believe that her voice was as cool and controlled as it was, when inside she was falling apart at the seams.

Sex.

That was what she meant to him and that was *all* she meant to him. He still wanted her, and he didn't see why his lies and deception should stand in the way of getting what he wanted—especially when he could throw his money into the ring and try and tempt her with it. Try and *buy* her with it.

Daniel looked at her frozen expression. He had been locked out and he wasn't going to beg.

'And what do you think your students and your fellow crew members are going to think?' he asked. 'Unless they're blind, they already know that there's something going on between us...'

Delilah hitched her shoulder in a dismissive shrug. 'Like you told me at the very beginning—who cares? Why should I care what other people think when I won't be seeing any of them again?'

She wondered how much longer he would stay on the liner and thought that it wouldn't be long. Off at the next stop, having pulled the plug on Christine and Gerry. When she left this cabin she wouldn't be seeing him again. She would make sure of that, however hard it might be.

She didn't look back at him as she let herself out of the cabin. She walked quickly—away from people, away from the possibility of anyone seeing her and guessing that something was wrong. She didn't want to bump into any of her students or any of the other crew members... didn't want them to ask her if she was okay.

She just wanted to get back to the safety of her own cramped cabin and give in to the tears that she was struggling to hold back.

She just wanted to go home.

CHAPTER SEVEN

DELILAH GAZED UP at the building in front of her. It wasn't one of those vast, impressive glass houses that broadcasted to the world that the worker bees inside were *very important* worker bees. By comparison this was a modest building, just three storeys high, a squat, square and rather old-fashioned red brick affair, away from the chaotic hustle and bustle of the city.

She didn't want to be here, but she had had to jump through hoops to find the wretched place and now that she was standing in front of it she wasn't going to retreat without seeing him.

Which didn't mean that she wasn't as nervous as a kitten.

In a sudden burst of anxiety she spun away from the building and headed to the nearest coffee shop, where she would try and rally her mental troops.

The heat of the Mediterranean sun seemed like a long, long time ago. Much longer than two months, which was when she had said farewell to the liner and to the friends she had made there.

Everything had been so chaotic.

Like a hurricane, Daniel had swept through them all and changed their lives in one way or another.

For Christine and Gerry, after what she had privately admitted must have been a horrible, horrible shock to the system, because they had both viewed the money he had flung down on the table as a hostile takeover, things had actually turned out okay.

Faced with the brutal facts of their financial situation, they had been forced to get their heads out of the sand and abandon their optimism that the tide was going to change—that they just needed a couple of bumper seasons, that hordes of culture vultures were waiting out there to book passages on their once-in-a-lifetime cruise.

And, Gerry had told her, Daniel's offer had been pretty fair—which had somewhat eroded Delilah's assumption that Daniel's sole interest had been to plunder and take for the cheapest possible price.

Which, of course, didn't excuse the fact that he had used her and lied to her.

Most the crew were to be re-employed, back on the liner, with six months of paid leave while the cruise ship was being renovated, and their salaries were now so inflated that they were overjoyed at the change of ownership. Stan, as Daniel had told her, had been over the moon at the prospect of running his own kitchen, no expense spared.

The other tutors had thought nothing of losing their jobs. Some, like her, had been part-time recruits and the rest, all in their mid-fifties, had been happy enough to use their talents in other directions. The liner had not constituted their sole income.

No one had been left with the corrosive bitterness that she had been left with—but then she had been in a unique situation.

As predicted, she had seen nothing of him, and had no idea how long he'd remained on the liner before leaving. She had hidden away, taking meals in her poky cabin and scuttling to her classes in a state of dread that she might see him sprawled in his usual chair, doing something and nothing in front of his easel.

He had not reappeared.

So much for his heated pursuit. So much for all that rubbish about still wanting her. He had given it one shot and then shrugged his shoulders and walked away. Literally jumped ship.

Delilah had told herself that she was hugely relieved, but somewhere deep inside disappointment had gnawed away at her, making her situation even more awful and painful than it already had been.

Everything had dissolved. There had been tearful goodbyes and promises to keep in touch. Many of the students had expressed an interest in the business she and Sarah would be starting, which was something, at least.

She had put a brave smile on her face. Several people had asked her about Daniel, asked her whether she would be seeing him again, and she had laughed and told them that it had been nothing more than a pleasant holiday fling.

All lies.

She had fallen in love and was she ever going to recover? Was there a Mr Right? A Mr Sensible and Suited To Her? The sort of chap she should have been looking for after Michael, who was going to elbow Mr Utterly Wrong out of the spot in her heart which he continued to occupy?

Even after everything had gone quiet.

Even after she'd returned to the Cotswolds.

After she'd done her very best to clear her head of him.

She still missed him. She missed him so much that she had gone through all the motions of helping Sarah and enthusing about their project like an automaton.

She missed him so much that she hadn't paid a scrap of attention to the fact that she had skipped a period, and it had only been when she'd started feeling sick and nauseous at certain smells and when certain foods were presented to her that she had twigged.

She closed her eyes briefly and relived that moment when time had stood still. Two bright blue lines had marked the end of life as she knew it. She could still taste the fear, the panic, and see the blank fog of confusion that had crashed over her like a tsunami. Then, when the utter shock had subsided, had come the numbness of just not knowing what happened next.

She opened her eyes and through the window of the coffee shop watched the crowds outside, scurrying about their business.

She had managed to find out, from Christine, where he was and how long he would be there. They, of course, were in touch with him, finalising the sale of their liner.

'He's not the predator we first thought,' Christine had confided. 'And his plans for the liner sound really interesting. Nothing we could ever have hoped to do in a million years… Literally catering for the rich and famous—and would you believe he's actually told me and Gerry that we can have three weeks a year free cruising for the rest of our lives? A way of keeping in touch with our beloved *Rambling Rose*. He didn't have to do that…'

Delilah's brain had stopped functioning at the word *predator*. That was what he was. A predator. He had obviously charmed Gerry and Christine, but she had no doubt that he would have done a pretty shrewd deal and then wrapped it up in lots of glitzy packaging so that he came out of it smelling of roses.

They might have been charmed.

They might have ended up thinking that he'd been a real sport and given them a good deal.

But *she* knew better than to judge a book by its cover. He was one of life's takers. She felt that he could have told her at *any time* who he really was. But he hadn't. Hadn't even come close. He'd been perfectly happy to string her along and she knew why.

At the end of the day there was no way that he would ever allow himself to become involved with someone he considered his inferior.

He played around with women, but in the end they were all potential gold-diggers and therefore only worthy of short-term meaningless dalliances.

Of which she had been one. One of a long number. He'd practically said so himself.

Unfortunately, even with that perfectly sound reasoning, she had still spent weeks thinking obsessively about him. She'd resisted telling her sister about her escapade, because she hadn't wanted any I-told-you-so lectures, but it had been hard. Harder than hard.

And now… Everything came with consequences, and sometimes those consequences lasted a lifetime.

She drained her tea—lemon and ginger—and took a deep breath before heading back out towards the building.

Winter was well and truly in the air. The days were getting shorter and there was a biting feel to the air that penetrated all the layers of clothes she had put on.

Thick socks, jeans, her thermal vest, a loose, long-sleeved tee shirt, a jumper, the long scarf which could wrap three times around her neck and a woolly hat pulled right down over her ears.

She barrelled through the revolving door of the building—a bit of an anachronism considering the age of the property—and was ejected into a modern marble interior that seemed more suited to a five-star luxury hotel than an office block.

But then she imagined that Daniel never did anything by halves.

Cool shades of grey were interrupted by towering plants and a semi-circular reception desk, behind which three snappily dressed women dealt with visitors with the help of their sleek, slimline computers.

The place carried the unmistakable whiff of vast sums of money being made.

At a little after eleven in the morning there wasn't the usual early-morning throng of employees hurrying to get to their desks, but there were sufficient people coming and going to allow her a few moments of unobserved privacy, during which she thought. Thought about what lay ahead…

Should she have warned him of her arrival? Would he have scarpered rather than have a conversation with her? He was only going to be in London for a couple of months. Renovations, apparently, to the office block in which she was now standing, gazing hesitantly around her. This was her window to catch him before he disappeared to the other side of the world. She needed to talk to him, whether she liked it or not, and the element of surprise had seemed like a good idea.

But she still couldn't convert her resolve into action. Her head was telling her to get the whole thing over and done with…her feet were refusing to co-operate.

And she felt horribly underdressed for the surroundings. Everyone seemed to be in a suit and carrying a briefcase. These were people who didn't waste time dawdling. These were *Daniel's kind of people.*

Up ahead, to the left of the semi-circular reception desk, were three subtly camouflaged elevators. Towards the back she could just about glimpse what looked like a private courtyard, and she assumed the building was designed around it, so that the employees had their own little mini-park to it in during their lunch break if they didn't want to head outside and face the crowds.

Gathering her courage, she headed for the imposing reception desk.

Would he even be in?

He was.

The blonde behind the desk wasn't warm and welcoming, but she didn't ask too many intrusive questions and the one side of the conversation Delilah heard, which was obviously conducted with someone else—perhaps his secretary while he was in the country—was brief and productive.

She was given a visitor's pass, directed to the lifts— or the stairs, if she'd rather—and told to make her way to the far right wing of the building.

Apparently she wouldn't be able to miss his office because it occupied most of the right wing of the building to which she had been directed.

A Very Important Man.

She would be going to see a stranger—not the man in whose arms she had lain night after night, who had made love to her as though it was the only thing he wanted to do in the world, the only thing he'd been born to do…

And just like that she was reminded of what she had lost, for coming out of the elevator was a couple…

The dark-haired woman was small and curvy, and gazing up adoringly at the very tall, very muscular dark-haired man who was holding her close against him.

This, Delilah thought with a pang of intense longing, was the very picture of a couple deeply in love.

She brushed past them and the man glanced briefly at her, barely registering her presence. A jolt of pure shock washed through her.

Those eyes! The same arresting shade of green as Daniel's…

She turned, watching their progress out of the building. That must surely be Daniel's brother… A De Angelis who had actually opened himself up to falling in love… Because the tall, striking guy was clearly head over heels in love with the small, curvy brunette pressed to his side.

On the spur of the moment she veered away from the lift and headed towards the staircase…

Daniel pushed himself away from his desk and stood up, strolling to the window and gazing down absently at the very impressive courtyard, with its fountain and its benches and carefully tended grass, which in the depths of winter, at just after eleven in the morning, was completely empty.

He had planned on having lunch with his brother and Alexa. They had, indeed, come to see the new premises with the intention of dragging him off to one of the many wine bars scattered nearby. But that had been before his secretary had informed him that a certain Delilah Scott was in Reception, asking to see him.

He turned from the pleasant view outside and couldn't contain a certain amount of satisfaction—even if that satisfaction was tempered with disappointment.

Two months. She'd walked away from him. He got it that she'd been furious with him because he hadn't announced his identity. He'd apologised. But he might just as well have not bothered, because his apology had counted for nothing. Nor had she made any attempt to understand where he was coming from.

He was rich—very rich. Most women would have been overjoyed, after their initial annoyance, to swap a so-called drifter for a billionaire.

Not her.

And that was probably why she had lingered in his head for the length of time that she had.

Unfinished business.

It could have been avoided, and then he wouldn't be where he had been for the last couple of months…thinking about her, feeling lukewarm about getting in touch

with a replacement, having cold showers on far too regular a basis…

He wondered how she was going to play it. Another
little spurt of anger because he'd lied to her? Before a reluctant but inevitable move towards him?

Maybe she'd fabricate some excuse about 'just passing
by' and deciding to look him up. Presumably she would
have found out where his offices were via Christine and
Gerry. She could have called in advance, but then that
wouldn't really tie in with some random excuse about
being in the vicinity, would it?

A darker thought occurred to him…

He'd offered to help her and her sister out of the financial difficulties they were experiencing. Had sufficient
time elapsed that she'd had time to work out just how advantageous it would be to have him on board?

That would be disappointing, but he knew enough
about women to believe that they were predictably susceptible to a bit of gold being dangled in front of them.
Even the most self-righteous couldn't resist and, frankly,
he hadn't met too many of those in his lifetime.

Sex for money.

No strings attached.

She was coming to take him up on the offer he'd made
to her two months previously and it irked him that he was
willing to let her back into his bed. He was, however,
enough of a realist to accept that if he didn't she would
probably continue to niggle away at the back of his mind,
and that wasn't going to do.

Time was money, and he just couldn't afford the unnecessary distraction.

The office block was pretty much up and running,
thanks to the amount of money he'd thrown at it. Work
had begun on the cruise ship and, again, things were moving along swiftly because money talked.

He anticipated heading back to Sydney some time before Christmas, detouring via Italy so that he could spend part of the festive season with his father, his brother and Alexa.

He wondered how Delilah would accept what was now on the table—because the offer hadn't changed. A limited time in which they would indulge their mutual desire.

He gave it a couple of seconds before he responded to the knock on the door—time during which he resumed his seat behind the big mahogany desk.

Delilah, her nerves at screaming point, wanted to hide behind the secretary who was now standing by the imposing wooden door that separated her outer office from her boss's.

Smoked glass advertised Daniel's presence in his office, but all she could see was a shape.

She thought how lovely it would be if that door opened and she discovered that her memories of him were all rose-tinted and wildly exaggerated. How much braver she would feel if she discovered that he was shorter than she remembered…squatter…less *overwhelming*.

But as she was ushered into the office every single one of those hopeful conjectures was wiped out by the sight of him, sitting behind an absolutely enormous desk.

This was and wasn't the Daniel she had fallen in love with.

Same striking face…those mesmerising green eyes… and the towering, muscular body of someone genetically programmed to be lean, who worked out so that there wasn't a spare ounce of fat on him.

Same overpowering presence…

Her breathing was shallow as she absorbed all of that and then everything else that was different.

His hair was shorter, cropped close, but still the same dirty blond colour. His skin was bronzed, so that there was the same peculiar eye catching contrast between his colouring and his hair.

He was wearing a suit.

'What a surprise.' He broke the silence and nodded to the chair in front of his desk. 'Why don't you sit down? You look as though you're in danger of imminent collapse.'

Delilah licked dry lips and thankfully subsided into the chair. Now that she was here, actually in front of him, all the cool she had hoped to have at her disposal had vanished. She was a mess.

'What brings you to London?' *As if he didn't already know.* He sat forward, resting his forearms on the desk, fingers lightly linked, head tilted questioningly to one side as he looked at her in perfect silence.

'I… I needed to talk to you…'

'About what? The fate of all the crew aboard the liner? I could go into the details, if you'd like, but suffice to say they're all happy campers…' He smiled, but the smile didn't quite reach his eyes. He was remembering the strident moral high ground she had taken the last time they had been together.

'I… No, I haven't come to talk about that…but of course, yes…it seems that you've re-hired a lot of the original staff…which is really good…'

'So if you haven't come for a little catch-up, then why are you here, Delilah? The last time we spoke you were in high dudgeon, and if my memory serves me right you stormed out of my cabin shrieking that you never wanted to lay eyes on me again…'

He'd missed those floaty shapeless clothes, which were nothing like the dapper suits that surrounded him. She was as nervous as hell and he wasn't surprised. Humble pie never tasted good, and she had chewed off a very large slice.

'I wouldn't be here if I… I didn't have to be…' Delilah muttered. He wasn't going to make this easy for her. She couldn't blame him in a way. On the other hand, what would it cost him to be a just a little friendlier?

So there it was… That hadn't taken long… He should be pleased, considering he'd always been a guy to cut to the chase, as well…

'So…' he drawled, relaxing back into the chair and looking at her with brooding intensity. 'Your venture with your sister…'

'Sorry?'

'The project you and your sister have sunk all your savings into…taken out a hefty bank loan to finance…'

'What about it?'

'Oh, I'm just thinking aloud…playing around with the reason why you've shown up on my doorstep two months after you stormed out of my cabin…'

'I stormed out of your cabin for a reason! You lied to me…' She had told herself that she wasn't going to go down the road of rehashing what had happened between them and resorting to old accusations, because that wasn't going to go anywhere, but the expression on his face…

Daniel lifted one lazily imperious hand to halt her mid-accusation. 'Let's skip Memory Lane,' he advised coolly, 'and bring things back to the present. When I was told that you had shown up here and wanted to see me, I confess I was a little surprised—but it didn't take me long to figure it out…'

'Why *am* I here?' she questioned jerkily. Surely he couldn't be *that* clever at reading situations? But then the timeline should tell him something, shouldn't it?

'Money,' Daniel said succinctly.

'Sorry?'

Suddenly consumed with restless energy, Daniel vaulted upright and began striding through his office, which had been kitted out in a style that suited the age of the building. His office in Sydney was the last word in modern. This was all wood and rich tones.

Not that he noticed. He was so damned *alive* to her... huddled in the chair, watching him... He was half furious with himself for even seeing her when he knew why she had come, and half triumphant that she was here at all, in his office, on the verge of caving in.

'It took you a while...' He stopped dead in his tracks in front of her and leaned down, supporting himself by his hands on either side of her chair, caging her in so that she automatically flinched back, nostrils flaring as she breathed him in. 'But in the end you couldn't resist the lure of the big bucks...'

His forest-green eyes locked with hers and his proximity sucked the oxygen out of her lungs, leaving her gasping and panicked.

Delilah's mouth parted in bewilderment.

'You want money and I'm prepared to give it to you... We've already established what the trade-off is...' He straightened, returned to his chair behind the desk, but now he pushed it back and stretched out his long legs to one side. 'And, seeing that you've tracked me down to re-establish what we had, *I* get to choose the terms and conditions...'

Something not quite audible left her throat.

She marvelled that she hadn't foreseen this—hadn't predicted that someone as arrogant and downright egotistical as Daniel De Angelis would put a completely different spin on her unexpected arrival at his office.

He thought that she had come running back, tail between her legs, so that they could resume where they had left off! And that she'd done it because he'd dangled his wealth in front of her like a carrot!

'And what exactly are these so-called "terms and conditions"?' she asked with glacial politeness.

'You're mine for as long as I want you...' He smiled, enjoying the thought of what was to come. 'And when I say mine, I *mean* mine. You...here in London...for the next few weeks...at my beck and call... In return I guarantee that I will sort out all the financial problems you and your sister are currently experiencing...'

'What a thoughtful and generous man you are, Daniel De Angelis.' She could barely keep her voice steady. 'But it's not going to work.'

She sprang out of her chair, walked in jerky steps to the window and took a few deep breaths as she stared down at the courtyard she had glimpsed earlier when she had entered the building. It was impressive. Like everything else she had seen of the premises.

She thought back to the casual way he had arranged that supper on the deck for them, his nonchalant approach to money, the ease with which he had seemed to *own* his surroundings, the lazy charm which she had found so bone-meltingly impressive.

All the hallmarks of a man born into money, accustomed to getting what he wanted at the snap of his fingers.

'Why not?' He frowned. 'Maybe you want to fix a price? Have a piece of paper signed by me so that you know what you're letting yourself in for?'

'Do you know something?' Delilah said, her voice high and shaky. 'I'm beginning to wish that I'd never come here! I might have known that you'd think the worst of me! Do you really and truly think that I made the trip here because I wanted to ask you for *money*? Because I wanted to trade my body for *cash*?'

She pushed herself away from the window but she

couldn't be still, so instead she stalked through the office, her arms wrapped tightly around herself, her nails biting into the tender flesh of her forearms.

'I feel sorry for you,' she said through gritted teeth, pausing long enough to look at him but then looking away again, because even though she was seething with anger some detached part of her still couldn't help but appreciate his overpowering masculine beauty. 'You're so caught up thinking that every single woman must be interested in your money you won't even allow yourself to think that some might not give a damn!'

'I don't imply that they're *exclusively* interested in me because of my bank balance.' Daniel wasn't going to rise to the bait. He was too busy enjoying the hectic flush in her cheeks.

He realised that this was part of the reason why he hadn't been ready to bid her farewell ten days into their fling… She challenged him in ways other women didn't and never had. It was the sort of thing that would get tiring after a while, but he hadn't yet had his fill of it.

Delilah's colour deepened. Oh, she knew only too well what else there was about this man that attracted a woman. The way he smiled…the look and the smell and the feel of him…the way he touched…his fingers, his hands…the way his mouth traced your contours until you were going crazy with want…

She blinked back the slow motion reel of graphic images.

'I don't care about your money, Daniel, and I haven't come here to try and barter my body for cash…'

'That's an ugly way of phrasing things.'

'I'm being honest.'

She'd lingered on the word *honest* and he frowned at her.

'Are we going to go there again? I didn't board that

liner with the express purpose of finding a woman so that I could establish a relationship with her based on lies… And if you haven't come here because of the money, then why *have* you come?'

He smiled slowly at her, the sort of wolfish smile that made her toes curl.

'You've missed me…' he mused flatly. 'Have you? Missed me?'

There was just the briefest of hesitations but it was enough for him to get the message that, yes…she'd missed him.

'There's something you need to know.' She said this before she could let that hot, sexy look on his face deprive her of all conscious ability to string two words together. She wrung her hands and gazed past him, through the window to the leaden grey sky outside. 'You're probably going to hit the roof, but I couldn't *not* tell you.'

Daniel stilled.

For once his agile brain was trying and failing to join the connections that would point him in the direction of knowing what she had stored up her sleeve.

'Spit it out, Delilah,' he said, but something was telling him that, whatever she had to say, it would be something he didn't want to hear.

'I'm pregnant.'

That flat statement left behind it a deafening silence. She didn't want to look at his face because she didn't want to see the dawning horror.

Daniel's thought processes had closed down. For the first time in his life he couldn't get his head around what she had said. He wondered whether he had misheard her, but when he looked at her face, drained of colour, there was no mistaking the sincerity of what she had just told him.

Yet he still heard himself say, 'You're kidding?'

'Do you really think I've come all the way down here to see you as a *joke*?' Delilah exploded.

Sifting through the fog swirling round in his head, he caught himself drawing the conclusion that she hadn't missed him…probably hadn't given him a passing thought until she'd discovered…

'Are you sure?'

'Of course I'm sure! I did three tests, Daniel.'

'Tests aren't always right.'

'It must have happened that very first time…if you remember…'

'I remember.'

Suddenly the generous dimensions of his very large office seemed too small. *Pregnant.* She was pregnant. Having his baby. He'd not given even a passing thought to having a relationship, certainly not settling down, and now here he was: facing fatherhood.

Life as he knew it was at an end.

The silence swirled and thickened and he surfaced from his daze to see her rising to her feet.

'Where are you going?' he demanded, shooting up as well.

'I'm leaving you to think about it.'

'Have you *lost your mind*?' He looked at her in utter amazement. 'You've waltzed in here and dropped a bomb-shell and you're leaving so that I can *think about it*?'

'It's a shock…' Delilah mumbled, edging towards the door—but not nearly fast enough, because he was in front of her before she could reach it.

'That's the understatement of the year!'

'And before you launch into some stupid speech about me coming here to try and get money from you because I'm pregnant, I haven't. I came here to tell you because you have a right to know and that's it. I don't want *any-thing* from you.'

What she wanted was the one thing he was incapable of giving. Love. Affection. Joint excitement at the prospect of having a baby with her.

But having a baby with her was the equivalent of a bombshell being detonated in his life.

Nowhere in all her secret romantic fantasies had she ever envisaged her life turning out like *this*.

'I can't have this conversation here.' He flung on his coat, then moved to stand by the door, like a bouncer at a nightclub, waiting for her to follow him.

Did she want a conversation? No. But a conversation was going to be necessary—like it or not. Bombshells would do that…would instigate a question and answer session.

One thing, however… There was no way she was going to let him think that she would be turning into a freeloader just because she was carrying his baby… She wasn't going to be one of those *gold-diggers* he had to be so careful about, because he was such a rich and important human being!

'I have a train to catch,' she told him.

'And you'll catch it,' he replied, in a voice of steel, 'just as soon as we talk about this. You're not paying me a flying visit and then disappearing so that I can *think about it*…and you're certainly not jumping to any conclusions that my role in this is to have a little think and then wash my hands of the whole thing. Not going to happen. This bombshell is going to have permanent consequences—whether you like it or not…'

CHAPTER EIGHT

SHE FOUND HERSELF tripping along in his wake, out of the office building, out into the bleak grey winter and, after five minutes of walking through a confusing network of small streets, straight into the dark confines of an ancient quintessentially English pub.

Dark suited her.

'I don't make daytime drinking a habit,' he told her, settling her into a chair while he remained on his feet, 'but I feel that the occasion demands it. What would you like? And don't even *think* of doing a runner when I'm up at the bar...'

'I wouldn't...' Although the thought *did* hold a certain amount of appeal.

She watched him as he headed for the bar. He'd slung his coat over the back of a chair and she greedily and surreptitiously drank in the long, muscular lines of his body, sheathed in a handmade Italian suit of pale grey.

He was the last word in sophistication, and she couldn't help but notice how people turned and stared. He was drop-dead gorgeous, and it was a timely reminder of just how out of place she was in his world. This was the world in which *he* belonged. Not her.

'Good. You're still here.'

'I'm not going anywhere.' She took the proffered mineral water from him. 'I know we do probably need to talk, but I just want to repeat what I said to you in your office.'

She shot him a defiant look from under her lashes. God, he was so beautiful, so urbane and sophisticated and carelessly elegant, while she...

One glance at her clothes and she knew that she would be plunged into unwanted feelings of inadequacy and self-consciousness. This wasn't the cruise liner, where the standard uniform had been *dress down and casual.* This was the city, where big money was made, and there was no room for the casual look. This was *his* comfort zone.

'Not interested.'

'You need to know that I didn't come here because I want anything from you,' she repeated fiercely. 'I know you think that you're a hot catch, and that you have to be on permanent guard because there are gold-diggers out there just dying to take advantage of you—'

'No one takes advantage of me.' Daniel's mind was almost entirely consumed with a future in which he was a father. 'I'm wary because I'm a natural target.' Experience had taught him that.

'But not for me.'

'Speech over?'

Delilah gazed at him with helpless frustration. 'I thought you would have taken the news a lot more badly,' she confessed.

'You thought I'd throw a tantrum? Shout? Hit things? Not my style. This is a problem that has to be dealt with, and throwing a temper tantrum isn't going to get either of us anywhere. And before you tell me that it's *your* problem and nothing to do with me—'

'I never said that.'

'You implied it. So before you decide to venture down that road again I'll tell you straight away that this is *my* problem as well and you won't be going through it on your own.'

Tears rose readily to her eyes and she blinked them

back. She'd been feeling tearful ever since she had returned to the Cotswolds. She had put that down to the fact that she missed him, that she couldn't see a way forward with a life in which he didn't feature. Now she understood that, however much she had missed him, her hormones were all over the place.

But she still resented the way he insisted on describing the situation as a *problem,* a *bombshell.* What other awful adjectives could he dredge up? she wondered? *Disaster? Catastrophe? Nightmare?* Didn't he have *any* sensitivity at all?

'Where are you living?' he demanded bluntly.

'Back at home with Sarah.'

'And the building work?'

'There were a few delays,' Delilah muttered, feeling about as comfortable as someone being pinned to a chair and questioned with a torch shining on their face. 'Halfway through they discovered some rising damp which had to be treated, and then the whole cottage needed treating, so everything has ended up a little behind schedule...'

'Behind schedule and over-budget?' Daniel guessed shrewdly. 'And presumably in a state of upheaval?'

Delilah maintained a mutinous silence, but he raised his eyebrows until she eventually shrugged grudging agreement.

'Pregnant and trying to cope with building work and general chaos?'

'There's a time line. It'll all be done in four weeks. The builders have assured us of that...'

Daniel burst out laughing and she glared at him resentfully. 'Since when do assurances from builders count for anything?'

'*You're* having work done on the liner. Are you telling me that you don't trust the time scale?'

'I pay them so much that they wouldn't dare overrun by a second.'

'Well, bully for you.'

'I don't like the thought of you having the stress of living somewhere there are builders trooping in and out, in the depths of winter... Chances are the heating will be down at some point and it'll be beyond uncomfortable. Unacceptable.'

'Hang on just a minute—!'

'No, Delilah, *you* hang on just a minute.' He was deadly serious as his green eyes tangled with hers and he leant forward, elbows on the table, cradling his drink in one hand. 'You don't get to do what you want. You're carrying my baby and this stops being just about you.'

'I get that, but—'

'There are no *buts*.'

'I have responsibilities to my sister. We have a business to get off the ground.'

'The situation has changed.'

'You can't just lay down laws, Daniel!' She could feel the power of him steamrollering over her, knocking aside every objection she raised, inexorably pressing her into a corner from which she would have no escape route.

She could feel control of her life being taken away from her and she resented it—because this was a guy who wasn't doing it because he cared about *her*... This was a guy who was doing it in response to the bombshell that had been dropped at his door.

'What did you think would happen when you came here to see me?'

'I... I thought that I'd give you some time to think things over...'

'And how much time did you allot to that?'

'You're busy, and you'd made it clear that you and I were in it for the very short term. You enjoy your freedom. I thought you'd take a few days…maybe even a few weeks…and after that…'

'I'm all ears…'

He leaned closer towards her and the unique scent of him filled her nostrils, leaving her giddy, making her lose the string of what she'd been telling him.

'And after that we could reach some sort of arrangement—if you chose to keep in touch at all…'

Wrong thing to say. He looked at her with thunderous incredulity. *'If I chose to keep in touch?'*

'I'm not saying that you would have vanished without a backward glance…' she backtracked hurriedly. 'But there's no need for you to take an…er…an active role… Lots of men don't…'

'I don't believe I'm hearing this.'

'Daniel, you have an empire to run! I looked you up on the internet… You don't even live in this country! Of course you can take an interest, but forgive me for thinking that you might find it a little tiresome to commute from Australia every other weekend!'

'I have no intention of being a part-time father.'

Delilah looked at him in bewilderment, because she had no idea where he was going with this.

'Well, what are you suggesting?' she asked cautiously.

'Let's start with the small stuff.'

'Like what?'

'The matter of you moving out of the Cotswolds.'

'That won't happen,' she said bluntly. 'It can't.'

'Your sister must understand this change in circumstances.' He looked at her narrowly. 'Except,' he said slowly, 'she doesn't know…'

'Not yet.'

'Good heavens, Delilah!'

'Well…'

'Well? You think she's going to give you a long lecture on being irresponsible…?'

She fought against the urge to confide in him. They didn't have any kind of relationship! 'She might…'

'Does she even know about me?'

'Not exactly.'

'Is that your way of saying not *at all*?'

He was outraged and frankly insulted when she blushed and shrugged her shoulders. He could almost understand her not confiding in her sister just yet about the pregnancy. It was a huge thing, and from what she had told him about her sister a warm hug and congratulations wouldn't have been her first response. Yes, he got that she might have needed time to absorb the enormity of her situation and then steel herself for sharing that particular confidence.

But to have kept silent about *him*…

Sheer male pride, but how many women would have *hidden* the fact that they'd been seeing him? He was accustomed to women doing their best to get him along to events where they could show him off to all their friends and family!

'Why should I have told her about you?' Delilah said defensively. 'We had a little bit of fun and then we went our separate ways. It wasn't as though you were going to be a continuing part of my life!'

'Well, once the cat's out of the bag you will have to explain that you labouring on a building site in the Cotswolds isn't going to do.'

'And what about *you*?' she threw at him. 'Are you going to emigrate to London so that you can be a part of your baby's life?'

Of course not! she thought bitterly. He would dish out orders and commands, have no problem with utterly disrupting her life—as if it hadn't been disrupted enough already—but he would make sure that *his* remained relatively intact.

It would be a major decision. Daniel knew that. But was there much of a choice for him?

He knew what it was like to come from a closely bonded family, knew the importance of having a father there as a role model. It was something he would not deny his own child, whatever the cost.

'I am,' he said, coolly and smoothly, and Delilah's mouth fell open.

'How *can* you?' she asked. Caught on the back foot, she could only think that he was having her on.

'What do you mean?'

'You can't just walk away from your home in Australia…'

'Because you assume that I'm as selfish as you are?'

'That's not fair, Daniel! I have a responsibility to my sister!'

'You also have a responsibility to our child, and frankly to me as well—considering I'm the father. I can effect a hand-over process at my offices in Sydney. The world is such a global village now that it's fairly immaterial where a head office is based unless it happens to be specifically based somewhere for tax purposes. Coincidentally, I've just finished work on my London office—there's no reason why I can't operate from there and go out to the Far East as and when the occasion demands.'

He would miss his boat and the freedom of going sailing when time permitted. He would also have to start looking for somewhere to live. The family penthouse in Knightsbridge wasn't going to do.

'I am prepared to change continents. You are prepared to do *what*, Delilah? You came down here in the expectation that you would impart your information and then walk away, safe in the knowledge that I had been informed, your conscience cleared, and you could carry on as normal.'

'Hardly as *normal*!'

'You didn't expect me to want to do anything apart from maybe clock in now and again when I happened to be in the country. Am I right? Maybe set up a standing order so that you could be solvent—?'

'I don't want your money.'

Daniel overrode her interruption. If she imagined that life was going to be anything but *abnormal* now then she had another think coming, and he intended to make sure that she was given no room to squirm away from her responsibilities and the changes he knew were going to be inevitable, whether either of them liked it or not.

'Did you think that I would be a little taken aback that you were having my child but aside from that would allow you to vanish back up to the country, leaving me to get on with my life undisturbed?' He laughed mirthlessly.

'You enjoy your freedom!'

'Not to the extent that I would allow it to take precedence over my responsibilities.'

'I don't want to be your *responsibility*! Just like I don't want this pregnancy to be a *bombshell* or a *problem* that has to be fixed. Neither of us expected this, but at least *I'm* not looking at it as some sort of catastrophe that has to be put right!'

'I'm not going to get lost in an argument about semantics. We have to deal with this, and you have to take on board that it's something we'll be dealing with *together*. I'm going to move to London and so are you.'

His voice was cool and inflexible, as was his expression. She could dig her heels in and tell him to get lost but she knew he would keep her hostage in the pub until she gave in.

And, as he'd said, he was moving continents simply to

be able to see more of his child. She was uneasily aware
that for her to refuse to move a few dozen miles would
smack of mulish inflexibility.

She might not want him in her life because it would be
hard. Seeing him would be a constant reminder of what
she wanted and what she couldn't have—a constant reminder of the limitations of their relationship. But, ex-
tracting *her* from the equation, wouldn't it be a good
thing for their child to have the presence of an interested
and caring father?

And she would still be there for Sarah. She would be
able to go up at least once or twice a week to help oversee the building project.

'I would have to find somewhere to rent in London.'

'Leave that to me,' Daniel said with silky assurance.

'And I would still want my independence,' she felt
obliged to inform him, just in case he thought that he
could call all the shots. That was a precedent she didn't
want to encourage. He was so forceful, so overpowering,
that it wouldn't take much for him to assume that what he
said was irrefutable law. 'And of course I would expect
you to…er…keep yours, as well…'

This was going to be a mature, civil arrangement, and
it was important that he understood that, however much
he was willing to adapt and contribute, she would not
expect him to change each and every aspect of his life.

She wasn't going take what he offered and then cling
like a limpet.

She wasn't going to let him suspect just how much she
wanted from him and just how painful it was for her to
accept that it was just never going to happen.

She was going to play it cool.

'What do you mean by that?'

'I mean that if you're willing to come all the way over
here, so that you can have a hands-on relationship with

our child, then I'm willing meet you halfway on that score and move to London—at least temporarily. I expect that as time goes on things might very well change on that front.' *Hope sprang eternal.* 'But I don't expect either of us to give up our lives entirely. You're free to carry on seeing other…er…women, and I'm free to…to—'

'Out of the question.'

'I beg your pardon?'

'The small stuff was the business of you leaving the Cotswolds. The slightly bigger stuff is the business of what I mean when I say that I want to play an active role in my child's life. That's something I can't do on an occasional basis.'

He paused so that she could digest what he was saying.

'We're not getting involved in a custody situation,' he informed her. 'You won't be out and about playing the singles game while I hang around and wait for some guy to bounce along thinking he's got paternal rights over my child. Nor will I be chasing behind women and kidding myself that I'm still a bachelor.'

Delilah could only stare at him. Bombarded by so much information, she was finding it difficult to sift through and pick out the salient points.

'And that's not going to happen,' he continued remorselessly, 'because we're going to get married.'

Delilah stared at him in utter shock. He was as cool as a cucumber, so cool that she wondered whether she hadn't imagined his outrageous suggestion.

'You've got to be kidding,' she said eventually, and he tilted his head to one side and looked at her.

'About as serious as the Bubonic Plague.'

'I'm not going to *marry* you!'

'Of course you are.'

'Oh, I am, am I? Are you going to drag me up the aisle and force me to say *I do*?'

Delilah was literally shaking with anger. Coming from a self-confessed commitment-phobe—a guy who had bluntly told her that he would only ever consider marrying into his own class, because there were so many gold-diggers out there and a guy like him couldn't be too careful—was she actually expected to take his proposal *seriously*?

'I won't have to. You're pregnant, and I can give you everything you could ever want. Both you and our child would benefit from every advantage money can buy. You would never have to work again, never have to worry about money again… You could have the sort of life you've probably only ever dreamt about…'

'It was never my dream to be rich—and I can't believe I'm hearing this!'

Daniel regarded her coolly. When she'd protested enough she would see the sense of what he was saying. She probably did now, even though she was still busy protesting.

'I have *never*,' she said in fevered whisper, 'dreamt of falling pregnant by a guy who isn't interested in a relationship! I have *never* dreamt about being someone's responsibility or putting them in a position they don't want because they've had a *bombshell* dropped in their life! And I have *never* thought that what I really want out of life is *money*.' She stood up, shaking like a leaf. 'I'm going to go now.'

'Over my dead body!' Daniel leapt to his feet.

After the token protest he had expected gratitude. Or at least some show of looking at the situation with common sense! Instead, she was acting as though he had insulted her in the worst possible way by suggesting marriage!

'You're being ridiculous!' He wanted to bellow, to shake some common sense into her. Instead, he held her by the arm as she was about to hail a taxi. 'You're not running away from me, Delilah!'

'I'll be in touch. But I won't be marrying you.'

'Why?' He raked frustrated fingers through his hair. He hadn't wanted to have this sort of conversation in his office, and he wanted to have it even less here. In the street. With the crowds swarming around them.

She looked at him with simmering resentment. 'You really don't understand, do you?'

'It makes sense.'

He looked down at her upturned face. The face that had haunted him for the past few weeks—ever since she had walked out of his life.

She still turned him on.

She was as obstinate as a mule, had rejected his offer for reasons he couldn't even begin to understand, was viewing the situation with just the sort of incomprehensible female logic he had never had any time for, and yet...

He still wanted her so badly it was like a physical ache.

And it wasn't just because this was unfinished business.

Could it be, in part, because she was carrying his child? Did he want to be a father? He'd never given it a passing thought, and yet he had to admit that there was something incredibly sexy about knowing that she carried his baby. Was it just some kind of primitive response to the evidence of his own virility?

He lowered his head and captured her mouth in an urgent kiss, his hand curving in the small of her back. He felt her melt against him. Briefly but completely. Then she pressed her palms against his chest and pushed herself away.

'Tell me that marriage doesn't make sense,' he said thickly.

Delilah was burning up, her whole body consumed by

a driving need that left her weak. How could she explain that that was *precisely* why it made no sense...*for her.*

'I'll...call you...'

'You don't have my number.'

'I have your office number.'

'That won't do. I want you to be able to reach me any time of the day or night.'

He was far from happy about her disappearing on him, and he wasn't the sort of man who had any patience at all when it came to waiting, but he could see the determination on her face and he knew that if he pushed it there was the danger that he would scare her off completely.

He gave her his number and watched as she put it into her contacts list. 'I need to be able to get in touch with you,' he said as she slipped her phone back into her bag.

Delilah looked at him with clear eyes. 'You never needed to before.'

'Things are different now.'

'I don't want to feel as though you're putting pressure on me.'

'Dammit, Delilah...!'

Their eyes met and for a few seconds her heart went out to him. He was just so endearing in his impatience, so appealing in the way he was looking at her, his green eyes alive with masculine frustration at this situation he couldn't immediately resolve.

The longing to touch him was so intense that she stuck her hands behind her back. That kiss he had dropped on her mouth was still burning, still making her realise how fast her brain cells could go into meltdown when she was with him.

'I... I'll call you,' she repeated as a black cab slowed to a stop alongside her. A black cab that would cost money she barely had.

What he was offering suddenly had such an appeal that

she had to fight against giving it house room in her head. He might be able to take care of her financially…it was true that if she married him she would never have a single financial worry in the world again…but that would be replaced by even more worries—for how on earth could she live with him when she knew that she would be waging a daily war with her own foolish feelings?

What *he* would see as a viable solution, a marriage of convenience, *she* would see as an agonising union with someone who could never return the love she felt for him.

Theirs would be a marriage of such unequal terms that it would be devastating for her mental and emotional health.

'When? I need to know…'

'In a week's time…or so…' She pulled open the taxi door before she could become embroiled in yet another debate with him. She slammed it shut and quickly rolled down the glass. 'You need time to think, Daniel, and to come to terms with the fact that I won't be marrying you…'

And then the taxi was pulling away into the impatient traffic and she was leaving him behind, already feeling the loss.

She knew that she wouldn't tell Sarah anything—not until matters had been sorted between herself and Daniel. She would confess everything as soon as they had reached some sort of solution, but at the moment a solution seemed far from being set in stone.

Move to London…

He would rent somewhere for her and she would be seeing him on a regular basis. He would be there for his child and she would be an add-on. His life would continue without her in it. Another woman would come along to absorb his attention and she wondered how she would feel when that happened.

How would she feel when, finally, he found the woman he felt he could marry? Someone rich and sophisticated?

She tried hard not to let her imagination run away with her, but over the next few days it was impossible to rein it in.

She was distracted—suddenly very conscious of all the building work happening in the kitchen, very much aware of how the disruption was beginning to get more and more unbearable. And yet she couldn't bring herself to think about leaving Sarah to get on with the project on her own.

She felt like someone wandering around in thick fog, waiting for a pinprick of light to announce a safe haven somewhere.

It was exactly a week before she contacted Daniel.

She had to brace herself for the sound of his deep, sexy drawl but when she connected with him it still took her breath away, leaving her winded.

'About time,' were his opening words.

In the middle of an important meeting he rose, signalled with a curt nod of his head that his CEO was to take over, and left the conference room without a second thought.

He'd kept many a woman waiting for the phone to ring. He'd never had the shoe on the other foot and he hadn't liked it.

It had, however, given him time to think, and he'd done a fair bit of that. He'd also put some things in motion—because at the end of the day he was a man of action. There was just so much thinking he could do, and then he needed to go beyond that point.

'Perhaps we could meet...' Delilah suggested.

'Where are you?'

'At home, of course...'

'I'll send my driver to collect you.'

'No!' She had yet to breathe a word to her sister, and the thought of some flash chauffeur-driven car pulling up outside the cottage for her sent a shiver of horror down her spine. 'I… I can come down to London…'

'When?'

'Well…'

'I'm not good at hanging around, Delilah,' Daniel told her abruptly. 'Time's passing and we need to find a way forward on this.'

'I realise that…'

'Then I suggest you get on the first train down and be prepared to stay longer than five minutes. I will ensure that my driver collects you from the station.'

'I'm perfectly capable of meeting you somewhere,' Delilah inserted quickly, because she was already in danger of handing over all control of the situation to him. He wielded power so effortlessly that it was easy to fall in with his expectation that whatever he wanted, he was entitled to get.

But, predictably, she was met at the station three hours later by his driver, and ushered to a long, sleek Jaguar with tinted windows that took her away from the bustle of the station, beyond the city and out of it.

Anxiously she dialled Daniel's number and he answered instantly.

'Where are you?' she asked.

'Waiting for you. Don't worry. You haven't been kidnapped.'

'I thought we'd be meeting…er…closer to your office…'

'Have you packed a bag?'

'I can't stay long,' she said hurriedly. 'I've told Sarah that I need to go to London for the night…'

'You're going to have to break the news to her some time.'

'I know that! Where exactly am I being taken?'

'It's a surprise.'

'I've already had my fill of surprises,' she told him honestly. 'I don't think I can stand any more.'

But, seeing that she was in his car, without the option of a quick escape, she could only sit back and watch as the clutter of the city was left behind, giving way to parks, trees, less foot traffic. It was a rare winter's day... cold, but with clear blue skies, barely a cloud in the sky.

She was delivered to a Victorian house with neat black railings outside and shallow steps leading to a black door, which was opened before she had time to bang on it with the brass knocker.

'Is this your house? Do you live here?'

His keen eyes roved over her. She was wearing so many layers that it was impossible to see whether she had gained any weight or not, but just thinking about it fired him up in a way that was sudden and powerful.

He dismissed the driver and ushered her into the house.

'Come and have a look around.'

'Why?'

'Because this is where you and our baby will be living. Here. With me.'

Delilah planted herself squarely in front of him, arms folded. 'Didn't you hear a word I said? I'm not going to marry you! And just looking at where you live shows me how different we are, Daniel! I don't come from your world and I don't want to marry into it! I *know* how you feel about women who don't come from the same background as you.' She sighed. 'What happened between us on the cruise was never meant to last. I was never the sort of woman you would have been interested in long term and just because I'm pregnant it doesn't change that. We're two people on opposite sides of a great big divide—'

'Five bedrooms, four bathrooms, countless other rooms...plenty of room for three...'

'You're *not listening.*'

'You don't want to marry me. I heard you the first time. I'm also hearing a load of rubbish about the fact that I have money and you don't.'

'It's not rubbish,' she persisted.

'Money shouldn't dictate the outcome of this situation.'

'But it will, won't it?' Delilah said bleakly. 'The man I met on that cruise was a pretend person. The real guy is here...' She looked around at the grand proportions of the house, the flagstoned flooring, the toweringly high ceilings, the priceless art on the walls. 'I don't *know* this guy...'

Daniel looked at her with a veiled expression. 'You didn't bring much with you.'

'I told you I wouldn't be hanging around.'

'No matter. I can get my guy to drive up to the Cotswolds and get whatever's necessary...'

'Necessary for what? What are you talking about?'

'We're going round in circles,' Daniel told her coolly. 'And getting nowhere fast.'

'I don't mind discussing whatever financial arrangement you want to make for the baby...'

'We need to talk about far more than that...and we can't talk here...'

'You mean in your house?'

'I want to take you somewhere special...'

'Where? Why? It doesn't matter where we have this conversation...'

'You'll need a bag...enough clothes for a couple of nights... I have a house in the Caribbean, Delilah... I want to take you there... We can relax... If you don't want to marry me I can't force you, but maybe if we're away from these surroundings we might find it easier to talk...'

He raised both hands to forestall her protest.

'It's a big villa… You can choose whichever room you want… Instead of arguing and getting nowhere we can at least try and recapture our friendship in a stress-free environment. I can't imagine how you must have felt when you discovered that you were pregnant. Money worries and then an unexpected pregnancy on top of that…tough.'

He smiled wryly and made no move to invade her space.

'A few days of sea and sand and sun might help us both find a way forward…'

Delilah's eyes widened. Little did he know it, but *he* was part and parcel of her stress. Cooped up in a villa with him? Crazy. How was *that* going to relieve her stress?

And yet wasn't he right? She felt herself getting more and more stressed by the second here. The prospect of sand and sun and sea was suddenly as powerful as the glimpse of an oasis in the middle of a desert.

Friendship. That was what they should be aiming for. The longer they argued, the less likely that was going to be. But maybe in different surroundings… Not here in London which felt frantic and claustrophobic, and not in the Cotswolds, which were all tied up with her financial worries and stress…

She found herself nodding slowly. What harm could a couple of nights do? And maybe if she could become his friend and remove the emotional attachment she would be able to deal with the situation better…

CHAPTER NINE

'Is THIS HOW you usually travel?'

In the space of one day Delilah had gone from arguing in London to sitting aboard a luxury private jet. She felt like an intruder into a world that might have been a different planet altogether.

With Daniel sprawled next to her she should have been as nervous as a kitten, but somehow the minute the jet had taken off she had felt herself relax. Daniel snapped shut the lid of his laptop and angled his big body so that he was facing her.

So she didn't want to talk about marriage and was adamant that he was the last person she would walk down the aisle with?

He wasn't going to press it.

So she wanted to make a big deal of their differences?

He wasn't going to waste time arguing with her about it. After Kelly, he'd sworn that a convenient marriage with someone independently wealthy enough to ensure his billions weren't the star attraction was the only kind of marriage he would ever consider.

But life had a way of pulling the rug from under your feet—although he'd never credited that he could ever be the victim of *that*. Control every aspect of your life and there could be no nasty surprises. That had been the theory at any rate.

She'd given him a way out, and he knew that he could

have taken it and kept his freedom intact, but the second she had told him about the pregnancy he had known that freedom didn't stand a chance.

He wanted the whole marriage deal. He wanted his child to have both parents. He didn't want her to get involved with anyone else. He didn't want to share his child, with weekend visits and watching from the sidelines while some other guy played the daddy role.

He didn't want to share *her*.

'It doesn't tend to work when I'm in London,' he drawled, eyebrows raised. 'Troublesome getting from my house to my office in a private jet... I find the car a much better proposition.'

Delilah didn't want him to make her laugh. They were going to stay in his villa. They were going to try to become friends. She was going to have to learn to put a little distance between them. But being witty came naturally to him, and he wasn't doing it because he cared for her, or because he wanted to get anywhere with her.

'What did you tell your sister?' he asked curiously.

'I told her that I was pregnant,' Delilah said on a sigh. 'I just didn't know how much longer I could keep it to myself. I mean, if I'm going to be living in London so that you can visit the baby I had to give her some warning...'

The last thing Daniel wanted to hear was that his role was being downgraded to ex-lover with visiting rights, but arguing wasn't getting him anywhere. He gritted his teeth in a tight smile.

'And her reaction?'

'Shock. I thought she was going to faint on the spot.'

'I don't suppose her shock was as great as yours when *you* found out...'

'It was the last thing I was expecting,' Delilah agreed, staring past him through the small window. They had been served drinks as soon as the plane had taken off and she nursed the orange juice she had requested. 'I was terrified,' she admitted. 'When I thought about having a baby all I could see were problems. It was like looking down a tunnel and not seeing any light.'

She focused on him and thought… *He's a friend…an ex who, thankfully, hasn't shied away from his responsibilities…who wants to provide support…that's the main thing…*

'I never thought that I'd be a single mum. I mean, it never occurred to me at all. I thought that I might end up on the shelf—but a single mother? No…'

Daniel didn't remind her that he had asked her to marry him. He wasn't interested in hearing another litany of reasons why it would never happen.

'I didn't think you would be as supportive as you've been,' she admitted, flushing.

'Because I'm a bastard who lied to you…?'

She looked away, reminded of the idiot she'd been to have fallen in love with a man who had never been in it for the long haul.

'There's no point rehashing that,' she said with casual nonchalance. 'The main thing is that you're going to have an ongoing relationship with our child and us becoming friends is a good idea…'

She was so *aware* of him—sitting so close to her that she could just move her hand and touch his forearm, feel its muscled strength and the brush of the dark blond hair on her arms under her fingers.

Becoming friends felt like the hardest thing in the world to do, but she was going to have to do it. She wasn't going to marry him—would never marry a man who didn't love her—but she was going to have to get used to a different type of relationship with him, however hard that was going to be.

'Tell me about where we're going...' she encouraged vaguely. 'Which island is it?'

'You wouldn't have heard of it.'

'Because I'm not well travelled?' she suggested, her voice cooler. 'I did geography at school. I was actually okay at it. I do happen to know about the Caribbean, even if I don't have first-hand knowledge of any of the islands.'

'You wouldn't have heard of it because I own it.'

Delilah's mouth dropped open and she stared at him in amazed silence for a few seconds. 'You *own* an island?'

'Not exclusively,' Daniel admitted. 'It's a joint enterprise with my brother. Not that either of us has actually spent much time holidaying there.'

He was a billionaire—there was no point in trying to play it down.

She didn't say anything, and eventually Daniel broke the tense silence with a heartfelt sigh. 'You're going to tell me that it's just another example of these different worlds we inhabit.'

'It's true, though, isn't it?'

'I can't deny that I've never had much experience of financial stress. My brother and I came from a wealthy family and we've both managed to make fortunes of our own.'

'I don't know why we're bothering with this trip,' Delilah heard herself say. 'We could have sorted out the money angle back in London.'

'Back in London we couldn't sort anything out without an argument.'

'I wasn't trying to be argumentative. I was trying to be practical.'

'The truth is, I thought that you could do with the relaxation... I get it that this will have been as much of a shock to you as it is to me and stress isn't good during pregnancy. At least, I wouldn't have thought so...'

For Delilah, that made more sense. He wanted to de-stress her for the sake of the baby, and he had the sort of bottomless wealth that enabled him to do it in style. Most men would have had to make do with a meal out.

Lots of men in his position, she thought guiltily, wouldn't even have bothered with the meal out—wouldn't have thought further than grabbing the get-out clause she had offered and running away with it. But he wasn't *most men.* She wanted to hate him because he had lied to her and strung her along, but she grudgingly had to concede that there was a strong streak of honesty and decency in him. He hadn't shied away from taking responsibility and now here he was, taking her on a far-flung getaway so that she could de-stress!

She followed his reasoning. They were to become friends, and that was going to be easier away from the grit and grime of London and, yes, from the arguing.

'What does it feel like to own an island?' she asked, intrigued against her will. 'What on earth do you do with it when you're not there?'

'Rent it out,' Daniel told her. 'It commands a healthy amount of money...'

'But you don't get there often to enjoy it?'

'Work,' he said flatly. 'It's almost impossible to take the time out.'

Delilah shot him a dry look. 'What's the point of work-ing so much that you never get to relax and enjoy the stuff you can buy with all your money?'

Daniel watched her narrowly. When he'd gone to San-torini he'd watched all those tourists and, yes, somewhere at the back of his mind had noted the comparison between himself and the laid-back holidaymakers.

When did *he* ever get to relax? He rarely took time out, and when he did he preferred solitary forms of re-laxation. Sailing...skiing... Did sleeping with women count? Women were a physical release… But complete and utter relaxation? No… He hadn't ever sought them out to provide that.

'Have you ever taken a woman to the island?' she asked, hoping that it sounded like a perfectly reasonable matter-of-fact question.

'Never.'

'Why not?'

'I marvel that I'd managed to forget how many "No Trespassing" signs you like to barge past…' But his voice was wry rather than belligerent.

'Friends know things about one another.'

'Especially friends who have enjoyed fringe benefits…?'

Delilah went bright red, and just like that her body fell into its familiar pattern, with her nipples pinching and tightening, her palms growing clammy with perspiration, and between her legs that hot ache that seemed to control all her senses until it was the only thing she was aware of.

'That feels like a long time ago.' She casually dismissed his husky suggestive remark and offered him a bright smile. 'Things are different between us now.' She cleared her throat and slanted her eyes away from his. 'So, when you've been to this island you've gone on your own?'

'Why not? It's great for snorkelling. It's surrounded by a reef and the water is very clear and very calm, The fish are so lazy and tame that they'd share your lunch with you if you gave them half a chance.'

'And you prefer to do all that on your own…?'

'I don't need a woman to spoil the peace by demanding attention and shrieking every time a fish gets too close…' he drawled.

'So what if *I* shriek when a fish gets too close?'

'You're different,' he commented drily. 'You're not

just any woman. You're the mother of my child... You should try and get some sleep now. We don't land on the island... We land on a runway on the mainland and take a helicopter from there. It's a long trip, all told...'

In other words he was no longer interested in chatting and he wasn't interested in her nosy questions.

Delilah shrugged and turned away. She knew that he had reopened his computer and could hear the steady sound of his fingers brushing against the keyboard, composing emails, reviewing important documents, doing all those things that kept him so busy that he seldom took time out to relax.

It was another mark in his favour that he was taking the time out now, when he didn't have to.

He was doing it because she was different... She was no longer a woman...she was the mother of his child. Her status had been elevated, but she missed being a woman he couldn't keep his hands off...

In the end she slept through most of the flight. When she opened her eyes the sky was bright blue outside the window and she straightened and peered past him to the banks of white wispy clouds.

'Are you excited?' she asked breathlessly, and he smiled at her.

'I think you'll enjoy the place.'

'Do you get excited about *anything*, Daniel?' she heard herself persist.

'I have my moments...' he murmured, green eyes locked on hers. 'Your hair's all over the place...'

He itched to brush it back from her face. He'd watched her as she slept and the urge to touch her had been overwhelming. He had amazing detailed recall of every inch of her body. Even before she had turned up at his office and announced the life-changing news that she was carrying his child she had managed to get under his skin in a way no other woman ever had.

She had preyed on his mind after she'd left. Why? Because, he'd told himself, she was unfinished business and he was egotistical enough to want to finish with a woman rather than the other way around. Egotism wasn't a good trait, but it was something he could deal with.

So he hadn't been able to get her out of his head...

So he hadn't been interested in replacing her with any of the women in his proverbial black book, who would have been overjoyed to have taken up where Delilah had left off...

It was just because they'd met under unusual circumstances. It was just because she'd had no idea of his true identity and he'd relished the freedom that had given him.

After his experiences with Kelly he had erected so many defences systems around himself and around his emotions that he hadn't recognised when his defences had been breached and she had breached them.

And he didn't mind.

In fact he liked it—liked it that she wasn't intimidated by him or impressed by his money.

When she had shown up in his office he hadn't been tempted to get rid of her. He'd formulated all sorts of reasons for her being there and rehearsed all sorts of arguments as to why he would be willing to take her back to his bed...where it felt as if she belonged...

The bottom line was that he'd never stopped wanting her. And more than that...

He'd watched her sleep, head drooping on his shoulder. He'd felt the soft brush of her hair against his mouth. Hell...

How was he supposed to have recognised the signs of something that was more than lust? He'd been in total control of his emotions for so long—how could he have been tuned in to the signs of anything that ran deeper than that?

And wasn't that why he was so adamant that there was no way he was going to let her go? No way that she would be able to walk away from him into the arms of someone else?

Just the thought of another man laying a hand on her filled him with sickening, impotent rage, and he'd had a lot of thoughts along those lines when she had disappeared back up to the Cotswolds. Pride had stopped him from pursuing her. That would have been a step too far. But she was here now and she was going to stay.

For the first time in his life, though, he had no idea what the rules of this game were. She didn't want him. He couldn't get to her through his money because she wasn't greedy and she wasn't materialistic, and he had lied to her. She was willing to try and forge a truce with him, but he knew that if he wanted more then he would have to use every trick in the book to get it.

And he did want more.

He just wasn't sure what those tricks to get it might entail.

Proceeding slowly—something that was anathema to him—seemed to be the only approach.

Delilah shoved her hair into something less chaotic and edged as far away from him as was physically possible.

The plane was coming in to land and she craned her neck to drink in everything as it descended and then bumped along a runway that was bordered by small hangars and beyond that waving palm trees.

As soon as the engine purred to a complete stop the heat seemed to invade the small cabin space and she was glad that she'd worn something light…a pair of cotton trousers and a loose-fitting sleeveless top.

'I feel almost guilty being here,' she confided as they headed out of the plane to make a smooth connection with a waiting helicopter. People bustled around them... the captain stopped to chat with Daniel...their bags were trundled in searing heat to the helicopter.

'Don't,' he commanded, looking down at her. 'You're pregnant and I don't want you to be stressed over anything. Or to feel guilty because you're here. Did your sister try and imply that it was somehow *wrong* for you to take a few days away?'

He helped her into the helicopter and then heaved his big body in alongside her, the two of them cramped in the confined space. The door was slammed down, locking them into the sort of intimacy that fired up all her senses.

She licked her lips and shook her head. 'Of course not. She understands the turmoil I'm going through...'

'And she agreed that the ex-lover you refuse to marry should be the one to try and help you with that?'

Delilah was spared having to answer that by the loud whirring of the helicopter blades as the aircraft tilted up and buzzed like a wasp, hovering and then swooping along, offering a breathtaking sight of navy blue sea and turquoise sky.

'Well?' Daniel prompted as the helicopter whirred to a shuddering stop on the island.

The flight had taken a matter of minutes and here they were. It was lush and green and a four-wheel-drive SUV was waiting for them on the airstrip. As far as the eye could see there was untouched beauty and the smell of the sea was pungent and tangy. She breathed in deeply and slowly and half closed her eyes, enjoying the heat, the slight breeze and the unique tropical sounds of unseen insects and birds.

'I can't believe this is all yours.' She opened her eyes, turned full circle and gazed at him.

'It's a small island,' Daniel said drily, ushering her towards the car while, behind them, she heard the helicopter begin to whirr into life, ready to lift off and go back to the mainland.

'But still…it's just so amazing…'

Privately, Daniel had never been able to stay longer than a handful of days on the island. Boredom would inevitably set in, even though the water sports were second to none.

'What else is there? Just a villa? I can't believe you don't come here as often as you can…'

She looked at him and then through the car window and then back at him, not knowing where to feast her eyes. Swaying coconut trees lined the sides of the road and through the tall, erect trunks she could make out slivers of blue, blue sea.

When everything had been worked out between them and some sort of visiting timetable arranged, she wondered how she would ever be able to compete with this. She had a vivid image of their child coming to a place like this for a holiday and then returning to England to spend the rest of the time with her in whatever modest house she might be living in.

And then she imagined their child coming here with Daniel and whatever partner had entered his life—maybe even one of those 'suitable' women. Because, with a child, he would doubtless be anxious to settle down and find himself a wife.

Had she done the right thing? She had stood her ground and refused to let him sacrifice his life because a mistake had happened, because she had fallen pregnant. She had refused to compromise when it came to love and the right reasons for entering into a marriage with anyone.

But now doubts began to gnaw away inside her. Worriedly she shoved them aside.

Ahead of them, the bumpy road was taking them up a small incline, and as the Jeep rounded the corner her mouth dropped open at the sight of the sprawling villa ahead of them. Banked by coconut trees and every shade of green foliage she could possibly have imagined, it was a one-storeyed building that was circled by a wide, shady veranda. Impeccably maintained lawns surrounded it on all sides, and as the car ground to a halt a plump dark-skinned woman emerged at the front door and several other members of staff spilled out from behind her.

Delilah thought that this must be what it felt like to be a member of royalty. Daniel took it all in his stride. He chatted with the woman, Mabel—who, he explained, looked after the house and all the staff when it was occupied, and made sure it was kept up to scratch when it was empty, coming three times a week from the mainland to check everything over.

'Your bedroom...' he paused and nodded to one wing of the massive villa '...is there. Mine is in the opposite wing. I'll get Mabel to show you to your room and then we can have some dinner and hit the sack. It's been a long day.'

So this was what it felt like to be friends. This polite, smiling man, who had once touched every part of her body, was now offering her the hand of friendship—which she had insisted on—and she hated it.

'Tomorrow,' he said, 'I'll give you a tour of the island, but don't expect anything much longer than half an hour. There are plenty of coves and small beaches. We can have a picnic on one of them...'

'And talk about how we handle this situation?' Delilah said with a wooden smile. 'Good idea. And it was a good idea to come here,' she conceded truthfully. 'I haven't felt so relaxed since I found out that I was pregnant.'

Daniel inclined his head to one side and shoved his

hands in his pockets. Even with her clothes sticking to her, and clearly tired after the convoluted journey that had brought them here, she still had that impossible certain *something* that fired him up.

And she showed zero sign of wanting anything more than a civilised conversation about technicalities. The girl who had given herself to him with abandon was gone.

'You never told me what your sister said when you informed her that you would be coming here with me...'

'I didn't tell her that we would be going abroad.' Delilah flushed and looked away. 'I just told her that I needed to spend a few days in London because I needed to sort some stuff out with you, and that we would probably have to visit a lawyer at some point to make our agreement legal...'

'I see...'

He didn't. And what he heard was the sound of her walking away from him. The way she hadn't been able to meet his eyes when she'd said that spoke volumes. He had asked her to marry him and, whatever excuses she had come up with, the bottom line was that she didn't want him in her life, and she felt guilty about her rejection because she was fundamentally such a warm, caring, genuine person.

And there was nothing he could do about it except play this waiting game and hope.

Delilah drew her knees up and gazed out at the distant horizon, which was a dark blue streak breaking up the cloudless milky blue of the sky and the deeper, fathomless blue of the ocean. The sand underneath her was powdery white and as fine as icing sugar.

Ground up coral from the reef that surrounded the island and the reef itself were responsible for the wealth of tropical fish, which were as tame as Daniel had predicted—bright flashes of yellow and turquoise and pink that weren't afraid to weave around her in the water.

It was paradise.

She should have been over the moon.

She was surrounded by the most amazing natural beauty. Water so clear that you could wade out for absolutely ages and still see your feet clearly touching the sand. Staff on hand to serve their every whim. The food was exquisite…

And Daniel had been nothing but conscientious. No longer the flirty, charming guy who had teased her and made her laugh, but guarded and serious.

They had talked about financial arrangements and agreed that getting lawyers involved would be a waste of time, because it was important to maintain the friendship they were so successfully cultivating.

The friendship that had replaced the fun and the sex.

'You're going to get burnt.'

Delilah spun round to see him striding towards her, a towel casually draped over his broad, tanned shoulders, his bathing trunks low-slung and emphasising the glorious muscularity of his body.

They'd been on the island for two days, and it wasn't getting any easier trying to hide the effect he still had on her.

'I'll be fine.' She smiled tightly at him and quickly averted her eyes. 'We're only going to be here for another couple of days, and I'm not going to waste this sun by sitting in the shade all the time. Besides, I've lathered myself with sunblock.'

Daniel steeled himself against the cool dismissal in her voice and draped the towel on the sand and lay down next to her.

Two days and he'd got nowhere at all. He'd never felt so impotent in his life before, and he didn't know what to do about it. She smiled, listened to what he said, seemed to take an interest in all the boring historical facts he dished out about the island, asked questions about the staff and the running of the place, but the polite mask never slipped.

Because it wasn't a mask.

He should never have lied to her. It had seemed perfectly reasonable at the time—a harmless piece of fiction that he could turn to his advantage. Except things had got out of hand, and by the time she'd discovered the truth they had both overstepped more boundaries than he liked to imagine.

She had made inroads into him without his even realising it, and when she had walked away pride had stopped him from going after her.

She had had time to come to conclusions about him that he was helpless to set straight.

Frustration tore through him.

'This heat is fiercer than you think,' he gritted. 'And the last thing either of us needs is for you to come down with sunstroke.'

Delilah's temper flared and she welcomed it. After two days of stilted politeness she had a churning sea of emotion inside, desperate for an outlet.

'I don't think I need you telling me what I should and shouldn't do,' she snapped. 'I appreciate that you've taken time away from work to come here on a rescue mission to get me to relax, but don't worry... I won't set back your timetable for squeezing me in by inconveniently coming down with sunstroke...'

'There's no need for the drama, Delilah,' he drawled, his mouth tightly compressed.

'I'm not being dramatic,' she returned in a high voice. She could barely look at him, and was angrily aware of just how easy it would be to lose herself in his extravagant good looks.

Hadn't he demonstrated, without having to say a word, just how detached he had become from her?

She was overwhelmed by the hateful feeling that she was being patronised.

Or maybe it was more than that.

Her thoughts veered off at a dangerous tangent and a series of heated assumptions were made. She'd thought that he'd been wildly generous in asking her here on this little break, was being understanding about the stress she had been through. And even though she had constantly reminded herself that this wasn't about *her*, the gesture had fed into her weakness for him. That was why it had been unbearable dealing with his politeness—that was why every solicitous helping hand had been a dagger through her heart.

Because she hadn't seen him for what he was and truly accepted it.

He had dropped all talk of marriage and had distanced himself. Maybe he thought that if he was too much like the Daniel she had hopped into bed with she might be encouraged into getting ideas into her head. He had proposed out of duty and responsibility, but she was sure that he must be quietly relieved to have been let off the hook.

And then there was the fact that he had brought her *here*. Not just on a little weekend break somewhere, but *here*. To an island he *owned*, where everything from the cool, elegant bedroom, with its bamboo furniture, to the exquisite infinity pool overlooking the sea, was the very last word in what money could buy.

Had he wanted to remind her how far apart their worlds were?

He intended to take an active interest in his child's life, but was this his subtle way of showing her that with marriage no longer on the agenda they were, as she had painfully pointed out to him, poles apart?

Suddenly it seemed very important that they talk about all the things they had somehow not got around to discussing.

Rigid with tension, she looked at him, relaxing on the towel like a man without a care in the world. She stuck on her oversized sunglasses and took a couple of stolen seconds to just look at him, lying there with his eyes closed against the glare of the sun.

'We haven't really decided anything...' She broke the silence tersely. 'And I'd quite like to get things sorted so that I can enjoy the rest of my time here without all that hanging over my head.'

Daniel opened his eyes and looked at her. 'Where do you want to start?'

'I've agreed to move down to London to accommodate you, so I guess I should know what the living arrangements will be...' Delilah wondered whether that concession had been the worst decision of her life.

'You'll have an apartment or a house—whatever you want and wherever you want it to be.' Daniel loathed this conversation, which smacked of finality. 'And naturally you will have a generous allowance...'

'I'm not asking for money from you,' Delilah said in a stilted voice. 'You can just pay maintenance for our child, like any other normal person.'

'But I'm not *a normal person*, am I? I'm extremely wealthy. and neither my child nor the mother of my child will ever want for anything.'

'And if...it's early days yet...if for some reason this pregnancy doesn't work out...'

I'll still want you in my life... That was what Daniel thought, with shocking immediacy.

'Then you can have your apartment back and I'll return to the Cotswolds...'

Her heart constricted and she was ashamed to realise that she would rather see him and suffer than never see him in her life again. How pathetic was *that*?

She twisted the knife inside her. 'Although maybe I'll stay in London and find somewhere else to live. Sarah will have become accustomed to my not being around, and in London I can...'

'Find a better job? A better life? Better dating scene? Mr Right?'

Daniel smiled coldly and Delilah flinched, because he just didn't give a damn, did he?

'Maybe all of those things,' she returned defiantly. 'Why not? But I'm not going to think about that. We'll have a baby together and sort out the details and then we'll both be free to go our separate ways. Will you want whatever's agreed to be legally put into writing?'

'Will you?' Daniel enquired, restless with a savage energy that was pouring through him like toxic waste. 'Do you think I'm the kind of man to give you something with one hand while keeping the other hand free to snatch it all back at a later date?'

He vaulted upright in one swift, graceful movement and stared down at her.

With the glare of the sun behind him, his face was thrown into a mosaic of shadows and angles and she was grateful for the oversized sunglasses hiding her eyes.

'I'll email my lawyer today,' he said, with considerable cold restraint. 'And have something drawn up for signing as soon as we return to London.'

'And visiting rights?'

'As many as I like,' Daniel gritted. 'And I'm warning you, Delilah, if you fight me on this I'll fight you back. In the courts if necessary.' He smiled coolly. 'And now that we understand one another, and the details have been worked out, I'm going for a swim—you can enjoy what remains of our time here without anything "hanging over your head…'"

CHAPTER TEN

DELILAH WATCHED HIM worriedly as he swam out, further and further. until he rounded the cove and disappeared from sight.

Of course he knew this island like the back of his hand! Didn't he? He might only have come to the place a handful of times…fewer than that, probably…but he wasn't a complete idiot. Just the opposite. He would know all about currents and the dangers of getting out of his depth.

She waited for fifteen minutes, her eyes glued to the distant horizon, reluctant to go back into the house until she could see him swimming back towards shore.

The sun was fierce and after a while she sidled under a coconut tree, where she tried hard to relax although her eyes kept flickering to the shore.

Eventually, after half an hour, she gave up and trudged back up to the house—where the first person she bumped into was Mabel, who was busying herself with cleaning.

'Mabel…' She hovered, feeling foolish in her swimsuit and sarong. The staff who looked after the huge villa and took care of the sprawling grounds, were friendly and smiling but kept a respectful distance.

Mabel turned to her, her broad smile going some way to putting Delilah at her ease.

'You should get out of those wet clothes, miss. You

change and give them to me and they'll be back in your room by this afternoon.'

'Er… I just wondered… What's the sea like on the other side of the island?'

Mabel's smile wavered, and Delilah couldn't blame the poor woman for her confusion.

'Because…' She hunted for a reason that wouldn't sound completely crazy. 'Because it looks so…so tempting to just swim round the corner and see what the other beaches are like…'

'I wouldn't, miss…'

'Why not?'

'The sea out here is unpredictable, miss, and once you get past the reef… Well…'

'Well, what?' Delilah smiled encouragingly.

'Sharks, miss… Barracuda… All sorts of things… And the water ain't calm, like it is close to the shore. So it's best for you to stay in the cove—or else Mr Daniel can drive you to some of the other coves… I could make a nice picnic lunch…'

Delilah smiled weakly. She had never been a strong swimmer, and she knew that she was seeing all sorts of potential dangers in a situation that *she* would have found threatening. Daniel was a man of considerably more experience than her. He was muscular, athletic…a man built to overcome hazardous conditions.

Hadn't he told her about all those black runs he had skied down? The surging, stormy seas he had successfully navigated in his boat where he lived in Australia?

But when, after two hours, he still hadn't made an appearance, worry began to set in with a vengeance.

She couldn't relax by the pool. She'd spread her towel on a chair, but the gorgeous view of the ocean, the blue sky, the softly swaying coconut trees that bordered the

land on both sides, could not distract her from the niggling suspicion that she had engineered an argument that
had irritated him to the point where he had disappeared
into the ocean. And God only knew where he was now.

Probably safe and sound and heading back to the
house. When she looked at it logically, she thought he'd
probably made it to the next beach and was calmly relaxing and thinking things through.

It wasn't as if they hadn't *needed* to talk about what
they had talked about. Sooner or later they would have
had to sit down and discuss future arrangements. And,
frankly, hadn't she seen just the sort of person that he
was? He had *threatened* her, for heaven's sake! Had told
her that if she did anything to try and curtail his visiting
rights he would fight her—and it hadn't been an empty
threat.

He was willing to play the good guy, but there was no
way he would allow her to cross him, so if he had stormed
off in a rage because she hadn't carried on being ame-
nable and pliable then *tough*.

They were both dealing with a difficult situation, and
if she hadn't been firm and businesslike then she would
have sleepwalked into him taking charge of everything.
Just as he had tried to take charge when he had asked her
to marry him!

Had she agreed to marry him—had she *given in* to that
treacherous little voice in her head that had urged her to
take what was on offer even if it wasn't ideal. because it
was better than nothing and because it would allow her
the forbidden luxury of still being a part of his life—she
would have ended up as nothing more than an append-
age, to be tactfully sidelined when the urge to sleep with
other women became more pressing than the novelty of
being a daddy.

That was precisely what would have happened—although she conceded he would have been diplomatic about it, would have made sure that any outside life was kept far from the prying eyes of the press. But he wouldn't have cared if *she* had known, because that would have been the unwritten codicil when they took their wedding vows. Marriage not for love but through necessity, and therefore not a marriage at all—at least not in the way she understood marriage to be!

And if she hadn't liked it—well, doubtless he would have shown her that tough, uncompromising side of him that she had already glimpsed.

She had a light lunch by herself in the kitchen. Mabel fussed around her but asked no questions about Daniel and why he wasn't there.

Delilah had no idea what she or any of the other members of staff thought about their peculiar sleeping arrangements. The fact they had come together but slept on opposite sides of the house. Did they gossip about that? Or maybe the super-rich who rented the property had their own peculiar arrangements so everyone who worked there was more than accustomed to odd sleeping situations. Who knew?

At night, the staff were all either collected and taken by boat back to the mainland or else they stayed in the collection of well-appointed little houses that formed a clutch at one end of the island. By the time six-thirty rolled around most of them had already disappeared.

There would be a delicious meal for herself and Daniel waiting in the kitchen, she knew. He didn't like anyone hovering around in the evening, waiting to collect their plates, and so, after the first night, he had allowed all the domestic staff to leave early—including the two girls who worked in the kitchen.

With no sign of him, and with darkness encroaching in the abrupt way that it did in the tropics, Delilah could bear the tension no longer.

It was a small island, and she was sure that she would be able to make her way to the next beach without getting lost. In fact it was practically impossible to get lost. But it made sense to wait until the place was empty, because although the staff might not be curious she knew that they might set out on a search party if she went missing.

The temperature had cooled by the time she quietly let herself out, pausing only to get her bearings and then purposefully walking in the direction she hoped would take her to the adjoining cove. She had a powerful torch, although the moon was full and it was bright enough for her to see without switching the torch on at all.

She had no idea how long she walked. At some point it occurred to her that she should probably return to the house soon—fortunately she had made sure to keep the lights on, so that she could orientate herself without too much difficulty. It didn't matter if they'd become fainter. As long as she could make them out in the distance she knew that she could return safely.

Getting lost wasn't a problem. Becoming exhausted, however, was, and it was so lovely and balmy, with just the softest stirring of a breeze and the soothing sounds of little insects, like peaceful, harmonious background music, that she decided to rest.

She'd changed into a pair of jeans and a tee shirt, and she was perfectly comfortable when she found herself a little mound of grass, where she nestled down and rested her legs.

She dozed.

It was impossible not to, because an overload of stress

had tired her out even more than walking the miles she had covered without realising it.

A loud crashing through the undergrowth woke her up with the unwelcome ferocity of a bucket of ice-cold water, and for a few seconds she was completely disorientated. She could still see through the trees and the bushes, and she could still hear the harmless sounds of the insects and the distant repetitive rolling of the sea, but she had no idea where she was until it all came back to her in a rush.

Daniel was missing.

She didn't care what they had said to one another. She just wanted him to be *safe* and she didn't think he was.

She struggled to her feet, backing away from the approaching noise, the sound of something methodically making its way towards her, and only heard his voice when she had spun around vainly, searching for the lights that would advertise the location of the villa.

'What in God's name are you doing here?' Daniel thundered, bringing her to a stop and probably, she thought frantically, disturbing every single member of staff who had chosen to stay on the opposite side of the island.

He stood in front of her like an avenging angel, hands aggressively on his hips and his body leaning forward, taut with belligerent accusation.

'I…' Relief washed over her and she just wanted to race forward and throw herself into his arms.

'Midnight stroll on an island you know nothing about?' he roared.

'There's nothing dangerous here! You said so yourself! No snakes…no big lions or tigers! You laughed when I told you that I'd be terrified of scrambling through all this bush on my own!'

'So you decided to put it to the test and find out whether

it was true or not?' He took a few steps closer to her. 'I've been worried sick about you!'

'Then you shouldn't have just jumped in the sea and swum away like that!' Her heart was racing, every sense heightened to breaking point.

'Dammit, Delilah, why do you think I did that?'

'Because you didn't want to talk about…about the arrangements for after I have the baby…' *Not unless those arrangements suited him—not unless he could have exactly what he wanted without her putting up any arguments…*

'And why do you think *that* was?' Daniel asked roughly.

He raked his fingers through his hair and glared at her. Coming back to the villa…realising that she wasn't there…he'd never felt so panicked in his life before. He'd been sick with fear.

What if something had happened to her? It would have been *his* fault. His fault for laying it on too thick because he'd been in a situation he hadn't been able to handle. Had he forced her into running away? He'd wondered whether she had gone to the staff houses—gone to see whether she could get one of them to take her back to the mainland on one of the boats that were kept anchored there, to be used if the need arose.

'Forget about dangerous animals! You could have fallen! Hurt yourself! You don't know the layout of this place!'

'And how do you think *I* felt?' Delilah yelled accusingly. 'You just took off! You didn't come back. I… I was worried. You went swimming. Anything could have happened. I thought I'd come out here and look for you…see if you'd swum to another cove…'

She didn't reveal the other more terrifying scenarios

concocted in her imagination. That he was lying in one of the coves, washed up and half dead.

'I was frightened,' she confessed with a hint of defiance.

Daniel looked at her, holding his breath.

'Were you?' He exhaled deeply. 'Because *I* was,' he muttered.

He took her hand and led her out of the clearing in which she had fallen asleep. It took them under ten minutes to get to one of the many coves scattered on the perimeter of the island, and during that brief walk there was nothing Delilah could find to say.

He had been worried.

Not about *her,* she made a point of telling herself. About the baby she was carrying...

But he was holding her hand...

Was it because he was scared she might trip and fall and somehow hurt the baby? Was that it?

She was dismayed at how pleasurable it was to dwell on an alternative explanation...

'I had no idea how close I was to the sea,' Delilah said. 'I mean, I could hear it but...'

'In the dark it's confusing just how far or how close you are because the island's so small...'

She shook her hand free and walked to the water's edge, kicking off her flip-flops so that the sea, as warm as bath water, could lap over her feet. She stared out at the ocean, silvery black and ominous, but every corner of her mind was tuned in to his presence behind her, and she drew her breath in sharply as she felt him approach her from behind, so that he was standing a few inches behind her.

'I shouldn't have disappeared,' he said softly.

'Where did you go for all that time?' She didn't turn

around. It was easier to talk like this, when she wasn't drowning in his eyes and having her brains scrambled.

'There's a very small inlet on the east side of the island. I remembered it from way back. I swam there. I needed to…think…'

'I'm not going to stop you from seeing our child. You didn't have to threaten me like that.'

'I know and I… I'm sorry. Will you look at me? I want to see your face when I…when I say what I feel I must say…'

Delilah slowly turned around and looked up at him reluctantly, because she really didn't want to hear what he had to say now that he had cooled down. She didn't want any more talk about signing things and lawyers.

'I'd never drag you through the courts,' he said gruffly. 'I said that in the heat of the moment because I was just so…so damned frustrated.' He shook his head but was driven to stare back at her, at her beautiful upturned face. 'I brought you here because…'

Delilah waited, confused, because he was a guy who was never lost for words. 'Because you wanted me to relax,' she reminded him.

'Because I wanted to take time out and show you that I could be the man you wanted…in your life permanently.'

'We've been through this…' But her heart still leapt, because she'd thought he'd stopped wanting to marry her. Yes, she'd told herself that she wasn't going to marry anyone for the wrong reasons… But it still kick started a thrilling response deep inside her, like a depth charge going off.

'We're good together, Delilah…and it's not just about the sex. Even though…' he couldn't stop his voice from lowering to a sexy, husky whisper that sent shivers racing up and down her spine…the sex is the hottest sex I've ever had…'

'You don't mean that,' she was constrained to point out. 'You haven't been near me since… Not that it matters… But all that lust stuff…'

'Have you wanted me to?' Daniel interjected. 'To touch you? Because I've wanted to—so very badly—but I didn't want to scare you away. You felt that you'd ended up with a man who'd lied to you and I couldn't take that back. But I wanted to… No, I *needed* to show you that I'm no bastard. I learnt a tough lesson years ago and it hardened me. I never thought that you or any other woman would ever come along and make me question all the things I'd taken for granted…'

'Things like what?' Delilah whispered.

'Things like how emotions could get the better of me… like how I could fall in love with someone and want her so badly that the thought of not having her near me every day for the rest of my life would be beyond endurance…'

'You *love* me?' She could barely whisper that in case she'd misheard.

'I love you and I want to marry you… And I want you to believe me when I tell you that I'll never lie to you again, that I'm good for you…'

She flung her arms around him. She wanted to hold him so tightly that he would never be able to leave. She wanted to superglue him to her.

'I love you so much, Daniel. You're everything that doesn't make sense, but I fell in love with you—and that's why I knew that I couldn't marry you. Because I hated the thought of you being trapped into being shackled to me when you weren't capable of attaching emotionally.' She pressed her head against his chest and felt the steady beating of his heart. 'You can't imagine how tempted I still was to accept your proposal…except then you stopped asking and I was gutted…'

She felt him smile into her hair. 'Like I said, I didn't want you diving for cover because I had no idea how far you'd dive, and I couldn't risk you going anywhere I couldn't follow. My darling, I love you so much... Will you do me the honour...?'

Delilah grinned. She didn't think she would ever stop grinning.

'Just try and stop me,' she murmured, brimming over with happiness.

* * * * *

LET'S TALK
Romance

For exclusive extracts, competitions
and special offers, find us online:

f facebook.com/millsandboon

🐦 @MillsandBoon

📷 @MillsandBoonUK

Get in touch on 01413 063232

For all the latest titles coming soon, visit
millsandboon.co.uk/nextmonth